self/less

AViVA is a multidisciplinary artist with international success, garnering more than 3 billion global streams of her music to date. Having always been a lover of stories and made-up worlds she has fed her passion for self-expression with a healthy lifestyle of creativity and writing.
When not writing music or touring the world, AViVA can be found in her home library either nose deep in a good book, fingers busy writing at the keyboard or otherwise occupied in her art studio, sewing or making something else she's dreamt up.

self/less

INK WYTCH

To my OUTSiDERS

WE WATCH BECAUSE WE CARE

Metropolis City's Platinum Jubilee

We celebrate this year, the year of Our Platinum Jubilee, and believe each of Us are to be congratulated for the great progress of Our City and its Council members in banishing all that plagued the Earth.

We are the Chosen People. Free from the *weakness of self*. Free from the *pain of art*. Free from the *persecution of religion*.

We the Chosen People have purged the Earth from forces that wish to harm Our progress.

We beseech you now, in our Seventieth year:

Continue watching. Continue listening. Continue working.

Help us to secure Our great City. We the people are stronger for what We have accomplished together.

We must remind you all, Our brothers and sisters, that no one is above the law.

Let Us congratulate Ourselves.

METROPOLISGOV.COM

LETTER FROM THE EDITOR

As the Occasion Season draws nigh, I am brought to great pride once again in Our Great City. Our Platinum Jubilee this year on Cleanse Day celebrates the Seventieth year Our City has been free of the great scourge of self-expression. That evil above all evils marred Our world, as We all know from Our history books. Even today.

I remember the videos depicting the war and destruction Our ancestors lived in, such chaos, all in the name of themselves and their own desires. Our Metropolis City Council has fought for seven decades for Us. To protect Us. To guide Us. To save Us . . . from Ourselves. With my daughter's partnership drawing near, I know this is a Jubilee I will be looking back on for decades to come.

Always remember: *We watch because We care.*

As a special tribute to Our fallen ancestors, Metropolis Magazine will be hosting free history workshops around the City for seniors and high-school students. (Please find the timetable in back of this issue.)

INSIDE THIS MONTH'S PLATINUM JUBILEE SPECIAL EDITION . . .

On Page 6:
The curfew explained: Clearing up misconceptions about Our heroes the City Patrol.
Our curfew, occurring at two hours past dark each night, has been in place since the second wave of Our Council's protection measures. As with all violations, anyone in breach will be automatically charged with engaging in illegal activity and will, in turn, be tried for treason against the Metropolis City Council. That is, they will be Sanitised. *To continue reading, please turn to page 6.*

On Page 19:
Tips and Tricks: Our latest techniques for family surveillance.
Our best kept secrets on how to check if you or anyone in your family or workplace may be suffering and require Sanitisation. *Find out more on page 19*

WE WATCH BECAUSE WE CARE

The Reformation of Our Metropolis

Dangerous Ideologies The Metropolis City Council enforced bans to protect its people. All citizens were victims in the war against self-expression, no one was safe. Any activities that could be identified as expressing individuality or creativity were deemed too dangerous. They were banned from Our City. These bans included art, music and a particularly dangerous activity: 'religion'. Many opposed these mandates due to extremist ideologies of *individualism* and sought to fight back. Many were violent in their protestations but Our Great Council knew the necessary course of action.

Reading Check: What were some of the activities banned for their danger to Our City?

A Time For Change At the time, many citizens of Our City deemed themselves above Our law. These people were removed from their toxic environments and cleansed. The cleansing process was what we now know as **Sanitisation**. This process exists for the benefit of all citizens caught breaching the laws of Our City Council. These individuals are dangerous and require immediate rehabilitation. This rehabilitation occurs at Council facilities before they are reintegrated into society. This process still occurs today, with excellent results.

Reading Check: What is the purpose of Sanitisation?

> See fig. 2.3.2 for a graph outlining the decline in illegal activities after the implementation of Our City's **Sanitisation** Programme and complete questions 1–4.

Did you know?

ANCIENT 'ARTIST' VAN GOGH CUT OFF HIS OWN EAR AFTER A PAINTING-INDUCED MANIC EPISODE.

part/one

one

I can feel the raw flesh rubbing against the inside of my heels. The blister just popped. Good, I hope I bleed all over these wretched satin shoes – my first pair of heels. *The first of three*, Mum said. Heels for Occasions. Today is an Occasion.

Actually, today is the 'biggest day of my life'. Today I will walk into the civic auditorium as a seventeen-year-old high school graduate and walk out –

'Name.' The man's grating voice cuts through my reverie. Mum tosses her hair across her shoulder and looks down her nose at the clerk.

'Luanna Veodrum and my daughter, Teddy Veodrum.' I don't bother caring about how she says our last name anymore, the emphasis she puts on it. Like she's speaking in italics. *Veodrum*.

'Row 57 A, B.' He doesn't look at her, and she narrows her eyes. *Everyone* looks at my mother. She's one of – if not *the* – most influential socialites in the City. He hands her two passes, a red one for her and a blue one for me. Another red pass sits menacingly on the bench. The clerk doesn't mention my father's absence. I copy my mother and clip my pass to the lapel of my dress. I swallow. *This is it.*

The door to the left of the clerk's temporary desk is open. I can feel the bodies of the other families behind us, all pushing, eager to get their names marked off and move inside the auditorium. I don't share their enthusiasm. If I could turn around and go home, I would. If I could go back to bed and wake up anytime but today, I would. I hate today. The more I learn about it, the more I feel like I hate this whole year. Today should be a time of grand celebration, my first Council Occasion: my Job Placement. Today marks the first of three ceremonies that signify the completion of my time as a child and student. According to the pamphlet, these ceremonies mark the emergence of my new life as a *worker, wife and womb keeper*.

Our Platinum Jubilee

THE FUTURE IS OURS

Help us celebrate all Our City Council has done for Us and our next generation of watchers, workers and womb keepers. Join Us for this year's Graduate Occasions. Outline of proceedings for this year on the reverse side of this document.

I trail after Mum, but the second I walk into the room I stop. Rows and rows of seats wrap around the circular auditorium, just stopping short of the imposing stage. This building was designed to fit the families of each generation, one Occasion at a time. But that's not what has my attention. Mum turns back to me and smiles.

'Pretty impressive, isn't it?' she says. I can't take my eyes off the colossal honeycomb dome above us. 'It took three thousand glass hexagons to make that dome. Each one cut by hand by master glassworkers.' She draws her eyes from me for a second to look up. 'Takes one's breath away to think about it.' Mum loves those things, the effort something takes, honouring work ethic and achievement when and where it's due. 'Hurry up Teddy, our seats are in row 57, and these stairs aren't going to walk themselves.' I sigh. I can feel the blood sticking against the back of my heels.

My mother ascends the stairs, the centre of attention. Some people stop her to fawn. Others are trying to be subtle, pointing just past us or looking around 'for a friend', but their eyes follow her. It's not hard to see why. My father might be one of the most influential councillors in Our City, but my mother is the voice of the people: the editor of *Metropolis Magazine*, Our only Council-sanctioned entertainment. For seventy years, that *institution* has guided Our City, and now my mother is at its helm. Hers is the voice of reason and trust, and we are the Council's poster family. She smiles benevolently, waving as sycophants call out for her attention. She stops, too, answering all the petty questions she's asked. It's worse than the pain my shoes are causing me. I don't know how she handles it at all, with a smile no less. Nothing slips through her façade.

As we settle into seats A and B, Mum eliminates my father's obnoxiously vacant seat C under the plumes of her skirt. I know it hurts her. His ever-increasing responsibilities on the Mayor's Table seem to have taken precedence over his familial duties, although I can't say I'm sorry for his absence. I slip my shoes off and bend forward to touch my heels. The sharp hiss of air I suck in is enough to catch my mother's attention. She clicks open her purse and passes me two band-aids. I take them with a grateful smile.

Of all the things dwarfed from our high seats, the long, black stage is not one of them. It's bare but for the vast banner hanging from the ceiling, as still as death, displaying Our City's seal, that eye. *Always watching.* There is a podium at the front of the stage. That's it; no guards clustered together in their charcoal uniforms, or eagle-eyed councillors. Yet I cannot shake the feeling of dread that settles across my shoulders like a heavy mantle. I turn to Mum and open my mouth. She looks at me, expectantly.

'Yes?' she asks.

'Nothing,' I say, shaking my head softly so I don't disturb the ornate twist of hair pinned precariously on top of my head. I turn back to the stage and swallow. *Why does it look so horrifying to me?* The band-aids haven't stopped the stinging, but they do help when I slip my shoes back on. I tilt my head back to look up again. The three thousand glass hexagons suddenly feel awfully close, and I notice it smells damp this far up.

I reach across and grab Mum's gloved hand with my own bare one. My hands are uncovered, as is tradition until I'm Partnered. She squeezes it tight and smiles at me. I smile back; a *real* smile this time. Together we rise, and our smiles are gone.

It has begun.

Our City and its People
With pride, truth, courage We stand,
Against all dark evil
Like self, creative or made
In Our predecessors' wake,
Those who couldn't share,

Our vision for Our People. It's time; We don't forget.

As we chant these words, I can feel Our voices resonating in my chest. I used to be filled with excitement, hearing everybody's voices united. I was proud to be a part of this. A bead of sweat runs down my back as the words rattle around in my head: *It's time; We don't forget.* As if we've ever been given the chance. As Our City's anthemic Creed comes to an end, I can hardly make myself move my lips. Nervous anticipation rips through me. I still can't tell if this is the beginning or the end.

'We watch because We care,' we all say together, standing shoulder to shoulder. Before the heat of our breaths has settled, a tall woman walks out from behind the banner. Her hair is grey, her suit is grey and, from up here, her watery, vague eyes look grey too.

'Our People,' she begins, her saccharine voice carrying clearly throughout the vast auditorium. 'It is my honour to be here with Us today, sharing in this Occasion. It is not every day We celebrate an Occasion such as this.' She pauses. 'It is once a year.' She smiles, and everyone laughs. Everyone except me. Her smile doesn't reach her eyes as they scan over us all, like she's scanning us for infection. I can't help but imagine her teeth are sharp and pointy. She gestures for us to sit, and in one sweeping motion over one hundred people comply. I can feel the force of Our action.

'This,' she continues, 'is the story of Our great achievement, the achievement of Our Metropolis City Council. It's the same story We have learnt as students at school each year; the City erected walls to protect Us, the City enacted laws to protect Us, and the City has made sure We are protected every year.' Everyone claps; the applause is not thunderous, it's polite, contained. 'We the People are gathered here today to celebrate Our City's youth. Today is the day they begin their journey of giving back to the City that has given them so much.' I glance at my mother. She has tears in her eyes.

'Our City has worked to protect *Us* – all of *Us* – and to save Us from Ourselves.' The woman suddenly grips the podium and leans forward. Her voice drops. 'I know I don't need to remind any of Us about Our responsibilities.' She stands up straight again and ruffles her papers, despite not having looked at them once. 'You know We are all born with those vile characteristics. The desire to create, to express.' She spits the words out as though merely saying them could infect her. 'They are evil.' She looks up towards the top of the large auditorium. '*We* are evil.' My heart quickens in my chest. It feels like she's looking straight at me.

'*That* is what leads to conflict. *That* is what led humanity to war and, in the end, mass devastation, nuclear fallout and the near extinction of Our very species. Within the walls of Our Metropolis, We're protected by Our City Guards, who patrol the very wall that saved Us from the slow death of Outside. That is why We obey Our curfew. We are simple people, and Our Great Council knows that We need protection from Ourselves.' She pauses again and steps around the podium. She places her hands on her thighs, formally bowing. 'Remember,' she says, her voice still loud and clear, and then everybody is back on their feet, bowing in the same stiff motion. 'We watch –' she begins.

'Because We care,' we respond, as is Our custom.

She nods curtly, and I see a small but satisfied smile playing on her lips.

'My name is Councillor Kathryn Corrumpere, I will now commence the proceedings and reveal who each of you will be, and how you will serve Our Great City, Metropolis.'

I remember her name from Our History classes. Kathryn Corrumpere is known as one of the greatest councillors of Our time, lauded for her exemplary work in the *Sanitisation of the Infected and Jurisdictional Control in the Sanitisation sector*. This is the woman behind the disappearances – the *relocations* of family members around Our City.

She's the reason Lisa is gone.

The thought of my best friend has me picking at the edge of my dress. How can these people accept their friends being taken and then *reintegrated*? And where? I still cannot work out where they are being taken.

'You will all be in the stages of completing your three month Internships – the service we've had you complete before you start your *real* service.' I roll my eyes; three months of slave labour. Mum elbows me and points to the stage. *Focus.*

Councillor Corrumpere continues. 'But that is not all. Today you will join us all as adults in a community that has *supported* you since your birth. And this year is particularly significant as We are also celebrating Our Great City's Platinum Jubilee. This year We are seventy!' The audience collectively jumps; she shouted *seventy* into the microphone, throwing her arms up in triumph. 'You're all here — Our City's brightest new lights, beacons of the future, ready to receive your jobs.'

She reshuffles her papers. 'Could all candidates please rise?'

The rustling sound is overwhelming as all the young people stand, fidgeting at clothes they've never worn, in shoes they don't fill. I swallow hard and look around the enormous auditorium. I'm not the only one stealing a glance.

I only recognise a handful of people — mostly girls, all from my School Code. We've shared the same classes since we were four years old. You would think after all that time together, we might have some kind of friendship. We don't. Lisa was my only friend. She was different from the other girls; she was more like me. *Or maybe I was like her?* Generally, students don't have much exposure to each other socially outside of school. I guess the City doesn't think it's worth it — once we're Partnered, previous lives don't matter. I spot Sarah Parker, looking around to see who's noticed her. It would be hard to miss her in the gaudy orange dress she's chosen. Unfortunately, we make eye contact. Sarah smiles. Correction: smirks.

I think back to school, when Sarah would mock Lisa for her family's lower ranking. Sarah's father, like mine, has a role in the Mayor's office, which will help our Job Placement, maybe even influence how we're Partnered. I loathe Sarah for every minute that she relishes in it, but I hate myself more, for not standing up for Lisa back then. *I was supposed to be her best friend.*

◉

'Pay attention!' Mum hisses beside me, and I realise they're calling the graduates to the front of the stage. I make my way down the stairs towards the pool of eligible young people. Standing amongst the crowd of adolescents, struck by the nauseating mix of perfumes and aftershave, I look around, still half expecting to see Lisa. *Wanting to.* Lisa would have laughed at my blistered heels. She would have put band-aids on at home before she left; she was always so prepared.

I smile at a girl who's playing nervously with a handkerchief beside me. She smiles back, and I feel a little less alone. I look around again, searching for a face I might recognise. I had promised myself I wouldn't be nervous. A part of me is worried that I might get the same job as my Internship, but I'm trying not to think of that exceptional torture. Anyway, it doesn't matter what position I get placed in – I will always have to watch myself. If losing Lisa taught me anything, it's that.

A vacant sort of resignation settles in my chest. I watch some girls giggling, their arms linked. Many of the boys are slapping each other on the shoulder. *Friends.* While we mill about, the 'great' Councillor Corrumpere is still talking. Like all the others, I hardly pay any attention. I move around, listening to the hushed chatter mixing with her speech . . . *Jubilee . . . I hope we're together . . . Chosen ones . . . anything but that . . .* someone bumps me. I look up and realise how close I am to the imposing stage.

'Alright, Children.' The Councillor calls us to attention, her spiel to the parents concluded. 'You are Our next genera tion, Our greatest achievement. You are the future of Our Metropolis City.' Her words have a silencing effect on the gathered youth. We are all still. She looks at us through her watery grey eyes. *Hungry.* I can see, now that I'm closer, her teeth aren't sharp, but I still can't shake the image from my mind.

'I will call Our children to the stage individually. Each will receive their Job Placement then return to their family seating. Please hold any applause to the end.' That last request is accompanied by a stern look at the gathered audience. *I don't think anyone would dare defy that look.* I feel a twisting knot of anticipation form in my stomach. *Stop it. This doesn't mean anything.* But still, it churns. A glance around tells me I'm not the only one.

'Pretty intense, huh?' I hear someone say. There's no reply, and I look around. A boy is standing beside me, smiling. It crinkles his freckly nose. I open my mouth to reply, but can't think of anything to say. 'Don't you reckon?' he asks. I close my mouth and nod. He nods with me, and the action makes his sandy hair flop over his eyes. He looks nice. Kind. A strange thought occurs to me: I wonder if I'm talking to my future Partner. *Could he be?* I swallow, then try to smile back, but he's already turned away. I didn't expect to feel disappointed. I'm not used to talking to boys. It's never encouraged, especially not at school. I want to ask what his School Code is. To find out what neighbourhood he's from. He turns back to me. 'Think this is so crazy. My new shoes are killing my feet!'

'Me too!' I exclaim. A few people turn to give us annoyed looks. I whisper, 'I'm not sure if we're allowed to talk.' He shrugs, looking around.

'Everyone else is?' This time I do smile. This talking to a stranger business is easy enough.

'Yeah, I guess with all us "chosen ones" gathered here there's too many to Sanitise.' I laugh awkwardly.

I have said the wrong thing. The boy's eyes freeze over and his face turns to stone. I want to kick myself. I don't know these people – I need to be more careful. *People don't joke about Sanitisation.*

I take a step closer and try to catch the boy's eye to apologise. Quickly he turns away, muttering about getting a closer view, and then he's disappeared behind the crowd of adolescents.

My attention returns to the stage as the audience breaks into a polite smattering of applause. And then there he is, the sandy-haired boy, marching stoically up to receive his job. 'We congratulate you, Charlie, on your appointment to electrical maintenance at the Metropolis substation. Your work will help us grow Our Great City.' Charlie shakes hands with Councillor Corrumpere, then walks across the stage to two more suit wearing councillors. *When did they get here?* He shakes their hands too, posing for a photo. I realise I need to start paying attention. I follow electrical maintenance worker Charlie until he's lost in the throng of people on the other side of the stage.

'We congratulate you, Helen . . .' Corrumpere continues from the podium. *There!* I see him climbing the stairs to his family's row.

'Teddy Veodrum.' I hear my name over the speakers. A few people from my School Code turn to look as I start making my way through the mass of bodies. As I move towards the stairs on the left of the stage, I can see that they're grated. Perfect for catching the thin heel of these stupid shoes. I wish this process were private, all of it. But we are not afforded the luxury of privacy – especially not at this time in our lives.

I can feel my hand shaking as I grip onto the metal rail beside the stairs. *Don't slip, don't get stuck.* I take two more steps and dare to take a glance out. The lights shining on the stage are so bright I have to look away. Blinking away the glaze of tears, I count five more stairs. I can see the councilwoman staring at me with her cold grey eyes. As I approach, I ball my clammy hands into fists by my sides. Every step I take, I can hear an echo. I glance around, then realise it's me. It's my shoes – they clatter across the stage. I feel like a lie. I don't wear shoes like this. I'm not a mother, a wife. *Yet.* Three more steps. I look up, and Councillor Corrumpere's pursed mouth breaks into her trademark saccharine smile.

'We congratulate you, Teddy, on your appointment at *Metropolis Magazine*. You will work with some of the greatest voices of Our City.' She extends her hand to me. I look out to the crowd, then look back, step forward and take her hand. Her grip is uncomfortably firm and her hand is cold, despite all the flesh it's been touching. I let go before she does. She doesn't tell or show me where to go.

'Kyle Reep,' she reads out. I look around for the exit, then walk towards the two men beckoning to me sternly from the other end of the stage. They don't smile. One of the councillors step forward and takes my hand. I notice a flash but can't see a photographer. He lets go, and the other man takes my hand – another flash from the camera. I'm sure I must look stunned.

'Down the stairs,' the second man says, already looking at the kid behind me.

I step off the stage then walk back to my mother, climbing the stairs up to row 57, to join the *elite*. No one would dare say it, but we know how it works. Your family name is the Council's ranking system. According to my father, Our Council needed a way to ensure their positions are filled, and using surnames makes overseeing this many people much more manageable. I take my seat and Mum pulls me in for a teary hug. She doesn't mask her joy. I try smiling, to look as happy as she feels, but I can't.

'You're so lucky,' she whispers in my ear. I wonder how much influence my father had in my new job, set to be working alongside her. A high-ranking position for our high ranking family. She sits back and dabs her eyes with a cotton handkerchief. I look down towards where I saw that boy go. His family don't look happy. I don't know if it's the distance or an illusion, but I swear I can see his mother frowning.

For the remainder of the ceremony, I'm stuck in a loop, watching each parent receive their child with different emotions. At one point, Mum squeezes my hand and whispers, 'I'm glad I'll be able to keep you close.' I squeeze back. Every family seems to have a different reaction: some are full of joyful tears for their child's new government role. Some jobs are obviously expected, the recipient greeted with a clap on the shoulder and a kiss. Others are unexpected – gasps of joy when an 'E' family find out their daughter will work in Sanitisation; clenched jaws when a 'Q' son gets a construction job. It takes hours. I think this is the reason they don't call us in alphabetical order. Jumping from 'T's' to 'B's' means there's no way to know when we're near the end. Finally, the last child is called.

Councillor Corrumpere smiles at the audience. 'You may now congratulate Our lucky recipients.' The auditorium erupts in applause – genuinely thunderous this time. Some people stamp their feet while others clap with their hands above their heads. I continue to watch the audience, noticing some people aren't clapping at all. My eyes slip back to the sandy-haired boy and his family. His mother is gripping his arm like a vice, while his father claps slowly, his eyes squeezed shut. Deep down in my stomach, I feel that knot twisting its way back in.

'You're so lucky,' Mum whispers in my ear, again. Following my line of sight, she gives me a look that suggests she knows what I've been thinking. I turn my attention back to the now-empty stage, the oversized banner of Our City's Eye gazing over us, *always watching*. My hands start to feel numb, a sensation that quickly spreads through my body. The longer we clap, the more I understand.

None of this is about luck at all.

two

It's dark by the time we make it home, just before curfew, which is two hours past sundown. Once we're inside, before Mum's even put her purse down, she starts her ritual of going from room to room, shutting blinds. I've seen her do it a million times, but tonight there's something different in the clipped way she marches from window to window. It sends a shiver down my spine as I watch her. I can still hear Councillor Corrumpere's voice in my head, reminding us of the need for constant vigilance of family and neighbours. *'Anyone can become infected, it's in Our blood. It is up to you as the next generation to maintain the strict vigilance that We observe; to ensure there are no outbreaks of the New Plague and that no infected person remains untreated.'* In Our City, everything is monitored. Measured. Careful. Neighbours watch neighbours. We know what to do. My teachers loved recap lessons on 'detecting infection', rehashing the three self-expression indicators: Uninhibited Rhetoric, Emotional Dysregulation and (my favourite) Secretive Behaviour. I once thought our home was a sanctuary, but my father showed me at a young age that even family is not to be trusted.

I cross my arms and wait. Mum trips on a corner of the hall rug, her handbag still hanging limply from her arm as she pinwheels for balance.

'What is it?' she asks. I ignore her, kicking off my shoes and leaving them in a mess at the base of the stairs. 'Teddy?' she says, carefully putting her handbag on its hook by the front door. I ignore her and climb the stairs to my room, shutting my door behind me. I take off my new coat, observing the thick black and white checks on the fabric.

My Occasions coat.

I consider hanging it in my wardrobe like I should, then decide

"

better of it. Instead, I dropkick the coat against one of the blue walls, leaving it in a crumpled heap on the floor. Blue walls to match the *theme* of our house. My mother hates blue, but it's my father's colour, and the choice was his to make. Blue is for senior government officials. I consider what my option will be, what role my Partner will have received. It's not fun trying to guess who I'll be Partnered with. A thought crosses my mind: *Does my father know?*

When I was young, I would pretend to be a sailor in the ocean, like our ancestors might have been, when there was an ocean. I loved the blue then. I can still remember Mum letting me sit in the washing basket as she folded clothes. I would scoot around the dining room, under the table, using an umbrella like a paddle while she laughed. That game didn't last long. One afternoon the two of us were in the dining room, and I was under the table, wearing my underwear on my head like a bandana, when I heard footsteps. My father was home from work earlier than expected. His low voice silenced us both, and his words are seared into my mind forever. Even at five, his threat to my mother was clear to me: if he caught me playing again, *she* would pay the price.

'She is not your daughter,' he had said. 'She is Our daughter.' We never spoke of that day again.

I reach around to my back, awkwardly grabbing for the zip of my dress. I could go downstairs and ask for help, but then we'd have to talk, and I don't want to hear Mum telling me again how lucky I am to have this placement and how great Partnership will be. How wonderful it is for *people like me.* That apparently innocuous statement. I finally wiggle out of the too-tight, too-long dress and leave it crumpled on the floor beside the coat, pulling on my favourite black jeans and a plain T-shirt instead of the skirts and blouses Council-approved for women. But no one needs to know what happens in here. My room *is* my sanctuary. Possibly the only place I feel safe.

I walk over to the window seat and reach behind the overstuffed navy-blue cushions. I find what I'm looking for immediately. The smooth leather of the notebook's cover is cool to touch, and comforting in my hand. I carry it to my bed and pick up the pencil on my bedside table as I settle down amongst the pillows. Drawing in a breath, I pull to mind the face of the boy I spoke to. It's already becoming a vague image in my memory. Councillor Kathryn Corrumpere's face is more defined. I lean back and start sketching.

Three raps on the door have me scrambling. I stuff the notebook under my pillow and lean back, but the door's already open before I can say *come in*. 'Why do you bother knocking if you're just going to come in anyway?'

Mum ignores me as she approaches the bed and sits down at my feet.

'What's wrong, Teddy?' she asks softly. 'What are you trying to hide?' Her voice hardens.

'Hide?' I feel the pencil snap in my hand, the tension in my fingers too much for the brittle wood. She points to the corner of the notebook, poorly concealed under one of the pillows. 'Oh, this?' I pull it out, waving it around. 'This is just a – a schoolbook.'

'Really? You graduated three months ago. Just catching up on some overdue homework?' She isn't smiling. Not even a little bit.

'Well,' I start to say, then she stands up abruptly and walks over to my door, flicking it closed in one swift movement.

She leans back against it for a moment, being typically dramatic. I fight the urge to roll my eyes. She stalks around my room, scrutinising everything until her eyes land on my new, crumpled coat and the discarded, expensive dress next to it. She sighs, then picks up both garments and opens my wardrobe. I lie back. *Great.* It's filled with clothing I'm not supposed to have. Things girls aren't supposed to wear. Hoodies, track pants. Mostly green uniform pieces stolen from the male lost property at school. Mostly stolen by Lisa. *Mostly.* I don't say anything, but neither does she, as she moves a green T-shirt aside to hang the coat and then the dress. She closes the wardrobe silently then steps forward.

17

'What is it?' she asks, looking at the leather-bound notebook I'm clutching.

'Nothing. It's just a book.'

She waves her hand dismissively and sits down. 'Cut the crap, Teddy. I know what that book is and what you're doing in it.' She reaches out to touch me, but I pull away. 'What is it?' she says again, softer this time.

'I don't want to do this right now, Mum. Or ever.'

'You know something, Teddy? You're not special.' The frankness of her words stings, even though I know she's right. None of Us are special. We're not anything, We are Our People, only as special as We are useful to Our Great City.

'You're not special because, despite this being some fancy year for Our government, they haven't changed a thing. No – thing. A few extra lines and some razzle-dazzle. It's still the same content. The same *thinly* veiled threat.'

I've never heard Mum talk like this before. I open my mouth to speak, but she holds up a finger, cutting me off. Her eyes dart to each corner of my room as if there might be a camera somewhere, watching us. If any rumours they used to whisper at school are true, there might be. Lisa never believed them. She thought her home was safe. But now she's gone, and so is her whole family. Gone to be *cleansed,* and preparing to start a new life by now, *I can only assume.* Somewhere else in this City.

'Teddy, they said the same things today as they said at *my* Job Placement twenty years ago. The exact same spiel. Did you know that?'

'No,' I say, confused by her change in tack. She sighs.

'I don't want anyone to report you.' She says it softly, and her voice breaks. It was a whisper, but I heard her loud and clear.

'Report me? Why would they do that?' My voice comes out louder than I had intended. I try swallowing, but my throat feels swollen. My eyes dart to the window again. The curtains are closed, but I still feel so exposed. Her eyes resume their dance to each corner of the room. *Does she know something I don't?* I know she would never sell me out, though. Luanna Veodrum would never sell out her daughter. Councillor Paul Veodrum, on the other hand . . .

'All parents were asked to do room checks last week,' she says. 'To provide updated data before Partnership.'

'Room checks?' I say, fighting the growing feeling of nausea.

'I guess it's, as Kathryn puts it, "to cleanse the pool".' She sits back down. 'I found the sketchbook on your bed. Open.'

I reach for the day-old glass of water on my bedside table and drink it down.

'Your father had been asked to do the check, but he's been so busy with work, I assured him I would do it.'

I open my mouth, scrambling for an explanation, but she puts her hand up, silencing me. 'The worst part, Teddy, is that this isn't the first time I've seen it. Don't you realise what you've been doing is dangerous?'

I want to say something in my defence, but I can't think.

My mind is exploding.

'Your father doesn't know.' I let go of my breath slowly.

'At least, I don't think he does. I asked him if he'd noticed anything and he didn't say he had, but that doesn't mean he doesn't know.' She looks away. 'There's a lot your father doesn't tell me.'

'I'm careful,' I say.

'Not careful enough. You know as well as I do that if your father did know, this conversation wouldn't be happening. You wouldn't be here anymore.'

'Like Lisa,' I say softly, and she closes her eyes. Mum had liked Lisa. She was a mile a minute and had a brain full of crazy thoughts, many of which she voiced, which was a worry, but no one had ever suspected her of anything. *Until they did.*

'Precisely. Because Lisa has gone, your father believes there is now a spotlight on you,' she says. 'You aren't supposed to have friends, let alone –'

'Everyone else has friends.'

'Strategic alliances are not the same as friendships,' she snaps.

I flop back against my pillows and stare up at the ceiling, letting my thoughts run through the list of illegal objects I have stashed in my room. Aside from my notebook, one red-coloured pencil Lisa pilfered from school and the contents of my wardrobe, there's also a small collection of rocks I carved into animal shapes when I was nine, paper birds Lisa showed me how to fold when we were ten and one of my most prized possessions, a collection of postcard pictures from the before time.

My grandpa gave them to me when I turned seven. He was watching me while my parents went out. He just walked in, like Mum had now, and caught me drawing. I remember being terrified, but he didn't tell my parents. The next time he was watching me, he gave me the postcards 'to look at'. They were a version of the Metropolis before the wall. A time I had never known. He said I could borrow them, but a week later, he disappeared.

'Grandpa,' I croak, my voice thick with emotion.

'What about him?' Mum says.

'He was Sanitised,' I say, sitting up abruptly. It's not a question. 'He never came home, never came to visit us after they released him.' I can feel the adrenaline seeping into my veins. 'Lisa was Sanitised. But I still haven't heard from her.' Mum looks at me, her eyes hard. 'I know people don't move back into their area codes, people are always moving, but I've never heard of anyone being banned from reaching out to their family. To colleagues.' I can feel my words rushing out, waiting for her to interrupt me . . . or to agree with me.

To explain.

I stop and draw in a breath. It burns the back of my throat. Mum doesn't move, doesn't say anything. She's trying to communicate something through her eyes. Something I don't want to know, something too dangerous to say out loud. Something I already know; have known in my gut for a long time. *We all do.*

I do a mental check of everything I've been told or taught about Sanitisation. I think about the list of offences you can be taken for, the grey trucks filled with men and women in their hazmat suits and perspex masks, lurking in the shadows until they're called to . . . to collect the *infected.* Their job is to take them, cleanse them, and then begin *reintegrating* them into society, taking them to new area codes with new lives, where they can *start over.* That's what we're told. It had always seemed too easy for me, too *clean.* Despite the fear of Sanitisation, there were always doubts. A niggling fear that it wasn't the reality . . . and that reality is so much worse.

I think of Lisa and her family, the Pechs. They were kind people. Middle class. Not what my father had wanted for us. *Middlers are acquaintances fit for middle people,* he had said. *We are not middle people. Remember, you're Teddy* Veodrum. *Remember where and with whom you belong.* He said those things to me six months ago after he saw us walking home from school together. It was one of those rare occasions he'd come home early. Lisa was an anomaly, a *middler* enrolled at my school, the highest coded school in Our City. I never thought of her any differently for it. Not until my father made that comment, even though we had known each other for years by then. Three months later, she was gone.

'Sanitisation is a lie,' I blurt out.

'Shut up,' Mum says, covering her ears. 'Just shut up.'

I've never heard her talk like that before. She dashes over to my window and pulls the already shut curtains even tighter, causing them to peek open at the sides, then she crumples onto the window seat, going still. So still, until her features squeeze tight and a sob escapes her lips. This time I've gone too far, but I can't unsay what I said. And I can't unthink it.

I can't unknow the truth.

That's why they teach us about Sanitisation using words like *cleanse* and *reintegration.* It's why we all wear formal shoes and clothes and celebrate Occasions that are rigged according to your family name in the City's hierarchy. It's the façade of trust. That same façade that shapes everything in this City. *Don't look too close, don't you dare.* That threat of death, of the loss of a loved one or your whole family, is a very persuasive motivator. But the City would never allow this to be common knowledge. They are here to help us. They *care.*

'I'm right, aren't I?' I say, but she won't meet my gaze. 'If people know what the City is doing, why hasn't anyone said anything?'

She draws in a deep breath, and for the first time, I notice the wrinkles around her eyes. It must be hard for her to think about her father being taken. They were so close, not like me and my father – a man who loves his position, his status, his authority more than his own family. I don't know if he even knows what love is. I feel a shiver run down my spine. *What if I end up with a Partner as cold as him?* I reach out to my mother and she takes my hand. I can't imagine how she must feel. Her father was taken and her husband works for the people who took him. I can't imagine what it must be like for her, helping perpetuate their lies.

She wipes her nose. 'The Council works based on fear. That's how all the councillors work. Including Paul.' She whispers my father's name, glancing at the door as if half expecting him to walk in. After all, it wouldn't be the first time he'd shown up unexpectedly. 'My mother was taken first. She was caught by her boss. Singing. Years later I heard a rumour she wasn't even singing, just humming, but her supervisor overheard and reported her to *Our* City.'

I've never heard her say it that way – loaded with disdain.

'Three days later, they knocked our door down in the middle of the night, and she was taken away.'

This is the first time she's ever talked to me about her mother. Grandpa used to talk about her occasionally, but Mum never did.

'They keep everything very hushed up,' she continues. 'I guess it doesn't look good for people to see these things happening every day. It might make people think things aren't running as smoothly as they'd like us to believe they are.' She leans closer. 'I don't want to tell you this, but you need to hear it – now more than ever, with your Partnership looming. The truth is this: people are taken every second.'

I want to ask how she knows all this, but I'm afraid that if I interrupt, she'll stop, so I just listen in silence, her words chilling me.

'Your grandpa started mixing with the wrong people. I guess he wanted to try to find out where they had taken my mother, to see when she'd be coming home. We still believed they returned people back then – many people still do – but it never happened.' She starts worrying her bottom lip while her hands wring in her lap. 'He woke me in the middle of the night, and we left.' Her voice is barely a whisper. 'I had five minutes to fit my life into an overnight bag before we moved into a new area and I was given a new name. I went from Luanna Burke to Luanna Westman.'

I feel like my chin is about to hit the floor. I try imagining my mother, perfect wife and model Metropolis citizen, sneaking out in the middle of the night to start a new life. It seems impossible.

'What are you saying?' I ask, grabbing her shoulder. 'What are you talking about?'

'We slipped into a new life with the help of some *sympathetic* councillors. There are always people willing to help if you know how to find them. Your grandpa got a new job and we had a new last name. No one questioned anything because the records all reflected it to be fact. For all our neighbours knew, we were just a typical relocated family. Many jobs require that kind of transience. Almost all blue-collar workers are needed to go where the infrastructure requires them. Anyway, people believe what they're told if you can be convincing enough.

'I was in my graduating year. The month following, I was Partnered with your father.' At the mention of my father, her tone shifts. I can't tell if it's regret or sorrow in her voice, or just long-accepted resignation. *He's nothing like her.* When I was young, I always knew it was my father's senior role as a councillor that made it so hard for me to talk to people at school. Lisa was the only one who didn't mind. Some kids were wary I would report them to my father, or worse – forced by their desperate parents to peacock their way into my orbit.

Mum wipes her eyes with the back of her cotton sleeve, smudging black eyeliner across her face in huge streaks. I take her hand, and try to give her a supportive smile. I've always felt like a circle in a box – no matter how hard I tried, I would never be able to reach the corners. I've spent my life assuming I was alone in that, but now it seems my mum and I might not be as different as I thought.

'So, if you managed to get away, why was Grandpa Sanitised?' I ask.

She shrugs. 'I guess they found him out,' she says, her voice thick with emotion. 'Or they were getting close, and he decided to sacrifice himself for us, so we could have our lives.' She shakes her head, and her dark brown curls bounce softly around her face. 'It's complicated, and it's dangerous, and there are many ways he could have slipped up.' I can see tears starting to well in her eyes again. 'Don't ask me any more questions, please?'

I want to, even more so now, but Mum looks so tired, I can't bring myself to do it. I sigh. But there's one more thing I need to know.

'Are you infected?' I ask. She smiles at me and leans forward to kiss my forehead.

'No more than you are, baby,' she whispers, the smell of her perfume both cloying and comforting as she hugs me then stands to leave. 'I guess my point in telling you all this is . . . I just want you to understand that if you continue doing these things after you're Partnered –' She can't meet my eyes. 'I don't want to lose my daughter too. Promise me you'll stop doing what you've been doing in that book?'

'I promise,' I say, feeling the lie tearing at my insides.

three

I am exhausted, yet sleep won't come. Mum's words keep playing on a loop in my mind, shattering everything I thought I knew about our world. For years I have fought with myself over the things we just talked about, trying to quash my theories about Sanitisation. I tried to silence Lisa, to tell her she was wrong, even though I was waging war within myself the whole time. I toss over again and let everything my mother just confessed wash over me. We could die for this. Really, truly die. Be dragged from our homes and then – I don't know. I feel the nausea build again. *What do they do to people once they're taken?* I roll over again. *And to think I tried to fool myself into thinking I was okay with all this.*

We were only five when we first learnt about Sanitisation. It was our third day of school. All the children sat in the white classroom; no one moved, no one even fidgeted. We were watching a movie about good children and bad children. It opened with grassy fields I had never seen before, as smiling blonde- and black-haired children chanted as they held hands in a circle. Then the scene suddenly changed. The sky went black, and grey vans surrounded the children as they were strapped to ambulance beds by men in white overalls. The van doors slammed shut, and the children were transported away.

I can remember some of the children in my class crying. They were told to be silent. I didn't cry. I was more scared of our teacher than I was of the men in the movie. I didn't think they were real.

I roll over and flip my pillow, pressing my hot cheek into its cool surface. We watched a different version of that movie every year, and each time, the children got older, just like we did. The last video we were shown was just before graduation. Lisa had already been taken. In that video, a man woke to find his Partner kneeling in the darkness, whispering unintelligible words, her hands pressed together in front of her chest. Black smoke billowed out from her nightgown. He panicked and called the Council Eye to report her. That film ended differently to the others. The men showed up in white marshmallow suits, perspex screens protecting their faces. The Sanitisation Crew raided their house, taking the man's wife out into the street, still in her nightgown. The woman screamed as her young child watched from the window, standing next to his father. I remember the unfamiliar ending on the screen:

See it, say it. Phone the Council Eye at extension 3-9-3.

I sit up. The videos never showed people 'Sanitised'. *Why hadn't I noticed that before?* After all these years, they never showed us the children *after* they had been Sanitised. *How had I been so blind?*

Within Our City walls, every citizen is promised safety. Every moment of our lives is prescribed, for our own good. We're told we're being saved from ourselves because we don't know what's best. We don't know what job we're best suited for; Our City does. We don't know who the right person to marry is; Our City does. Whether we have children is determined by Our City; it's for our own good. Just like we were taught in seventh grade. After all, how could they let everyone make their own choices? We don't know if we're capable of managing that kind of responsibility. *We* don't, but Our City does. We don't know if we're infected, but Our City does.

Each year is planned, each moment accounted for – until you step one foot out of line. Then you're Sanitised. Sanitisation, that miraculous process where they take you away, cleanse you, then prepare you for reintegration into society. It's all just a huge *lie*. If they're lying to the entire City about that, then what else are they lying about? I feel bile in my throat. My room feels hot. Suffocating. I throw back my covers, rush over to the window and tear open the curtain, revealing the inky black night. I open my window and the cold air hits me, filling my nostrils with the sweet smell of grass and dew.

The watery moonlight casts pale shadows over our neighbours' red-tiled roofs. In our suburb, we live in unison. Every car is black, every house is white, and the lawns are trimmed with exquisite precision. I rest my head against the glass. Even the beads of dew that cling to those perfectly manicured blades of grass look carefully constructed. The leaves on the trees are dancing, their rustling a soft murmur in the silence.

The wind is absolutely free, I think. It's the only thing that can't be controlled and shaped by Our City.

Something moves. I see it in the corner of my eye.

A cat?

I scan the neighbours' front lawns. Any pet unlucky enough to be out at night would be punished, as would their family. There it is again, the same shadowy movement. I see it clearly now – a shadow slipping across the night. It's taller than a cat, tall enough to be – no. I open my window wider and stick my head out. *Yes.* I think it is a person. A scene unfolds in my head: my grandpa slipping out into the night with Mum behind him, their bodies enveloped by the darkness as they make their way towards a new life.

Something pushes from inside me. I want to follow the shadow. To find out who it is. A sliver of my mind cries out for me to stop, begging me to climb back into my warm, safe bed, to forget everything and go on blindly, but I can't. Now I know too much, I must go. Ignoring this isn't an option.

I cross my bedroom and press my ear against the door. I want to feel the cool night air hit my face. I want to be *out* while the rest of the City is trapped inside. I can hear the shower running in my parents' en suite. That means my mother will go to bed soon and won't be coming to check on me again.

I quickly change out of my nightgown into my black jeans and pull a dark hoodie over my T-shirt. My hands are shaking so much I can hardly get my arms into the sleeves. I creep over to my window, feeling that tug inside me again. *If the shadow's gone, there's no point in going out.* If the shadow was gone, I would do this anyway. *Will* do this. A rustling in a bush three houses down catches my attention. Glancing back over my shoulder for a final time, I clamber over the ledge and fall more than jump into the pristine flowerbed below.

four

All I can hear are my footsteps and my heart thumping. If I'm caught, I'll be killed. This chilling realisation hits me as hard as my feet are hitting the pavement. *Are they as loud as they sound to me?* I swallow a lump of spit and glance over my shoulder. I haven't given myself a chance to stop yet. I'm afraid if I do, I'll turn back, run home to the window I left ajar and climb into my warm bed. I don't want to do that. I don't want to be that person. If the Council is going to dictate what the rest of my life will be like, I deserve to feel alive, even if it's only this once, a tantalising first and last taste of freedom before even my bed becomes a place where I'm watched.

My pace quickens, and I glance over my shoulder again. *You're just paranoid.* My Partnership is something I had never been worried about. Not until this year. I had even been looking forward to it. As children, we were forbidden from associating with the opposite gender except for official school business. Even during the three-month break between school ending and our Partnership Ceremony, we weren't allowed to mingle *in public.* I didn't have to be invited to the secret gatherings to know they were happening. Considering I barely associate with people of my own gender, let alone boys, I wouldn't want the pressure of that illicit life. But it was a moot point. I'd never be invited, because of my family.

Lisa always told me she couldn't bear to go anyway. *Why spend extra time with people we hate?* She was right. I turn down a street to my left, keeping an eye on the shadow's brisk and somewhat erratic movements. *Haven't I been down this street already?* Lisa's worry was that she'd end up with a Partner she hated. 'It will be a perfect scientific match,' I told her. Now my fear is ending up with a Partner who's married to the Council before he's married to me.

I stop and look around. *Crap.* I hadn't realised how far I've walked. I thought I would remember the path I've taken, but the shadow seems to be far more familiar with this City than me. I don't recognise where I am. I can feel the panic rising in my chest. We've been weaving through so many streets I'm not sure I could find my way back now. The big white houses of my suburb have been replaced with small grey cinderbrick terraces, huddled close together. I don't recognise these places, these streets, but I've had little reason to go out past the narrow wedge of my suburb so it's unsurprising. I know from school that Our sprawling City is built within the confines of the Great Wall. The ultimate barrier to protect Us from the devastation outside. *Nuclear fallout.*

We are the Chosen People.

Us.

The chipped paint on the wooden fences looks old and uninviting in the moonlight. I wonder why these people don't have perfect walls like those in my neighbourhood. Each of these box-like houses looks the same, but unlike my suburb, these homes are all vacant-looking, devoid of any life or colour. *It's like a concrete maze.* There are so many things I don't know about this City. Every crack in the pavement feels like it's screaming at me to look closer. *What else don't I know?* My attention snags on the shadow as it ducks down a side street. My blood chills in my veins when I hear the sound it is scuttling away from.

The crackle of radio static carries across the deadly silent street. I thought we had been too lucky, or the shadow had been too smart, had known where to twist and snake through the streets, but it appears our luck is out. A louder crackle of a static sends me darting up the road, following the path the shadow just laid. My sore feet and aching heels protest as I skid around the corner just before they come into view, light packs attached to their padded vests. Guards.

I hear them approaching, their studded boots clinking in unison. I peek around the corner. There are at least ten of them, coming faster, each marching step ringing out into the night.

There's no time to think. I sprint. Behind me, I can still hear the unsettling crackle of radios as I run down the side street and into an alley. I stumble over something, an empty can, and it rattles against the stone wall. *This is how I die.* I reach the end of the alley and look up and down the dark street. No guards, but I can still hear the hiss of their radios over the thump of my heartbeat. I turn right and run faster than I have ever run before, knees jarring every time my sneakers hit the pavement. I feel hot tears running down my cheeks. Each step propels me further from the guards. The tears continue to flow, and as I keep running, I realise they aren't for me. They're for my mother. *This was selfish. Stupid. I can't leave her alone with him. I can't leave her like this.* I ignore the pain and run deeper into the City I thought I knew.

I stop and heave air into my lungs. I've never run like that before. It hurts, but I relish the pain shooting through my legs and burning in my lungs. *It feels like freedom.* I stop and hold my breath for a second, listening, and glance behind me to make sure I'm alone. There is no sound around me, and there are no houses. Satisfied that I have left any immediate danger behind me, I finally look up, scanning the towering buildings that surround me. The rusty smell in the air clicks a memory into place. I have somehow made it to the warehouse district. I've only been here a few times, picking up furniture with my parents. The deserted area looks different under a shroud of darkness. Old shipping containers loom overhead, stacked in tall columns between each of the rusty brick and metal warehouses, some built long before the wall was erected. I creep over to the closest warehouse. It was once green, but now has only tiny chips of the colour left on its exterior.

I sit down on a step and close my eyes for a second. I have no idea how to get home now. During the day, I might be able to find my way back to Downtown, where the City Council Buildings loom over us, casting day-long shadows. Once there, it would be easier to navigate my way home.

I was ten years old the first time I was allowed to see these buildings. We went there on a school trip. Lisa and I huddled together, terrified by the enormous buildings; thousands of bricks stacked higher than anything I'd ever seen. As we got older, it wasn't the buildings that frightened us, it was the cameras. We first started to notice them there, then everywhere. They weren't just on the corners of the Council Buildings, they were at the shops and at our school. Everywhere we went, Lisa would point them out. But carefully. After all, if we could see them, they could see us. I wish she were here now. *This wouldn't have scared her.* I let myself imagine for a second that she was the shadow. That she had come back to get me.

I take a deep breath. Lisa isn't here, and I can look after myself. I look around again. I *do* recognise where I am. If I head straight back the way I came, I will end up in Downtown. But now I can't stop thinking about the cameras. Watching . . . because they care. They are everywhere. Plus, I'm at *least* forty-five minutes from home. *No wonder my legs are so sore.* I begin to realise that I may have just made the biggest mistake of my short life. But there isn't much time to bemoan my choices, because I hear a rustling sound metres away from where I'm standing. It's too loud to be a rat. The shadow slips out from between two closely stacked container columns. I can't believe it. It's definitely the same person, the slight figure I saw huddled in the corner of the darkness.

'Hey,' I call out softly.

The figure startles, then makes a mad dash across the expanse to the next row. I blink twice as she – *she!* – darts across the open space, her hair lighting up bright pink in one of the few floodlights that still work.

'Hey!' I call out again, then I leap from my step and follow her.

'Wait a second!' I see another flash of her pink hair and then she disappears from view.

I come to a complete stop as a fist connects with my stomach.

'Stop following me!' hisses the girl.

'Who are you?' I whisper, clutching my stomach. Her hand covers my mouth.

'Shut. Up.'

I try to speak, but the girl pushes me against the wall and a sharp pain shoots through my shoulder. I almost scream at the intensity of it, but I bite it back to a whimper when I see the look on her face.

'Do you *want* to get us killed?' she snarls.

I reach back and touch my shoulder, and my fingers come away bloody. I can feel a nail digging into me. I pull away gingerly, feeling my skin resist as I tear it off the long-rusted nail. A loud hiss escapes my mouth. The girl lets me go, but puts a finger against her lips.

'Stay the heck away from me,' she says, and slips behind another container.

I press my hand against my shoulder, trying to stop the oozing blood, then peer around the corner after her. The crackle of radio breaks the silence, but I can't hear any marching boots. *Yet.*

'I told you to get lost!' the girl says over her shoulder, her voice louder.

I don't care what she says, I've come this far. I step out to follow her and a large hand covers my mouth, then forces a cloth into it. I struggle against the grip, gagging at the fabric suffocating me. The movement jars my shoulder, sending ripples of pain down my back.

This is it. This is how I go.

Taken by guards, anonymous and alone.

Will my parents even know I'm gone?

five

I open my heavy eyelids. The air around me is stale, and I can tell I'm being carried. No, not carried – dragged.

It takes a few moments for my eyes to adjust, but when they do, I recognise the pink-haired girl stomping ahead of me. I'm being dragged by a tall man whose long hair is spiked up along the middle of his head. If I weren't so terrified, I'd probably think he looked ridiculous. But I am frightened. I can feel the blood pumping around my body, my mind rushing to find an escape. I'm being towed on a wooden pallet. *They must think I'm still passed out.*

I can't hear any footsteps behind us, so I risk a glance. My pulse is thumping in my neck. We turn down a long corridor, and tiny clouds of dirt fly up into my face every time the pallet jolts over some loose stones.

No one's there.

As I stare back at the darkness behind us, green tiles with dim yellow lights suddenly appear around us in the corridor.

The unknown seems like my best option. My *only* option.

I must make my move now. If I wait, it will be too late.

I twist myself around blindly, ignoring my shoulder's protest, then take off into the darkness. Someone is quicker. Before I know it, big hands are around my waist, and that cloth is being shoved in my face again. A bitter smell bites at my nostrils, and I'm fading.

I wake up slumped over uncomfortably. I kick, but my legs won't work. I can feel them, feel the stinging pain but they . . . *won't*. I look down and immediately see why. My legs are bound. No, *I'm* bound – tied to a rigid metal cafeteria chair. My wrists and shoulders are restrained too. I try pulling a hand free, but it won't move. I start to panic. I can feel the pressure rising in my chest. Desperate, I struggle until I somehow manage to bunny-hop forward. The metal chair makes a loud, scraping sound on the concrete floor, and the horrible noise sharpens my ears. Now I can hear something else. *Shouting.* I'm not alone in here. That wakes me up a bit.

'Are you completely useless?' The words are loud but mangled in my head. 'You have one job, and you can't even do that right, you skinny little worm.'

I open my mouth, but nothing comes out. Then I see her. A woman. Angry. Screaming.

She's screaming at someone out of the ring of light. Then she turns and storms towards me, and in a heartbeat her cruel, lined face is inches from mine. She's so close I can see the spit pooling in sticky, white puddles at the corners of her mouth. Her hands are on her hips.

'What about you?' she snarls. Her breath is warm and sour, and I can't help it, I gag.

'Excuse me?' she demands, kicking my shin.

I bite the inside of my cheek to keep from crying out.

'. . . That is why I need some answers. Because right now, I don't think I need you, you prissy bitch.'

Dizzy, I try focusing on the woman in front of me. On her thick midsection and beady eyes twisted in rage. Her hands, perched on her waist, are . . . grotesque. Each finger is swollen and strained, like when you fill a cleaning glove with water. Mum called it a balloon. *Mum.* I groan.

'What was that?' she shouts in my ear, her hand clamping down on my wounded shoulder. I bite back a scream of pain. She shoves me and walks off. I can see her calling someone over, then the girl with pink hair steps into the light.

'Luckily, I didn't get Link to kill her *and* you on the spot!' the old woman shouts. Pink looks angry. I don't have the energy to feel angry right now.

'Luckily, *I* was there to keep Link from killing her there. Listen,

Paula, she's injured, she fell against a nail up there. Let's just throw her back up.' The girl shoots me a look. *An apology?*

'I brought you the girl, didn't I. You can see she's useless.' But . . . *why?* A cry escapes from my lips.

Both pairs of eyes shoot to me, and the woman turns her back on the girl and takes a step towards me. 'Now you're crying?' *Am I?* 'Little bitch.' She steps forward again and grabs my ponytail, pulling my head back so far I think it's going to pop right off my shoulders.

'I'll give you a reason to cry.' Her free hand finds my shoulder wound again. I jerk, screaming, but I can't move far with my hair still in her other hand. I can feel her fingers now, pressing into the open wound.

Pain obscures my vision as it fills with spots. I try to blink them away. *Why is she doing this?* I find the woman's face again through the bright light. She's flexing her balloon fingers. *I didn't do anything wrong.* I sob, I can't help it, it just comes out. *I did* do something wrong. All of this is my fault.

'Who are you?' she says through clenched teeth. I suck in a sharp breath, trying to speak, but the words won't come. I can't seem to slow my breathing either. The woman starts to talk again — to yell, but it's hard for me to hear anything above the roar of pain in my ears. My eyes won't stay open. I am sliding into nothing.

'Answer me!' The woman's face is inches away, and the lights are making my eyes sting. I'm searching for something familiar to hold on to, something to focus on. I can hear her clearly now. 'I said, what is your name?' The woman shoves my chair as she stands up and crosses her bare arms against her chest. I blink a few times. She's looking down her nose at me, but she's not tall. Her pants are rolled at the hem, too — men's pants, lots of pockets . . . Probably where she hides people's fingers. *I bet she hates other people's fingers.* The thought of it makes me smile and, before I can stop it, a gurgle of laughter escapes my lips.

'Something funny?' Her spit lands on my cheek, and I imagine my eardrum exploding from the volume of her voice. 'Tell me,' she says, her voice suddenly soft. *Is that a smile?* Her teeth are entirely yellow. She squats down in front of me, her hands on my knees. I brace for pain, but it doesn't come. 'Tell me,' she says again. I can feel the hairs on the back of my neck prickle. Somehow this approach is far, *far* worse. I can feel the spit foaming in my mouth. I try to swallow it, but I can't even breathe. The soft grip turns vice-like, and I swear I can feel bruises forming, one for each of her stodgy fingers. I want to shout at her, tell her to stop, but the words won't come out. My voice is nothing more than a croak, and my throat feels dry. Foreign.

She shoves my chair again and walks away. I watch her move out of the pool of light, my eyes straining to see through the harsh lights. They're watering. *Or are they tears?* I can see the pink-haired girl. She reaches forward, gripping the older woman by the forearms. Balloon-fingers pulls back and slaps her. Her pink hair bounces from the impact, her cheek smeared with blood, then she leaves, casting a glance back over her shoulder. *Is she crying?*

Now we're alone. I grit my teeth against the agony I feel in my body as the woman steps back towards me. Paula wipes her hand on her white singlet, leaving dark red smears, then steps closer, her voice low and threatening.

'Kit told me you followed her, which makes me think you're a spy or, as you like to call it, *Council Eye.* Now, Kit doesn't think so, and maybe she's right. But guess what? She's not the boss; *I am*, and I think you're a spy. So, *Sunlight,*' she snarls the word at me, 'what do you think I should do with you?'

Suddenly there's a loud screech of metal on cement, and a burst of cool blasts through. I drink it in as best I can. A boy runs over to us, huffing, then notices me tied to the chair. He freezes, and his eyes widen in shock. The kid can't be much older than ten.

'Ss-sorry Paula. I —' he pants, trying to draw his eyes away. He's been running.

'WHAT?' she roars, stepping in front of me to obscure his view.

'Jamie sent me; my sister, Meg . . . she's having another attack a-a-and the medicine's all gone.' The boy looks around her, and I catch his eye.

'What do you mean, *all gone*?' she says, pushing him back towards the door.

'She used the last of the puffers earlier this week. This is the second attack in a week. Sh-she can't breathe.' The boy looks stricken.

'Oh, fuck.' Paula turns around to face me again, and her mask slips for a second. There is no concern on her face to match her words; instead, I see a glimmer of satisfaction. I don't think she was surprised by the boy's news, and the way her lip curls . . . she's certainly not concerned.

Then her mask is back.

She looks from me to the boy at the door, who's bouncing uneasily from foot to foot, and then back at me. Her eyes narrow into two black slits. 'I don't have time for pieces of shit like you.' She turns to leave, then swings back, fist raised, and I realise.

Meg isn't the only one who is clearly expendable.

six

I sit up gasping for air. Everything hurts. The air around me is warm and smells sweet. Blinking in the dim light, I realise I'm back in my own room. Twisting my neck to look around sends a shooting pain into my shoulder. I flick on my bedside lamp. The clock reads 4.45 am, and my quilt is skewed around me as if I slept fitfully.

What? How?

The last thing I remember is the face of that woman. Paula. My shoulder aches. My legs ache. I glance at my desk, scan my room: everything is in its place. My shoes are in a crumpled pile on the floor near my window, next to the swinging foot.

Foot?

I pull the covers up to my chin. The pink-haired girl is perched on my window seat.

'You should be more careful,' she drawls, not looking up from the notebook she's flicking through. *My* notebook. I force back the desire to throw my alarm clock at her head. Some of my memories are hazy. Her presence and then her absence are not. I grit my teeth as I turn to face her properly.

She looks at me. 'People have been *Sanitised* for less than keeping a diary with hand-drawn pictures in it!'

'What?' I ask, my voice coming out in a croak. She left me there with that monster. *What kind of person doesn't help in a situation like that?*

'This.' She waves my notebook in front of her face like it's a fish. 'I think you should be more careful. Sanitisation is not the way *I'd* like to go.'

'What would you know about that?' I snap, then swallow. My throat feels like sandpaper. She ignores me, unfolding her long legs and crossing the floor to my bedside in two long steps. Her eyes are bright, glowing in amusement. It makes me even more irritable.

'I'm Kit,' she says, waving a hand tipped with long pink nails.

'Your nails match your hair,' I say before I can stop myself. I've never seen anything like that colour.

Kit rolls her eyes, then sits on the end of my bed, smiling at me. The smile doesn't look friendly; it's more like the smile of a predator about to eat its prey.

'I don't care who you are,' I say, trying to sound nonchalant and regain some dignity. 'You just left me there for dead.' I'm surprised at the strength behind my words, even as I try to keep my volume down. The last thing I need is for Mum to walk in.

'I helped you! How do you think you got back home?' she says, peeling off her jacket. She throws it on the floor and I recoil, snatching at my sheets. Her arms are covered in black inky swirls. *Is that what infection looks like?*

'What's that?' I say, drawing my legs up.

'These? They're tattoos.' I wait for her to continue, but she just looks at me. 'You don't know what tattoos are?' She whistles low and slow. 'They're harmless, chill out. They're just art.'

So, it is *an infection.*

'Listen. You're wrong,' she says. 'I might have left you in that room. But I did help. You're here now rather than down there.' She rolls her eyes. 'Or dead. Which means I helped you.' She looks at me, holding my gaze for a moment. No smile. When I don't reply, she shrugs, then starts picking at her nails, chipping off little flakes of pink onto my quilt.

I draw in a full breath then let it go slowly. I think about Mum, asleep in the room down the hall, and guilt starts bubbling to the surface. Her alarm will be going off in one hour. Then my thoughts slip back to last night. The face of that woman, her thick fingers. It makes my skin crawl. Maybe Kit is right. I don't know how I got back here, but I can only assume it's thanks to her. I lie back against my pillow, but it hurts my shoulder, so I sit up again. She stops picking for a moment and looks at me, head cocked to one side.

Watching. I ignore her. Once I've rearranged myself, she nods as if satisfied and goes back to her picking.

I pull back the quilt to get up, to get away from her, and discover I'm still wearing my jeans and T-shirt from last night, both of which are ripped and stained with dirt and blood. *My* blood. The shirt has one significant tear along the right shoulder. *Where did my hoodie go?* Kit shrugs as I look back at her in horror.

'Did you really think I was going to change you? We're not *friends*, Teddy,' she says.

'How do you know my name?'

Kit indicates the notebook over on the window seat. I shake my head. Great. *Now everybody knows about my notebook.*

'Sorry, you'll need clean sheets too,' she adds, not sounding sorry at all.

I stand up and stumble, and in a flash she's by my side, steadying me with a firm hand. I lean on her gratefully. I don't understand how someone can be so hostile one moment and so kind the next. Looking down, I see that my bedsheets are smeared with dirt and blood. Mum will freak out if she sees this.

'Shit, I need to sort this out before my mum –' My eyes land on the door.

'She's still in bed, I think. When we got back all the lights in the house were turned off. The heat was on though.' Something in her voice sits uncomfortably close to envy. She leads me over to my desk and sits me on my chair. Then she walks off, opening my wardrobe door.

I look over at my window. The curtains are open a crack, but it's still dark outside. Kit paws over my belongings for a while, then turns to face me. 'It's Wednesday morning.' She's holding the ridiculous green dress my mother bought me for the Partnership Ceremony. She wrinkles her nose, and I can't help doing the same.

'I know that,' I say, still irritated. 'I have to get ready for my Internship. It's my last day.' She hangs the dress up and then grabs it again and moves it, burying it deep within the folds of other equally horrendous dresses. I slide my wardrobe door across to the other side. Now we're reflected, side by side. I look shocking. My skin is swollen around my collar, and my arms are bruised. My face is smeared with dirt, framed by the bird's nest of hair on top of my head. I meet her eyes in the reflection, and see that she's holding in a laugh. I feel sick. 'I can't really remember any of this.' I gesture to my body. She looks at me and, for a second, seems genuinely concerned. Then she rolls her eyes.

'That's the Underground for you,' she says, shrugging, then turns and walks away.

I turn to face her. She's stripping my bed. 'The *Underground?*' I ask.

'I tried to find some clean sheets in here – couldn't. I didn't want to sneak around your house.'

'In the hall cupboard next to my door,' I say on reflex. She nods curtly.

'If you have any disinfectant or a clean bandage, I can fix you up.' She expertly bundles the dirty sheets into a neat ball, all the scum carefully concealed on the inside.

'What's the Underground?' I ask again, but Kit's completely ignoring me. She throws the ball of sheets towards me, then lies back on the stripped bed, hands behind her head. 'Tell me,' I push.

A split second later she's sitting back up. She slides open my bedside-table drawer and begins lining up my belongings along the top: a lip balm, old school notes, the Ceremonies brochure.

'The place you just were. Where you got this.' She turns to face me, wiggling a long finger up and down my dishevelled body. 'It's down there.' She points down below our feet, then turns back to my drawer.

I glance at my now cluttered bedside and the time on the clock flashes forward: 5.02 am. *Shit.* I really don't have time for this.

'I'm going to take a shower before my mum wakes up and sees me like this.' I snatch an assortment of clothes from my wardrobe. 'I'll bring some first-aid stuff back up, then you are going to explain *exactly* what's happening. You'd better not leave,' I add, trying to make my tone menacing, but I don't think she's even listening as I slip out the door.

I know the code to override 'ideal' cleansing temperatures, so I set the shower temperature manually – hot. As hot as it will go. The floor-to-ceiling screen fogs up almost instantly as I close the temperature panel.

It stings, but it feels good to burn the blood and dirt off my body while I try to piece everything together in my mind. *Who is Kit? What is the Underground?*

I select my favourite body wash and wave my hand under the dispenser. It buzzes while it squeezes a generous amount into my palm. Instantly my olfactory senses are filled with strawberry and vanilla. I hadn't even known these things were a luxury until I became friends with Lisa. Her house had manual soap pumps. One scent: soap. One night we worked on an assignment too late and I slept over. The soap didn't smell bad, but it was slimy and stung my eyes. Afterwards, I asked her mum if they had any other soaps. She just laughed at me and walked away.

I shake my head, letting the thoughts wash away with the swirly red mixture of soap, water and blood. I cover my head in shampoo and try to loosen the more stubborn crusty layer around my shoulder. That proves painful, and even this soap stings a little as I discover grazes across the back of my shoulders, elbows and knees. I let the water wash over me while I massage shampoo out of my hair. It feels like the hot water is loosening my muscles and washing away some of the tension the last twenty-four hours have inflicted. No matter how hard I scrub, one thing in particular is still bothering me: Paula. Even the hot water can't stop the shiver that runs down my spine as I think about her expression when the boy told her that girl was dying. I saw her apathy as clear as day.

I step out of the bathroom dressed in what is possibly my most hated garment – a black blouse with black fabric buttons, lots of them, and a ruffled collar. I don't do the buttons all the way up to my neck. I always wait until I'm walking in the front door of Maree's cafe, about to start my shift, to complete that final indignity. I'm also holding off on wearing the ridiculously full skirt and apron that finishes off my uniform, opting instead for a pair of black sweats until I have to go. Mum hates these pants. She still can't understand why I won't wear the silky pyjamas she buys me.

I grab the box of first-aid supplies from above the kitchen sink and a packet of chips from the pantry. Part of me hopes Kit has left, so everything can just go back to normal. But I know she'll still be there, and a more significant part of me feels happy about that. Walking down the hallway, I notice how still and quiet the house is at this pre-dawn hour.

I pass my father's study and look at the closed door. It's been almost ten days since he was last at home. The initial sadness I noticed in my mother seems to have turned, mostly, to resignation. Apparently, his work for the Mayor is more important than being at home. Sleeping at work is expected when you can't even travel in a vehicle after curfew. I reach out and brush my fingers over the cold doorknob of his study door, swallowing a lump in my throat, then I drop my hand and walk away quickly, without looking back.

I take the stairs slowly because everything hurts. The soothing warmth of the shower has worn off, and my shoulder is back to a sledgehammer-smashing-my-arm level of pain. I open my bedroom door. Kit is still here. I let out a breath I didn't know I'd been holding. She's sitting on my bed, crosslegged, with her eyes shut.

'What are you doing?' I ask softly. One green eye pops open, then the other.

'Meditating,' she says, rolling her neck, one eyebrow raised. I nod, perplexed, and cross the floor, putting my collection of supplies down on the carpet. Kit doesn't join me, so I wave the packet of chips in her direction.

'I brought some snacks to eat while you tell me what the hell is going on.'

Her eyes almost pop out of her head as she unfolds her legs and jumps off the bed.

'What are these?' she murmurs, snatching the foil packet from my hands and settling cross-legged on the floor.

I can hear her munching behind me as I close my bedroom door. When I join her on the floor, she has her eyes shut again, and that look of peaceful contemplation is back on her face. I wait . . . and wait. It's like she's never had a salt and vinegar chip in her life. She chews slowly, as if savouring each mouthful.

'I can't believe you guys *aren't* allowed to have music, but you *can* have these. It's crazy!' she says with her mouth full. 'This is a fucking rave in my mouth!'

'A what?' I ask, and her bright hair shakes as she laughs and keeps munching.

'A party. Music . . . dancing.' She grabs another handful. 'Guys . . . girls . . .' She wiggles her eyebrows. Stray crumbs fall onto my carpet, and I resist the urge to pick them up. I still don't know what she's talking about. 'You live in such a bubble,' she huffs, licking her fingers.

'Listen, Teddy,' she says slowly, like I'm a child. 'I don't know why, but *you* followed *me*. I didn't know you were there until I was down near the warehouse entry point. It probably wouldn't have mattered, except those dumb-ass guards were wandering around down there. Creeps. When you called out to me, that alerted them – them *and* that dickhead Link, who grabbed us both and took us Underground.' She starts wiping her hands with one of the alcohol swabs I grabbed from the bathroom. *At least she's a hygienic weirdo.* 'From what I gather, Paula thought you were from another clan trying to steal our supplies, although I told her I didn't buy it. *Then* she thought maybe you were Council Eye, but you were clearly too dumb for that.'

I open my mouth to make a retort but realise that won't help. I take a slow breath instead, but Kit clams up.

'Clan?' I nudge, hoping to get something more out of her. Kit tears open another swab and begins unbuttoning my blouse. I push back her hand.

'Look, you want me to patch you up or not?' Sighing, I unbutton my shirt, pulling it off my shoulders gingerly.

'There are five clans; each has a role in the Underground to keep things going. When the Underground formed forty years ago, everyone was really –' I hiss as she presses alcohol onto the open wound. 'Everyone was amicable and worked together. But over time, the clans each had different ideas about how things should be run. So, the fighting began, and now they're all quite separate – except for the roles we each play to keep supplies coming in, waste going out, electricity, even some water.'

She sighs, and her breath is warm against the back of my neck. I hiss again, biting back a scream. 'Yeah, the needle will have that effect,' she says. I wince. 'It's just some stitches, you'll survive. Anyways, like I was saying. Now things aren't so peachy; the clans are more like gangs really.'

I try to turn and look at her, but she shoves my head down. Not violently, but practised, like she's used to dealing with difficult patients. 'Anyway, Paula is the head of my clan. Clan Ember. She's really pissed at the moment – which isn't good, because she's pissed at the best of times.' Kit stops tugging on my shoulder and sits back. I can feel her sharp eyes appraising me. Then she moves around to face me and gestures with one hand as if to invite questions, while expertly picking through the medical spread on the floor.

'So, you're infected,' I begin. Kit stops and looks at me, and it all spills out. 'Which means *I'm* infected. Which means I'm going to be caught and Sanitised –' Things are all making a horrible kind of sense. 'Are *you* Sanitised?' I ask slowly. Maybe the Council doesn't kill everybody? Perhaps they're dumping them . . . U nderground?

'No, I'm not,' she says, grabbing my arm. 'I wouldn't be here if I were. Listen! Would you sit still, you freak? You'll tear those stitches! I am *not* Sanitised. If I were, I'd be dead.' I see Lisa's smiling face flash across my mind. *Dead.*

seven

I glance between Kit and the clock as she takes her time picking through the bandages. 'Can people still get the infection . . . down there?'

'*The* infection?' she asks, rolling a bandage in between her now-not-so-perfectly-manicured nails. 'No one can Teddy. Not up here, or down there. It is a con. A government sham. There is no such thing as *the infection*.' She punctuates each word by throwing an unrolled bandage at me.

'Then why are you down there?' I ask. She doesn't speak, just glances at me occasionally while she expertly bandages my now stitched-up shoulder. She finishes by patching the grazes on my elbows, then sits back.

'I'm down there because the City called my mother "infected".' She spits the word. 'When she was pregnant with me, she didn't know my dad – if you know what I mean.' I don't, but something in her tone tells me that now is the wrong time to interrupt. I sit, waiting.

'Go on,' I encourage, but Kit waves me away with a roll of her eyes. She crosses her legs again and lies back.

'You better get ready for work. Mummy will be coming in at any moment,' she says dismissively. I don't move, and she sits back up. 'Look,' she says, 'someone reported my mum, but she was warned. She didn't have any time – she just had to leave.'

I nod, willing Kit to continue.

'This whole city is surrounded by one big-ass wall, so going into the dead outside lands isn't an option – unless you want to die a slow, agonising death in a desert wasteland. That means the only place to go is down.'

For a split second, I feel like I have a grasp of what's going on, but then it's gone. Kit sits back up, grabbing the last handful of chips.

'So, Paula is your mother?' I ask cautiously. Kit starts coughing so hard I think she's choking.

'Oh, God, no! Eugh. She wouldn't be anyone's mother. She's the Clan Head for Ember, our leader. I love the woman but noooo, not my mother. But y'know, she's always been good to me, so I'm loyal to her.' Her eyes glaze over. 'My mother is dead. She died when I was three, from a chest infection. Paula took me under her wing. I'm pretty important to her, I'm sure of it.'

'No one dies from a chest infection,' I blurt out, then instantly regret it.

She drops the packet upside down. 'Not up here maybe,' she snarls, scrunching the empty foil bag in her fist. 'Up here, everyone is perfect and healthy and normal, and if you're not, you're killed.' She prods my chest with her fingernail, and I can see the muscles in her arms flexing. Then she shrugs and pulls her finger away. The fingernail has left a little crescent moon on my chest. 'I'm *so* sorry. I meant to say, "Up here everyone is perfect and healthy and normal, and if you're not, you're

Sanitised."'

'About your mother. I – I didn't mean –'

She snatches my black work shirt and tosses it to me. 'Get dressed,' she says in that condescending tone. I pull the blouse on silently, doing up the tiny buttons.

She stands up, and an awkward silence settles around us. 'I hadn't known about Sanitisation – about what they were really doing, until yesterday,' I say softly.

She stomps away, then spins to face me. 'You're so brainwashed up here you can't even see the most obvious truths staring you right in the face. I'm free down there, and that is all you need to know.'

I swallow hard. I remember learning about the atomic bomb shelters that were built long ago, like a mirror of the City, beneath our feet. But they remained unused, a relic of the past. Our People are lucky. None of those bombs reached Our Great City. But what if she's telling the truth, that people are escaping? Down there. I stand with great difficulty and face her.

'So you're saying there's a world under our feet, and I've *been* there?' I don't bother hiding my disbelief. 'To the *Underground*?' Kit nods.

I've got so many questions for her, but they will have to wait. Soft, peachy morning light is filtering in.

'I don't think you're *that* free,' I say. Kit narrows her eyes. 'How are you going to get back there? You're hardly incognito.' I point past her to the window. She looks, then turns back to me.

'I'll figure it out,' she says.

There's a soft knock on my door, and I spin around so fast I'm sure I've ripped the stitches in my shoulder.

'Teddy, good morning!' Mum calls softly through the door. I spin back, and Kit and the medi-kit are gone. I look at my window – nothing – then to the wardrobe, just in time to see the mirrored door slide softly shut. I walk over to my door, trying to plaster my best early morning look on my face.

'Hi,' I say, opening the door. Mum's still in her robe. *Weird.* 'Are you running late?' I ask. She smiles and pushes my door wide open, stepping inside my room. I'm glad I'm wearing my work blouse. She pulls me in for a hug, squeezing tight. I feel my muscles tense.

'I slept so poorly last night I decided to go in late. After all, this is your last day of Internship at the cafe.' She raises her eyebrows at me. 'I know how much you're going to miss working there, so I thought I could drive you.'

If anyone knew how much I had hated the last three months, it was Mum. I never held back on my complaints about Maree the Tyrannical. She's always been surprisingly sympathetic. 'I was so worried about you after our . . . talk,' she murmurs into my hair. Her hand is pulling me closer. Right. Over. My. Shoulder.

I can't help the tears of pain that well up in my eyes. She pulls me back. 'Oh, darling, I know. It must have been a lot to take in. It wasn't fair of me to put you through that. Let's just forget it happened. You'll be Partnered soon, and I'm sure you'll be very, *very* happy.'

I smile and wipe the tears away.

'I'm going to have a shower and make some coffee and then we can go to work. I see you're *almost* ready.' She glares pointedly at my sweats, and I shrug. 'An extra half hour. How does that sound?' She smiles. I smile.

'Sounds perfect – now, let me enjoy it!' I push her out of my room as playfully as I can.

'Half an hour, Teddy, you'd better not go back to sleep.'

I close my door, then press my ear to it, listening to her retreating footsteps. I don't pull away until I can hear the water running from her shower.

'*Owwww!*' I moan.

'Let me have a look at your shoulder,' Kit says, stepping out of the wardrobe. But I don't step any closer. I just glare at her through narrowed eyes.

'Your expression this morning has been priceless! It's like you met a unicorn.'

'A what?' She opens her mouth to explain, but I interrupt. 'Never mind. You *did* just tell me there's a whole city of drifters and vagabonds living beneath the City's feet.'

She rolls over onto the bed, laughing. 'Oh, that's rich! Like we're mythical hobos, sucking on the teat of Our perfect Metropolis!'

I rub my temples with my two index fingers. 'So, what do you actually do?' I ask, fully prepared for her to fly off the handle again.

She smiles. 'Well, like I said, each clan has a key role: water, supplies, food and electricity. It all takes work to keep things running. There's an unwritten hierarchy; our clan – Ember – being the most important.' She picks up a jar of lip balm from my bedside table and starts spreading it on her lips.

'Why?'

'Partly because we are the largest and partly because we collect the supplies from Sympathisers around the City and then distribute them *fairly* to each of the clans. Without us, no one eats . . . that sort of power gives a clan superiority, y'know?' I shrug, not knowing at all. 'And I'm a healer.'

'You have your Job Placement?'

'Don't be a moron, Teddy, it doesn't suit you. Down there, we don't get *placed*. We pick our calling.'

I stare at her, wondering what I would pick if I could choose. *What if I chose wrong?*

'We dance and sing and draw,' she says, waving my pen around. Then her eyes light up. 'But we also fight. And there are plenty who use their time for spirituality and religion. There are all sorts down there. We have monks – especially Clan Hashé, and there's even a group of nuns in Clan Gaia! It's all about people expressing themselves. I, for one, am a Witch.'

'A what?' I say. The words are in English, but they don't make any sense to me.

She gestures to the tattoos covering her arms.

'Eh, I think it would all be a bit too complicated to explain to you right now, but basically I believe that we all have the power to control our own destinies and influence those of the people around us. Don't look at me like that. You can't honestly tell me that your mind isn't being *blown* by all this. There are so many great books from the old times before the big war, and games – some people like to gamble while they play, betting their supplies.' She laughs, shaking her head. 'I'm not much of a gambler myself. I'm all about reading books and music and *dancing*.'

It all sounds so crazy I feel like I shouldn't believe her, but it all seems too *real* for her to be making it up. 'Dancing?' I ask.

'Of course! To music – you would love music. I listen to it, dance to it, sing along . . . Sometimes I just let it soundtrack other things.' She gives me a wiggly eyebrow look. 'Anyway, it's my turn to ask a question,' Kit declares, dropping to the floor opposite me. 'What's the deal with your dad working for City Council?'

I consider the facts I know about him – the truth – and there's not much.

'I don't know. I know Dad's high up there.'

'Yeah, but like, what's the *area* of the Council that he's in charge of?'

I rack my brain. 'I think he started with a role in the workplace industry. Giving Job Placements. He told me I was going to get a good job, and I did. I don't know if that's because he actually knew or –'

'Oh, come on!' She cuts me off. 'As if you don't know what area your dad works in. Geez, I told you what *you* wanted to know.' For the first time, she looks genuinely annoyed. Ripped off even.

'I'm sorry, I can't tell you what I don't know. I know he just got a promotion and works with the Mayor now, on the "Mayor's Table". I don't know any more than that.'

'Bullshit!' She crosses her arms. 'Bulllll. Shit. You're just pulling more of that Metropolis party-line bullshit. There's no way you don't know.'

'I don't even know where he *is* right now! I haven't seen him for almost two weeks.'

She rolls her eyes. 'He's your dad! I'm pretty sure he's told you what he does.'

'Up here, people don't talk much. *Especially* about things to do with the City Council.'

She just raises an eyebrow and tilts her head, like she's trying to decide if I'm lying.

I shake my head slowly. 'You really have no idea, do you? That relationship doesn't mean *anything.*' It's not until the words leave my mouth that I realise the weight of their truth. I don't know him, and I don't trust him. I don't even care that I haven't seen him. There's always been a heaviness in my stomach, which I assumed meant I cared about him. *But what if it's something else?*

'I've seen how your mum treats you. I've heard her with my own ears. She cares about you. Relationships do matter.' Kit's right. But I think my mum is an exception.

'You knew my dad worked in the Council. Is that why you're here? Is that why Paula thinks I'm a spy? Bet you told her that too, didn't you?'

'No –' she tries to cut in.

'Because your questions are pretty specific.' I can't think of anything else to say. She opens her mouth, then I cut her off. 'Look, I think you should go.' I turn away from her but can hear her standing up. I pull on my petticoat and take off my pants. Then I pull on the skirt and do the belt up at my waist. I want to get my apron from my wardrobe so I turn anyway.

'Look, Teddy, I'm sorry for pushing. I – we – it's . . .' She sighs and shrugs. 'Veodrum is a name most people know.' I swallow. Kit's right.

'I found that out by looking at your name in your sketchbook. I swear I didn't know before I met you tonight though. I'm asking about it because it's always good for us to have info. To know where and who they're going to strike next. It's nothing personal. We're up here on the surface picking up supplies all the time. Sympathisers have been whispering about some serious eyeballs on them – more than ever before. Some have even quit. But we still need to eat. Teddy, I didn't know who you were when you got taken down to meet Paula. Trust me, she has nooo idea who you are. If she knew who your dad was, well –' She looks sheepish. She doesn't need to spell it out. 'Do you have any more questions?' she asks softly.

'A million,' I say. My shoulder still hurts. 'But I can't think clearly right now. We should probably talk another time. Anyway, I have to get downstairs before my mum bursts into the room again.'

'I guess you're right.' She walks over to the window. 'I'm going to head back down and try to dampen the constant fire of rage that is Paula.' She rolls her eyes. 'I'll try to get back here later.'

She leans down quickly, reaching under my bed to grab her coat. I look at it properly for the first time. It's a thigh-length caramel suede jacket with fluffy white woollen trim. It's like nothing I've ever seen before.

'You cannot be thinking of wearing that out now,' I say. 'You'll stand out enough as it is.' She looks down at herself and frowns.

'I really didn't think I'd still be here after the sun had come up.'

I walk over to my wardrobe. 'Borrow this.' I throw her a grey coat and scarf. 'You can wrap the scarf over your head to cover your hair, like this. It's going to be a cool morning. Nobody will question it.' She makes a disgusted face at herself in the mirror as she pulls on the coat, buttoning it at the front.

'Mmmm, I feel *so* fashionable right now,' she says sarcastically.

'You'll need this too.' I hold out a skirt. It's long enough to poke out the end of the coat. If someone sees her pants, pink hair will be the least of her problems.

She shakes her head. 'Ahhh, no thanks,' she says, but I insist. 'Alright, but turn around,' she says in a mock scandalised tone.

I don't. She doesn't put on the skirt.

'Seriously?' I turn around, then hear ruffling.

'Okay, done,' she says.

'You should probably go, before it gets too busy out there.'

She's staring at herself in the mirror. Her black top is tucked into the full blue skirt, one of my old school skirts. She's opening and closing the jacket.

'Fine, but I must say I could really rock this Metropolis costume party you have going on! I actually look cute!' She winks at herself in the mirror, and I can't help cracking a small smile. She spins around, making the skirt flare, then throws the grey coat open in a dramatic flourish.

'Some women at home wear skirts like this, for dancing in. You'll have to come watch sometime. Flamenco!' She claps and stamps clumsily. The idea of dancing intrigues me, but I don't think I want to face Paula again anytime soon. 'Okay.' She snatches her own jacket from my hands as I start putting it on a hanger, and strokes it gently. 'I'll be back to collect her soon. If she's gone — *you're* gone.'

It sounds like she's joking, but her eyes say she's serious, and she draws a finger menacingly across her throat. She laughs at whatever horrified expression is on my face, then wraps the scarf around her head. 'All I need are sunglasses, and I'd look like Marilyn Monroe.'

I don't know who that is, but she seems thrilled with herself.

She walks over to the window and waves. Surprisingly, she looks *almost* normal. Well, Metropolis normal.

'You know, I think you're alright, Teddy.'

I hadn't expected that from her. I smile more freely now.

'Yeah, I think I am too.'

She laughs a big laugh and climbs onto my window ledge.

'Teddy!' my mum calls from downstairs. I turn to the door.

'Coming!' I shout over my shoulder.

'See ya again soon . . . friend,' I hear Kit say, but when I turn back to the window, my room is still except for my curtain blowing softly in the breeze. She's gone.

eight

I was quiet after Kit left. Mum drove me to work, but she didn't press me. I've spent the better part of my shift trying to figure out how everything Kit told me fits in with what I found out from Mum.

I pick up the next dirty plate and dump it into the tepid water. The stench of meat and garlic is lingering in the air from the lunch rush, making me feel sick. *Sicker.* I've spent all morning thinking about Sanitisation. If I had known about the Underground earlier, maybe I'd have been able to save Lisa. To help her escape.

I sneak a quick glance at the clock – there are only two hours left of my shift. My *last* shift. I lean against the sink and take a deep breath, glancing up to see Maree glaring at me with beady eyes as she walks past. She owned, ran and cooked at this cafe with her husband until he died a few years ago. Maybe she was a happy person back then, but now she is a wench, and her life is literally my idea of a living nightmare.

'You do a good job for your last shift. I don't want a slacker.' She slaps my back with a tea towel, hard, as she walks out. It wakes up the ache in my shoulder.

'Alright, I'm off.' Jane, my co-slave, walks over to the sink and dumps the dishes from her tray into my water. She doesn't even bother to empty the half-full milkshake. I pull my hands out quickly.

'What is wrong with you?' I snap.

I didn't know Jane until she was given the same Internship as me here, three months ago. She came from a different School Code. I tried to be nice to her, but she seemed determined to make life hell for me. On our very first day, within the first hour, Jane spilt a bowl of soup and a milkshake onto my perfectly pressed apron and blouse. Then she told Maree I had shouted at her. In response, Maree threatened to fail my Internship, which would have jeopardised my

Job Placement *and* Partnership. That was all before we'd said more than five words to each other. Since then, Maree has watched me like a hawk, and flits over Jane like she's a fragile dove.

'We don't get off until four,' I say while I empty the water from the sink.

'*You* need to work till four. I, on the other hand, just feel so sick.' She swoons, collapsing against the sink. A stack of freshly washed and dried plates topples back into the milkshake- stained dregs just as Maree walks in.

'Jane, are you sick?'

'Oh, Maree, I feel so –' She fake swoons again. 'I think I may pass out. Thank goodness the lunch rush is over. Maybe I could do a simple job for the last two hours of my shift?' She sighs and clutches her stomach, groaning slightly. I grit my teeth.

'Teddy and I can do the rest of your shift. You go home, Jane. Early mark for sickness!'

Jane surprises us both by pulling the crusty Maree in for a hug. As she does, she winks at me over our boss's back. I imagine what Lisa would say: *Jane is just jealous.* She always says people are jealous of us. *Said.* I'm not sure who would be jealous of Lisa now. I quickly squash those thoughts. Jane waves her hand evilly at me, then walks out of the cafe, groaning occasionally.

'Teddy, go serve or clean outside. You just seem to make more mess in here. Look at all these dirty plates.' She shoves me out of the kitchen, snatching the scrubber from my damp hands.

Every table I wipe down and every perfect grey plate I carry feels more like a lie than it ever has. *Look at you, perfect plate. No one cares about you, we're just puppets, you and I.* Everything I thought I knew has been decimated. I'm starting to feel paranoid, too. *More* paranoid. Mum's 'welcome home' ritual of running around shutting curtains was always creepy . . .

I shake the thought from my head.

I survey the remaining tables. Jane was right about one thing.

There aren't many people left, just one small group of mothers and their toddlers sitting at a round table. I notice one little boy with red hair. He's fidgeting – nothing unusual for children that age. But when the other mothers aren't looking, his mum keeps grabbing his leg under the table. The little boy hits his hand on his head, and she snaps her grip away and laughs with the other mothers. I bend forward to pick up a cloth napkin that 'fell' onto the floor, sneaking a closer look. The little boy's leg is covered in half-moons like the one Kit left in my chest with her fingernail, except these aren't indentations. Each small crescent moon on this boy's skin bubbles with blood. As I stand up slowly I notice the mother glaring at me. I put my head down, spinning around quickly – too quickly. One of the glasses falls off the tray I'm holding, and I close my eyes, waiting for it to shatter.

Nothing.

I open my eyes and see the glass is being returned to the tray. I follow the hand back to its owner. A boy, seventeen or eighteen at the oldest. He doesn't have a Partnership Seal on his neck so he must be seventeen. Like me.

'Here you go,' he says. He's standing close, but I keep my eyes down. The mothers have stopped talking to watch this unusual interaction, and I'm keenly aware of their attention as I nod curtly and shoulder past him. The tray is heavy and its weight tugs against my shoulder, against Kit's stitches. I turn around slowly and look at his face for the first time. Wavy chestnut hair falls into his eyes, and I notice a smile playing on his lips as he cocks his head to one side and brushes the hair from his eyes. They're so light they're like ice.

'Thanks,' I mumble, avoiding eye contact. We really don't talk to boys unless we *must*. I glance at his face again. A part of me sparks up, telling me I know him, but I must be imagining it. If he were from my School Code, I would know him. Even if we weren't encouraged to talk to our other-gendered peers, it was still expected we knew them. For acknowledgement, and formal events. For Partnership.

'No worries,' he calls from behind me softly. I hear a chair scrape as he sits down at an empty table, far away from the table of mothers. I glance back at the child with red hair. He's not fidgeting anymore.

'Who is that?' Maree asks abruptly, not even looking up from the meat she's deboning, and I nearly drop the tray again. She's grumpy and too suspicious – *basically, an old version of myself*, I think humourlessly. I decide to ignore her. 'I asked you a question!' She puts a stubby finger on my chest, smearing what looks like pig's blood on my apron as I try to move past her. I examine her face, both eyes squeezed into a thin line.

'I don't know, Maree.' I push past her finger, my back pressed against the large oven that takes up half the wall of the already cluttered kitchen.

'You know him.' It's not a question.

'I don't know him. I *have* seen him around though,' I lie. 'I think he's from my School Code.' I meet her gaze and she gives one sharp nod, satisfied. She snatches a pad and pen from the counter and her apron flaps around her short legs as she bustles out of the kitchen. I sag against the sink, grateful for the privacy, and try to clear both my tray and my thoughts, while my stomach twists in a knot. I pick up my empty tray, ready to go back out and pack down some tables, but pull up short – Maree is standing at the doorway, staring silently at me.

'What?' I ask, trying to keep my voice steady.

'Did you hear me, Teddy?' She narrows her eyes until they become little black beads disappearing in the folds of her pink skin. I shake my head. 'He said he'd wait for you to come back.' I shrug, confused. 'The boy outside.' She points a stubby thumb towards the window. 'You.' She points at me. 'He didn't want to be served by me, he said he'd wait for you.' I swallow hard.

'Oh, that's . . . really weird.' I put down my tray and reach forward to take the pen and pad out of her hands. As I walk outside, I can feel her eyes boring into my back. *What was I supposed to say to her?* I force myself to slow my steps as I walk towards his table. *What does he want from me?* I stop and pretend to straighten a fork at a table.

Barely a metre away, I realise why I'm frightened.

I know too much.

I straighten up and risk a glance back.

I can't trust anybody now. Maree is glaring at me through the kitchen window, and the mothers have stopped talking again. I square my chin and march forward. When I reach his table, the boy smiles, broad and confident. His eyes reflect the bright afternoon sun, and my stomach drops. *Maybe he's Council Eye.*

◎

'Here you go, one veggie sandwich with a side of chips and a chocolate shake.' The food looks sad and dead as I put it down in front of him.

'You want to sit?' he asks. I hug the empty tray to my chest like armour, hoping he can't see that my hands are shaking.

'No thanks,' I say. 'I'm working.' I hope my tone doesn't come across as angry. *Why do I care what he thinks?* If he is Council Eye, being nice probably won't do much, but pissing him off definitely won't help either. *In what upside-down world would I ever sit with him?*

'Suit yourself,' he says, grabbing a chip and crunching down, not breaking eye contact for a second.

'Will that be all?' I ask, looking back over my shoulder, the first to break our staring competition.

'What time do you get off work?' he says, popping another chip into his mouth.

'In an hour.' *Why did I say that?* I should have lied. 'Why?'

'Just wondering,' he says, flashing that open, honest smile again. I shake my head. I want to trust him. His smile makes it seem like everything is okay. I take a step backwards.

'Can I get some sauce, please?' he asks.

I turn and start walking back to the kitchen. 'Sure,' I mumble.

As expected, Maree is ready for me, armed with more questions. She's holding a knife as long as her arm, casually, as if she hasn't been watching the whole thing from the front window.

'What did he talk to you about?' she asks, returning to her

work. *Chop.*

'He was asking about the chips,' I reply. *Chop.* 'He wants some sauce.' I almost drop the bottle as she slams her knife down tip-first into the aged wooden board.

'My chips need no sauce. They are perfect!'

'I said that,' I say, throwing my hands in the air dramatically. 'I told the boy everything we serve is handmade, fresh on the premises.' She shakes her head. 'That's why I was out there so long, explaining that your cooking is known City-wide to be perfect, as is.' She nods, and I swear I almost see her smile. 'But he still wants the sauce.' She hisses as I grab the bottle from the shelf behind her and return to the mysterious customer.

'Thanks,' he says, grabbing the bottle a split second before I let go, brushing his fingers against mine. 'My name's Jamie, by the way.'

'Okay,' I reply.

'Oh, you're funny,' he says wryly. It catches me off guard. I'm not sure how to respond.

'So, what are you doing after you get off work?' he asks. I'm sure Maree is watching again, probably cursing her salami, wondering what the hell problem he has with his food now.

I stifle a smile.

'I'm sorry, I have to get back to work,' I say, tucking a strand of hair behind my ear.

'Yeah, this place is *hectic*,' he says, gesturing to the vacant courtyard. The mothers have left. Absently, I wonder what punishment that little boy will get once they're in the privacy of their home. The thought makes my arms prick with goosebumps.

'You cold?' he asks, noticing. He bites into another chip, never breaking eye contact. *He didn't use the sauce.*

'I need to go back. Enjoy your lunch.' It's my turn to put on a winning smile. I don't want to spend any more time talking to him, so I turn on my heel and begin crossing the courtyard.

'Bye, Teddy. I'm sure I'll see you soon.'

I stop, only for a fraction of a second. A chill slithers down my spine, and it feels like my legs are turning into jelly.

How does he know my name?

I force my jelly legs to keep moving, one after the other until I make it back inside the kitchen. He's not a normal boy: he's either Underground or Council Eye. Neither option is good.

Not good at all.

nine

It's been four days since my final shift at the cafe and five days since I was in the Underground, and there's still no word from Kit.

I've spent a lot of time gazing out my window and staring at the journal I promised not to touch. I haven't, either. It's been so hard, though. Now that the sun has set, the temperature is starting to drop. I try to think about what might happen after Partnership – well, not after Partnership, after the final cer emony, the Sealing, where the City Seal and year will be marked on my neck in white ink – forever. It reminds me of those dark marks on Kit's arms. What had she called them? After that, it's all over . . . or it's just beginning. I rub my neck, imagining what it will feel like to have '70' stamped there forever. The skin is smooth under my fingers. I hope I can stay in this same suburb. Not because I love it – I don't – but I need to stay close to Mum. I think she needs me now more than she ever has. Now that my father has all but disappeared.

I grab my empty cups and make my way downstairs. Despite the seriousness of the situation, it gives me a little thrill to think about all the imperfect secrets we hold in our house, like a silent protest to my absent father.

I'm not blind to the fact that this week really is the last time I'll be able to do things un-Partnered, without my parents, without my own children. I swallow. The Partnership and Sealing have been in Mum's planner with big red circles around them for months. Now that we're so close, I feel like those bright red circles are leering at me.

Mum's been on a wardrobe rampage. I thought she had settled on the green dress Kit stuffed in the back of my wardrobe upstairs, but every day she's come home with a new selection of dresses and shoes, and every day I've said *no*. At the kitchen sink, I imagine squeezing into the pale pink tulle dress that's still draped over a chair.

'Ouch!' I cry out as I accidentally pour boiling water over my hand instead of into my mug. I hold my hand under the tap and let the cool water soothe my burnt skin.

After a minute, I take my hot mug over to the kitchen island and sit down with the latest edition of *Metropolis Magazine*. We've had the latest edition of this magazine sitting right here in the kitchen for as long as I can remember, and I have been reading it for as long as I can remember reading. Other than schoolwork and government publications, there isn't anything else to read. I flip through the pages. *This flimsy little magazine is going to become my life.* I've seen how Mum lives and breathes this all-consuming job. *And she still hides those secrets.*

I flip through the glossy pages and skim over the articles . . . *if you notice anything strange in your Partner, please contact the . . . children don't play. It's essential to support new parents in creating good habits in their children* . . . My mind wanders back to the red-headed toddler at the cafe, and the bloody marks on his leg. That image is in stark contrast to the cheesy smiling families in the magazine's editorial. I wonder if their smiles are as fake as my own.

After two pages sharing the latest approved clothing for the upcoming Occasions, I'm bored. I think about Kit's jacket, still hanging at the back of my wardrobe. Definitely not something that would be featured in this publication. I have checked the pockets of Kit's coat. Twice. Once to see if there was anything interesting hiding in there, something that might provide some extra insight into Kit's existence. And then a second time, to see if she had left a note. She seems like the note-leaving type.

I slam the magazine cover shut. Everything feels colder. Shoving the magazine under my arm, I carry my mug upstairs. I consider slipping outside for a walk, but it's already sundown. Someone would notice. Someone's always watching.

I open the door to my room, and there's Kit, sitting crosslegged on my bed. I jerk to a stop, and tea arcs its way out of my mug and onto the floor.

'Meditating again?' I ask wryly, trying to mop up the wet patch with a discarded shirt I grab off the floor.

'Hah. You may mock me now, but I'm the most aligned bitch you'll ever meet!'

I glance up at her, and she smiles ruefully, stretching back against my pillow, her pink hair a stark contrast to the crisp white. 'You have a good day?'

'Eh,' is all I manage by way of a reply. She stretches and jumps off the bed, crossing the floor in that way she does. Moving without moving. She takes the mug out of my hands.

'Thanks.'

'Hey –' I start, but she's already back on my bed, slurping away at what's left of my tea.

I perch awkwardly on the end of my bed like my mum does. 'So, what brings you back?' I ask, trying not to sound too interested.

'My jacket,' she says matter-of-factly. A little ball of hope I didn't realise I'd been holding drops. I wait for her to say more. She doesn't. I glance at my clock. Mum will be home soon.

Kit yawns.

'Something weird happened at work the other day,' I start to say. 'A customer –'

'Were they infected?' She sticks her arms straight out with a flourish and groans. 'Zombie style?'

'What's a zombie?' I ask, but she waves my question away.

'Go on, dummy!' When I don't immediately continue, she interrupts again. 'Waiting!'

I begin by telling her about the marks I saw on the little boy's leg. I'm surprised by her reaction. Kit's tough-gal bravado disappears for a second. She asks questions about the cuts, what the child had looked like. *It's like she really cares.*

'So, then you dropped a glass?' she asks.

'No. I *almost* dropped a glass, but some guy was there. He caught it for me.'

'That seems like a normal thing to do.' I don't say anything. She really doesn't understand normal. 'So, was he cute?' she asks. I don't say anything. 'So, he *was* cute, huh? Interesting . . .' She stares at me and wiggles her eyebrows.

'Honestly, I don't know what you're talking about,' I mutter, pulling my legs up under my chin. Kit smiles one of her infuriating *I know* smiles and waits for me to continue.

'He was nice – to look at – but he was also a bit smug and really, *really* weird.' I lean closer. 'He asked when I finished my shift. That's really weird.' I look up to see a puzzled expression on her face.

'Did he tell you his name?' she asks. Something in my head whispers, *don't tell her.* I don't know if I can trust her yet.

'No.' I'm surprised at how easily the lie slips out.

Kit shrugs, moving on. 'Anyway, what's so weird about that, Ted? He just wanted to hang out.'

I'm exasperated. Kit randomly pops into my house, peppers me with questions and then BAM, *I'm* the one who's crazy for thinking something is weird. It seems appropriate, so I borrow the finger quote marks she always uses when talking about Sanitisation. 'People don't "hang out" here, Kit.'

She sighs and takes the last sip of my tea, completely ignoring me. *Yet again.* 'I've enjoyed this. I think I'd like another.'

I take my cup back, trying not to snatch. 'Anything else, ma'am? Could I interest you in some food?'

Kit pretends to seriously consider her options then she nods, her eyes bright. 'You know, you're right. I think I would like to grab a bite.' I can't help laughing at her enthusiasm. She lies back, her ink-covered arms splayed across my white pillows. I hope the colour doesn't come off the –

'What do you call those again?' I ask, pointing at her arms.

She crosses them quickly.

'Tattoos. I told you that. Don't scrunch your nose at me!'

'I'm not!'

'You are.'

'It's just, they're not going to –' I don't know how to say it, so I gesture rubbing an arm on my blue doona.

'Stain? No, they're not.' She rolls her eyes. 'I'm sure I told you this. They're permanent. In my skin. *Under* my skin. Never coming off.'

'Oh,' I say. 'It *is* just like the Partnership Seal we get. On our necks. At the Sealing Ceremony.' She nods slowly.

'Yes, they are just like that, except I *want* mine. I've seen that Seal thingy on people in the Underground. Lots of people get them covered up. Hidden behind other art.'

'Why?' I ask, unsure why anyone would want to do that.

'No one wants to be a slave, Teddy.' She lies back, letting her words sink in.

'Well, speaking of slavery, can I get you anything else? I'm going to get another cup of tea,' I say, standing up.

'I want some different chips.' I raise an eyebrow. 'Don't get me wrong, they were amazing! I just want to see what other wonders you have available in this culinary paradise.'

'*Okay.*' I walk over to my door, and she follows me.

'Actually, I wanna come with you and check out downstairs. I've never been *in* a house on the surface before – except for your room and that top landing. Which is, no offence, pretty boring.'

I glance back at my room, trying to be offended, but she's right.

I shake my head. 'No way. Mum's due home any minute.' She pushes past me, dismissing my fear with a flick of her hand.

'Meh. I'll hide if I have to.'

◉

Kit watches everything I do from her seat at the breakfast counter. Everywhere I walk in the little blue and white kitchen,

I can feel her watching. I fill the kettle up at the sink, then pull an extra mug out of the cupboard.

'I wish I had a kitchen I could just pop into,' she sighs. I turn around and lean on the bench behind me.

'You don't have a kitchen down there?' I ask, blowing steam casually off the top of my mug. She shakes her head, grabbing the salt and pepper shakers and rattling them softly.

'They're like maracas!' Again, it's like we're speaking a different language.

'No kitchen?' I prompt.

'We have a kitchen, but it's a big one.'

'For your family?' I ask. She puts the shakers down hard, and little grains of salt and pepper fly out across the bench.

'No family. Remember?' *Stupid.* 'And anyway, that's not what I mean. There is a kitchen for each clan. We all share our meals together in a big dining hall.'

'So, you don't get to just eat what you like?'

She laughs bitterly. 'No, we don't, *and* despite the fact that we have Sympathisers up here helping us –' 'Sympathisers?' I ask.

'Yeah remember, the people who help us out. People like you.' *Am I helping her out?* 'They leave food, old clothes, medicine, that kind of stuff in places around the City. I told you, my clan distributes the supplies. Where did you think we got them from?' I try to reconcile all the new information I've learnt over the last few days. I pass her a steaming mug. '*Anyway*,' she continues, 'despite Sympathisers' donations, the resources are still spread really thin. We share everything equally, so the food needs to last. Especially now that things are going missing.' 'Going missing?' I wait for Kit.

'Like I said, Clan Ember is the most important clan. The supplies are *our* responsibility – running, collecting and distributing. We're the heartbeat of the Underground.'

'So who lives down there?'

Kit slurps her tea, her face contorting. 'That is hot!' She blows on the mug fiercely. 'I told you the other day, all sorts. But basically, there are two kinds of people who end up in the Underground. Escapees – we like to call them transplants – and Trues, people like me, who were born down there. That's mostly the younger people and children.'

'Children?'

'We have every age, every stage.' I take a sip of my own tea, processing this new information. 'Don't look so surprised. Just because you're an idiot drone who doesn't know what exists at the end of her own nose.' I put my mug down hard, its contents sloshing over the side. 'In fact, most of the Sympathisers are family members of transplants. If it weren't for their supplies, we'd all slowly starve to death.' Kit continues. 'My suspicion is some councillors know about the Underground, and I'm not talking about our insiders – they're just desk drones.' She holds up a finger, cutting off my questions. '*Different* to ignorant drones like yourself.' I bite back my retort. 'No, my theory is that some of the high-ups know. But never tell anyone I said that.' She looks up, wielding a pen at me like a knife. '*Ever*, you hear me?' I nod. 'Especially not Paula . . .' She trails off.

'So, no help-yourself kitchen then.' I try to keep my voice casual, bringing the subject back around.

'Nope. We are in tight quarters. Heaps of people live in dorms – shared rooms – and the bathrooms are the same. We share *all* the resources. Showers are primarily cold – unless you get up before the other hundreds of people.'

'Well, that sounds . . . crappy.'

Kit gives me a strange look. 'It is.' I consider offering her a shower here, but I know she will take it personally. She picks up the mug I set in front of her and hugs it with her hands, breathing in the steam.

'It really sucks in winter when it gets freezing. Everyone wants a hot drink, but electricity is precious, so no tea or coffee, outside of breakfast time. Sometimes we get hot chocolate at night, if it's someone's birthday or if you know the right person in Clan Lux. I have a few friends there, mostly guys.

Very smart and *very* fun.' She wiggles her eyebrows again.

'It's winter now,' I say.

Kit's face drops. She starts tapping her long pink nails on the mug. 'Trust me, I know,' she says, looking up. 'Why do you think I want my coat back?' She winks at me, then the tough-gal façade disappears for a second, before snapping back in place.

'I should probably be going.' She slams her cup down on the bench.

'You've hardly told me anything.' I open a cupboard behind me and pull out a packet of biscuits. She pauses for a second, then snatches the pack out of my hands, tearing it open.

'Three more questions,' she says, holding up three crumby fingers.

'How do you get enough clothing?'

'Supplies, sewing. We have teams that make clothes from everything – you'd be surprised how wasteful your city is. Once something is *out*, every shop *has* to throw it out. So, we take the Sympathisers' donations and make them cooler.' She eats another two biscuits.

'Have you got any friends down there?' I ask. She raises an eyebrow, licking the tips of her fingers.

'Yes, I have friends. I'm a friendly person. I have some girlfriends, and some boyfriends and some special friends – if you know what I mean.' She winks. *I can guess.* 'Most of the people who work with Paula . . .' I don't like the way she whispers Paula's name, as if she's scared of her. 'They suck. Mostly. People like Link. He's the worst. Generally, my friends are from my clan, it's easier that way. One of my closest friends is

a guy called Jamie. He's really cool.'

SMASH.

Kit is up and helping me before I have a chance to pick up the pieces. My mug slipped from my hands the second she said his name. 'Only a few big pieces to pick up,' she says cheerily, offering me a smile. 'You okay?'

I nod over-enthusiastically. 'Yeah, I think my hands were a bit wet.' We clear up the mess, and I take the shards over to the bin.

'Okay, so last question.' She smiles, taking her place back at the bench.

'Umm . . .' I try to buy some time. 'Okay, what did you mean when you said supplies are going missing? Who's taking them? It must be hard, especially since there isn't enough stuff around anyway.'

For a second she's silent.

'That's more than one question.' She narrows her eyes at me. 'Remember I told you about Sympathisers, that we collect their donations and then distribute them Underground?' She waits until I nod. 'Well, lately the supplies have been disappearing before we can pick them up.' I open my mouth to speak, but something shifts, and I get the feeling she's about to burst into tears. 'It's getting worse,' she says finally.

'What is?' I ask.

'We're really struggling now, more than ever. With more missing supplies, everything needs to go further. But it's not just that. The more important the supplies, the more likely they're missing. Medicine, food . . . We can make do with clothing scraps. Even food can stretch for a while. But medicine.' She shakes her head. 'You don't understand.' Her voice drops to a whisper. 'It's not just about the supplies. When things get tough down there, the people get tough. *Tougher.* It's more violent. Everyone is hungry and cold and on edge. I hardly ever pick up supplies anymore because I'm always needed as a healer. Last week someone lost their toe to frostbite!' I chew at my lip. 'Every shift I have at the medical centre, I see more and more people come in, and not all their injuries are because of the cold. I've seen arms twisted out of their sockets, missing fingers, shattered kneecaps. There's only so much I can do with my bare hands.' She shakes her head briskly. 'People will do terrible things to get what they want or what they need for their families.'

'Are more people getting sick, too?' I ask.

'Yes.' Her big green eyes fill with tears. 'One little girl I work with, Meg, she needs a new puffer.' The name tugs at a memory but I can't place it. 'The refill usually comes with the medical deliveries, but . . .' Kit swallows. 'Without it, her body will choke her to death. It's really serious.'

'Asthma. It's so weird to think that a young person would have a disease like that. Only really old people or babies get something like that up here.'

'It's not that hard to imagine,' Kit snaps. 'Maybe after you spend some time in the Underground, you'll realise it's not as nice as it seems.'

'I didn't find it very nice,' I say, turning around to the pantry.

'Hah, well at least I'm free,' she says. My hand freezes on the second packet of biscuits.

Don't bite, you know she couldn't survive a day up here.

Something about Kit's tone and the look in her eyes make me think she's in her own cage . . . not so different from mine.

I turn back and slide the new packet towards her, and she perks up.

'You know, sometimes we get a delivery of these exact cookies,' she murmurs thoughtfully through crumbly lips.

'They're my mum's favourite,' I explain. 'Speaking of my mum, she'll be home soon so I think we should wrap up this house tour and go back to my room.' I gesture for her to follow me back upstairs.

As we reach the top step, I can hear the front door unlocking and Mum's shoes clicking on the floorboards in the hallway.

'Teddy? You home?' Mum's voice winds up the stairs.

Kit's eyes light up. 'Perfect timing,' she says, ducking down to peer through the balustrade.

'Of course. I'm just up here,' I call down, grabbing the back of Kit's T-shirt and shoving her into my room, just as my mother pokes her head around the corner and looks up with a smile on her face.

'I've bought some new shoes for your Partnership tomorrow. I'll bring them up to you, then I'm just going to have a shower.' She puts her handbag down and starts making her way up the stairs.

'Why don't you have a shower first?' I ask, trying to sound casual.

'Because I want to show you these!' She pulls a pair of shoes out of a bag and holds them up. 'Aren't they lovely? I thought you'd really like them.' She's holding another pair of heeled shoes for Occasions, but she's right – for the first time, I *do* like them. They're black and beaded and look more like a boot than the usual satin slip-on style. The heel is only an inch, and wider than most options she brings me. They still have a tapered toe, something I'll have to get used to, but with black silk ribbon laces at the front they're . . .

'Wow,' I say, as she reaches me at the top of the stairs.

'I *know* you, daughter,' Mum says, smiling knowingly. She presses the shoes into my arms. Her eyes flick quickly to my bedroom door, which is only open a crack. I hope desperately that Kit isn't peering through that crack. 'We'll have to talk about the laces. They might have to change – for now.' She silences my protestations with a hand. 'You can show me what they look like on, after my shower.'

I nod as she walks off towards her bedroom. I stay frozen in the hall till I hear the shower running. I've been holding my breath.

When I turn around and step into my room, Kit's standing by the window wearing her own fluffy jacket. On my bed there's an empty mug and my coat, skirt and scarf.

'You off already?' I ask the obvious.

'Those are cute.' She juts her chin towards the shoes in my hands. 'Really cute, actually.' She takes a step closer. I put them down and pick up the scarf.

'You should keep this,' I say, holding it out to her. She looks at it, then back at me.

'It's ugly.'

I shrug. 'I know it is, but so is losing an ear to frostbite. Anyway, I was just going to throw it out. I've got a new wardrobe coming with my Partnership and the Sealing.'

'Well, if you were throwing it out anyway.' She takes the soft scarf from me slowly and wraps it around her neck. The grey colour suits her hair.

'Teddy!' Mum calls out. 'Can you please get me a towel?' 'Well, I suppose you'd better get going then,' I say.

'You know I only visit for the food.' Kit waves the unopened packet of biscuits in her hand before stuffing it into one of her coat's deep pockets. 'Thanks for the rag!' she says, then jumps out of my window and into the night.

ten

My room feels so still now Kit is gone. I walk over to the window and stare out into the darkness, imagining her darting through the streets, a flash of white and pink, leaving a trail of biscuit crumbs behind her.

Mum knocks on my open door and pops her head around, hair still wrapped in the towel I dug out for her an hour ago. 'How was your day?' she asks, sitting on my bed right where Kit was sitting earlier. I see a younger version of my mother for a second, and try to imagine her with bright pink hair. What would her life have been like if she'd grown up in the Underground? If her relocation with my grandpa had been down, not across. *What about Lisa?* I had considered asking Kit if she knew her, if there was a chance she'd escaped. But I know it's futile. If Lisa had made it down there she would have found a way to contact me. She would have told me.

'Hello? Earth to Teddy,' Mum says, waving a packet of pink laces in front of my face. 'You okay?' I don't know. *Am I?*

'Yeah,' I say, smiling as I walk over to the bed. 'It's just weird, not working or schooling.' I shrug. 'Thanks for the shoes.' I step around the mattress so she can see them on my feet. She stands up.

'Re-lace the boots with these, *please*.' She hands me the pink silk laces. 'To go with the tulle dress downstairs. You have a big day tomorrow.' I roll my eyes, and she walks out. 'Do it now, Teddy,' she calls over her shoulder, shutting my door behind her.

I throw the pink laces at the wall and pull up the end of my mattress. The cool black leather of my sketchbook feels good beneath my fingers. I open it and flick through the filled pages, and some of my tension slips away. All my sketches jump out at me. Faces are my favourite thing to draw. I keep turning pages until I see a drawing of Lisa. I pause. She's sitting on my window seat, smiling broadly. As I flick through the book, I feel the hairs at the back of my neck stand on end. *I should put it back. I should tear it apart. Burn it.* I freeze. *No. Never that.*

I walk back to the window. The new moon has left the streets shrouded in impenetrable blackness. I turn to a fresh page and lie my pencil on its side, covering the blank white page in thick black strokes. Covering the lies . . . *or revealing them?*

I turn to another page and run my fingers across its smooth surface. *Full of possibilities.* This is the first time I've sat down to draw since I promised I wouldn't. It was a promise I knew I couldn't keep, but I still made it. I shut my eyes and let my pencil dance across the page, then open them slowly and see Kit's face. It's not realistic. I play with her hair, bringing it to life, the way it flicks and bounces whenever she moves her head. Next, I move on to a light sketch of the boy from the cafe – Jamie.

I stare at the drawing for a while, then shade in the dark shadows I noticed under his eyes. *How does he fit into all this?* I don't know if he's the same Jamie that Kit mentioned. I turn to a new page. The side of my left hand is covered in a silvery smudge – it's a dead giveaway. I look out into the night. Right now, there are teams of people darting from place to place, collecting supplies to feed, clothe and heal the thousands of infected people hiding Underground. No, not infected.

Infection is a lie.

If supplies are being cut off, who is doing it? Is it Sympathisers, scared of getting caught? I've overheard customers at the cafe whispering that security was being tightened, more patrols, more surveillance. The rumours say it's Jubilee related – all the planned gatherings, and processions. Events announced in *Metropolis Magazine* reflected that idea too. Mum hasn't mentioned any of the specifics to me yet. From what I've gathered Our Occasions are the catalyst for the other events. But if the people, the *Sympathisers*, stop donating from the goods to the Underground . . . the impact will be devastating, regardless of the reason.

As my hand hovers above the page, Paula pops into my head.

I haven't drawn her yet. I start by outlining what I can remember: her short hair, the heavy lines across her forehead. I try to capture the shape of her mouth, its constant cruel smile. Kit's voice rings in my head while I work. *Clan Ember collects and distributes the supplies.* I start another sketch on the same page, this time capturing Paula's body and her clothes – *her pants.* Kit told me that everyone uses what they can find, that they make do, but Paula's pants were clean, albeit worn. They were guards' pants, and they fitted her perfectly. *If the supplies have been missing –* I think I hear something, and slam the book shut. *What was that?* Silence. I open the book again and start another sketch, not caring that the graphite on my hand is smearing everything on the page. The sound of my pencil scratching is all I can hear.

Something doesn't fit. Kit said she rarely picked up supplies anymore because of her time spent in the medical centre. My pencil has taken on its own life. Racing across the smooth paper . . . *Kit is just trusting what Paula tells her.* I put my pencil down. *Trusting Paula.* I look down at my finished sketch and flick the book away from me before I can stop myself. It lands on my floor with a soft thud, with Paula's face staring back at me. I have captured it perfectly, exactly how it sits in my memory: the moment Paula's mask slipped. That is where Kit has made a mistake. *Trusting Paula.*

I pick up the book and shove it under my pillow. My room feels hot. Suffocating. I rush back over, pulling the curtains and sliding the window wide open. My face is instantly hit with a rush of cold air. It burns my cheeks. I reach forward to close the window slightly, and just as I reach for the latch, I notice a slip of paper sticking out from the metal handle. It's stuffed in so tight it's barely moving despite the wind. I pull it out and open it. It reads:

Warehouse. Tomorrow night. Midnight.

K

eleven

Today is my Partnership. The second of three challenges I must face before beginning the next chapter of my life. I went to bed thinking about Kit's note and woke up this morning with Mum hovering over me like an annoying wasp. 'Wear the pink dress I hung on your wardrobe door,' she said, then grabbed the discarded pink laces from the floor and stomped out with my new black boots.

Now I'm in the kitchen swathed in pink tulle scarfing down cereal while she busies herself with her morning 'tonics'.

'You look lovely,' she says, not looking at me. 'Today Partnership, next week the Sealing, then on to your future.' She downs the little glass of green liquid and squints. 'You really do look stunning,' she says again, actually looking at me this time.

'Thanks,' I say. I don't feel it. The dress is layers of pink silk and tulle. I didn't know how to put it on, so I spent half the morning doing and undoing the twenty-three buttons on the back, simply trying to line them up. I couldn't ask Mum for help – not with those stitches on my shoulder. I glance at myself in the reflection of one of the million mirrors Mum has around the house. I suppose the wispy silk neckline, loose over my collarbones, does look nice. I put a significant effort into my hair too. I usually tie it in a simple bun or a ponytail, but today, part of me wanted to care. *This is it*, I think as I retwist a curl hanging from my temple. Since my Job Placement, I've felt nothing but dread, but now I can't hide from the excitement that's brewing.

'Your hair looks amazing!' Mum exclaims, circling around me to look at the back. I had to use my old textbook. We were *tested* on it, actually given a grade on how well we could do our own hair. Lisa and I would spend hours 'studying' for our exams. I hated it, she loved it. 'How are the shoes?'

I wriggle my toes. They're remarkably comfortable but I decide not to tell her. I don't want the woman knowing she's won this round of our shoe battle.

'The pink laces ruin them,' I say wryly.

Mum sighs. 'Yes, I'm sure you think so, you can go back to black laces after today. You *might* even be able to wear the same shoes to the Sealing Ceremony – with green laces to match the green lace dress.' I scowl, not bothering to hide my irritation.

'Your father won't be coming today, Teddy, but he will be at the Sealing Ceremony next week. In fact, he will be the person giving the Seals.' Her voice is clipped. I hadn't asked, but still, relief floods out of me. I glance up at her, toying with the questions I've always wanted to ask and never dared. *Is she happy he's not around? Does she miss him?*

I never feel so distant from her as I do when we talk about him. My father, the invisible wedge that drives its pointy end into the middle of our life whenever the topic comes up, whether he is around or not.

'Do you miss him?' I ask. Her head snaps up as she looks at me, startled by my question. 'I mean, when he's not around – do you miss his company?'

She smiles one of her *Metropolis Magazine* smiles at me. 'Ahh,' she says knowingly. 'The nerves are really starting to set in. I understand.' She pours herself another cup of coffee and sits down opposite me. 'I was nervous too, but I was lucky. Your dad is very handsome, which made the whole process a lot smoother.' She winks, and I wish I hadn't said anything. I'm always struggling to understand what she really thinks of my father. Despite everything he puts her through, she caters to his every whim. She's his smiling devoted wife. The perfect mother. *Where is* his *devotion?* We're taught to expect equality, but I've never seen it in our home. The expectation of equality that we're taught is something I can only hope for. I think back to the woman who cried on my bed a week ago.

'Is it true the matches are scientific?' I ask. I am nervous, but not for the reasons she thinks. I know I should cut myself some slack. Lisa and I talked about it a million times. Having someone so close to you, who knows you so well; you could reveal those hidden parts of yourself, *without fear of Sanitisation.*

'Scientific, psychological, they look at your intelligence levels. Perfect pairs.' She smiles at me like I'm a child. 'But you need to be careful too.' She's still smiling.

There was no way I could have known about the Underground or the truth behind Sanitisation. It wasn't as if they published those things in *Metropolis Magazine* and I'd just missed that page.

I swallow. Mum knew about Sanitisation all this time.

'What about before?' I ask. She looks at me, puzzled. 'You know, *before* the laws. I don't think they always had Partnering, did they?'

'Eh,' she says with a dismissive wave. 'There was no Partnering back then. I guess people would "fall" in love.

Toxic, self-indulged behaviour.' *She's hiding something.*

'What about if you love someone who you're Partnered with?' I ask.

'That's okay, I suppose. Very convenient. But you still need to be careful.'

How many times does she want to tell me that?

'What about if you love someone that you're not Partnered with?'

She stiffens in her chair. 'That doesn't happen.' She puts our dishes in the sink. 'It used to happen before, sometimes, and I'm sure it would have caused all sorts of problems. It's probably one of the reasons they set up Partnership in the first place. Eliminate all this self-centred behaviour, all this "me" talk. It's not about who you *want* to love – it's about who you *need* to love. Who Our Council *needs* you to love, to best serve Our City.'

She smiles again, but I can tell I have hit a sore spot. I try switching to something lighter.

'Did men and women hang out before? Get to know each other before they were Partnered? It seems so rushed. You find out your Partner then you're Sealed one week later and bound to them for the rest of your life.'

'Perhaps, but look at all the mess that "hanging" out got Our City into.' She leans back against the bench. 'Nothing good comes from selfishness, nothing but heartache for everyone.' She closes her eyes, and I feel the sting of betrayal. It's like she's forgotten everything she told me last week.

As if it never happened.

'What about all those things you said to me the other night –'

She slams her hand on the table, and I jump.

'Remember what happens to people when they get too close to the edge,' she hisses, then she leaves abruptly, calling over her shoulder, 'Brush your teeth. We need to leave.'

twelve

Mum doesn't talk to me for the whole trip. We drop the car off with the valet and walk up the stairs, into the same massive domed building where I received my Job Placement. I expected her to continue her icy attitude throughout the day, but she softens as soon as the car door opens. Luanna Veodrum is back. *Proud mother and devoted patriot.* She's wearing a mask too, like Paula.

I had expected something different from the last time I was here, but the huge foyer is much the same, with check-in desks lining the far wall and swathes of young people all dressed in their finest. The anticipation in the air is palpable, as excited teenagers mill around with their families, getting ready to receive their life Partners. This is the second and final day we can wear any colour we like . . . *in theory.* I tug at my dress. *I've never had any choice.*

We register at the desk with a different but equally bored clerk, then walk together into the main auditorium and up to our seats. We are sitting in the same seats, in the same row. I look up once more. The honeycomb ceiling takes my breath away. *Again.*

'Still stunning,' Mum says, smiling at me. I can't smile back. 'I mean you.' She elbows me playfully. The room might be the same, but the energy is different. More intense. The talking is hushed. Every wall is covered in fine red and gold fabric. It's all backlit, so they look like sheets of flame. The material is moving, and I wonder if they're using a fan to create the effect. Nervous young eyes dart around the room, including mine. This is a life-changing day.

I didn't think I would feel the same buzz as the young people around me – not after the weird conversation with Kit last night, and this morning's bizarre encounter with my mother – but the energy in the room is infectious. I swallow.

What if I'm wrong? What if they get it wrong?

I slip my bare hand into my pocket and feel a pair of silk gloves. They will be placed on my hands by my Partner, to symbolise our Partnership. Then in three days our necks will be Sealed – tattooed – with the Metropolis City Seal and the date, at our Sealing Ceremony. I feel past the gloves, deeper into my pocket. The tip of my finger brushes the slip of paper, Kit's note, and a thrill passes through me.

I swallow. I can't go. Shouldn't. Something flutters in my stomach. *I might.* I look towards the imposing stage. I have so few choices in my life, and I still don't know what decision I will make. All I know is that after today, nothing will ever be the same again.

'It's almost time,' my mother says softly. She squeezes my hand supportively as the lights are dimmed, and I smile back weakly.

It's almost time.

The audience falls silent, and we stand – hundreds of people in one motion – ready to recite the Creed of Our Great City.

The ceremony has begun.

The voices from the stage echo around the cavernous auditorium, but all I can hear is a ringing in my ears. I glance furtively at the empty seat next to my mother and pretend not to notice how once again she artfully conceals its emptiness with the ample folds of her red dress. All the parents here today are wearing red. I am sure I learnt why they wear red, but my thoughts are so heavy I can't remember now. *Was it for the celebration?* No, not that.

Blood.

It's to symbolise blood. The blood of their own flesh – their children, now being birthed into adulthood. I look around at the sea of men and women in crimson suits and dresses.

I swallow and try to bring my attention back to the proceedings. Today, the stage is set up differently. The black banners hanging from the high domed ceiling have been replaced with bright crimson flags that match the parents' garb. Councilman Parker, a friend of my father's – Sarah's dad – leans forward, his hands gripping the sides of the lectern. I imagine my father standing in that spot next time we're here, and the thought sends a bead of sweat rolling down my spine. I don't recognise the two other councillors who stand at either side of the stage, chaperoning the nervous teenagers to their fates. There are two raised platforms in front of the lectern, facing each other. Standing on one of the platforms is a girl, waiting to be Partnered. She is the tallest girl I've ever seen. I imagine her new heeled shoes and the raised platform aren't helping her much. They haven't gathered us at the front of the stage, so everything is even slower this time, as we sit with our families, waiting for our names to be called.

The councillor is standing, staring at the girl. She shifts nervously and accidentally rolls her ankle – *ouch*. I notice Councillor Parker shoot her a look of disgust over his glasses. Even from my seat up here, I can see that his hair is combed over his head, smoothed down with so much gel that the lights on the stage create a shiny halo over the bald patch he's trying so desperately to hide. He calls out another name: *Hector Crumb*. Her Partner. I look sideways at my mum. She's pulled one of her gloves off and is picking at her nails like Kit does. I glance around. *She shouldn't take them off.* Not here.

Hector Crumb staggers onto the stage, looking around like he's lost. He's an exceptionally short boy. A councillor steps forward out of the shadows, Councillor Margay. She visited our School Code during our final week to discuss the Occasions, explaining the process of each ceremony. I hadn't noticed her earlier. She's dressed in the same grey that Council members always wear, but there is a red sash tied across her chest. Hector and the tall girl stand facing each other.

'Now you will take each other's hands . . .' Councillor Parker drones, his voice flat and emotionless. Councillor Margay steps forward and places a white cloth over their hands, symbolic of the bed they will now share. I swallow. 'Now, the gloving.' The girl puts her hand into her pocket and starts pulling out a pair of crushed gloves, light green to match her dress. She passes them to the

Councillor who in turn passes it to the boy. He drops one in their awkward exchange. I want to look away, but I can't. The councilwoman bends down to pick up the glove, but so does the boy, and they bump heads. I bite the inside of my cheek to stop a giggle from escaping. The tall girl glances across to Councillor Parker, who looks like his eyebrows are about to fly off his forehead. I look around the audience and spot Sarah a few rows down, snickering.

Finally, the boy is holding the gloves. He takes his new Partner's hands and pulls each glove on, 'Sealing' their Partnership.

'Say the lines,' Parker says through pursed lips.

'As I dress you now, I see you as a whole,' the boy says. The girl nods, and there is an awkward silence.

'Torabelle?' the councilman nudges.

'As you dress me now, I see you as a whole,' she mumbles. Then they're holding each other's hands, repeating the lines we've been waiting our whole lives to say: 'We see each other now. Now we will grow together to serve Our Great City. We, the Chosen People.' The pair step down from the raised platforms and walk off the stage. They're both smiling, as if those words have made their fears disappear. I find I'm clapping, even though their shaking voices are still rattling in my head. *I see you as a whole* . . . What is going on here? I look over at my mum, but she's playing with her own gloves, slapping them on her palm in a half-hearted clap. I sigh. Everyone settles back down and another pair are called to the stage. I laugh to myself when I recognise one of them. Up there on the podium is the sandy-haired maintenance boy. He's holding the hands of an olive-skinned girl I don't recognise; his face is glowing as he pulls gloves onto her hands, clearly satisfied with his match. Maybe my mother's right, maybe Partnering with someone attractive might make it easier. I doubt it, though.

'Teddy Veodrum.' I hear my name, but I can't move. After watching pair after pair cross the stage and repeat those same lines, my skin has started to crawl. I want to get out. To escape. I realise I'm sliding down in my seat.

How did they get to my name so quickly?

'Teddy. Get up,' my mother whispers as she pinches my arm. 'Ouch!'

'Get. Up,' Mum says again, a knife-edge to her voice. Her gloves are back on.

I begin to make my way to the stage, grateful for my new shoes. I don't think I could have made it down all these stairs in any of the other pairs. Not with everyone watching me. *Not just watching, judging.* I can hear the rapid thumping of my heart pounding in my ears. I'm acutely aware of hundreds of eyes on me, but my ears are flooded with the thump of my heartbeat. I walk across the front of the stage to the large staircase, swathed in red. Now that I'm closer, I can see that the raised platforms are much taller than they looked. *Maybe that first girl wasn't that tall after all.* There's a ringing in my ears. I touch my pocket in a quick panic, worried the gloves might not be there. *Did I leave them on my seat?* No, they're here.

I hold on to the railing with a shaky hand as I climb the stairs to the stage. The woman at the top greets me with a smile that looks like she's trying to hold in gas rather than convey happiness. The two platforms are even taller this close. Each one has its own small set of stairs to climb.

I don't hear my Partner's name being called. I can't hear anything, I can only feel everyone's gaze boring into me from all around the circular space.

I'm directed to a platform and climb up the small ladder and onto the narrow top. I swallow, but my mouth is dry. I try to relax my hands and stand still while I wait for my Partner to join me. I can see some movement out in the crowd, but the lights are so bright I can't make out anything else. I try not to sway. Out beyond those lights, there's a sea of hundreds of faces, and I suddenly feel very exposed. *My secrets.* My heart starts to race. *Can they see them?* I glance at Councillor Parker standing behind the lectern. He's peering at me with cold eyes above his square glasses.

Does he know I've been into the Underground? Does he even know there's an Underground?

I train my eyes on my Partner's feet in front of me.

'I said, hand me the gloves,' Councillor Margay thunders. I fish in my pocket, praying the note from Kit doesn't fall out. *Why did I bring it with me?* I pull my hand out and pass the silk gloves to Margay. I grit my teeth and slowly look up, starting with his shoes. Then I stumble back and, for a second, teeter on the edge of the platform.

'No, no, no,' I hear myself saying.

'Don't be foolish, girl,' Margay snaps. 'Stand up straight and be silent.' I steel myself and force myself to meet my Partner's gaze while he pulls the gloves onto my hands.

'As I dress you now, I see you as a whole.' His hands are as gentle as mine are trembling.

'Speak,' the councilwoman hisses.

'As you dress me now, I see you as a whole,' I say, my voice a whisper. We join hands and then repeat the lines I've been dreading saying all morning: 'We see each other now. Now we will grow together to serve Our Great City. We, the Chosen People.'

'Congratulations,' I hear Councillor Parker say from the lectern. Somewhere in the distance, I know the crowd is clapping, but I can't hear it.

All I can focus on is the young man standing before me.

Jamie.

thirteen

The cold night air whips against my face as I weave silently down the side streets and alleyways I know so well in daylight. I redirect my course twice to avoid roads where known Council Eyes live, and dodge the ever-increasing packs of patrolling guards. Their radios hiss and pop, the static jarring me from my racing thoughts. It's a welcome distraction.

Tonight, every sound is amplified, and I feel like I'm racing some wild beast through the dark streets. As I stop to catch my breath I hear voices close by. I try to breathe quietly, but I've been running fast. A group of guards is milling about at the end of the street, rifles slung casually over their shoulders. I crouch in the shadow of a fence, my pulse beating rapidly in my neck. The guards don't seem to be moving. I count six of them, hanging about like cockroaches. One wrong move and they'll be on me, and I'll be . . . dead.

I redirect my course, running down a back alley, then squat down. I can see the angled lenses of three Council Eye surveillance cameras glinting behind a streetlamp. I curse to myself silently. Still, I'm grateful to be out of the house, albeit illegally. My insides are still reeling from the Partnership Ceremony.

Everything is wrong.

When we got home from the ceremony, my mother was almost in hysterics. Happy hysterics. She had read the profile they handed to us when we left. It turns out my Partner, Jamie Guise, is destined to be a City Councilman.

Just like my father.

The icy night air filling my lungs can't dampen the fire of rage burning within me.

Is this something he planned?

I lean back against the wall and close my eyes, then open them again.

More guards.

They're everywhere tonight. I stand up slowly, making sure to keep my back against the wall. I'll be able to ask Jamie if this was his plan soon enough. I'll see him again at our Sealing Ceremony. A few more days and it will be him and me, and 'Our' City. I look back the way I've come, but forward is my only choice. I just need to keep my footsteps light.

But before I can take a step, a radio spits and stutters until I hear a voice. It sounds distorted and distant. *Disruption at Walker and Press Streets. All available units required.* The radio crackles and returns to its low hiss again, then two guards rush past the mouth of the alley. They run rhythmically, right in front of my face, and I'm so startled I almost scream. With two hands clamped over my mouth, I feel my heartbeat throbbing in my chest, watching them retreat under the lights, rushing up the street until their dark grey uniforms dissolve seamlessly into the road. *A perfect camouflage.* I wait until I'm satisfied they're gone, then I dart across the main street, feeling the road crumble beneath my shoes. The Council doesn't care about streets this far from Downtown, this far from the 'nice' suburbs. Lisa's street was okay, but she'd once told me that the place where her grandparents lived was terrible. I hadn't believed her, and we'd had a huge fight.

My mind drifts back to the different people I'd seen today at the Partnering. Sure, everyone was dressed up, but not to the same standard. I wish I had paid more attention. *Jamie Guise*, I muse. He even had the nerve to tell me his real name at the cafe. *How did he know me?*

I try to stick within the shadow of the trees and fence line, but I can sense the cameras everywhere around me, blinking like eyes. I'm thankful for my hoodie as I slink past more fences. I pause to check for guards, then slip into the warehouse forecourt. My mind slips back to Lisa. *What would she have said about all this?* I don't think she would have been surprised at all.

The sight of the looming containers and giant warehouse buildings would once have filled me with childish fear. In fact, up until a week ago they did. Now I'm relieved to be under the safety of their shadow. The cracked cameras here have no eyes, smashed, from I don't know what. I try focusing my brain on two tasks: listening for guards and setting my feet down, so I don't trip over.

I think of Kit's note: *Warehouse. Tomorrow night. Midnight. K*

For a second, I consider the possibility that I'm being set up. There are so many variables. Kit, Jamie, even my father.

After today I'm not even sure if I can trust Mum.

Of course, I can . . .

When we were children, Lisa and I used to talk about our future Partners, listing the qualities we hoped they'd have. She always valued status, like my family. I always wanted trust.

Someone I could talk to and share my secrets with. Now I'm Partnered to someone I don't know. *But he knows me.*

I feel stupid. No one should trust anyone here.

Everyone watches everyone. Even family can't be trusted.

Considering the reasons Kit might want to meet now, I stumble on some gravel, but keep walking. *It could be a trap.* I hear the crackle of a guard's radio, and my breath catches in my chest. I spin around, looking for shelter, then drop to the ground. The sound of marching boots slapping against pavement is loud. Not just one or two pairs, either. A lot.

I press myself against the rough ground and half lie, half crawl my way to a container. I see a sliver of space between two stacks of rusty shipping containers, relics of a time long past. I'm not sure I'll fit, but I don't have a choice. I slip into the crack and make my way down. The narrow space opens wider, as if the containers were pushed together on an angle. I stand.

'I didn't think you were gonna show.'

I swallow a scream and spin around to find Kit leaning against the side of the container, her arms folded and a small torch in her hand. I rub my fingers against my temples.

'Hi,' I say, once my heart stops jumping out of my throat. 'I had to reroute for two separate sets of guards. Can you believe that? What's happening tonight? Are there always this many patrols out?'

Kit just rolls her eyes. 'I guess it's something to do with this big Jubilee.' She shrugs. 'Maybe they think something's gonna happen. Eh, I never pay much attention to them, although this is a fairly important day, isn't it?'

I notice a flash of light behind me and spin on my heel, finding myself face to face with –

'Jamie,' I say. A sick feeling forms in the pit of my stomach. 'What are you –'

My new Partner steps forward, moving his torch out of my eyes, and I shift, letting him pass. 'What is going on?' I ask slowly, trying to maintain control.

'I'm not sure if –' Kit begins, but I cut her off again.

'Not sure if what? If you want to tell me what the fuck is going on?' She steps back with her hands up. I've never spoken to anyone like that before. It felt good.

'Did he tell you we've met before?' I ask.

Kit looks between us, shocked.

'You *met* her?' she asks him.

'I went to her work,' he says sheepishly.

'Were you going to tell me?' she demands.

Jamie ignores her, pretending he's keeping a lookout. Kit's silent for a beat, then she turns to me. 'Were *you* going to tell me?' she demands.

'I did, *remember*? He was the guy at the cafe who asked what time I got off work.'

'You didn't tell me he was *Jamie*.' She runs her hands through her hair.

'Was I supposed to? How was I supposed to know your Jamie was above ground, anyway? Maybe one of you wants to tell me what on earth is going on?' I cross my arms.

'Mmmm.' She looks at Jamie then back to me. 'He's not a bad guy, Teddy, he's one of us.' She says that last part cautiously.

'*Us?* Oh, so I'm part of your "us" now?' I spit the words out. 'I thought *we* were us!' I say, pointing to him and me. 'How long have you known I was going to be Partnered with your friend?'

She ignores my question. 'You're part of this, yes. You're a part of the Underground now, a Sympathiser if you will. You're in this now.'

I step forward. I have had it with being told what to do.

It ends now.

'I don't remember *asking* to be a part of this –' I say, my voice growing louder.

'Shhhh,' Jamie hisses. 'Guards are everywhere tonight. We need to be quick, Kitty.'

I tense my hands. *Kitty?*

'*You* chose to leave your room that night, Teddy. That's on you,' says Kit, poking her finger into my chest. I swat it away, and Kit leans back against the cold rusty metal wall. I stare at her for a moment, then look back to Jamie.

'So, what's the deal with my Partnership to him then?' I ask Kit, not taking my eyes off him. 'I guess it's all a ploy. Some little piece in a *bigger* game?' Kit starts to nod.

Jamie cuts in. 'Did she tell you about the people who are sick? The missing supplies?' he says.

That's not what I'm asking.

'So why did you go to the cafe, Jamie?' I ask, answering his question with one of my own. I turn to Kit. 'And how did you know he was my Partner?'

Kit tenses, picking at the paint on her long nails.

Jamie's the first to crumble, with both of us glaring at him. 'I wanted to suss you out,' he says, turning to face me properly. 'No one was suspicious. I've been going to Maree's with my family for years.' I open my mouth, then close it again.

'With your family?' I finally say, and see Kit and Jamie exchange a glance.

'This is so typical,' Kit says as she slumps back down.

'Can one of you please just tell me what is going on?' I ask, sitting down hard in the cold dirt opposite her.

Kit sighs. 'I've known him forever,' she says. 'Since I was five, I think. That's when they brought you down to the

Underground, wasn't it?' Jamie nods.

'Yeah,' says Kit. 'I was five, he was seven.'

'Nice history lesson, but that still doesn't explain how he's ended up Partnered with me.'

'I'm getting to that, okay? Just shut up and listen.'

Keeping her voice low, Kit tells me initially none of this was planned. 'I've spent the last three months looking for any clues to lead to a breakthrough on the missing supplies. Jamie was scheduled to be Partnered and start his new role in the City Council and we've been trying to find the right Partner for him, for ages. Then when you showed up, right at the start of the Occasions season – i t was perfect.' I look between the pair of them.

'How do you possibly –' I begin to ask.

'We have people on the inside. The Sympathiser network exists within the City Council – remember the desk drones?' she says, and Jamie shifts uncomfortably beside her.

He won't meet my eyes.

Kit goes on. 'Paula was certain you were a spy. I knew you weren't, but I had to give Paula a good reason to let you go. When I left you in there with her,' she gives me a pointed look, 'it was to find Jamie. I told him what had happened, that you had followed me and, well, we didn't have much choice. We had to choose you. To get you out.'

'We?'

'Us,' she gestures to herself and Jamie. 'It was that or remain

92

Paula's prisoner, so I'm *sorry* for saving your life!' She looks at me indignantly. 'Your dad being a councillor was actually nothing more than a happy accident. I didn't find that out until I took you home and had a little look around.' *Is this just a set-up?*

'Paula took some convincing. "How can we trust she'll do what we want?" she kept saying. I just told her we'd keep a close eye on you in the lead-up, and once you were Partnered – well, then you're your Partner's property.'

Huddled against the wall, trying to draw some warmth into my body, I stare at her in shock. 'Why me?'

'I just told you why –' Kit says.

'I know what you said!' I snap. My head is swirling. Part of me feels hurt by the prospect that my entire life is now a sham . . .

but part of me is relieved. *No secrets.* Isn't this what I wanted?

'Like Kit said earlier,' Jamie says gently, 'you would be a Sympathiser. We both would be – except, well, I'm a Dual Citizen, which is only slightly different.'

I open my eyes. There's so much to take in. I pinch the bridge of my nose.

'So, you can create fake Partnerships and make someone a citizen up here, but you can't get a little medicine?'

Kit sinks onto her knees. 'I'm a True, I was born in the Underground. Jamie was born up here, then moved Underground. Dual Citizens are a *very* select few who have an identity in the Metropolis but are really escapees. They can leave the City and go Underground anytime. They stay with relocated family or generous Sympathisers.'

But what about me?

'People get relocated a lot in this city,' I say, thinking about Lisa's family, about the day she just didn't come to school. Along with everyone else in the street, we got a letter notifying us her family had been taken for treatment. Then her house was empty, and a week later a new family had moved in.

'People believe what they want to believe,' says Jamie. 'In my *Metropolis* family, I have elderly grandparents living all around the

City. Everyone in my neighbourhood knows I have to go and stay with them regularly, to help them.' 'Oh,' I say lamely.

'Any file can be edited; any facts can be altered . . . if you know the right people,' he adds.

Some of the arrogance I thought I'd sensed in him seems to have worn off. I wonder what it must feel like, only half living in two worlds. I imagine how unsettling that would be, having to split your time between locations. I've been living in two worlds, in my head, for a week – Jamie's lived like this his whole life.

'It's great though – I really do get the best of both worlds! And now you will too – mostly.' He smiles at me encouragingly. 'We won't be going Underground very frequently; it will be more people like Kit slipping in and visiting us. When needed.'

His words take me by surprise. Days ago, I was in my room wondering what my Partner would think about Kit popping in to have tea and biscuits. Now I'm here at the warehouses, at night, *with* my Partner, who's telling me that Kit will be a regular house guest. My head is spinning. I nod slowly, but I still don't fully understand.

Kit clears her throat. 'Your main job is to be a good citizen and help Jamie look good; to become a model couple. Perfection means fewer questions. While you do that, *we* need to figure out what's happening with these supplies.' I glance at them both.

'Have you considered it could be Paula?' I ask. Jamie shakes his head, warning me, but it's too late.

'What?' Kit says, her voice sharp and wary. I glance back to Jamie, but he seems suddenly compelled to check the batteries in his torch.

'I understand it might be difficult to hear, but she *could* have something to do with it. I mean, it is her "people" doing the collecting.' I adopt Kit's quote marks when I say 'people'.

'It's another clan stealing from us, Teddy,' Kit says through clenched teeth. 'You've only been here half a second. You don't know anything.'

I nod slowly, and look back to Jamie, hoping for some backup, but he's now reading the label on his torch with intense concentration.

'Let me make this clear, Teddy,' says Kit. 'You don't make the calls around here.' Her eyes flash. 'Got it?'

'*You're* the one who just said I'm a part of this. You just told me I'm being Partnered with Jamie to become a

Sympathiser.'

'Sorry, you misunderstood. Your job is to be a pretty little silent thing on Jamie's arm, so no one asks questions while we do the work.'

'Excuse me?' I stand up.

This isn't any different from being Partnered by the Council — it's still someone else choosing my path. I steel myself.

'Kit,' Jamie interjects, but she cuts him off.

'Teddy, you're too deep in your "world" to have any useful insight. You met Paula once. So, I'm just saying —'

'Yeah? Well, I'm just saying we need to keep our minds open.' Jamie nods slowly. *Does he agree with me?*

'We?' she spits. '*We?* A few minutes ago you didn't want to be part of any "we"!' She points to Jamie. 'We need someone we can trust — not some Metropolis lunatic who wants to start throwing blame around like it's a grenade!' Kit stands up, balling her fists at her sides.

I can feel a headache growing. 'If you had seen Paula's face when I was down there that night —' Cutting me off, Kit shoves an open hand in mine and goes to leave.

'Teddy, you were right to tell us,' Jamie replies, his voice still gentle. He puts a hand on my leg. 'Kit and I have actually had

very similar conversations before — haven't we?'

I'm momentarily distracted by his lingering hand.

Kit throws her hands up. 'Jamie is right. You were right. We've all had this conversation; it's *so* obvious. Gee, Teddy, I'm sooo sorry.'

'She's been a tyrant your whole life,' Jamie cuts in again. 'Look at your arms.'

Kit pulls her arms across her chest, and I watch another of their wordless exchanges, then Jamie looks at me, his gaze lingering, a sad smile playing on his lips.

How can she say I'm not a part of this, after being literally dragged down into it? Sure, I followed her, but I didn't follow her *down there*. I didn't want any of this. They're using my life as a part of their game, manipulating the entire course of my future. I want to turn to them and shout, I DON'T CARE!

But I do care.

No one speaks.

You've taken my entire life.

After a moment of silence, I get up, ready to leave.

'Paula has asked me to watch a certain site tomorrow night,' says Kit. 'To keep a lookout, and see who has been stealing the supplies. But the last few nights, I've been watching a different location. I was going to ask you and Jamie to watch my usual spot, since I can't be in both places at once.' She clears her throat. 'Yesterday, I floated that idea with Paula. Not for you to go, just Jamie. So we could watch both locations.'

Intrigued, I sit back down. 'Paula said no.' Kit sighs. 'And even though I *still* think it's another clan, she *did* say no too fast. It was suspicious, even I could see that. So, I've agreed to watch the new spot, only I'm enlisting you and Jamie to watch my normal spot anyway.'

'Are you serious? You just went off at me because I said I *think* we need to consider Paula and now you're telling me you think that Paula is suspicious?'

I've had enough of this. I hesitate when Jamie grabs my hand.

'It's because she suspects Paula that she went off like that,' he says.

I stare at his hand gripping mine, then quickly look at Kit, but she won't meet my eyes. 'Kit has been so unquestioning and supportive, there's no reason for Paula to be suspicious of her. Even the way she convinced Paula to accept our . . . the arrangement. She trusts Kit enough to have let you go so we could execute this plan.'

He drops my hand, and it hangs limply.

I don't expect the rush of anger that hits me. I'm sick of them talking about our Partnership like it was all their decision, like it's just some plan to 'execute' and I'm just going to play along. *But I will, won't I?*

'I get it,' I say, crossing my arms. 'This is a sham,' I wave my hand between Jamie and myself. 'You're a lunatic,' I point to Kit. 'And *I'm* going home. See you next week, *Partner.'* I turn to leave, but Jamie grabs my hand again.

'I know it sounds sterile,' he says, 'and this probably wasn't the best way to tell you –'

'You think?' I snap, yanking my hand out of his gentle grip. *But when would be the right time? After years of living a lie together?*

'I don't know how I feel about this. Any of it,' I say.

Jamie shrugs. Kit nods.

'I think you do,' she says.

'What's that supposed to mean?'

'I don't think you would have come tonight if you didn't know how you felt about it.'

'If I had known he was going to be here –' I point to Jamie, 'I probably *wouldn't* have come. I am not some "chosen person".

No one is.'

Kit laughs. 'Yet here we all are.'

'We said it today,' says Jamie. *"We, the Chosen People."*

Those City Council fools don't know how right they are.' I cross my arms against my chest.

'Teddy, there is going to be a change. I know it. The fact that you're here tells me you know it too. And it's not something so out of the ordinary. Not everyone is *born* into their life.' He gives me a look, like he knows something I don't know.

I rub the back of my neck, looking at them both. Kit isn't scowling anymore, and Jamie has that same earnest look he's had since the first time I saw him. I pull my hood back on and crouch down.

'So, when are we going?' I ask.

Kit smiles and pulls out an old street map. 'Tomorrow night. You two will be going here.' She clicks on her pocket torch and shines it over a small red circle on the paper. I recognise the location immediately.

'The cafe?' I ask.

'Exactly,' Jamie says with a sly grin. I consider him lurking around the cafe. I thought it was just about me, but now I realise he could have been casing the joint.

'I guess I was there for a few reasons,' he says. 'You were just a pleasant coincidence.'

Kit's snort of disgust distracts me from his lingering smile, and I'm grateful for the darkness to hide my burning cheeks.

Blushing? Seriously?

'So, you're telling me that Maree is infected?'

'Teddy! How do you not get it by now? There. Is. No. Such. Thing. As. INFECTION.'

I look at Jamie, and he nods.

Since when did I need his confirmation?

'Kit's right,' he says matter-of-factly. 'It's a scare tactic. But yes, essentially, you're right too – she is what you Sunlighters call "infected", and what we call a Sympathiser.'

I'm floored at the connection. 'Why didn't you tell me?' I ask, struggling to fit this new information into every suspici ous look Maree gave me, her insane following of *every* rule. The fact she *hated* me. And all this time she was on *their* side.

Maybe she was afraid of me?

'We didn't know where you stood. Your dad is a power player; your mum too, in her own way. Maree has been a Sympathiser for thirty-five years. We couldn't put her in danger.'

And I've been panicking that Maree was going to report me.

'You were – are – so new to all this, I didn't want you to get anyone into trouble. I didn't want you to get *yourself* into trouble,' Kit says.

I narrow my eyes. 'Forgive me if I don't believe my safety was your main priority.'

'Are you finished?' Kit says.

Jamie cuts her off. 'Enough!'

'I need some space.' Kit stands and turns sharply, walking away. Jamie sighs before slipping out into the night to follow her.

My head is still spinning as I lean back against the rusting container. Even with Kit's irrational faith in Paula she obviously sees some truth in what both Jamie and I are saying and that makes me feel more confident that I'm right.

Paula has something to do with the missing supplies.

After a few moments, it becomes clear they're not coming back. Gathering my thoughts, I creep out from between the containers and start making my way back home, through the cold, dark streets.

fourteen

On my way to meet Kit, I had been shivering, the damp air seeping into my clothes and chilling my bones. Now, the heat of our fractured meeting is still coursing through me, and I welcome the cool mist that lands on my cheeks as I jog down the silent moonlit streets.

The journey home is peaceful. The guards that had swarmed like flies before are gone. For a second, I think I hear the crunch of marching boots from an approaching patrol, but after crouching in a bush for a moment, the sound disappears. The darkness can play tricks on you. It has been just an hour since I left the warehouse, but for some reason, the journey back home feels like it's taking forever.

The mist has started to turn into rain. I pull my hands into my sleeves and start pushing myself, running hard for the last leg of the trip.

Approaching my street, I decide to make a quick diversion, ducking left and looping back around. As I approach my house from a different angle, I squint through the rain. It looks like a figure is lurking near our front door. I slow behind a tall pine tree. Feeling around, I pick up a fallen pinecone and toss it out into the street. The shadow freezes. *Surely this isn't my imagination.*

I close my eyes and count to three. When I open them, the shadow has disappeared.

I slip through the window, into the warmth of my room, then look outside again, searching the milky light for the shadow. *Nothing.* I close the window and make sure it's locked. I turn around and feel my way over to the bedside table, fumbling for the lamp switch.

Warm light floods the room.

'Hello,' says a voice.

I fall back and trip on the corner of my rug. Righting myself, I take in the full picture. Jamie is lying back against my pillows, his legs crossed at the ankles. My notebook sits open on his lap. 'I didn't think you'd *ever* be coming back. I was actually starting to get worried.'

I glance at my notebook in his hands and feel the colour rise to my cheeks. If he's been looking at my book, he will have seen my sketches . . . of him.

'What the hell are you doing here?' I hiss, trying to keep my voice low.

'Waiting for you to get back so I can talk to you without our emotional wreck of a friend.'

He yawns, stretching his arms high above his head, and I try to ignore the muscles flexing along his arms.

'I've been here for at least half an hour. I seriously thought you'd be faster. I wouldn't have come, otherwise.' I notice a muscle tic in his jaw, as if he's fighting back a smile.

'How do you know where I live?'

He uncrosses his legs and moves to sit on the side of the bed, facing me.

'How do you think Kit got you back to your room?

She certainly didn't carry you by herself. Anyway, I only just turned the lights off. I've had time to flick through this entire book.' He looks at me ruefully. 'Twice.'

'Then who was at my front door?' I ask again, more urgently this time. He furrows his brow.

'Wasn't me,' he says matter-of-factly. 'But if you want me to take a look around . . .' He gets up from the bed and makes his way towards my door.

'No!' I jump forward. 'No, no. It's okay. I'm sure it was nothing.' I shrug.

I hope it was nothing.

He walks back towards my bed and turns the book around to

face me. It's my drawing of Paula.

'Is this drawing real?' he asks. I raise an eyebrow. 'I mean, is this something you saw, or did it come from your imagination?' 'It's real,' I say, trying not to be annoyed.

'I've seen it too,' he says, his face suddenly serious.

Having Jamie here in my room makes me feel just like I did when I first met him at the cafe. Awkward and shy.

'You can come and sit down here, you know,' he says, patting the bed beside him. I look at the spot and consider it for a second. He won't stop looking at me, and his clear blue eyes are now practically glowing with laughter.

It's like he can read my mind.

There are rumours about Partners being together before their Sealing, but they're just stories. He mimics my raised eyebrow and pats the spot beside him again. 'I don't bite.' His eyes are still twinkling.

'Why are you here?' I ask, ignoring him. 'I'm sure it's not just to break in and look at my stuff. You'll get a lifetime of that soon enough.' He sighs, standing.

'I'm here to apologise for leaving so abruptly before.' He seems sincere. '*And* to tell you —' I draw in a breath. I'm not sure I want to hear what he has to say. After he'd put the gloves on my hands at the Partnering Occasion, I had thought — hoped — that maybe it was a coincidence, us being Partnered. I don't want him rubbing in how fabricated this all is . . . h as always been.

'— that I agree with you. One hundred per cent. I think it's Paula.'

I blink. Twice. Then, finally, I sit down on the bed.

'Seriously,' he continues. 'I've been watching the deliveries on and off for months, like Kit. There is *nothing* to indicate it's another clan stealing supplies. Or the Sympathisers. I live with them! I'd know.'

He sits next to me on the bed, closer than he needs to. I can feel the warmth radiating off him. 'The only thing that remains the same is that every time I watch, Paula's "people" are always there.'

'People like Link?' I ask.

'Yeah. I hate that guy.' Jamie's face contorts, and I think back to my blurry recollections of the man who dragged me into the Underground. His pointy hair.

Like knives sticking out of his head.

'If I'd been there, I would never have dragged you back to Paula.' He tries to take my hand, but I pull away, eager to steer the conversation back to Paula.

We hear a slam from somewhere in the house. I freeze.

'You need to go.'

'What?'

'No, now – you need to go now.'

'But we're talking –'

'Go!'

My door opens a crack, and Jamie dives onto the floor on the far side of my bed.

'Mum!' I cry out. 'What are you doing awake?' I hope she doesn't notice that I'm fully dressed, and my voice is three octaves higher than usual.

'I'm just checking on you.' She's dressed too. At two o'clock in the morning. *In pants.* 'I could hear talking.'

'Yeah, I've just been practising what I'm going to say to Mr Guise at the Sealing.' Instead of being satisfied with this, she steps into my room. I look down at my feet, and Jamie winks at me from where he's lying.

'You *can* call him Jamie, darling. And you don't need to practise what to say.' She walks over and sits down on my bed. I can feel my stomach trying to claw its way out of my throat. 'You're right, Mum, I should just go to bed. Try to sleep.'

'You know, my first night with your father, the night of our Sealing, I was *so* nervous.' *No, no, no, no. Stop talking!*

'He took my hands and pulled those gloves right off! It was – ' She closes her eyes at the memory, and I steal a glance at Jamie, still lying at my feet. He meets my eyes, his own twinkling with laughter.

'It's fine, Mum, I've got it, I'm not worried about that stuff. I was talking about his parents, anyway; I want them to like me.'

'Oh, how could they not love you?' she exclaims. 'You're going to be the mother of their family line. I've got this booklet for you –' she pulls a small booklet out of her pocket. Her *pants* pocket. *Are we just ignoring what she's wearing?* She hands it to me.

YOUR FIRST NIGHT AND BEYOND

A woman's duties in the Metropolis Master Suite as wife and womb keeper.

On the back cover is a picture of a lavishly decorated and overstuffed bed, one side of the bedcovers pulled back. There's a woman lounging on it, wearing what looks like a slightly silkier, sleeveless version of the nightgowns Mum's been trying to get me to wear for years.

'Just have a little flick through it,' she says, giving me a look. 'You need to learn a few things. I know it's late. I'm going to make a cup of tea. I might bring you one too, to help you sleep.'

I shake my head, stuffing the embarrassing booklet into my pocket.

'No, thank you, I'm fine.' I try to smile as convincingly as possible.

'No need to be shy – once you start reading that I doubt you'll be putting it down. I'll be downstairs with tea, ready to answer all your questions! Only one week to go – best to be prepared!' She gets up and walks out of the room, closing the door behind her.

Wow, so weird. It's two in the morning . . . and those pants.

'What was that she gave you?' Jamie asks, popping up beside me.

'You heard her, she might be back any minute. Now go!'

'Okay, okay,' he says, putting his hands up. 'But I just want to let you know, you need to tread carefully with the whole Kit–Paula thing. Kit's mother died when she was a baby, so she doesn't cope very well with abandonment.'

'Do any of us?' I mumble, thinking of my father. He shrugs a nod.

'I guess, but for as long as I've known Kit, she's been searching for "her people".'

I think about Kit's confidence. She's never seemed like someone who would struggle to find friends. I assumed it was easy for her.

'You're saying she doesn't make friends easily?'

'Yeah, well, for as long as we've been friends, I've seen Kit go in and out of other friendships and phases,' Jamie says. 'She has impossible standards. I think she's fighting a battle within herself.

She loves being the centre of attention, but she wants to be "one of the gang". But when she stops being the boss, she feels threatened so she starts pushing people away before they can push her away. Like a defence mechanism.' He shrugs.

'But she's stayed friends with you,' I say. Jamie shakes his head.

'*I've* stayed friends with *her*. She's tried to push me away a few times, but I see past that tough exterior. She's not so tough at all. The only things that have ever stuck are her work as a healer and working with Paula – despite what she did.'

'What did Paula do? You said you've seen Paula make that face before.'

'She's evil. You know why Kit's tattoos cover her arms? It's to cover the scars.' I frown.

'From her "initiation ceremony",' says Jamie, 'into Paula's inner circle when she was fourteen. Paula's rules say you have to be tough and rough to survive. It's eat or be eaten. I've seen Paula kill members of our clan for less than stealing. A wrong look can have you kicked out and stuck fighting with the

Outskirters.'

'Are they another clan?'

'They're the clan-less – people who have been accused of crimes by their clan Underground. There are some unwritten rules – things like stealing aren't tolerated in the Underground. Some Outskirters choose to live clan-less – they never join or just leave their clan once they're eighteen. They're so different they can't handle being under the leadership of a Clan Head. If they are caught, it's up to the clan they steal from to decide the punishment. Generally, it's best to stay away from them. For most people, being clan-less is a death sentence. You either starve to death, or someone will shank you in your sleep for whatever food you've managed to scrounge. Some Outskirters band together like gangs. It's not a nice life.' I shudder. 'If Paula gets the impression anyone will question or challenge her power, she eliminates the threat before it can become one.' He grabs my hands and closes his eyes. 'I just don't want anything else to happen to Kit. I know she flipped out tonight, but she really cares about you. She's been so excited about you, ever since the other night. *Her Sunlighter friend.* She's just a bit messed up – but you're right. We all are.'

Something about his tone has me thinking there might be something more than friendship between him and Kit. I try to push it down, to think about Kit's experiences, the tattoos she wears to hide her scars, but my mind keeps coming back to the two of them.

'Are you and her . . .?' I ask, trying to sound nonchalant.

Jamie closes the gap between us in one step.

'Why? Are you jealous?'

I stuff my hands into my pockets. One of them brushes the booklet, and I feel myself blush. I can't believe he overheard that conversation.

For a moment, I want to know everything about him. The soft purple pre-dawn light has a calming effect. His eyes are now glued on the world outside my window, and I take the opportunity to really look at him, his broad shoulders and muscular arms. He is tall, taller than average, and his hair has been recently cut. He turns and catches me staring.

He's the first to speak. 'So, you're jealous?'

I blush again, and swallow the lump forming in my throat.

'No – I'm, it – it doesn't matter,' I say, clearing my throat.

What is wrong with me?

He holds out his hands.

'Neither of us has been Partnered before, and neither of us have ever been adult Sympathisers. So, let's just figure this out – *together.*'

I take his hands, and let him pull me closer, and I can't tell if it's in the tone of his voice or the way his eyes are staring into mine, but I feel . . . safe. All the things that are going wrong seem to wash out of my mind.

But I can't let them.

'No,' I say, pulling away again. 'None of this is normal. I'm not supposed to know you. You were not supposed to know you were going to be Partnered with me. This is only because of your dual citizenship.'

They're using you. They're using you. They're using you.

But so is the Council.

They're lying too.

He steps closer to me, and I find myself moving closer again too. 'You need to learn that things don't always happen the way you think they will up here – or down there, for that matter.' His voice is soft. We can hear my mother banging cupboard doors in the kitchen. He pauses. 'If you want to keep the people you care about safe, *you* need to be careful.' I can feel the heat radiating off him as his face comes even closer to mine. Then he bends down and tears a page out of my notebook.

Paula.

'Hey! What are you –'

'Kit needs us. The whole Underground needs us. Not to mention the people up here who are trying to help, too. If what we suspect of Paula *is* true, everyone is in a lot more danger than we know. Especially with people like your father –'

'What? What do you know about my father?' I say, stumbling backwards.

What's he talking about?

'He's not the man you think he is. From what I've heard, no one seems to be quite sure who he is at all.'

'How do you know that?' I ask, my brain tripping over all the questions that bubble to the surface.

'There are only fifteen senior councillors who work directly with the Mayor. Your father is now the most senior councillor on the Mayor's table.' I swallow a lump of nervous tension, ignoring the pinched feeling at the back of my neck. I can hear my mum's footsteps on the stairs. Jamie reaches for my hand, squeezing gently. I let my guard slip and squeeze back. 'Meet me in the park opposite the cafe tomorrow night. Midnight.' He pushes my window open and cold air fills the room. 'Let me know what you learn from that booklet,' he says, winking. Then he's gone. I step forward and close the window.

Just in time.

'Wow, it is cold in here! Shut that window, Teddy,' says Mum from the doorway.

'I will,' I say irritably, grateful to the cold air for washing the heat of embarrassment off my face. Mum puts a steaming mug on my bedside and wishes me goodnight, leaving the door open a crack behind her.

She's suspicious.

I flop down on my bed, letting all the recent events swirl around in my mind until my thoughts are a huge, tangled mess. *Jamie suspects Paula, Kit is brainwashed by Paula, and Jamie seems to know more about my father than I do.* I make a mental note to ask Mum about Dad's new role in the morning. *Is that why he's performing the Sealing next week instead of the Mayor?* I toss that thought to the side. I can't think anymore.

I close my eyes and let sleep take me.

fifteen

As I wait for Jamie, crouching behind a tree, I regret not bringing a warmer jacket. Soupy mist slips into every crevice it can find, and I blow on my fingertips in a futile attempt to warm them.

What is it with Jamie?

I can't piece it together.

Was he going to kiss me?

I swallow. I'm sure it's after midnight by now. I blow on my fingers again and try to ignore the cold that's needling its way into my body.

I asked Mum about my father's new role this morning over breakfast, but she didn't seem to know any more than what she'd already told me. *Unless she's hiding something.* At this point, that seemed likely.

It doesn't take long for my thoughts to slip back to Jamie. I try reminding myself I don't know him. *Our Partnership is wholly fabricated.* I shiver. *He's been friends with Kit since they were children; maybe she should become the Dual Citizen.*

They'd be better suited. It doesn't matter anyway.

I'm not jealous.

I don't have to have anything to do with him – other than for show, which would be completely fine. My parents hardly ever see each other. I look around again – no sign of him. The more I think about our Partnership, the more I find myself wishing it were real. I bite the inside of my cheek to distract myself.

Want and reality are two different things, Teddy.

I hear the soft crunching of leaves behind me, and before I can turn, I feel his warm breath on the back of my neck.

'You're early,' he whispers.

'You're late,' I respond, turning to face him. He breaks into a smile, teeth glinting in the low light.

'Sorry, I got held up,' he says.

Held up where?

'Seen anything interesting?' he asks, rubbing his hands together.

I shift my weight and shake my head. He steps closer, and I try not to be distracted by his smell: pine trees and wood smoke, as if he's been near a fire. I point to the storage roof of the cafe.

Head in the game.

'We need to get up there.' I try to focus, distracted by his proximity.

Is he always this warm?

'Yeah. I think I have the best way to get up there too.'

'Oh?'

Suddenly he presses his palm against my mouth. His eyes find mine. *Quiet.* He takes his hand away. We're inches apart. Then I hear it: a low rumble. Almost imperceptible. I can't tell which direction the sound is coming from, but whatever it is, it's moving fast. Jamie's eyes are trained on the main road behind us. I break my eyes away from his face and turn to face the street, just in time to see a Sanitisation truck rumbling past. The bright green Metropolis slogan leers at us in the darkness.

Remember We watch because We care.

I try to retreat, but there's something blocking me. I realise I'm pushing back into Jamie's *very* solid chest. I'm too afraid to be embarrassed.

This is how I die. This is how we die.

'It's okay. Calm down,' he breathes softly into my hair. His breath is sweet, like he's been eating an apple. I swallow and try to calm myself. I have only seen the Sanitisation Crew once before. They had been presenting to the school after our annual Sanitisation video screening. We were ten. Lisa told me they were bad men. I told her she was wrong, that they protect us. I was scared.

Lisa was right. Those bad men took her.

'The truck is ours,' he explains in a whisper, and I'm instantly flooded with relief – and then panic. 'It's fake. We use it to gather the supplies from different collection points. There is too much for us to carry, so we needed a truck that wouldn't be stopped by guards. Next time we see it – and we will – look for the colon after "remember".' He sees my confusion. 'If it's our truck, it won't have the colon.' He smiles again, then stands up. I grab the back of his jacket to stop him. 'What?' he asks. I can see his eyebrows furrowed in the dim light. I point out the route we will take if we approach the cafe from the street.

'It's too risky,' I say. I direct his attention to the courtyard. 'Maree will see us straight away. Our job isn't to collect, it's to watch. She's going to be moving around, so we need to make sure she doesn't see us.' He nods slowly. I continue. 'We need to go back out and around. We can loop outside the park and then cross over the main road. Once we double back, we can climb up the fence and onto the storeroom roof.'

He shakes his head. 'Going onto the street is too risky,' he says. I frown, preparing to argue.

Would he be questioning this if it were Kit's suggestion?

'You haven't done this before,' he says.

'I grew up here,' I retort. 'And I worked here; I think I can work out the best route to get to our lookout.' He still doesn't seem convinced. 'If you didn't want me to come, why did you invite me?' No response. 'You'll just have to trust me. If we go through the park, we'll come out right in front of the cafe. Maree will see us. If we cut across the main street, we'll remain completely undetected.'

'Fine, we'll go your way,' he says, throwing his hands up. He's not exactly frowning, but I notice a hint of irritation in his voice.

He clearly considers himself the leader of this expedition.

Both of us remain in a half-crouch as we press into the shadows of the tech tower. The waxing moon is mirrored on the building's polished chrome exterior, a weak imitation of the real thing. The building houses the supercomputer and electricity plant that powers the entire city. Running my hand across its cold metal surface, I feel a soft buzz at my fingertips. There's a zap, and I quickly pull my hand back. They only have one tower to supply electricity and communication to the whole Metropolis – not because Our City abhors tech, but because the Council understands that technology has power. In school, we learnt that before the New Plague, technology was so advanced, people could send photos instantly to anyone, and then the pictures would disappear just as quickly. That kind of communication is too free. *It would be too dangerous, too hard to control.* The City Council needs to control Us, every inch of Our lives.

Jamie gestures for me to stop, and we both turn and face the street. Once we cross the road, we'll be at the fence. This is the most exposed part of the journey. I start to wonder if he was right to doubt my plan.

This seems far riskier than the park.

But before I can say anything, a cloud passes over the moon and everything goes black. Jamie grabs my hand and I follow him, half-running, half-stumbling across the road towards the fence. The linked metal is three metres tall and runs straight around the back of the cafe's storeroom. This is the only way to get to our lookout, to watch Maree's delivery to the Underground. *I can't climb this,* I realise. I glance over at Jamie, but he's already halfway up, gripping the fence like a monkey. I take a deep breath. He's done this before. I bet he thinks I'm useless.

Just some Metropolis girl, too afraid to get her hands dirty.

'Grab my hand, Teddy.' Halfway back down, Jamie reaches out. 'I can piggyback you up if you don't think you'll make it?' *How humiliating. He thinks I'm completely useless.*

I imagine what Kit would do. She'd probably climb up and down a half-dozen times just for fun. I take Jamie's strong hand and reach up to grasp the fence with my free hand. Straight away, the metal digs into my fingers as it takes my weight.

'See, it's not that bad,' he says, slowing his pace to match mine.

'So much . . . fun,' I manage to say through clenched teeth. When we reach the top, he leans over, offering to pull me up onto the flat rooftop, but I ignore him. Instead, I drag myself up without grace, but with independence – far more valuable.

'Good plan, in the end,' he says cheerily.

How could any sane person be cheery after that?

We crouch-crawl along, then flatten onto our bellies, bits of rooftop debris catching in my shirt.

'This really is the perfect spot,' he whispers.

I look down. He's right – we have a clear view of the whole cafe courtyard and out the back.

'What do we do now?' I whisper. I know the answer, but I want an excuse to keep talking. To figure him out.

Somewhere below us, a floodlight flicks on, and he puts a finger to his lips. I lean down, my cheek pressing onto the roof.

'Who is it?' I mouth.

He shakes his head.

I lift mine just enough to peer down and see Maree wheeling out boxes on a dolly. I can feel Jamie tense beside me, but we're fully concealed in shadow, thanks to the angle of the floodlight.

'They can look up here all they like, but they won't see anything!'

I turn to him triumphantly and realise our faces are inches away. I meet his eyes and feel a blush rise to my cheeks.

'It really was good thinking,' he whispers, but I'm barely listeni ng. I want to lean forward and close the space between us.

But he's not here for you.

I look back down at the cafe, hoping desperately that he can't read my thoughts.

We watch Maree continue pushing boxes out into the courtyard, two at a time. I wonder what's in them, but I don't want to annoy Jamie with too many questions. I still can't fully grasp that there are people all around me in this city, putting their lives at risk to help a network of people they've never met.

After what feels like hours of silence, I have to speak. 'What do Sympathisers get in return?'

Jamie gives me a strange look.

'Well, they're taking a huge risk!' I add defensively.

'They don't *get* anything,' he says. 'The satisfaction of having helped people is enough for some. Other people might do it to stick one at the City Council. I dunno.' He sighs. 'Why are *you* here? You're helping.'

I don't take the bait, although he has a point: I am technically a Sympathiser now. I can't tell him that part of my reason for coming tonight was because I wanted to see him again.

'It's really peaceful out here,' I comment, ignoring his question. Maree walks out with a bowl of pasta and sits down on one of the boxes to eat. She looks so small and frail from up here.

'Most things are peaceful at night,' he murmurs, rolling onto his back. 'Thanks to you, we are *right* on schedule. Now, all we do is wait.' I don't move.

'You *can* relax a bit, Teddy.'

Finally, I roll onto my back beside him.

'You hadn't been out at night before, had you?' he asks, gazing up at the stars.

'Is that so surprising?' I say, trying to keep the defensiveness out of my voice.

He's not trying to criticise you.

'Not as surprising as finding out an entire world exists underneath your feet, I guess,' he says.

I roll back onto my stomach. He's right, I would never have guessed it, but I'm more surprised that I wasn't actually all that shocked. It was like I had always known something was happening.

'Who else knows?' I ask, but he doesn't answer. He's staring at me, each light breath puffing a little white cloud into the cold night air. I close my eyes, and for the first time in weeks I start to relax. It almost feels like we're two ordinary people chatting idly . . . as if lying outside after curfew, looking at the stars, was something ordinary people did. I want to move closer to him.

I shouldn't.

His face is so close, his bright eyes glowing in the moonlight. I swallow, leaning closer, and a bubble of peace grows in our merging breaths. I want to luxuriate in the moment, but a familiar rumbling breaks the stillness we're holding between us. Jamie rolls back onto his stomach, wriggling forward to look down into the courtyard.

'Showtime.'

The fake Council truck rolls into view, and the door pops open around the other side. I check the slogan. There's no colon.

Jamie puts his finger to his lips and points down. Maree walks out of the cafe carrying a fresh bowl of pasta.

'You need to stack the boxes into the truck before you eat,' she says curtly, her voice cutting through the silence. 'Last week took too long, too risky.'

The driver comes around the back of the truck, opening the doors. When he steps into the floodlight, I'm not at all surprised. This is the first time I've seen Link properly. The shoulders of his leather jacket are spiked and match his hair. His whole look is a warning.

He doesn't look especially strong, but he carries two or three boxes at a time as he stacks them into the back of the truck, disregarding Maree's request.

Once Link sits down to eat Jamie speaks again. 'They do the same thing every time,' he mutters.

'What usually happens?'

'Sometimes they pick up from two or three locations before they do the drop-off to the Underground.'

'What about the patrols?'

'It's timed. Better to have one fast drop-off with a team of people emptying the truck, than a parade of people carrying boxes around the City all night.'

I nod. It's a sound approach in theory . . . but if supplies are going missing, it's not working. But it doesn't look like the problem is here at the collection. I roll my neck and shoulders, thinking it through, when a loud crash smashes me from my thoughts. Maree stands frozen, shards of porcelain around her shoes, which are stained red with pasta sauce. I follow her terrified gaze. A stream of guards flows steadily out of the park. I hadn't noticed Jamie move closer, but now I feel his lips brushing against my ear. 'Interesting development.'

I nod slowly, not daring to speak as guards rush in and out of the storeroom and cafe, like ants fleeing a destroyed nest. Two of them grab Maree, gagging her with the strings of her own apron. It hangs around her neck like a child's bib. She struggles in their grip, her meaty arms twisting between their rough hands.

'Look,' Jamie says, gently pressing my cheek to turn it towards the truck. I don't want to look away from Maree, but then I realise what Jamie is showing me.

Nothing is happening.

The entire courtyard is filled with guards, about twenty of them, but no one has approached the truck. Link is casually leaning against it, watching with a glowing stick in his mouth.

Is he breathing out smoke?

The sound of more smashing plates and shelves echoes up to us. Beyond the cafe I can see the storage room billowing thick grey smoke. Seconds later the windows explode, and flames shoot out, making the nearby guards scatter.

I scan the scene. There are no other trucks, no Sanitisation vehicles in sight, just Link's phoney one. I strain my eyes, desperately trying to find Maree in the commotion. Then I spot her, the apron still hanging limply from where it's been tied around her mouth. She's not fighting anymore; her wilting body hangs limp over a young guard's shoulder. He looks like he's struggling with her weight. I notice a dark stain on the floor. A puddle . . . something thick and dark is dripping, pooling around the guard's boots. Someone calls to him and he turns around, Maree turning with him, and I cover my mouth to stifle the cry. Her forehead is marred with a large gash streaming blood.

Is she dead?

I freeze, until Jamie's hand on my shoulder brings me back.

There are tears on my cheeks.

How could I have hated her so much?

Guilt gnaws at my insides.

I turn to Jamie. He's running a hand through his hair, his face white. I look back at a guard, laughing with Link. We don't need any prompting. We turn around and army-crawl away from the edge and out of sight. Jamie stands up as we reach the dark side of the roof near the fence.

'We need to warn Kit,' I say, thinking of her waiting alone at the location Paula demanded she watch tonight, desperately hoping he knows what this means.

Something snaps into place, and Jamie's eyes lock onto mine. 'We have to beat the truck.' He's already jumped down onto the fence and offers me a hand. 'Come on.'

I don't have time for pride; I grab his hand and swing onto the fence. As we climb down, I'm *almost* too preoccupied to notice the pain digging into my icy fingers. We jump a metre to the ground and hit the pavement running. I don't know where the next collection spot is, but Jamie seems to know, so I follow without question. Even with a head start, there's still a chance the truck could beat us.

We run and run, turning down streets and crossing roads, not checking for guards or trucks. I can feel my lungs burning and my legs locking up. We haven't slowed for at least two kilometres. *Don't stop now*, I keep chanting. *You're not some useless Metropolis girl. Come on! Kit needs you!* I'm screaming in my mind, but eventually, I can't keep going. I need air.

'Jamie!' I gasp.

'We need to get to Kit before Link does,' he spits over his shoulder, still moving. I know he's right, but my body doesn't care. I stumble, trip, and finally, Jamie stops. He helps me to my feet and waits until I take a normal breath, then he's off again, slower than before, but still too fast for me to keep up.

'You were right about everything,' he says over his shoulder.

He doesn't sound angry.

Not at me, anyway.

'I should have forced Kit to listen earlier. If anything happens to her . . .'

His sentence hangs in the cold air. If they *Sanitise* Metropolis citizens for 'being infected', I can't imagine what they would do to someone who isn't supposed to exist. Someone from the

Underground. For a second, I feel a wave of nausea coming on, but I don't have a chance to let it hit me as Jamie picks up the pace again. Coursing through the streets, we pass empty windows staring back at us like lonely black eyes. The air filling my lungs still burns, but I care less now. *This all has a purpose.* I follow Jamie, not paying any attention to the streets we're careening down. Then he stops. My hands fall instantly to my knees as I gulp down air, filling my heaving lungs. After a minute, I'm able to look around.

'Wait, why are we here?' I say, suddenly noting the familiar houses. We're only streets away from my home.

'Are you serious?'

'No, I mean why are we *here* near my house?' I feel like I've missed the punchline. He looks at me for a moment then turns right, walking straight up the footpath.

I grab the back of his shirt, pulling him to a stop. 'Why didn't you tell me it was in my neighbourhood?' Jamie ignores me and keeps walking.

'Jamie, if you had told me, I could have given you a dozen different ways to get here.'

He stops abruptly and walks back to where I'm still standing on the footpath.

'Well, we're here now.' He points down the path. 'So, let it go.'

I curl my hands into fists by my sides. 'I don't think you trust me; I don't think you're listening at all. I *live* here. Why wouldn't you just ask? Why do you think you know everything?' I pant. 'You and Kit both think you're so smart. You think no one else in the world knows how to do anything. You might be *pretending* to be from the Metropolis, but you're not. *I am.*'

'Not *everything* is about you, Teddy,' he says, then turns and walks away. 'Are you coming?'

Reluctantly, I follow Jamie through the white picket gate. I thought I'd feel better after saying those things, but I feel worse.

I take in the pale yellow standalone terrace, its white trim glowing in the milky moonlight. *Wait, I know this house.*

Inside, the walls are painted pale pink and all the windows are trimmed with white, to match the outside . . . I know this because I've been here before.

Why are we here?

I practically grew up here with Mrs Lowry, one of our oldest family friends. She was friends with my grandpa – before he was Sanitised.

Murdered.

'Jamie, what are we doing here?' I ask. He pulls me off Mrs Lowry's garden path and into the garden.

We didn't see Mrs Lowry much after my grandpa was taken. My father said he didn't think she was a good look for us.

'Kit is somewhere around here, and by the looks of things, we beat that dipshit Link,' Jamie says, ignoring the tension between us.

'She's probably in the garden shed,' I say. Jamie raises his eyebrows, surprised.

'I know this place. There's a perfect viewing spot in the front corner of the shed. You can see down the side path to the entire backyard.'

Jamie nods slowly.

'Also, not sure if you know this, but Mrs Lowry isn't home tonight. She goes to stay with her son and granddaughter every weekend.'

'How do you . . .' Jamie asks, but his question peters off.

'She was friends with my grandpa,' I explain.

'But she's always here. We've had deliveries from this location for years,' he says, shaking his head.

'Through the trees on the left.' I point. 'We can slip into the shed through a secret back door Mr Lowry made for me to play in.'

'I thought children weren't allowed to play in the Metropolis?'

'Duh, that's why it's secret!' I say. His low throaty chuckle slips inside me and untangles some of the tension I had been holding in my muscles. I'm about to smile when I notice his jaw clench.

'Shhh.' He grabs my arm and pulls me back into the foliage. Silently, he points to a figure running down the path towards the front door. It's too small to be Link, and we haven't heard the truck arrive. *It's too tall to be Kit.* Once the shadow reaches the front door, it crouches down, playing with keys and glancing furtively backwards. Something about the way the shadow is moving seems familiar.

'Paula?' Jamie whispers in my ear. I shake my head.

This person is a woman. But it's not Paula.

There's a click of the lock, and the door opens. The figure slips inside, and lights flick on. Just before the door shuts, she steals a look out into the darkness. Light spills across her face, and my heart freezes.

I know exactly who it is.

sixteen

'Are you sure?' Jamie says again in disbelief while we creep towards the garden shed.

'I think I know my own mother,' I snap.

He shrugs, and I can tell he doesn't believe me. *I* don't want to believe me. I mean, in the past it would make sense for Mum to be at Mrs Lowry's house. But not now. And not in the middle of the night. While Mrs Lowry is out of town. Jamie motions for me to follow him.

'What the hell are you doing here?' We both bite back a shout as Kit grabs us from behind, one hand on each of our shoulders. 'You had one job. One task.' She spits the words in our ears through clenched teeth. 'Or are you both so stupid you forgot?'

Jamie launches into our story. 'We went to the cafe. Maree was prepping the boxes for pick up, then –'

I cut him off. 'Link arrived with the truck to pick up the boxes. After he had packed everything away, the City Guard arrived.' I hold Kit's gaze. 'It was some sort of set-up. Link was *working* with them.' Kit looks frantically between Jamie and me. She rubs at her arms absentmindedly. She's dressed only in black jeans and a tank top, and her skin is covered in goosebumps. I pull the edge of my jacket down against the cold as Jamie continues explaining how the guards tore the cafe apart, his voice low and rushed.

'It was all but burnt to the ground – and before you say anything, it wasn't Sanitisation people. It was City Guards.' Kit shakes her head.

'Kit,' I say, 'the guards knocked Maree out, maybe even killed her.' Saying the words makes me start to panic. 'I don't know where they've taken her, there was blood everywhere.' *And now my mum is inside that house. We have to warn her, to get her out somehow.* Jamie puts his hand on my arm and squeezes.

'We need to move,' he says.

'You sure Link was in on it?' Kit asks. Jamie and I exchange a glance, and he peers back to the road.

'They were laughing,' I say to Kit. 'The guards and Link, like they were old friends.'

'Laughing, clapping each other on the back,' Jamie adds.

'What?' she asks defensively, wrapping her arms around her shoulders. Even in the limited light, I can see her disbelief. Finally, she speaks. 'Wait. You think Link is going to send the guards here?' She looks at me. 'Paula didn't want me there. She must have arranged this, to set up Maree.' She looks at Jamie, her gaze sharp. 'Obviously, she didn't want any witnesses.' She sits down heavily, crashing into the crisp dead leaves with a crunch. Jamie's arm brushes past mine as he reaches for her. I notice the tears in her eyes.

'If the guards know you're here. If Paula told them . . .' Jamie says, trying to pull her back into a crouch. I step forward to help. I fight the urge to rush into the house and drag Mum out. I turn back to Kit. Tears are rolling silently down her cheeks. She nods slowly, as if her head is too heavy to hold still.

'What if you're right?' she whispers. 'What if Paula has been behind it all? How else would the guards know Link?' she mumbles. I hear more shuffling sounds coming from the house, like something heavy is being dragged about.

How am I going to explain my way out of this one?

Kit starts rubbing her arms compulsively. I don't say anything.

'Why?' she exclaims, too loudly. I glance anxiously at the window. '*Why* would she do this? Why steal from other clans and put the Sympathisers at risk? And all her people Underground . . . and me,' she finishes in a whisper. Suddenly, she lunges towards me. I freeze.

'I'm so, so sorry!' Kit cries softly into my neck, enveloping me in her arms. She squeezes me tight. Too tight. I try to loosen her grip, but she won't let go. 'I was *so* horrible, but I guess you were right. I just didn't want to believe you. *I'm* the idiot.' She finally releases me, wiping her nose with the bottom of her top. 'You were both right.'

I hadn't expected this from her. She looks up at Jamie, and he gives her a warm smile. I look away, feeling like I'm intruding. Kit sighs. 'I think I even knew it deep down.' She starts rubbing her arms again, and for a second she's elsewhere, completely lost in her thoughts.

I close my eyes and listen. I can hear the sound of the approaching truck.

'Where does Link think you're going to be?' I say quickly. Kit looks like she's about to be sick.

'There.' She points to the garden shed beside us with a shaky finger.

We need to move.

'Follow me,' I say. 'If you see my mum, don't say anything. Let me do the talking.'

'Your mum?' Kit asks, and I hear Jamie shush her.

'Guys, we need to warn Mrs Lowry,' Kit says in a whisper.

I had almost forgotten about her. 'She's not here,' I say. Kit looks confused.

'What?' She narrows her eyes. 'I definitely saw someone putting out boxes.'

Jamie sits down next to her. 'It's Teddy's mum,' he says.

'What the hell is going on tonight?' she cries out, and we both lunge forward to cover her mouth. I can still hear the truck, its low rumble getting louder.

Link's almost here.

'We need to move deep into the house, to hide and warn Mum. I don't think we're going to have time to get out of this now,' I say, standing up, but nobody follows.

'So you're just going to go say hi to your mum?' Jamie asks. *Shit.*

'We can't stay here. We're sitting ducks. If Link is just collecting, he'd expect it to all happen outside. And Kit would be in the shed. We need to go inside.'

'And what if the guards come and we're stuck inside?' Jamie asks. I sigh.

'I don't know yet, but we have a better chance of hiding somewhere in there than out here.'

'I can see it now,' Kit mumbles. 'She's only ever been looking out for herself. For *her* position.'

'Who?' I ask. I start pacing, trying to think of a story to tell Mum.

'Paula.'

I stop. 'What do you mean, her *position?*' I ask. I hadn't considered the possibility that Paula could lose her position as Clan Head. I thought it was like being the patriarch of the family: you just always are.

I lead our small party down the path that runs beside the house and fence letting this new information sink in. Once at the back door, I fumble with the rocks looking for the fake one that holds Mrs Lowry's spare key. When we're inside the house, I carefully lock the door behind us.

Kit stalks over to a drawer and yanks it open, pulling out a sharp knife.

'Anyone can become a Clan Head,' she says, spinning the knife across her knuckles. 'The Underground laws state that unless a Clan Leader dies of natural causes, whoever takes down the previous head becomes, by default, the next leader. They just need to eliminate whoever is in power.'

I frown. 'When you say "eliminate", you mean –' Kit slams the blade tip-first into the bench.

'Kill them,' Jamie answers. I swallow, looking at the quivering blade.

'Which I would never do!' Kit says. Too softly.

Suddenly the room feels too silent. We freeze in the darkness as the thud of a truck door slams shut somewhere outside. 'Subtle,' Jamie mutters under his breath.

'Sounds like Link's about to collect the goods,' I say, trying to peer through the lacy curtains into the dark night. A loud sneeze from outside makes us freeze, then we all duck instinctively at the sound of heavy boots marching down the side path.

'Down,' I whisper, and we drop onto our knees, crawling frantically deeper into the house.

seventeen

'Teddy?' I freeze as I hear my mother's voice, a whisper behind me.

I stand up slowly to face her. She's standing in the doorway of what appears to be a linen cupboard. 'I thought I heard your voice,' Mum says frantically. 'What on *earth* are you doing here? It's after curfew!'

'Seriously? *It's after curfew?* What the hell are *you* doing here? What the hell is going on?' I try to keep my voice low while I spit out the excuse I concocted in the kitchen. 'I saw you leave the house; I was worried. I – I had to follow you!' 'You saw me?' she says, her face lined with concern.

Great. Now Mum thinks this is her fault.

I feel sick. *Sicker.* I cross my arms, glaring, and shake my head.

'You saw me, huh?' she repeats, raising an eyebrow. I'm fumbling for something to say when Kit pokes her head around my shoulder and sticks out her hand.

'I'm Kit, from the Underground. You must be Teddy's mum.' My mum steps out of the cupboard and looks up and down the corridor, then shields the light of the tiny torch she's holding.

'Teddy, seriously?' She steps closer to me then stills, her eyes landing on Jamie, who is so close behind me I can feel his warm breath brush my neck.

'What the hell are you all doing here?' she asks Jamie. Her hair is pulled back in a tight bun – I've never seen it done like that – *and* she's wearing those pants again.

'You were out here last night?' I ask. She ignores me as she pushes the three of us towards the door.

'I'm from the Underground,' Kit says again.

'It's a network of –' I start to explain, but my mother cuts me off.

'I know what it is,' she snaps, her voice sharper than I've ever heard. 'Get inside.'

She shoves us into the cupboard. I put my hands on Kit's shoulders as we walk into the linen cupboard . . . which isn't a cupboard at all. After a few steps, it opens into a room. A light is flicked on near the doorway shedding a warm orange glow into the space. I haven't seen anything like this before. It's filled with strange objects I don't recognise, and the air is musty, but spiced, like nutmeg and cinnamon. The walls are covered in pictures. Some look real, like photographs, and others fake, like the drawings I do, but rich with colour. I step closer to the wall and look at one picture of several flowers in a vase. It's not a photograph, but the texture of the image looks soft and wet. I touch it, surprised to find the surface completely hard and dry. Turning around to take in the remainder of the room, I notice that the walls are covered with more pictures like this, and clocks – so many clocks. There's a machine on a wooden table in the corner of the room, with a big metal horn and a handle. I step over to it, running my fingers across the dusty surface. I grab the crank –

'Don't touch that!' Mum snaps from behind me. I pull my hand away like I might get burnt.

'What is this place?' I ask, unable to keep the awe out of my voice.

'This is our meeting place,' my mother says as she sits down on one of the overstuffed floral couches. She looks out of place amid the multi-coloured madness of the room. I spin around, taking it all in. My mother points to some wooden panels, and Jamie lifts them, covering our entrance and turning the space beyond back into a closet again.

'Wait, *whose* meeting place?' I ask, walking over to where my mother is sitting.

'Sympathisers,' Kit says, as if it's the most obvious thing in the world. Mum just nods. Jamie walks over and sits beside where I'm standing, in an armchair opposite my mother.

How is she not freaking out right now?

'Maree was compromised at the cafe,' he explains, as if this is all going to make sense to her. 'A patrol of guards intercepted the pick-up, but "our guy" remained untouched.'

It annoys me how much I'm comforted to hear him talk.

'They were friendly!' Kit chimes in. 'The guards and Link.' She's sifting through thin squares of cardboard, stacking them in piles near the big metal horn and wood machine. I notice traces of tears still on her cheeks.

'What about Maree?' Mum asks, looking at me. Before I can answer, we hear a loud thud. My mum slinks over to the wall, moving silently, then carefully unhooks one of the pictures and presses her face to the wallpaper.

'What's she doing?' I ask Jamie in a whisper.

'Looking,' he says. Kit dims the lamp somewhere behind us. We wait in silence, listening to the different sounds, all amplified now we're shrouded in darkness. I shift uncomfortably. Eventually my mum puts the image back on the wall, and Kit brings the light back up.

How do they all know what to do?

'Your guy's out there now,' says Mum. 'So, you think Paula is behind this? I wonder if she's going to send guards here too.' She settles back in a chair, crossing her arms across her chest.

'You're sitting down?' I say.

'I was getting ready to leave when I found you three in the house. We can't go now, Link is still outside, and if what happened at Maree's happens here, well, we're better off in here than out there,' my mother responds, finality in her voice. 'There's no way to leave now. We'll have to wait them out.'

The secret room suddenly feels tiny. I look up and notice how low the ceiling is. How the slant of the roof mimics the slope of the staircase above.

We're trapped.

We lapse into silence. Jamie puts his head back as if taking a nap. Mum's eyes are shut too. Kit quietly sifts through the cardboard squares, occasionally pulling out round black disks and spinning them in her hands in the shadows. I can't hear Link's boots stomping anymore.

Absolute silence.

Then there's the sound of a truck door slamming. Mum's eyes snap open.

'How long have you known about the Underground?' she asks me, leaning forward.

'Since after my Job Placement. How long have you known?'

'Since I relocated with your grandfather,' she replies.

'Why didn't you tell me?'

I notice pain cross her face at the question.

I jump up and start pacing around the room. 'Why have you kept this a secret from me?'

A photograph stops me. It's Mrs Lowry and some other people I don't recognise, *and my grandfather.* I point to the picture and turn to face my mum.

'We don't have time for this now,' Kit says, stepping over the pile of black disks and leading me back to the others. My mum reaches out for me, but I pull away. I can't let this go.

'I think,' Jamie starts, not giving anyone a chance to protest, 'Paula didn't want Kit to go to the cafe, or she would have seen what went down there . . . she wanted her to come here.' We all nod.

'So, following that logic, Paula didn't want Kit to witness what Teddy and I saw. *But* she knows Kit is way more stubborn than that, and would either send someone else or just go there herself anyway.'

I swallow, looking furtively at my mum. She's listening.

'Either way, it's a win-win for Paula. If Kit did see the scene at the cafe, they'd have her under their thumb, and if she fought back, they'd take her out because she knows too much. If she came here – bam! Simply get her captured and taken away by guards.' Jamie's earlier words ring in my ears. *Eliminate the threat before it has a chance to become one.*

I look from face to face as his words sink in.

My mother frowns, while Kit stares into space, having been

sucked back into the vortex of Paula's betrayal.

'It makes sense,' Kit says, the first to break the silence.

'Maybe she was hoping I'd be here too?' Jamie adds. 'She knows we would never have gone along with any of this. That's why she's been getting Link to do all her dirty work. Getting him involved.'

'Wait a minute.' My mother turns to me. 'How do you know Paula?' 'What?' I ask.

'I don't even want to get started on how you seem to be best buddies with your Partner. I can't quite figure out how this managed to happen.' She waves her hand at Kit and shoots

Jamie a dangerous look. 'But *you* know about Paula too?' 'She doesn't just know *about* her,' Kit chimes in.

'I've met her.'

'You met her? *How?*' she shrieks. I stand up, walking away from my mother.

'I've been in the Underground. I've been down there.' I turn around, pulling the jacket off my shoulder and yanking down my shirt to show her the puckered but healing wound. The stitches are starting to dissolve into my skin already.

I turn back to face her, straightening my clothes.

'How could you be so . . . foolish?' she says, shaking her head.

'How could you lie to me for seventeen years?' I reply.

She blinks rapidly, but two tears still slip out, rolling down her face so fast that she hardly has time to wipe them away.

'Why would you put yourself in such danger, Teddy?'

I think of Grandpa. I look back at his photo, hanging on the wall.

'The same reason you're here, I guess – it's in my blood.' I sit down next to her and let her put her arm around me.

'I saw a shadow moving outside my window the night of my Job Placement, and I followed it. I had to. The shadow was Kit.'

Kit looks up at the sound of her name.

'Then I was taken into the Underground.'

Mum pulls me closer. She looks different. Older. I notice the small lines in her face, and silver hairs for the first time. I wonder whether she similarly sees me differently tonight. Not just her little girl.

She's been locked in a time capsule in my head, I realise, and it's time for me to let her be who she is. To see what she's capable of. She looks over at me and smiles, putting her hand softly on my knee.

'I'm sorry,' she whispers, pressing her head into my shoulder. She's the second person to apologise to me tonight.

'Ah, guys?' Jamie says tentatively.

A door has just slammed open, rattling the tiny room. My mother sits up, and we all tense. We'd been hoping that Link had gone.

In an instant, the energy shifts and everything hangs on a knife's edge. I look around. There's enough evidence here to have us all Sanitised a hundred times each. And there is nothing but a couple of pieces of chipboard between us and – Boots.

It sounds like there are hundreds of them. The little room shudders as doors are slammed and plates are smashed. The memory of what the guards did at the cafe flashes in my mind. I look at our small party. Kit is balled up on the floor, ashen-faced, hugging her legs. My mother hasn't moved from the edge of the couch, her back straight and eyes forward. Jamie is the only one who looks relaxed. I reach out towards him, then pull back. There is nothing he can do for me now. Maybe not ever.

A loud voice penetrates the room. 'Yep, bud. This is it, last stop tonight.'

Jamie turns to us and mouths, 'Link.'

'I'm gonna get into some shit with Paula,' Link's voice drawls through the wall.

'Didn't find that little pink pixie chick?' asks another voice I don't recognise.

'Kit? Nah, couldn't find her anywhere. Guess none of your people found her? She was meant to be in that shed, but it was empty when I got here.'

'Nobody here tonight. Just a bunch of trash,' the unfamiliar voice growls. There's another thud, and some of the frames on our side of the wall tilt. The guards outside our room guffaw with laughter.

'She wasn't at the cafe either. Fuck, Paula is gonna flip.'

Again, something hits the wall, and it shudders. I look at the chipboard hiding us at the back of the cupboard. The voices continue. *So close.*

'Just say she's a lazy bitch and didn't show up for her post.'

The men laugh. I look over to where Kit is on the floor, still hugging her legs, jaw clenched. Jamie steps up silently and whispers, 'We need to see what's happening.' I grab his arm to stop him.

'No,' Mum says. 'Let him look.'

He takes down one of the skewed frames and presses his face to the small hole cut in the drywall. I hope no one on the other side can see him. We all tense.

'Well, if this is the last stop, I guess there's no harm in going through the goods,' Link says. The voices become softer.

'I won't talk if you don't.'

I imagine their sleazy nudges and raised eyebrows.

'Oi! James!' Link shouts, and Jamie lunges back so fast he almost trips over the rug at his feet.

'Yes, sir?' a younger voice asks, followed by what sounds like a baby elephant running into the room.

'We can take it from here, brother. Thanks again for helping us clear out the rats.' *Brother.*

We look at each other, and Kit opens her mouth to speak.

'We haven't cleared them out yet, *brother.*'

It's a new voice, seeping into our hiding space, and we all freeze. Kit and I look at each other, eyes widening as we recognise the speaker.

Kit mouths one word to me: *Paula.*

'And,' Paula continues from the other side of the wall, 'I do think there's *some* harm in going through the goods.' Her voice is laced with disgust. My mum stands and goes quickly to Jamie's side. He moves so she can peer out. 'I think we need to renegotiate our terms, Link. If you can't follow simple instructions, then are you *really* going to be suitable as a leader when I'm gone, you low-life piece of shit?' she growls.

'Kit was nowhere,' says Link. 'Not at the cafe. Not in the shed.'

Something smashes against the wall, and one of the frames slips off its nail. Jamie lunges forward to break its fall, and it smacks against his hand. He grimaces at the pain.

'So, why didn't you look SOMEWHERE ELSE?' Paula shouts. 'She was on watch, she's not going to be out in the open waiting for you to find her, you fucking idiot. Can't you do anything right?'

'I did manage –'

'"I did manage" blah blah. If that dumb girl wasn't so damn righteous she'd have been better suited to do what you do. At least she's got some brains.'

Link mumbles some retort, but Paula cuts him off. 'Get out of here, you incompetent fool!'

I swallow and listen as Link's heavy footfalls get softer until they fade away.

'Well, Captain, nice to see you've stayed around at a job for once!' she continues, her heavy boots thumping as she moves across the room. Every movement is amplified in here. I find myself speaking to my grandpa, wherever he is: *Please keep us safe. Please protect us. Please.*

'Your guards have trashed the place,' she continues.

'It'll send a message to the old lady when she gets home . . . Sympathisers are a dying breed.'

I hear a bark, and it's so unexpected I reach out and grab Kit.

'That's her laughing,' Kit whispers.

'Look, I know it all seems a bit unfair and confusing,' Paula croons. 'I know Councillor Raeburn has let me have *all* this power, and I'm just a *city sewer rat.*' Jamie clenches his fist. 'But I was once higher up the ladder than you, *Captain,* and believe me when I say

I'm going to get there again. I will NOT
      have my own men treat me with disrespect.'
      We all jump as her voice goes up an octave.
      'In just under three weeks there will be a new Commander of
the Guard. C'est moi. Now, Councillor Raeburn has known me for
a *very* long time. Raeburn has accepted my proposition to finally
eradicate the Underground, in exchange for my
      reinstatement into Metropolis life.'
      Does my father know anything about this?
      I look at Mum, but her face reveals nothing. Jamie replaces the
picture on the wall. *Paula is a Clan Leader . . . for now.*
      'How do you plan to do it?' the Captain asks. I can hear his
voice shaking.
      Paula's snarl is so clear it sounds like she's in the room with
us. '*You're* going to do it. I don't care how. Starve them out, smoke
them out – hell, light a fire and burn them out! I'll be standing strong
with my gun at the exit when those rats start running.'

eighteen

As we listen to Paula and the captain march upstairs, the atmosphere in the small room is tense.

We're trapped.

I watch Kit anxiously rubbing her hands up and down her scarred arms. Jamie is pacing across the thick rug. I glance over at Mum. She's sitting still as a statue on the couch, her eyes closed.

I think I have a way to stop this.

'We need to leave,' I say, loud enough to grab their attention. 'Shhh,' Kit hisses.

'We can't stay here, we need to leave, while they're upstairs.' 'Oh yeah? And where are we going to go?' Kit says.

'Out the cupboard, down to the kitchen, then into the shed. Link already looked there. Anyway, Link's gone.'

Jamie nods. 'She's right.' I allow myself a small smile of satisfaction.

'Then we need to move now,' Mum says, crossing the floor in two steps and pulling the wooden panels down. Kit switches off the lamp completely, and we make our way out of the safety of the secret room.

Mum opens the closet door a crack, and we peer out into the bright room; the light stings my eyes. I can hear the guards stomping around upstairs, and the occasional bark of laughter, confirming Paula is still up there with them. We step out into the bright corridor, and I'm instantly hit by the state of the house. It's like the scene at the cafe, except worse. Plates and lamps are shattered, and feathers and stuffing are still floating in the air; it looks like every soft furnishing in the room has been slashed. Family pictures lie in broken frames on the floor.

'Let's go,' Mum says, her voice breaking as we move into the kitchen, avoiding puddles of food splattered all over the black and white floor. I fumble with the lock on the kitchen door.

'All that waste,' Kit says, shaking her head. I finally manage to open the door. Everything sounds too loud. We creep out of the house and I shut the door, turning to lock it behind us.

'Don't bother,' Mum says. We move around the side of the house. Looking up, I can see that all the lights upstairs are on.

SMASH. Something flies out the window.

I'm surprised no one has called Sanitisation authorities.

I look down the path, out into the street, where a Council vehicle idles with its lights on.

Of course. The neighbours think it's being dealt with.

'So, what are we going to do?' Kit asks, slumped on the dirty shed floor. No one says anything at first. Mum sits in the shadowy corner, eyes shut, arms crossed, lost in thought. Jamie flexes his hands. I tug at the strings of my hoodie.

'We've been thinking about this all wrong – *like sheep,*' Mum says. We turn to look at her. She shifts forward. 'We have a Metropolis-sized problem now, so let's solve it in a Metropolis way.' I blink a few times. She's looking at us like we're all just a bunch of dumb kids, and perhaps she's right. After all, we did just bust in here with no plan and a corrupt legion of City Guard hot on our heels.

'We need to call in the troops,' I say after an age, breaking the silence.

'Who?' Kit asks. 'The other Sympathisers?'

'She means the Metropolis Sanitisation Authorities,' Mum says, locking eyes with me. She nods curtly. 'Exactly. And we need to do it now.'

'But there are guards already here –' Kit says, shaking her head. Jamie silences her with a hand.

'No, Teddy's right. The City Council is a complex political organism,' he explains. 'From what my Metropolis family have explained to me, it's like an octopus. The parts are all connected to one big main head – the Mayor. Its size is both its strength *and* its weakness, because each arm can be doing something the others don't know anything about.' My mother nods approvingly, and I feel a rush of pride for Jamie.

'So, we call Sanitisation, and they take Paula,' I say. 'Once you're in the wheels of the system, you can't just *ask* for an appeal because "there's been a mistake".'

'Yes, I doubt they'll want to wait till morning, especially not in this suburb,' Jamie muses. His head is bowed, to avoid bumping his forehead on one of the low beams in the shed. Opening the tiny shed window a crack, Jamie leans out, then ducks back in quickly. 'Some guards are leaving. No sign of Paula.'

'We're running out of time,' I say, standing up and brushing off my pants. 'So, where's the phone?' I've already started making my way over to the door.

'Oh yeah? And what are you going to say?' my mother demands, splitting her sharp gaze between me and the window.

'I'll tell them I have a crazy aunt,' I say. Kit and Jamie both give me a *really?* look. I just shrug weakly. Mum reaches out and pulls me back over to the dirt floor where she's sitting. She's tall, almost as tall as Jamie, and looks graceful in all black despite having to contort herself to fit in the small, awkward space.

'No. It needs to be real enough that the Sanitisation Crew will believe it. I'll tell you what's going to happen.' She looks out the window again, then gestures for Jamie and Kit to sit down beside me. Sandwiched between my friends, I feel safer. 'You're *all* going to stay here. I'm going to take Teddy's fantastic idea and go out there and call the Metropolis Sanitisation Authorities.' I shake my head, but she's not finished. 'I'll tell them I just caught my daughter *Teddy Veodrum* painting. I'll explain that we're staying at a friend's house.' A tight knot of panic twists around my throat, making it difficult to breathe.

'Won't they know Teddy is younger than Paula?' Jamie says slowly. I look around the small space, desperately searching for answers on their stricken faces.

'They won't look. They never do. Sanitise first, paperwork later. By the time they get to her file, one of our people on the inside will have wiped everything on Teddy.' Kit's voice from the night before rattles around in my head: *We have people on the inside. The Sympathiser network exists within the City Council – desk drones.*

'Sweetie,' Mum's voice is soft again, 'you're going to take Paula's place.'

I feel like I've been shot. I pull myself up from the dirt. 'What are you talking about?' But I had already been thinking about it. *If Sanitisation wipes my identity . . . what happens to me?*

She looks out the window. 'I'm sorry, I thought you'd already been told how this works. You will be the new leader of Kit's clan.' I don't speak. 'It was *your* idea to Sanitise Paula. You know what that really means now.'

'It could have been any of our plans. I mean, technically it's *your* plan,' I scramble back.

Kit speaks for the first time. 'We're literally using *you* to eliminate her.'

My mind floods with the memory of Kit in the kitchen, playing with the knife: *The laws of the Underground state that unless a Clan Leader dies of natural causes, whoever takes down the previous head becomes, by default, the next leader.*

I shake my head, suddenly filled with untenable rage.

No.

I didn't sign up for this.

I can't leave.

I was going to be a Sympathiser and help people survive in the Underground, not *lead* the Underground. Selfish, incoherent thoughts swirl through my mind. I can't look at anyone.

'Teddy, you chose to leave your bedroom that night. Whatever you started, it's your responsibility to finish it,' Kit says softly behind me.

'Shut up! Just shut up!'

Jamie springs from the shadows, his hand gently covering my mouth as his other arm wraps around me.

I can feel my hot tears rolling onto his hand while my throat burns, bile fighting to escape.

I force my breathing to slow. 'We can still get away,' I say softly. When I'm finally sure I won't vomit, I continue. 'Like Mum did. I can get a new name – we're not Partnered yet; we can change our names.'

'Not this time, Teddy,' Jamie replies, his voice hollow. 'You'll have to be wiped from the system. Like I was.' I look at my mother, still confused.

'We'd be setting up Paula at the expense of using your profile. It cost Grandpa everything to relocate us, and he *still* ended up Sanitised.'

Jamie leans closer. 'We don't want to pique any notice on the system. Not right now. I lived Underground for months before I became a Dual Citizen. Everything we do has to be in tiny steps if we want to remain unnoticed, and we don't have time for that now.'

'So, what does this mean for me then?' I ask. Kit scoots over and puts her arm around me, and the weight of it anchors me in the conversation.

'Teddy will move to the Underground with you two. I'll continue my work, possibly be relocated – it depends on what story they need. I may become the creator of a monster, or a hero for turning in my own daughter – and so close to her Sealing.' She gives me a sad smile, and I know this isn't easy for her either.

'I wish none of this had ever happened,' I whisper.

'It wouldn't have mattered if you had never found out,' she says, pulling me into a hug. 'I would still have been here tonight, and without your warning, I most likely would have been taken by the guards, just like Maree. And Kit too.'

I picture mother as I saw Maree, her long thin body limp over the shoulder of some anonymous guard. I can't help the tears that start escaping.

I don't want to leave her up here alone.

I don't want to start over.

I don't want to be a leader. Jamie's words about Kit flick in my head: *But when she stops being the boss, she feels threatened so she starts pushing people away.* I don't know how this is going to change things between us . . . and Jamie. I consider what this change means for our Partnership. *It means we don't have one.* I wipe my eyes and pull away. Everything had just been starting to feel normal, in the most abnormal kind of way.

'There's nothing you can do about it now,' my mother whispers, her head resting on top of mine. She takes my hand and slips something into it. 'I'll be in your heart wherever you go. You be the captain, and I'll be your crew,' she says softly, her breath rustling the hair beside my ear. Then she is gone, the shed door banging softly shut behind her. I look at the small silver ring in my palm. It's engraved on the inside: *love is all.*

I twist it over in my fingers and try to remember where it came from. It was my grandmother's, a gift from her father. My grandpa had given it to Mum, right before he was Sanitised . . . *murdered.* I slip the ring onto my finger; it's a perfect fit.

'You'll be okay,' Kit says, rushing to my side. Her hand moves in slow circles on my back. 'We all will be.'

'We need to see,' I say, opening the door. I slip out into the cold.

'Teddy!' I hear Kit whisper from somewhere behind me. I ignore her.

If this is who I must be now, I won't be told what to do anymore.

I step into the garden bed, disregarding the flowers I'm crushing under my shoes. *Where is Mum?* I peer around the house, through the kitchen window.

I watch as my mother, standing illuminated in the moonlight, puts the phone down in the kitchen, then turns, making her way slowly back to the corridor. *She's trying to get back to the secret room.* She slides out of view.

'They're here. The van's out front,' Jamie whispers excitedly.

It seems too quick, but he's right, I can hear the purr of the Sanitisation van. Soon it's competing with the noise in the house. I notice the guards toss something into the corner of the kitchen. I risk pressing closer to look in through the open window.

'Don't,' Kit says, putting her hand on my arm. 'We can't risk being caught.' I shake her arm off, but crouch back down in the crushed garden bed and spin my grandmother's ring on my finger.

'What are you talking about?' Paula's voice is rough and clear. I can hear heavy footfalls, and the kitchen light flicks on. We press ourselves against the wall below the sill.

'*Miss*, you've been reported as needing help for artistic impulses. We've come to take you to where you can be treated. *Sanitised.*'

'That's impossible, I never –' Paula rebuts.

I can't resist. I kneel back up, ignoring both Jamie and Kit tugging at my jacket, and peek over the ledge. Paula looks different tonight. Cleaner. She's wearing a coat, all buttoned up. Clean and new. *Not very scavenged.* I look back to the corner where I thought I'd seen my mother. She's gone. *Her clothes!* I suddenly realise. If they see her, they'll take her too, solely based on what she was wearing. I peer into the house, but she's nowhere. The crooked guards also appear to have left.

'I believe there's been some mistake,' Paula says, looking around, wild-eyed. 'This residence is under Metropolis City Guard lockdown.' A loud hissing sound drowns out Paula's shouting. Sanitisation workers connect some strange tubes to her face, and soon she collapses. They take no pains to catch her. Two other people step forward. It's impossible to see any distinguishing features through the massive suits they wear.

Protecting themselves from infection.

A guard appears, and another. A Sanitisation worker steps forward and pulls out a flashing tablet. 'Captain.' The Captain reads whatever is on the screen, his eyes opening wider as he scans the tablet.

'Yes, sir,' the Captain says, saluting. 'Sorry for any confusion. MEN!' The remaining guards appear from the shadows in the house. 'It's time to head out,' he instructs them. Then he leaves, without a backwards glance at Paula. I dare to look down the side path and see a procession of guards marching away, up the street.

If one of those men looked to their right, they would see us.

All three of us. I move my attention back to the house.

'Is this the victim, Ma'am?' The voice cuts through the din. 'Yes. That's her.'

I hear my mother's voice, and relief washes over me like a cool wave. Both Jamie and Kit peer through the window beside me.

'What happened here?' the man with the tablet asks, indicating the disarray in the lounge room.

Mum steps into view and I can't contain my gasp. She looks stunning. *Where did she get those clothes from?* I'm in awe as I watch her holding her handkerchief to her eyes. She's fully dressed in a red skirt, with her hair pulled up into an elaborate bun. She looks every inch the councilman's wife.

A woman devoted to Our Great City above all else.

'I told her I would have to call you, and she flew into a rage. I hardly knew what to do.'

'That's all we need to know. Thank you for calling us, Mrs Veodrum.'

'Is this your residence?' the leader asks. I still haven't been able to see his face. 'We can take you to get medical assistance if you're feeling any bodily distress, or drop you to your registered place of residence.'

I watch as my mum tips a hand against her forehead, always keeping the handkerchief by her face. She steps forward.

'Medical, please.' The two other crew members carry Paula out on a stretcher, and the man beckons my mother to follow him. I watch her, not wanting to miss a second.

This might be the last time I see her.

I wipe away the tears that are rolling down my cheeks. She

stops. *What's she doing?*

'I'm just going to make sure the back door is locked!' she calls out. I can't hear any response. The three of us crouch down. 'I will see you again,' she says through the open window. I jump up, but before I have a chance to do anything, the window slams shut and I hear her heels against the wooden floors as she walks away. I turn around, sliding my back down the side of the yellow house to sit in the dirty garden bed.

I listen to the purr of the windowless van fading away, taking my mother and Paula with it.

'You know you're going to be okay. Right?' Jamie says, eventually. I feel his leg press against mine, and draw my knees up under my chin and shake my head. No, I don't know that.

I don't feel okay right now.

'We need to get going, so take some deep breaths.' *I'm not a child.*

I look up at him, my eyes heavy with tears of anger and sadness. 'Your mother is a tough woman.' He smiles, standing up and brushing the brown earth off his dark jeans. 'She's going to be fine. She's been doing this a long time.'

'Holy shit,' Kit says from behind us. 'Your mum was incredible.'

I had been thinking the same thing. Kit stomps onto the path facing us, hands on her hips. 'So Paula was just going to starve the whole clan out. Have guards with machine guns at every exit and shoot us as we scrambled out, sick and starving?'

This is a version of Kit I haven't met yet: deeply angry and afraid. *Everything she does is for those people — her brothers and sisters in the Underground.*

'It's not just our clan,' Jamie says. 'There are thousands of people across all the clans. It would have been genocide.' He offers his hand out to me and I take it, letting him pull me to my feet. 'We need to go now, Teddy. Dawn is coming.'

They start walking silently back onto the street and I follow, glancing at the neighbours' houses. I wonder how many eyes are watching us now. Would they talk? Would they be contacting the Sanitisation Crew right now? Three young kids just walked out of Mrs Jenny Lowry's house into the street. I swallow nervously at the thought of one of them recognising me, calling tomorrow, using the name *Teddy Veodrum*.

I almost laugh, imagining their confusion when the operator informs them that there's no one by that name on their system.

I'm just Teddy now.

Teddy from nowhere.

Teddy from the Underground.

part/two

nineteen

I lean over to Kit. 'Is every birthday like this?' I ask. Kit pauses, wiping hot chocolate from her mouth with her sleeve.

'Nah, Rita is kind of a big deal. Lew likes to treat his favourites, and everyone lurves Rita.'

Kit waves at the birthday girl. Well, birthday *woman*, really. Rita is wearing a red dress that clings to the curves of her body; it's like nothing I've ever seen before. Her bare skin shimmers as if she's been dusted with stardust. She spins around, clapping and stomping in time to the rhythmic beat. The floor in the centre of the enormous dining hall is packed. Everywhere I look, bodies are moving and undulating to the music. *Music!* I still can't believe what I'm hearing as the enticing new melodies wash over my skin and fill my ears.

Towards one side of the room, a group of people are playing instruments − *a band*, Jamie explained. They're performing on a raised platform under pulsating red and blue lights that cast ghoulish shadows across their faces.

'Let's go,' Kit says, grabbing my hands and leading me into the fray.

'Ugh, I don't know,' I say, pulling back.

'Don't be such a drone.' She spins me around, and I knock into a man who leers at me. I look away quickly. 'You'll have fun!'

Standing amongst the mass of sweaty bodies, I can see the band up close. Towards the back of the stage looms the tallest man I've ever seen. His green hair is spiked into three sections in the centre and shaved around the sides. His eyebrows stand out against his pale skin. They are green too. I look away abruptly after he catches me staring. *Mental note: Don't stare at anyone.* I swallow, trying to ignore the nervous feeling that's growing in my stomach.

'Are you just going to stand there?' I turn and find Jamie

standing behind me.

'Wanna dance?'

'Hey, Jamie,' a girl says, interrupting us. I take a step away from him instinctively.

'Hey, Zelda, this is Teddy – she's the new boss.' The girl narrows her eyes at me. She has metal studs in the corners of her bottom lip. I recognise her from the dining hall yesterday, but we hadn't been introduced yet.

'I'm Zelda.' She holds out her hand and I take it, noticing the large tattoo of a W on her waist as her top stretches up.

'Z manages to clothe us all in *interesting* ways.'

'Sometimes . . . when I'm feeling creative. Mostly I deal with room allocations here in Ember . . . I used to do supplies. Maybe now –'

'No clan talk tonight, okay? We're at a party.' Jamie cuts her off, but I'm interested in what she was going to say.

'Fine,' she huffs. 'It's good to see you back, Jamie, I hope you're staying down here with us for a while now.' She glances in my direction. 'I'm sure you will.' Then she turns and starts walking back into the crowd. 'Bye, Teddy grrrl.'

'You'll like her. She's got a sort of love–hate relationship with Kit.'

I roll my eyes. *Who doesn't.*

I twist around looking for our friend but the surge of bodies on the dancefloor makes it impossible to see.

'Where's Kit?' I ask Jamie turning to face him. My breath hitches in my throat. He's staring at me in a way I don't really know how to describe. *Hungry?* I open my mouth to speak, but a girl bumps into me, and I fall against him. Too stunned to react, I watch the dancer as she passes us, her long slender body moving in fluid motions, a stark contrast to the somewhat erratic music.

'Ready?' Jamie asks, his lips pressed against my ear. The warmth from his breath sends a shiver all the way down to my toes.

'For what?'

Before I have a chance to respond, Jamie's hands are on my

waist and he lifts me into the air, spinning me around. He puts me down, then takes my hands, moving my arms in time with the music. I glance down at my black jeans and T-shirt. Compared to some of the other people here I look woefully underdressed. All around us are couples in bright colours like I've never seen. A man waves to Jamie, whose hands are now on my hips, trying to coax some sort of movement out of me. The man's eyes look dark and deep-set, like they've been outlined in the same make-up Mum uses. *Mum.* The thought of her sends a pang through my chest, but before I have time to think about it, I feel Jamie's lips graze my ear.

The heavy erratic beat starts to morph and change into something more upbeat. Then it stops, only for a second, and everyone raises their hands and claps. *One, two, three.*

Then the music starts again, washing over me, and the bodies start moving faster. Looking around, I struggle to see where one person ends and another begins. I look back, locking my eyes on Jamie's. He's smiling.

'This is a lot,' I say, but my voice is lost over the ever-increasing volume of the music. He smiles and nods. *He so didn't hear me.* I glance over his shoulder. Everyone is lost in the sound, and their own movement. *If I do move a little, no one would notice.* That's when I realise *I'm embarrassed.* I consider for a moment what Lisa would do. *Lisa would love it here.* I draw on my courage and reach forward, draping my arms loosely around Jamie's neck, copying some of the other couples I've seen. I draw in a deep breath and shut my eyes.

As soon as they're closed, I feel everything still. I can smell something sweet but pungent in the air. *Liquor,* the same as Mum's 'tonics'. Before I can start overthinking, I let my muscles relax and wait for the music to wash over me again. I begin to move my hips, not worrying about who I might be bumping into. I just let my body go. After a few seconds of stiffness, it feels like a dam has broken inside me, and I let the rhythm of the music rush through my veins. My muscles loosen up even more and I start to move in ways I never have. When I open my eyes I notice Jamie staring at me again and I look away, feeling the heat of embarrassment flood my cheeks.

'You're a natural,' he says, pulling me closer. I sneak a look back up into his eyes, then the spell is broken when I feel a hand on my shoulder.

'Hey, Teddy! Sorry, I lost you – I saw an old . . . friend. Anyway, glad Jamie has been keeping you safe.' I turn around, offering Kit a smile, and a cool wave of disappointment hits me as Jamie lets go of my hips, gently pushing me towards her. I turn around, but he's already moving through the crowd. I take Kit in – her hair is somewhat more tousled than I remember.

'Let's go somewhere we can talk a bit better,' Kit shouts over the music. I nod and let her take my hand as she leads me through the dining hall. The lights start changing at dizzying intervals as we snake through the crowd. I look around at the bodies, some moving in rhythm while others thrust manically to the backbeat.

We move out into the corridor. There are people everywhere out here, too: sitting on the floor, leaning against the walls. Some are still dancing, the bass's drone carrying out of the repurposed dining hall. A guy turns around to stare at me, his eyes heavily outlined in black kohl, his forehead tattooed with what looks like a band of feathers *and knives*. His eyes meet mine.

He winks.

I look away quickly, and then, despite my better judgement, I look back. Now the woman he had been . . . *talking* to . . . has turned to glare at me.

'What're you looking at skank?' the woman shouts. Kit steps in front of me.

'Back off, Mina.'

'I'll back off when this ray of Sunlight goes back to where the sun don't shine.' A few onlookers start laughing. I fidget, my feet still uncomfortable in my new donated guards' boots that are one size too small but *will definitely stretch*, according to Kit.

'It's okay, Kit,' I say, putting my hand on her shoulder. She looks at me; her rage is palpable. I draw myself up to my full height.

'I'm not going anywhere, *Mina*,' I say, then pause with my mouth still open. I was sure the second half of a comeback would come out once I started speaking, but apparently not. I close my mouth and fold my arms like Kit does when she's particularly sassy. Beside me, I notice Kit raise an eyebrow, and we wait. The other woman, Mina, stares at me for a moment, then does something I hadn't expected.

She spits.

Not in my face, but on my new, ill-fitting boots.

'Come on, Doom,' she says, grabbing kohl-eyes by his blue ponytail and marching off down the corridor.

Once they turn out of sight I let go of a long breath.

'Not bad,' a voice says from behind us. We turn around to see Zelda standing with a guy beside her. Now that I can see her in clear light, she looks even more imposing. . . *or impressive*. Her jet-black hair is streaked with red at the front, and her skirt is ankle length, except for the slit that goes up to – goes right up. I look at the guy beside her. He has shoulder-length white hair pulled back in a low ponytail, and a scar across his left cheek.

'This is Mark,' Zelda says, sliding her hand down his chest seductively.

'Good to see you both, we've got to go.' Kit takes my hand, and we start walking away.

'That was rude,' I say, looking back over my shoulder and giving them a wave.

'They're rude.'

'Why?' I ask, but she just huffs and pulls me into another room.

I'm immediately struck by the smell. *Blood.* I look around, trying to see where it's coming from. There are small round tables all around the edges of the room.

SMACK.

I scramble to push Kit out of the way as a half-naked man hits the wall beside us. Everyone at the nearby tables jump up screaming and cheering. Wall guy gets up, leaning forward. The sweat glistens off his back, and now I can see that his face and knuckles are covered in sticky, congealing blood. Before I can say anything, the man begins barrelling towards us. I skirt out of the way as two bodies careen into the wall. Their flesh thuds against the concrete with a sickly thud and they slide to the floor, leaving behind a sticky trail of blood on the grey concrete.

'Shit,' Kit mutters as she drags me back into the corridor.

'What was that all about?' I ask. I can feel my heart still racing. 'They almost smashed into us.'

'Yeah – fight club. I wasn't sure if it was on tonight, with Rita's party and all. Guess it is.'

✗

'Some people are thrilled you're here,' Kit says breaking our silence. It's like she's read my mind. 'Others are happy 'cause you got rid of Paula, but they're not happy with the replacement per se . . .' I don't comment as we walk into another room. Again, it's packed with people sitting around. I still can't wrap my head around how many people are down here. *And this is just one of five clans!*

'What is this place?' I ask softly. Kit leads us around the room, as my eyes hungrily devour all the pictures hanging from the walls. There are hundreds of them, from the floor to the ceiling. Some are framed, some unframed. Paintings, drawings, photographs. I spin around in awe. There are pictures on every wall except one. That wall has the most gigantic bookcase I've ever seen. Spanning the wall's entire length, the bookcase is easily six metres wide and four metres tall. A metal ladder leans against the shelves, begging to be climbed.

'Welcome to the library,' Kit says, a smug smile on her lips. I'm awestruck. 'This is –'

'I can guarantee there isn't a book on those shelves like anything you've ever read before.'

I take a step closer, not even worried that I'm gawking. *Incredible.*

'I didn't even know there were that many books in the world,' I say absently.

'Pshh, that is not even a drop in the bucket, lady. You have no idea.' She's right, I really have no idea at all.

We sit down hard on some floor cushions. I lie back, letting my back stretch out. That dancing has really tired me out. Sitting back up, I notice Kit has grabbed a book and is reading it. *The Delta of Venus*. I shrug to myself, surprised. She never seemed like she'd be that interested in space.

I look around the library, taking in the walls of paintings and people. Even here, this late – *although apparently 10 pm isn't considered late by Underground standards, since most people don't get up until 10 or 11 am* – the room around us is full. Many people are reading, some are even *drawing*! I feel a sudden urge to draw. I haven't drawn anything in the three days I've been down here, and it's not like I've been starved for new material.

✗

I hear his voice before I see him. Turning around I find Jamie is standing at the door to the library.

'There they are,' Zelda says matter-of-factly as she walks towards us, Mark in tow. Jamie pulls away, stopping by the huge bookcase, pulling down a book. Jamie puts the book in front of me, *The History of Art*. The three of them sit down on the surrounding cushions. I feel Jamie's leg press against mine.

I open my mouth to speak, but the atmosphere in the room suddenly shifts. I wonder what's happened for a second, before I turn to look around, my gaze snagging at the entrance.

Link.

Everyone watches as Link saunters in, one arm slung over the shoulder of the woman standing next to him. Some people shout and wave to him. Apparently, some people thought *he* was going to terminate Paula, all of them completely unaware of the part he played in her plans. He does a round of the room, giving us an obvious wide berth. Link's entourage doesn't acknowledge us, but eventually Link does.

I see it.

One dirty look.

He sits down at a table at the far end of the room, surrounded by his people. I look away.

'Urgh, the life sucker is here,' Kit says, shoving the book into one of the large pockets of her fluffy coat.

'What?' I ask.

'Link, he just sucks the life out of everywhere he goes. Asshole.' Zelda chuckles beside her, and I steal another look. His whole crew sit around him, but somehow, he still seems taller than all of them. One girl, younger than most of his group, gets up and starts walking over to us. I nudge Kit.

'Leelo,' Kit says, standing up as the girl approaches. Her boots make her look taller than she really is.

'Kit,' Leelo says flatly.

'This is Teddy.'

'I know.'

I offer my hand for her to shake; it seems to be the general greeting down here. She gives me a tight smile but makes no move to shake my hand.

'Nice to meet you,' I say, turning my shake into a wave.

Lame.

'Cool,' she says, not looking at me. 'Can I talk to you about something?' she asks Kit. They walk away from the table, and I lean over to Jamie.

'What's her problem?' I whisper.

He shrugs. 'Leelo's Kit cousin. She was a nice kid who used to hang out with us quite a bit, but she got friendly with some of the people in Link's crew, and she's been sour ever since.' I look over to where they're talking. Kit shakes her head, pink hair flicking. Leelo shoves her in the shoulder then walks away. I stand up, half expecting to see Kit fight back. She doesn't.

Kit walks back over to us. 'Eugh!' She sits down hard on the vibrant cushion. 'She is such a ratbag – was I that annoying when I was her age?'

Jamie laughs, nodding with Zelda.

'Why did she shove you?' I ask, looking back to where Leelo is now slumped in the arms of a guy who appears to have more metal in his face than skin. *Doesn't that hurt?*

'I wouldn't let her get out of her shift. She wants to go play Stix with her new boyfriend, but I said she had to honour her rostered shift.' Kit runs her hands through her hair. 'I'm not going to cover her shift every time she wants to go gamble away her supplies. Y'know? It's like, do what you want, sure, but working in the medical centre isn't a joke. She shouldn't have begged me for a job there if she couldn't hack it.'

'You shouldn't let her get away with that behaviour,' Jamie says softly, leaning forward and taking Kit's hand. I feel a rush of jealousy at the gesture, and it startles me.

'She's just learning to pick her battles,' Zelda retorts, grabbing Kit's other hand across the table and squeezing it softly. I look at the communal hand-holding, and it abates some of my jealousy, but also – *weird.*

I glance back at Link and his crew, and his angry eyes burn into mine. Something tugs at me, urging me to stand up to him like I did to Mina, but another part of me gnaws away. *Learn to pick your battles.* I shoot Link a wry smile, and he looks away with a snarl.

Something tells me there will be many more battles ahead.

twenty

'Are you ready?' Kit asks for the billionth time.

'No,' I say. She levels a look in my direction. 'Yeah, fine, whatever. I'm ready, can we just get this over with?' I shift awkwardly. It's been a week since the big birthday bash.

Just over a week living Underground.

Most of our time has been spent preparing for this stupid 'swearing-in' ceremony. I lean down and retie my shoelaces. My one-size-too-small boots have been replaced with a pair that fit *perfectly* – a gift from Jamie. I also received another gift – a brand-new packet of pencils along with a note from Mum. She was proud of me, she said, and that we'd see each other soon. She also sent a list of proposed new supply drop-off/pick-up locations.

'We need to assess the options and pick six new drop-off spots,' Kit explains, still fussing with my hair.

'I know,' I say. *I'm so hot.*

'After we get a chance to run over them, I'll send a note back to your mother, and confirm that meeting with Mrs Lowry. Okay?'

'Okay,' I say dismissively as I fidget in my new clothes. 'Are you hot?' I ask. She rolls her eyes.

'It's the middle of winter, you're just freaking out.

You have no reason to!' Kit puts a heavy circlet of metal on my head.

'Is this a crown?' I ask in horror, remembering the lavish crowns ancient royalty used to wear. *Frivolous displays of wealth, while thousands were murdered or starved to death.*

That's what the history book said. *Not a lot has changed . . .*

'No, it's not a crown – it's a tiara.' She looks at me sheepishly.

'Why?' I ask, narrowing my eyes.

'Because it looks so pretty on you, and Paula never wore it, and it's part of Ember tradition . . . honestly, I think it makes you look kinda badass.' She smiles.

'Well, badass *is* what I was going for,' I say wryly, raising one eyebrow.

'Yay!' She steps back and holds up a mirror, and my eyes open wide. My appearance is a shock. I stare at the black kohl she's drawn around my eyes . . . and down my chin *and* across my nose.

'Kit.'

'I'm not going to apologise. You look like a queen, and you're wearing a crown, and you're going to be the Queen of the Freaks now, so you might as well get used to it.'

I harumph. 'You can dress me up however you like, it doesn't mean everyone is going to bow down to me.'

'You don't need them to,' she says softly, taking my hand and leading me to the door that goes into the dining hall. 'You just need to show them that you don't care if they do or don't.'

I let her words sink in, *show them you don't care if they do or don't* . . . Kit sweeps the door open and Jamie steps forward, taking my arm.

'It's time,' he says, his eyes light up as he takes me in.

✗

I am overwhelmed, seeing everyone in Clan Ember gathered here in one place. Not because of the two thousand odd people spilling out of the dining hall, but because of how many emotions there are. Looking out into the sea of faces, it's evident that not everyone wants to be here, and not everyone wants *me* to be here. But here I am, and this is happening.

I walk between Jamie and Kit, feeling hotter with each step, as eyes sear into me. Some people are here to mourn Paula's end; others to celebrate her demise. So much has happened in such a short time – not just for me but also for these people. My biggest challenge so far seems to be remembering everyone's names and working out where their allegiances lie. Turns out if you mention the wrong person, an everyday conversation can get violent *very* quickly.

I shift uncomfortably, the stupid tiara starting to feel heavy on

159

my head. As we approach the opening towards the back of the room, I take a step back, running into Jamie's solid chest.

'Woah there,' he says with a chuckle.

'What's he doing here?' I ask, hoping my face doesn't betray the panic I feel as I look up at the table I'm supposed to climb onto. 'You didn't tell me he was going to be here.'

Kit shoots Jamie a look, and in a second they're both in front of me.

'We didn't want to tell you because we didn't want to freak you out.'

Why is he here? I say through clenched teeth.

'As Paula's *official* second, it is Link's right to be the master of ceremonies.' I look between them, confused.

'He gets to swear you in,' Jamie says.

'I had hoped he would defer to me since I was sort-of also her second,' Kit says.

'*Was*,' Jamie emphasises. 'Anyway, he refused. So that's why he's up there. The ceremony will be exactly as we told you, it's just that Link is doing it.' They smile at me, but their smiles are tight-lipped; forced.

'You both suck,' I whisper, straightening my shoulders and pushing past them. Using the bench as a step, I climb onto the old wooden table and face Link.

⚔

As Link drones on, my attention fades out as I scan the gathered crowd. I've surprised myself over the last week. Things haven't felt as strange as I thought they would. The different customs and behaviours haven't *shocked* me in the way I thought they would. It's almost as if I knew this was here, and I was waiting to find it.

'Teddy?' Link asks, his eyes slits as he waits for my response to a question I didn't hear.

'Could you please repeat that?' I ask.

Link growls. 'Do you accept your probation period? We're one week in, and two remain. During such time your position is immune

160

to physical attack, as state the rules of Clan Ember. After this time passes, you accept that your life is the price for a new challenge to the leadership of Clan Ember.' Oh yes. The probation, aka my murder-free safety net.

I clear my throat. 'I accept,' I say, trying to ignore the challenge in Link's eyes. He hates my guts, and I mean *hates*.

'Give me your hand,' he says. I glance over my shoulder to where Kit and Jamie are standing with Zelda and Mark.

Kit smiles at me reassuringly, looking like a proud mother.

My eyes lock onto Jamie's. He gives me a small nod.

I turn back to Link and hold out my hand.

'Other hand,' he says, rolling his eyes. I hold out my right hand, tensing my muscles to stop it from shaking.

He pulls out a knife and holds it up so everyone in the room can see.

'With this knife, we shed your blood to seal the deal and make us one.' Those words – *and make us one*. A shiver runs down my spine, and then panic sets in as I get a good look at the ridiculously sharp blade Link is holding. I watch in petrified horror as he cuts a slice down my right hand, and suck in air as the pain rips up my arm.

'Repeat after me,' he says. *Blood for blood – to serve and to sacrifice.*'

I repeat the words, feeling the weight of them sink into my bones as my blood oozes down the bright silver length of the blade. A shudder rips through me.

Not so different from the Partnership after all, I think . . . not for the first time that day.

twenty/one

Kit keeps talking while I'm shovelling heaped spoonfuls of grey porridge into my mouth. I don't think I'll ever get used to the texture. I genuinely can't figure out how they manage to make it both thick and dry, yet somehow soggy, too.

Disgusting.

Today is Monday. It's the final week of my probation period. Just the thought sends a shiver down my spine. I put my spoon down, the metal sinking into the grey slop. I *will* have to eat it; being Clan Head doesn't mean I can waste food. Absently, I rub the bright pink scar that crosses my right palm. Kit removed the bandage last night, but it's still very tender.

I sigh, then continue spooning the grey slop into my mouth.

Not that anyone really wants me to be Clan Head.

Kit and I are the only people in the dining hall this early. Long wooden tables fill the cavernous space. The dining hall is the only place food is served in our clan. Lights hang low and cast a warm glow over each table. The benches are soft and smoothly worn down by years of hands, plates, and cleaning cloths wearing away at them.

I grimace as Doom and Mina walk in, arms around each other. I don't think I'll ever get used to the *PDA*, as Kit calls it. Kit and I are sitting up the back, at our usual table. It's long enough to fit eight people, but it's rare that anyone will join us. Usually, it's just Jamie, Kit and myself. Our conversations are always the same. *Don't do this, do more of this, that's great, probably wait until* . . . I'm sick of being coached and talked to like a baby. *It's like they don't think I can do the job.* Toying with the dregs of my breakfast, another thought bubbles to the surface, not for the first time. *Why didn't one of them just take on the damn role?* Kit's still talking, but I'm barely listening. I know what she's explaining. It's all *my* work. Ever since I've moved down here, she's been running around trying to keep things going the old way. Most of my changes have been met with resistance from *someone.*

'Did you have any more thoughts on the reallocation of the storage rooms? Zelda said there were some changes we could make to increase living quarters,' I ask, pushing my bowl away.

'Mhmm, we'll talk about it later, hey?' Kit says standing up taking my bowl.

Always later.

Even Kit, my *friend*, has a hard time accepting my ideas. She and Jamie insist that I'm the best choice, that my knowledge of the *above ground*, as they call it, gives me a fresh perspective – but every time I try to offer some of that perspective, it's met with resistance. I tried to argue that Jamie would bring the same perspective, but all my protestations have, so far, been silenced.

I look around the hall. More people are starting to trickle in. Unsurprisingly, most of them avoid looking at me. I'm caught by surprise when two young men meet my eyes and smile. One of them even waves hello. I look away quickly, uncomfortable. *Great, now they'll think I'm a snobby bitch, just like everyone else does.* It's just that I'm still not used to the easy way men and women seem to mingle here. Like there's nothing wrong with it.

There is *nothing wrong with it.*

I've noticed some people have Partnership Seals on their necks, many tattooed beyond recognition, just as Kit had told me. One woman caught me staring once. Her Seal was covered with an intricate, colourful tattoo of a flower. Its leaves disappeared into her green hair. *Having a good look, ya perve?* she'd shouted, before shoving past me.

There are so many different people here.

No wonder Paula enjoyed being leader. She'd have thrived on this kind of chaos.

Kit seems to think the three-week probation should comfort me; that the knowledge my would-be murderer, *aka Link*, won't be eligible for leadership if he attempts anything during this period. After the three weeks, however, *anyone* can make a leadership grab.

She slides back onto the seat and pushes a cup of water across the table to me.

It's so early, Jamie isn't here yet either. In the Underground, everyone is just waking up, despite the fact that half the 'morning' is over. People keep different hours down here – we get up when the City goes to bed so we can collect supplies and sneak around. Something I still haven't done since I moved down here.

I take a sip of water. It still wigs me out that above us, in the Metropolis, people should be well and truly in bed by now. *Except for people like my mother.* I allow myself a small smile. I'm excited I get to see her today. I'm excited every time Mum visits our planning meetings, because each visit is a sign that she's okay. *They haven't found us out . . . yet.*

I finish the water then slam the empty cup onto the table. I've got one week left, then the clan vote: a unanimous 'no' means I get kicked out. No one will explain to me what that means. Otherwise, I'm still in, just leading with a target on my back until I build up enough of a following that the clan becomes my armour. Looking around the room and seeing how many people are trying desperately to ignore me, I know that this is not going to be an easy feat. Kit seems convinced it's unlikely anyone *will* challenge me, but the strange looks and unfriendly eyes make me question her confidence. *Nothing* is impossible down here, especially with people like Link gaining supporters and just – *lurking*. At home, I knew when the day would start and when it would end. Down here, it doesn't end, it's just one long night. I'm worried I'll have to start sleeping with one eye open.

'Earth to Teddy. We need to get moving, I don't want to be late again.' Kit breaks into my thoughts, slamming down her own cup.

'Geez, you can talk!' I say, grabbing our empty cups and taking them over to the kitchen door. There are three chutes: food scraps, utensils and dishware. The metal hits the side of the chute, clattering all the way into the big plastic tubs below.

As I walk back over to Kit, my thoughts circle back to my most common worry: *Link*. I've only seen him twice since the ceremony, and something about that doesn't sit right. *What is he planning?* Whatever it is, I know it can't be good.

I've mentioned my concerns about Link to Kit a few times, but she just blows them off. Jamie is more cautious. He's been in and out since the ceremony. We had dinner last night, just the two of us at our table – the first time we'd been alone together since we danced at Rita's party. I feel heat flood my cheeks at the memory, the feeling of him being *so close*.

I follow Kit out of the dining hall, keeping my eyes peeled for him. Three times I've tried to find Jamie, only to discover he was on the surface. Kit told me that Jamie's the one who's been taking the notes to and from my mum. Last night, without *Officer Kit* there to monitor our conversation, he told me a few things about Link. *Link had some dirt on Paula, so he was never punished for all the rules he broke down here. Everyone knew what he was doing, but he wasn't even initiated formally. Whatever he had on Paula, it must have been good. Link was always Paula's 'guy'* . . . Jamie spat the words out. *There's some big whacko ego trip going on in his head. I think he's a real threat.*

As Kit and I exit through the dining hall, a man shoulders past me and I fall back a few steps.

'Go back to where you came from,' he growls at me.

'Hey –' I say, spinning around, but he's gone.

'Asshole,' Kit says, shooting daggers with her eyes into his back. She's wearing the scarf I gave her. I'm happy she took it because she wasn't lying, it is bone cold down here.

Together we turn and start making our way through the dark corridors of Clan Ember. The most urgent thing that needed attention when I arrived was a complete overhaul of the Sympathiser supply chain. We walk past the sorting room. The piles of supplies are more extensive than I have ever seen them. I stick my head in to see if I can spot Zelda. One of the sorters waves at me and I wave back, feeling one small tangle of tension loosen around my insides – *a friendly face*. Since Paula's been gone, more and more people are finding random pockets of supplies. It's clear Paula had been using

Metropolis's 'the left hand doesn't know what the right hand is doing' principle to maintain her control down here. She'd made sure it was impossible to track who was doing what and where things were happening or being stored. *Something I've been trying to change.* Paula had been hiding everything she'd stolen underground; people just hadn't been looking. Now, with Zelda and Rita's supervision, they are finding things, and it is a good thing too, because with the pause on supplies, we were in danger of running out of everything.

Just as I'm about to join Kit in the corridor, she bursts past me, shouting, 'Hey, Tony! Get this stack of bandages to the medical centre this morning. These are urgent things – not "do it when I feel like it", alright?' *Always bossing.*

I do trust Kit – *I think.* But I don't understand why she has been fighting me on all my ideas.

It feels like I'm just a puppet to her.

I shake my head. I need to stop thinking like that. *She's my friend.*

Despite Kit's reprimand, Tony is lying back on a pile of clothes, reading something – back to front?

'He's reading the wrong way,' I say under my breath, and Kit gives me a look.

'Manga,' she mutters. 'All he does is read his stupid comics; he gets them from his boyfriend in Clan Degout. Plus, how are you so sure you know which way is the wrong way?' she asks, then smiles and walks out of the room. *There is no wrong way down here.*

✕

We keep walking deeper into the Underground, weaving through corridors. I'm glad Kit seems to know where she's going. This is the third time we've left the clan's central hub, and every time we do, the same creeping feeling crawls up my legs. At first I thought it was because of the lack of lights, and the sticky floor. The walls here are different, too, the green tiles replaced with . . . nothing. Just rock. I reach out and drag the tips of my fingers across the sandy surface. When I pull them away, they're sticky. *Gross.* I wipe my fingers on my pants, then shove my hands up under my armpits.

'What is with the lights out here?' I ask.

'What about them?'

'There are less here,' I say slowly, looking back the way we came, the warm glow of light beckoning for me to return.

'Conserving power. It's something Clan Lux put in place. These parts are used less frequently, and by fewer people, so why light them up like the living spaces and private quarters?'

Kit pulls out her torch and flicks it on, and I do the same, casting cool light along our path.

We've been meeting Mum and Mrs Lowry twice a week for the last two weeks since I became Clan Head, with extra communication going to them – care of Jamie, as I have now learnt. I take a deep breath of musty air. These meetings are my bi-weekly sanity check. An opportunity to pretend that things are – well, not normal, but still. The first meeting didn't go smoothly. Mrs Lowry was still mad about what happened to her house, and no one could find any information on Maree. Pair that with Kit not being very . . . sympathetic . . . and the result was a short and explosive meeting. I didn't get to exchange one word with Mum.

'Kit,' I say, stopping by one of the remaining yellow lights and reaching out for her arm. The light's warm glow casts eerie shadows on the wall.

'Yeaas?' she asks slowly.

'You *did* send Mrs Lowry the latest intel on the new guard routes, right?'

She nods curtly. I know I should trust her with my life, but I struggle to. I can't stop thinking about her blind trust of Paula. *It doesn't speak well of her instincts*. Plus, she's too eager to keep things the way they've always been. Now Paula is gone, Kit thinks everything can go back to normal, but she doesn't want to accept that normal was flawed. If Paula *had* been working with the guards, then I'm sure more members of the Council know about the existence of the Underground. And I haven't said it out loud yet, but I can't shake the feeling that we're all living inside a ticking time bomb.

'Yes! Teddy, she's up to date,' she says, crossing her tattooed arms. 'And we have the new confirmed locations, *and* we're running late! You know how irritable Mrs Lowry gets when we keep them waiting.'

'You know why I'm nervous?' I say. It's not really a question.

'Yeah, I know – this new drop-off, pick-up thing you've come up with is about to start, and now it's time to see if it works.'

I nod, and we start walking again. It took a while to get Kit to come around, but she did. Now we're about to start picking up supplies again.

'This is going to be fine. Your plan is brilliant. We'll smash this,' Kit says, squeezing my arm. I can't help smiling at the rare compliment. 'Now let's go! I don't think I can sit through another lecture from that woman.' I follow Kit down another corridor, our torches casting light on the sticky walls. We stop in front of a tarnished metal door. She looks at me, one eyebrow raised, and I nod. She turns the handle, and we step into the room. As we do, a thought rolls around in the back of my mind.

What does Kit really care about?

✗

'You're late,' Mrs Lowry clips from her flimsy metal fold-out chair. Her white hair is pulled back into a tight bun, making her look as severe as she sounds. Once she was a round, jolly woman who would bake cakes and tell me stories about princesses in castles, and dragons . . . even though she shouldn't have been. But when my grandfather was taken, she changed. I didn't see her as much, and when I did, she was distant and cold – *like now.*

I sit down at the small table next to my mother. We smile at each other, and she squeezes my hand. She looks tired. Older, since we said goodbye.

Things have gone very differently from what we'd planned. As in, nothing has really changed at all. The Sanitisation was processed, and Mum didn't even need to leave our house. She told my father what had happened – the amended version – and he had accepted it with a nod. *What was it that she had said? Disappointed, but not surprised.* Apparently after that, she hadn't seen him at all, only receiving updates from his secretary at the Council.

'How's Paul? Any word about my –'

'Your Sanitisation was discussed – is discussed – but no one would dare ask any questions of me, now your *father* is working with the Mayor.' She purses her lips, and I don't push any further.

Opposite me, besides Mrs Lowry, Kit shifts uncomfortably on the hard metal chair. With four of us crammed into the tiny room, it feels like we should be rationing our breathing. A single bulb hangs low and ominous, hovering over the small metal table cluttered with notes and maps. It swings gently, propelled by the force of the invisible wind as we wait for Mrs Lowry to speak.

She looks across at me with narrowed eyes. 'As I said, you two are late.'

'Yes, we are so sorry, Mrs Lowry,' I say, hoping Kit can conceal her trademark eye-roll. 'We were in another meeting,' I lie. I appreciate what this woman does for us, and how much she has helped over time, but that doesn't change the fact that she doesn't fully understand the life people lead down here. She's not the benevolent grandma figure I had thought she was. I'm starting to get the impression she's motivated by whatever *she* can get out of her good deeds.

'Look, Teddy, we're not down here because we want to be, and I'd like to get topside as soon as possible. I rather wish you and your mother's actions hadn't removed the option of meeting at my home.' She gives my mum a look. 'It was infinitely more civilised there.' I swallow, pleading silently with Kit to hold her tongue. Under the table, Mum grabs my hand and squeezes.

'Due to the increased number of guards, and the pressure of this year –' Mum says.

'What pressure?' Kit interrupts.

'Jubilee, dear,' Mrs Lowry says, as if Kit were a small child.

'I know that,' she says through gritted teeth.

Mum continues, ignoring the tension in the room. 'Some big

things are happening this year, because of Jubilee. The Occasions are being used to demarcate the *chosen generation*. There are new accommodations for Partnered youths, to help them live their best so they can serve their City best. There are also new roles we've never had in the City, *and* the spectacular Jubilee Festival that is planned for the end of the year.' At this, Mum sits back in her chair. It was something the editor of *Metropolis Magazine* would say, not my mother, the Sympathiser – y et somehow, she is one and the same.

'Right,' Kit says as she goes back to picking her nail polish.

'We can't stay here long. Even since our meeting last week we've noticed an uptick in patrols.'

'And an increase in those annoying cameras. Watching everything, always bloody watching.' This outburst from Mrs Lowry is a surprise. 'There are also some rumours.' 'What rumours?' I ask.

Mum rubs her temples with her long fingers. 'About Sanitisation. Some people are talking about . . . well, they're talking about the truth, suggesting that it's not a sanitisation but a culling. Of course, I've only heard people talking about the *nonsense other people have said*. No one has said any of this to me directly. They're all trying to curry favour with me, now that your father is the councillor of the hour.'

'Being the *Met Mag* editor probably doesn't hurt your position either,' Kit adds.

I rub the back of my neck.

'Okay,' I say, before we digress any further. 'As you understand, my plan was, primarily, to ditch the truck.' Everyone nods. 'We need to streamline the process. Have small teams making the collections. Always on foot, never alone. All supplies need to be arranged so that we can carry them. We'll go out more frequently and grab smaller amounts.'

'About that,' Mrs Lowry interrupts. 'The brief you gave us said *backpacks*. I'm not sure where you expect our Sympathisers to keep getting these packs from?'

'We'll obviously swap them every time we pick new things up, and drop off the empty ones,' Kit says, playing with a dagger she's pulled out of the side of her left boot. Mrs Lowry raises an eyebrow, and they exchange a look for a tense second. Kit understands how delicate our allegiance with the Sympathisers is, but typically, she doesn't care. I glace sideways at Mum. Her cheeks are sallow, and her eyes have dark bags under them. She gives me a weak smile.

'Alright, give us the final approved locations then let us get out of here,' Mum says, her tone business all of a sudden.

I nod, and Kit begins explaining the new pick-up locations. With the risk of Council members knowing about the Underground and Sympathiser activity, Jamie and I came up with a fortnightly roster of sites on a three-month cycle. We agreed it would work because the gaps between time and place will throw off anyone who is monitoring our movements.

'You do realise that this is a trial?' Mrs Lowry says, narrowing her eyes. 'These collections are of utmost importance. As the largest clan, you are the only people who are to be on the surface making collections. There has been *far* too much exposure with this Paula incident, and we've yet to find out how deep the City Council's knowledge of the Underground really is.' I glance at Mum, but she's gazing at her hands, playing with her wedding ring.

'I understand the danger,' I say curtly. 'That's why this change was my priority. Ensuring pick-up locations are not at the homes or workplaces of Sympathisers is vital. It won't be a popular idea on either end, but we need to protect *our* people going above ground, and we need to protect *your* people, who are risking their lives so we can have basic supplies.'

Mrs Lowry nods as Kit continues listing the new locations for this month.

'. . . and lastly, inside Chang's Park.' Kit passes our list over to Mum, who cross-checks it against the copy they have.

'We're relying on a smooth transition into the new leadership,' Kit says. 'Nothing can go awry.'

Mrs Lowry fixes a long look in my direction.

'Until next time, ladies.' She raises her eyebrow at Kit, as if 'lady' is a stretch in her case. Then she stands, indicating the meeting is now over.

'Thank you for coming down here, we really appreciate the risk involved,' Kit says, extending her hand. They surprise me by shaking hands.

I hang back as everyone files out of the dingy meeting room, hoping to catch a moment with Mum in private. I run over my plan in my head.

Paula thrived on the chaos and general disorganisation down here. That's what enabled her to deceive the entire Underground. I don't really want to *force* things on people, but of all the things Kit has told me, one thing has really stuck: that there's perpetual chaos down here.

'You need to watch out, Teddy,' Mum murmurs as she gets up and pulls me into a hug. 'There are people down here who

aren't happy about your arrival.'

That includes me, I want to tell her.

'Your probation is almost up. I've heard some people are trying to stir up trouble.'

I feel my muscles tense. *How has she heard any of this?*

She's not saying anything I don't know. I'm not blind to the dirty looks and whispers. I know Kit and Jamie sense it too. Jamie must have told her when he delivered the notes. *Why would he tell her?* I feel an inappropriate flutter in my stomach at the thought of him.

She pulls away, her face ashen. 'The people down here, they're not going to do anything that will hurt the Underground . . . but if they can turn the majority of Clan Heads against you –' She drops her voice even lower. 'I don't know what they've told you, but I do know that being down here without support can be worse than being Sanitised.'

My stomach flips. I know in my gut that Mum's right. Last week I saw a man tied to a chair for three days because he stole another man's shoes. I tried to intervene, but got nowhere.

We don't talk to get action down here, girl. Take your big ideas and blow them out your –

'Just watch out for the people who stood with Paula,' Mum

says.

My gaze follows Kit, who taps at her wrist from outside the room.

Mum shakes her head. 'No, not Kit. You can trust her. She wouldn't be here with you if she didn't believe in you.' She hugs me again. 'You *can* do this, you just need to trust yourself. And *be careful.*'

She's right. People down here are wild, and even though we're meant to be working together, the clans really do feel like gangs. Mum pushes a strand of hair from my face, and I'm suddenly overwhelmed by a wave of homesickness. 'They're just not used to the order you're trying to bring.'

'Luanna, are you moving down here now too?' Mrs Lowry calls out impatiently from the hallway.

I wish.

Mum pulls me in for a final hug. 'I love you, Teddy.'

'I love you too,' I whisper, and then I'm alone, with a million questions lingering on my lips, feeling the body warmth seep out of my bones.

twenty/two

'What?' Kit probes as we begin walking back towards the dining room, where Jamie is waiting for us. 'I'd recognise that look a mile away. Speak up.'

'It's nothing,' I reply, but the lights as we head back into the heart of the Underground are making it impossible to hide from Kit's probing eyes. 'It's just something Mum said.'

'What did she say *now*? You know you can't take everything she tells you to heart. You *had* to move down here, she knows that. To be honest, I don't know why she doesn't move down here herself . . .' Kit launches into one of her monologues, and I nod, not listening. I don't *want* to tell Kit what Mum said, or what I'm thinking. It's as though if I don't say anything, it isn't a real problem. I stop abruptly, and Kit turns to face me, silent.

I look around to make sure we're alone, but my voice still comes out as a whisper. 'She told me to be careful.' Kit raises an eyebrow. 'You know, to watch out for all the stuff that's brewing down here.' She sighs, but I go on. 'It's just made me think about all those people still devoted to Link and Paula.'

'Don't worry about it,' she tries to flick the issue away, but it weighs heavy between us. 'Jamie and I support you one hundred per cent. This is meant to be. *Seriously!*

Both Jamie and Kit are influential here in the clan. Having them around me has helped me to be accepted, somewhat. But I'm not sure it will be enough to guarantee my safety.

Kit starts walking again, and I trail behind. We've barely made it five metres before the piercing trill of an alarm begins to sound.

'What's that?' I shout, covering my ears with my hands.

'It's our alarm system,' Kit replies, her eyes wide.

'What for?'

'Fire.'

After a stunned second, we both turn and start running in the direction of the sound. 'What can we do?' I shout as we zigzag through tunnels. She doesn't reply, and I wonder if she's heard me. 'Kit?'

'It means bad news. This far into the Underground, the exit points are limited.'

I have no idea where we are as I follow her expertly weaving through the corridors. Kit starts shouting over her shoulder. 'An uncontained fire will mean –' Suddenly she stops, and I crash into her back. She turns to face me with a flash of urgency in her eyes. She's blocking my view, but I push past to see what's happening. I feel the eyes of the gathering crowd all turn to face me. Their angry gazes and curious eyes follow me, waiting to see what I'll do.

We walk closer to the fire in question, and I can see now that it's small, not designed for destruction – just enough to smoke out the alarm.

A warning.

Smouldering against the wall, the remaining flames cast ghostly shadows across the yellow graffiti before us.

Down with Sunlight. BRN BRN BRN

I can hear people talking and realise the alarm has stopped. I start to feel claustrophobic as people push through, shouldering their way forward, clawing against the growing crowd to see what's happening. Their eyes look first to the wall, then to me. I can feel the smoke stinging my eyes and burning my nose.

'This is her fault.' A girl steps forward, pointing a long finger in my direction. She looks about the same age as me. Beads of sweat roll down her tattooed forehead, making the blue inked barbed wire look slick across her brow. She takes another step forward, and an older man joins her.

'She's from up there, she don't belong here.' I swallow hard and quickly look away from the pair.

She doesn't belong here.

I bite the inside of my cheek hard, trying to focus my attention.

More voices join in. I try to block them out, but it's impossible.

Why her?

This isn't our choice.

She's brought her Sunlight dramas with her.

Sunlight scum.

I can feel tears stinging my eyes, threatening to tumble out. Kit steps forward and grabs my hand. She squeezes it tight.

'Who did this?' I demand, my voice coming out stronger than I had thought it would. The people nearest me shuffle, clearly uncomfortable with me speaking up.

'Let's go,' she says softly, tugging my arm. We glance at the fire again.

'This fire is *not* my fault. Whoever *set* the fire put our Underground at risk. Someone will pay for this mistake.'

'Don't make things worse,' Kit says.

'We need to put the fire out,' I reply, trying to twist out of her grip, but she won't let me go.

'We don't have anything to use.' She meets my gaze.

I shake my head. 'Let go,' I say, ripping my hand from her grip. I shoulder through the crowd towards the smouldering fire. *I'll stomp it out.*

She stares at me a long second, then shrugs and begins pushing her way through the crowd until she's beside me, both our pairs of boots stomping out the remains of the fire. It feels like we're part of some strange performance as we stamp on the fire until it's nothing more than a pile of ash. I feel my cheeks burning as the whispers turn into a soft din of chatter. A few people step forward as if to help, and I look around, desperately trying to find a friendly face. My search is futile; most of the gathered crowd don't bother to hide their disgust.

As Kit and I step away from the wall I notice more people have arrived from another corridor – this is an intersection, I can see now. Whoever started the fire wanted as many people to see it as possible.

'We're done here,' Kit says, reacting to one of the louder

'whispers' near us. I try to keep up as she shoulders her way through the crowd, some people thanking her or patting her on the back. I feel the heat of their anger.

It wasn't me! I want to scream. *It wasn't my fault!*

I know they'll blame me regardless. I'm the new one – not only am I their 'leader', I'm an unwelcome guest – from above. I square my shoulders and look back into the crowd one last time. They have no idea what danger they're in.

If I'm not accepted and chaos reigns, a fire will be the least of their worries.

twenty/three

Kit, Jamie and I sit in the dining hall, silently huddled around our usual table. The bright lamps nurture the dull headache in my temples into a full-on avalanche of pain. Kit munches down her tepid mashed potato, but I'm not hungry. I stare at my plate, pushing peas around. They're cold now. Kit and I were too late to serve ourselves dinner.

If you miss a meal, you eat whatever's left. If everything's eaten, you don't eat. If you complain, you don't eat.

That's what Mark explained to me the first night I was late for dinner. That night, I didn't eat. Tonight, by the time Kit and I made it here, all that was left were the unappetising plates put together by kitchen staff: mashed potato, peas and some kind of soy protein, sitting drearily under the 'warming' lamps at the food counter.

I take another mouthful of mash then breathe in through my nose. Smoke lingers in the air, slithering through the air ducts. I pick up a pea and squeeze it between my fingers. I can feel eyes burning into my back but the mood isn't bad. I look around and see more people filtering into the hall, late. They're crowding around the old wooden benches and tables, setting up games with chips and wooden pieces. A band sets up in the corner. Still people throw furtive glances in my direction and whisper.

Gossiping.

'Those idiots. Are you okay?' Jamie grabs my hand and squeezes, his eyes bore into mine and I look away, overwhelmed by a flood of emotions. *Why does he still care? He doesn't owe me anything.* I look back to him. *He's just trying to understand what just happened.* I sigh.

Jamie was the first to support my changes to the pick-up and drop-off procedures. In fact, he's supported everything I've suggested. Not once has he expressed any doubt that I'm the right choice for leader. Kit, of course, has had her own moments of scepticism, but never Jamie. I break his gaze for the second time and he turns to Kit, waiting for an explanation. *It isn't hard to see why everyone likes him.*

Kit goes to interrupt, but I put my hand up, stopping her. 'You can't deny I'm the "Sunlight" they're referring to. It's just like Mum said.'

Jamie looks from me to Kit, confused.

'Your mum? What did she say?' he asks, reaching out. I pull my hand back, crossing my arms and stretching my legs up onto the bench.

'I think she just said for Teddy to be careful,' Kit explains, trying to gloss over it. She exchanges a look with Jamie. I pretend not to notice. 'Which is nothing I haven't said,' Kit continues, 'and that's why it's important now more than ever that you keep your head down and just get through the week.'

I feel sick with anticipation. I have less than seven days to prove my new plans will work. To show that I am valuable. To make the clan *want* me to stay.

As Mum said, *being down here without support can be worse than being Sanitised.* If I can't get people to support me, I won't survive – and I don't feel like this week is off to a great start.

'Forget it,' I say, harsher than I had intended. 'It's clear I'm not welcome here. It's time for someone else to take over. I said from the start that it should be one of you.'

'Really? Things get a little bit tough and you just back off?' Jamie crosses his arms. 'For some reason that just doesn't resonate with the Teddy I know.' *You don't know me.*

Kit nods, and he continues, leaning forward to stop anyone eavesdropping. 'Do you really think that the type of people who *don't* want you to be Clan Head really want anyone else to be? We're talking about a small group of power-hungry maniacs who will only ever be happy with themselves being in charge. They'll always be hanging around.'

I know he's trying to make me feel better, but a quick look

around the room cools the warmth of his support. A table of young people hold my gaze. *Great.* I stare back at them, and a girl with flame-red hair and a black leather jacket narrows her eyes and draws her finger across her throat. Clichéd, but it's effective.

'She's someone I *would* watch out for though,' Kit says softly. Jamie meets my eyes and nods. 'I agree,' Jamie says. 'Petra Tack.' 'What about her?' I ask.

Kit leans forward. 'She's like, *with* Link, I think. They're like this power couple of evil. They manipulate people.' She leans

closer. 'Some people say they're *siblings.*' I feel my skin crawl.

'They trick people into thinking they're *good*, that they're "here to help". That's why they have so many followers,' Jamie says. 'Look how many people are over there, hanging on her every word.' He shakes his head. 'But they're no strangers to blackmailing the dumb few who trust them with their secrets.'

Kit nods. 'I've treated people in the medical centre who've had injuries they couldn't explain. A young boy once came in with both his arms twisted out of their sockets.' I feel the food in my stomach start to rise.

'It took three of us to hold him down so the doctor could reset them. Afterwards, he wouldn't tell us what happened. Only that it was an *accident.*'

'That sort of injury is never an accident,' Jamie says. 'And Petra and Link are the only people cruel enough to do it or condone it.'

We sit in silence, finishing our meals.

'I haven't done anything to these people,' I say finally. Kit just laughs.

'Your existence down here is enough. Link *and* Petra want to be in charge. You're stopping that from happening.'

Jamie throws his cutlery down so quickly the flimsy metal flies off the tables and slides across the floor. He stands, pressing both fists on the smooth wood.

'They don't care where you're from, Teddy. The fact is, *you* pulled down Paula, not them. Kit was wrong, you're not *stopping* their leadership from happening. You literally *stopped* it. Link was called the "Underlord" for a *year* until Paula punished him for it. The fact is, he wants power, and he knows the system, 'cause he's a True. If you're approved, and someone kills you, they take your place, *and* they get their probation too. If they're already well-known and well-liked down here, there's almost no risk to them. *But –*' Jamie raises a finger. 'If you're *voted* out, the new leader is voted in.'

'Which would be a little harder for a cretin like Link,'

Kit finishes. 'He's got a following, sure, but he doesn't have enough people to win the whole clan over like that.'

'So, for Link to become Clan Head, he needs me to be approved, then he needs to be the one who murders me?' 'Yep, exactly!' Jamie says victoriously.

I stare at him – *weird tone.*

He leans forward. 'But *I* think you need to find a way to take him out before he can get to you.'

'So what?' I say with a huff. 'Then the next person who wants to take over can try *their* hand at killing me?' I push my plate away. 'Sorry, guys, but I don't really want to be killed.'

'Okay,' Jamie cuts in. 'Say you drop out. Do you really think there's anyone else here who's suitable?' He spins around on the bench and looks out into the sea of people. I look at a table of Trues, about our age, though a few look a bit younger, maybe fifteen. They're laughing as one of them plays with their dagger, stabbing in-between his fingers as fast as he can, into the wooden table. Next, Jamie gestures to a table of families. Children run around the table, knocking into people and ducking away from slaps, dancing to the music of the band that's just started up. Parents drink and eat, shouting and laughing with each other. Women arm wrestle while men sort piles of knives, trading and testing them out together.

Jamie's right. No one in this room stands out to me as remotely suitable. No one except Jamie or Kit, both of whom deny they can do the job.

Why do they think I *can, of all people?*

'That fire really threw off the dinner service. A lot of people will be hungry tonight,' I say with a sigh, trying to change the subject.

Jamie smiles. 'See? That's exactly why you're right for this job, Teddy. You see these things. You have that Metropolis order in your head, you'll be able to help us set up better systems, so people don't get "first-come-first-served" meals!'

'No, I mean, whose fault is it that they're hungry? It's *mine.*'

'Don't you think we would have said something if we didn't think it was going to work?' Jamie's eyes blink bright blue and earnest from behind his tawny lashes. I can't deny he *looks* sincere, even if I can't fully believe what he's saying.

'I guess,' I sigh.

'Look,' Kit says, sitting back at the table and picking at the remains of all our dinners, 'at the end of the day, you know how the Metropolis works. No one here gets it like you do, not even Jamie. These suckers all forget that most of the people down here came from the City anyway. Paula just managed to brainwash them into thinking that everything associated with "up there" was evil. The idiots forget that's still where all their food, medicine, clothes, *everything* comes from. We all came from up there at some point.'
'Except you,' I tease.

'Of course, I'm from outta your world.' She stands up and spins around. 'You *know* you're the rightful leader, so you might as well get used to it.'

Kit smiles and grabs our now empty plates, carrying them over to the chutes. She's right. *I made my fate.*

twenty/four

The lights across the dining hall dim significantly to save our limited electricity and serve as a reminder that it is now 'late evening'. I nod my head along to the band as the music amps up a notch.

'Okay team, I've got an all-nighter tonight,' Kit says as she returns to our table. As one of the senior medical staff, Kit often works overnight. Every clan has its own responsibilities, but all clans share the three medical centres.

We say our goodbyes and Jamie and I begin walking back to my room. Someone always walks me to my room. At first, I thought it was so I wouldn't get lost in Clan Ember's maze, but more recently it feels like a safety precaution. When it's just Kit and me, or the three of us together, we chat and joke around, our laughter rebounding off the dark green tiles. It's different now that it's just Jamie and me. There's something about the way he keeps pace next to me, something *intimate*, as we weave through the dark passageways. People bustle past carrying boxes marked 'distribution to outer suburbs only' as well as musical instruments and other contraband – *Not contraband.*

There's a sharp hissing sound, and I notice a group of people spraying paint onto a wall in bright, elaborate colours. I'm still getting used to the fact that art is legal here.

Occasionally Jamie's hand brushes against mine as we walk. I try to convince myself it's by accident – just the movement of each step. But somehow, I know it's not. Every few steps, he glances at me. I push my shoulders back and straighten my spine. There's a loud thud, and I stumble into him as two children run past shouting at each other. He smiles at my reaction. I'm constantly inundated with new sounds. Fighting, music, laughter. *So much laughter.* Life is so hard down here, yet I've never known people to laugh so much, so *easily*. At first, it made me uncomfortable, but now I wish I could laugh with everyone. I still don't feel like I'm allowed to, though – only with Kit and Jamie. To everyone else I'm still an outsider, a witness to their jokes but not a part of them.

We round a corner and I stop for a second as the lights are dimmed further, now barely a whisper. Every lamp we pass casts a looming shadow of Jamie against the wall. I look at the hard cement floor, trying to ignore his gaze. It's hard to believe our ancestors built this place. An atomic-bomb shelter. *What would they think if they could see us now?* With my head still down, I look at Jamie's worn boots and notice his pace begin to slow. I glance at him, his eyes shining through his mop of messy brown hair.

'So?' He's looking at me, arms crossed in front of his chest.

The corridor is deserted.

'What is it?' I ask, suspicion creeping into my voice.

'I spoke to Michelle – the head of Clan Gaia.'

'Oh.' I push away the disappointment. *What were you expecting?*

'She sent a note today saying she wants to meet you. She's heard a lot, and I think it would be an excellent idea. You need to build allies – more than just me and Kit. You need to let the other clans know that you're on their side, and Michelle heads the second biggest after ours.' I cross my arms then uncross them again, letting my hands hang limply by my sides.

'Don't you remember what Kit said five minutes ago about me keeping my head down and lasting one more week?' I say with a huff. He laughs, deep and resonant, then takes a step closer, closing the narrow gap between us. My pulse quickens, and I glance up the corridor to see if we're alone.

What does it matter if someone sees us?

'I know what Kit said, that's why I waited to tell you now,' he murmurs. 'But I also know what I'm saying. Michelle could be a useful ally. She's the youngest Clan Leader in the Underground. I know Kit wants you to keep your head down. She'll probably say you shouldn't meet Michelle, but that's more because of some grudge she holds against her . . . even though they've never even met!' He's waving his hands vaguely, and I laugh. That sounds very, *very* Kit. My thoughts are interrupted as he takes my hand in one of his, sliding the other behind my back. I exhale, and lose the sensation of being watched for the first time since I left the embers of the fire. Now both his hands are around my waist. 'Anyway.' He tucks a loose strand of hair behind my ear, leaving the skin burning where his fingers skimmed my flesh. 'How do you feel?' I don't know how to answer. I know how I feel right now.

Confused, angry. Hungry . . . for him.

And afraid.

I blink slowly and breathe in his musky scent, like damp forest soil at midnight. We're standing so close I could count his eyelashes. I take a breath in to speak, then press my hands into his chest and push him back.

We're no longer alone.

Coming down the walkway is an old man carrying a basket filled with bread rolls. The chains on the waist of his pants clink with rounds of keys.

'Excuse me,' he mumbles in a thick accent. Once he's out of sight, the moment has passed.

We start walking again. I can feel the air between us tingling.

We turn the last bend before my room and Jamie stops. He smiles at me, the same warm smile he gave me that afternoon in the cafe. I wish I could think of something to say, but I have nothing. We walk the last few metres in awkward silence until we reach my door. Something is different. My hand flies out to grip his arm.

'What the hell?' Jamie says.

'What is it this time?' I say, stepping forward.

Three notes are screwed into my door, curls of metal springing out of them. Whoever put these here wanted everyone to see. Jamie steps past me, tearing the notes down. He's silent, and it's terrifying. I turn to check if anyone is nearby, but there's no one.

You are not our leader

BRN Bitch *BRN*

Sunlight scum

twenty/five

My bed is lumpy, and my shower was cold. I'm lucky I got a shower at all. It was too late to have a hot shower. In the Underground, your showers are always cold unless you get up really, *really* early, before everyone else. I'm fast learning that cold is the general temperature of most things down here.

Jamie wouldn't leave. He waited outside the shower room, just five doors down from my own room, then escorted me back those same ten metres. After we got back to my room, Jamie insisted he come in again. It was nothing like the first time I had been alone in my room with him, though.

I watched him pace, furious. I'd never seen him so mad, so passionate about something. *Assholes*, he barked, pacing back and forth. *Who do they think they are?* I'd stood there silently, watching him swear and mutter to himself. *When I find out who did this.* But I already knew. I still know.

Link.

I begged him not to tell Kit. She was already trying to control *everything* I do. She won't let me be alone at all if she finds out. Finally, I managed to convince him to leave so I could sleep.

I'm not sleeping, though, and the silence is almost deafening. I take some deep breaths, rolling my grandmother's ring between my fingers. It has a calming effect. I bring the silver ring close to my face and read the engraving inside the thin band again: *love is all.* The dim light from my lamp makes the silver shine brightly, even in my dingy room. My 'room', which feels more like a cell, is about one-quarter of the size of my Metropolis bedroom.

I slip the ring back on my finger and turn over to face the patched metal door. I'm feeling sick from everything that has happened today. Jamie's been gone for half an hour. I managed to convince him I was okay, but I haven't been so successful in convincing myself. I need to sleep, but I can't. Part of me is mad at myself for insisting he leave, just like I'm still annoyed that I pushed him away in the corridor.

What is wrong with you?

Eventually I resort to counting the rivets on the back of the door. It doesn't help, though; my mind just won't shut down.

There is no denying I'm the target – *the outsider*. I don't *want* it to be about me, but I know even Kit, who looks for the rational and not Teddy-centred reason for everything, wouldn't be able to find an alternative this time. I consider what Jamie said about meeting Michelle.

He might be right. Maybe it is time for me to start building allies.

Several times, I've asked Kit about meeting the other Clan Heads, and almost always received the same answer: *Not now.* It's starting to feel like she means *not ever.*

They're dangerous, and you're still too new to all this. They've all been doing this much longer than you. I don't want them to take advantage of you. They're not to be trusted. And Paula was? I roll over and hit my head on the back of the metal cot. *Why is everything metal down here?*

Grumbling, I get up off the bed and open the tiny cupboard built into the wall, where my grey backpack holds my notebook. It feels heavier than I remember, reliable and comforting in my hands. I shove the bag and the remainder of my old life back into the cupboard and shut the door. *You've got fifteen minutes.* Kit's voice echoes in my head from when we went to collect my belongings. *I'll help you,* Jamie had offered as we crouched under my bedroom window.

No, I need to do this alone.

Shaking off the memory, I walk over to the desk and grab a pencil from the packet Mum gave me. Then, sitting cross-legged on the hard cot, I open to a new page and draw a straight line down the centre, relishing the smoothness of the pencil on the paper. It's soothing. I draw a plus at the top of one column and a minus for the other, and begin listing the pros and cons of meeting up with

Michelle.

Pros: She's young and might relate to me. She has the second largest clan so she must be good at influencing people. I need to see what other clans look like (they can't all be the same).

Cons: She could be working with whoever 'they' are. It could be a trap, and they could try and kill me. Death.

I put the pencil down.

Those are some pretty compelling cons.

But at this point, it's either be killed by Michelle before my probation is over, or be killed by Link afterwards. I turn the page and start sketching. Without thinking, I begin to draw figures – people around a fire.

When I finish, I look at the page in my hands and see what I've drawn. It's the scene from earlier. I'm not sure if the details are accurate or if they're just fake faces I've conjured from my imagination, but the page is covered in them. A sea of angry sneers and furrowed brows. And in the middle of the drawing is one blank face.

Me.

I snap the book shut and put it on the floor beside me, finally allowing myself to enjoy the solitude.

I *am* going to meet Michelle.

At this point, I don't have anything to lose.

twenty/six

The next morning I navigate the familiar route to the dining hall. It doesn't feel like morning. It never does. Living down here feels like one long, never-ending night, and when I feel the way I do today, it's not such a good thing. I just want to feel the sun on my face and see some blue sky.

As I enter the big dining hall, I'm instantly hit with the buzz of activity around me.

'Give it back!' a boy shouts as an older girl runs past, brushing against me. Her coat is studded with nails, and it scratches my arm as she dashes past. She's holding a ball above her head. 'GIVE IT!' the boy shouts.

I keep weaving through the bustling hall. This morning it seems like *everyone* from the clan is here. Not a single table is free, and children sit in circles on the floor, munching their toast under the gaze of watchful parent-teachers. After breakfast, they'll start their lessons in reading, writing and hand-to-hand combat – much to my initial horror. *You never know when you gotta go*, Kit had told me with a smile, holding up her fists. *It's almost like our entire existence is punishable by death or something.*

The delivery women and men sit with huge empty bags at their feet, like deflated parachutes, ready to be filled up in the supply room, so they can begin their deliveries across the clans.

The young messengers are my favourite group to watch. I hear them laughing as I grab a bowl and fill it with what looks like rolled oats and dried raisins.

'Never have I ever . . .' one of them starts, his voice dropping to a whisper until the whole group bursts into laughter again, one of the girls so overcome with the giggles she rolls back, bumping into an old woman. The woman's bowl flies from her hands, landing with a splat. Steaming with rage, she grabs the child by the ear. The girl shrieks and her mum jumps up from another table. As the two women start shouting at each other, the children scatter, keen to avoid being punished for the wasted food.

I sidle past unnoticed and stand in line, waiting for my breakfast. The couple in front of me are locked in each other's arms. The taller man's hands keep straying to the seat of his partner's pants and the other keeps elbowing him. *But then he pulls him closer.* I crane my neck, looking for my friends. Jamie raises his head from further down the line and holds up two bowls. I smile and step out of the line, jogging over to meet him.

'Thanks,' I say, taking the bowl from him as we walk over to our table.

'Of course,' he says. 'You okay?'

'Yeah, I'm fine,' I say with a smile. 'I've decided I do want to meet Michelle.'

His face perks up a bit at this. 'Hey, maybe don't mention the notes to Kit. She's in one of her mad-at-Zelda moods, and we'd have to mention Michelle so I don't want her to explode,' he says. I roll my eyes as we sit down at the table. Zelda and Mark say hi, but Kit just nods.

She pushes her empty bowl away and cocks her head to the side. 'Wow, you decided to make it!'

I look over at Jamie, who shakes his head almost imperceptibly. *Ride it out.*

'*I'm* the one who worked all night, and I still managed to get here.' She grabs her mug and takes a swig. 'These buffoons were out half the night, and *they* still made it.' She slams her cup down, spilling coffee over the table. 'What were you up to?'

Her eyes bore into me, and I lift a spoonful of the cement-porridge up to my lips, willing myself not to blush.

'You think I didn't hear?' she asks. I choke down the gooey concoction, not bothering to chew. 'Don't lie,' she says, before I even have a chance to answer. 'I can't believe you brought a *cat* down here!'

I feel the tension slide out of me. *She's not talking to me.*

Zelda pushes her hair back off her shoulders and shrugs. 'I rescued a kitten,' she says, smiling. Kit narrows her eyes. 'They get killed if they're out at night. If he's got no collar, then he's got no family. You know that's Metropolis law.'

'Yeah, and the law down here says that no one can have pets!'

Zelda crosses her arms. 'It's not official.' 'I say it is,' Kit retorts.

I square my shoulders, sitting up straighter on the bench, and open my mouth to speak. *Kit's not in charge.* But then I glance around the table. Zelda is pouting, but I realise it's just a performance. Mark rubs her back, and Kit starts eating his leftover porridge.

They've all been friends since they were children and I'm learning this is how people react down here; angry and openly emotional, but they all seem to understand the subtle unspoken conversation. I haven't felt so homesick as I do right now. *But even at home, I didn't have what they do.*

Zelda pokes out her bottom lip. 'Rita said he could live in the sorting room.'

'Alright,' Kit says with a resigned sigh.

The conversation moves on, and I shift uncomfortably on the bench. Not telling Kit about the notes on my door feels awfully close to lying. I glance at Jamie. Then suddenly I remember: last night Zelda and Mark went to the surface for the first pick-up at the new locations!

'Any news from above?' I ask Mark as he takes a sip of the sludge they call coffee down here. Even though I haven't known them for that long, Zelda and Mark seemed like natural choices to be on our new pick-up team, primarily because they've both worked in supplies for years.

'Nothing new, other than the increased patrols,' he replies. 'But you two are going up tomorrow night, aren't you?' Kit looks up, smiling for the first time. She wiggles her eyebrows. 'Be careful,' Zelda adds. 'It's crazy right now, so many guards.' 'They're like cockroaches,' I mutter.

'They are!' Zelda agrees, laughing. 'That is such a good

description.' I smile, happy to feel like I'm a part of the conversation.

'And you're going to see Michelle today?' Kit asks, not looking up from her porridge.

I glance at Jamie, confused.

'Um . . .'

'Like I said, Michelle asked to see you,' Jamie explained. I feel my brows pinch.

'But I only just told you I wanted to go.'

'I know. Look, Michelle is kind of –' 'Weird,' Kit says smugly.

'I was going to say, *different*. If you don't tread carefully, Michelle can –'

'Turn into a blood-sucking monster?' Kit offers.

'Helpful,' Mark says, shoving her off the bench.

She laughs. 'She'll see what I mean,' she says, tapping her teeth.

Jamie slams his cup down, levelling a look at Kit. 'She is unique, and so are you. I think that's why you might get along. Anyway, I had already said yes because it's easier to cancel something than wait a week to do it.'

'So when am I seeing her?' I glance over at Kit, trying to gauge her reaction. She looks past me and waves then winks at someone over my shoulder. Within a second her bright eyes are locked onto mine, and she smiles.

'Today,' Jamie says, and I notice Kit roll her eyes.

'I think you have some lessons to learn, and I'm sure Michelle is one of them,' she says.

'Do you know her?' I ask tentatively. I notice Zelda smother a laugh by picking up her mug.

'*No*. But I also don't need to – I'm not the one with enemies.' I'm taken aback, but she's right. She shrugs. 'Look, I know we haven't talked about it much, but I understand you feel like Link is a threat. I know that the more allies you have, the

better you'll feel. I just don't want you to –' 'Die?' I ask, raising an eyebrow.

'No, silly – I don't want you to have a new best friend.' With that, she stands up and goes to talk to someone behind me. I look at the others, shaking my head.

'Well, that went surprisingly well.'

'That was amazing,' Zelda says, her eyebrows halfway to her hairline.

Jamie turns to me. 'Forget about Link and Petra too. I'm going to suss everything out. They're playing a political game, remember that. They don't want to take you out overnight. Their plan will only work if they can turn *everyone* against you.'

Cause that makes me feel better.

'And to accomplish it by next week,' Kit adds as she re-joins our group, standing behind Jamie and resting her elbows on his shoulders. I tense.

He is not yours.

'Yes,' Jamie says, nodding slowly, 'and there are so many people here who are on your side! Think of Zelda and Mark.' He gestures across the table and they pose, smiling with their hands under their chins.

'Zelda and Mark who have supplies to sort, and a kitten to feed,' Zelda adds, flashing a wink to Kit as they get up from the table. 'Good luck,' she says to me with a smile, and they head off.

'Let's get going,' Kit says, grabbing my hand and pulling me up from the table, away from my now-cold oats. 'We have something to show you before you go to meet Draculette.'

twenty/seven

Kit power walks through the clan, and I struggle to keep up. I have no idea where we're going. We pass my room and I hold my breath, hoping Kit doesn't notice the holes screwed into the metal door. As we pass, I feel Jamie's hand press gently against the small of my back. I relax at his touch. We take bend after bend. It could be weeks before anyone found you if you got lost in these tunnels. These are the same tunnels where the clan-less Outskirters linger. Kit stops abruptly and checks over her shoulder, then slips between the walls to our left and shimmies down a corridor only a sliver wider than Jamie's shoulders. It would be easy to miss, nothing more than a shadow in the monotonous dark walls.

'Where are we going?' I ask. Jamie chuckles behind me, and I feel the sound of it send a warm tingle down my spine. Kit just keeps walking as if I haven't spoken. We stop in front of a tall metal door, and she pulls out a key that slides effortlessly into the oversized lock. After three rhythmic clicks, the heavy door swings open.

'In,' Kit instructs us, still glancing over her shoulder.

Once inside, she heaves the door shut, and the overpowering silence hits me.

'Welcome to your new home,' Kit says. She throws the key on the desk in the middle of the room, then she turns to face me with her hands spread wide. 'Whaddya think?'

'I can hardly see,' I say, just as the lights buzz on and Jamie whoops softly from the doorway.

I lean against the table. 'Where are we?'

Now lit up, the room reveals itself to be as impressive as it is disappointing. It's hard to see past the mess that covers every surface. Books, papers and piles of food are everywhere, along with tons of unopened boxes. There is a small bed in the corner and a door to another room. Kit walks over and opens it, poking her head in.

'This is Paula's old quarters – neat, it looks like she never even used this bathroom,' she says from the door.

'It has its own bathroom?' I ask, stepping towards her.

'Yeah, this place is fancy! She was hardly here.'

'Why not? There's so much space,' I say, spinning around and taking in the oversized room.

'Honestly, I have no idea,' Kit says, and I feel my heart squeeze for her as a shadow passes over her face. *She's hiding that darkness inside.*

'It was used more like a storage space,' Jamie says from the other side of the room, his arms loaded up with boxes of tissues. 'I thought it was time we upgraded our new Clan Head.' He shoots me a wink as he puts down the boxes.

'We need those at the medical centre!' Kits says, launching forward to snatch one of the small boxes and hugging it to her chest.

'She really has a lot of stuff in here. It looks like a store.' I move around the room, looking at all the supplies that would be invaluable to the Underground.

'How did you *not* know what was going on?' Jamie asks, snooping through another box. I look at Kit in time to see the hurt flash across her face as the shadow around her darkens. It's not just the betrayal, which I think she's still processing. It's the feeling of having been stupid, for not having seen the signs.

I understand exactly how she feels.

Kit shrugs and ignores him. I smile at her. *Blind faith can be powerful.* In two steps she's next to me, her hands gripping my forearms, her eyes challenging and severe. 'Why do you think meeting Michelle is a good use of your time?' 'Because she needs allies,' Jamie answers.

'I was asking Teddy.'

'And I was saving her having to answer your stupid question.'

'Oh, so I'm dumb *and* stupid now? Nice.'

'What? I never said you were dumb –'

She shoulders past him and starts flicking through the piles of papers. There's an intimacy in their friendship that I envy. I questioned Kit about it not long after I moved down here. *Ew. He's like my brother!* she'd said. That left me to assume the fighting was familial . . .

'Teddy needs to keep a low profile!'

'She needs allies!'

'She has us!'

'I thought you were okay with it?' I say, stepping between them. Kit turns and glares at me.

'I am,' she says through gritted teeth.

'Riiiight,' I say softly, walking away and leaving them to their bickering.

I start organising supplies into piles: food, tools, medicine and miscellaneous. If there's anything that I think will be useful to the three of us, I put that it in a separate pile – currently the smallest. Going through Paula's things doesn't reveal much about her. As Jamie said, the room feels like a storage space. There is nothing personal here.

I notice that the room feels warmer. I turn around and see Jamie climbing off his knees, the orange light of a heater happily blinking in the corner. *Fancy indeed.*

'Great. Teddy, you'd better get ready, you're off to meet

Michelle,' Kit snaps. 'Take a knife; you'll probably need it.'

'Are you being serious?' I ask her, glancing at Jamie.

Kit looks between us, then rolls her eyes. 'Of course, you won't take *my* word for it.' She climbs onto the table, sitting cross-legged on top, disregarding all the papers. 'You need to understand how dangerous she is. If she thinks you're weak – if *any* of the Clan Heads think you're weak,' she draws a finger across her throat, reminding me of Petra, in the dining hall.

These Underground people certainly have a flair for drama.

'I'm not exaggerating,' she says. She climbs off the table, sending a shower of loose papers to the floor, and starts loading a bunch of supplies into some big backpacks that Jamie found in another beat-up cardboard box. With her back to me she continues. 'Every Clan Head would *love* to grow their own clan by absorbing another.'

'Look what I found,' Jamie says, dusting his hands off on his jeans.

'Paula's file,' Kit says softly stepping forward to snatch it from his hands. He lifts it high over her head and passes the green folder to me.

'Legend says it's where Paula kept everyone's *secrets*. You might get a better understanding of what you're up against.' Jamie winks at us both. Kit rolls her eyes, shouldering an overstuffed bag.

'Have fun meeting pointy teeth.'

'What?' I ask, but Jamie just waves her off.

'Ignore her, she's just a pest,' Jamie says, shooting Kit a look.

'I've got to get these to the medical centre and start my shift,' she says, her voice icy – and then she's gone.

Neither Jamie nor I move for a moment, letting the dust settle after Kit's hurricane of energy passes.

'I'll be walking there with you.'

I try not to show it, but I feel better knowing that.

I don't need him.

I'm certain Jamie would never suggest something that would put me in danger, and Kit knows that too.

'So, what do you think of your new room?' he asks finally, crossing his arms.

'Other than the mess, it's . . . perfect. I can't believe it has its own shower too!' I say, stuffing more valuable supplies into the other packs Kit left behind. The room looks bigger now that the piles of supplies are getting sorted. I notice a mattress in the corner – a *real* bed, not one of the thin cot rolls. It's still wrapped in plastic. Unused.

Did Paula ever sleep?

'Why didn't you guys show me this place when I first came down here?' I ask Jamie, trying to clear the thought of Paula and her mysteries from my mind.

'I don't know. One of Kit's decrees. Honestly, I don't think she was ready for the change right away.'

'For someone who didn't want to become the Clan Head, she sure loves being the boss.'

Jamie laughs and nods, hoisting a full pack onto his back. I pass him another, and he pulls it onto his front.

'Yes, she does.' Our eyes meet, and I move towards him.

I want to be closer to him, to feel his heat, but the overstuffed bag keeps us at a distance.

'You coming?' he asks.

I open the green file and almost drop it when a photo of Link stares back at me. I shut the file and slide it into the side of the smaller bag then follow Jamie out of the room.

✕

We walk together in silence, loaded up with supplies, until we reach the sorting room. It is buzzing like I've never seen it.

'More goodies?' a woman calls out from across the overstuffed supply room. People are busy everywhere, tossing things into piles and stuffing them into bags for inter-clan distribution. 'Excellent! Kit told us there was more to come. Can't wait to see what else that betraying bitch was hoarding – s tuff has been literally coming out of the walls.'

Rita smiles, soft wrinkles crinkling the corners of her eyes. I haven't seen her since her birthday party, but she looks just as radiant working down here, her skin still sparkling. 'People should be worshipping the ground you walk on, girl!' I sigh.

If only they were.

Before I can respond, Zelda runs across, stepping over black boxes filled with random objects; cans of food, socks, toilet paper. She grabs both the packs I'm carrying.

'You do an amazing job in here,' I say, gesturing to the buzzing room.

'Shah!' Rita says, her curly orange hair bouncing as Jamie puts his arm around her. 'Things are generally good – unless Tony is working.'

I notice a few people chuckle. 'I do what I can to keep things moving. I'm glad you're making good friends down here.' She looks at Jamie beside her, then smiles, winking at me. I feel the heat rush to my cheeks. I brave a glance at Jamie, but he's already turned around, handing his packs off to Mark.

Did he hear what Rita said?

'This one's a good egg,' Rita says, reaching up to scruff his hair as Jamie turns back to her. I look away. It feels like I'm intruding on a private moment. 'You know, Teddy, you should come and hang out here with us sometime. We like to change things up around here – variety!' Rita shouts.

'It's the spice of life!' everyone else in the room replies, whooping and cheering. I notice Zelda roll her eyes as she holds a tiny black kitten in her arms.

Jamie and I bid Rita goodbye and wave to Mark and Zelda up the back. It feels good to know there are people down here I can trust. *Correction: People I think I can trust . . .*

This is just complicated.

'Not everyone is against you,' Jamie says, as if he's been in my head. He's right. It's nice to have people smile when they talk to me.

I can do this.

I feel the back of Jamie's hand brush mine, and I pull away, swapping my grip on the folder I had rescued before Zelda took the supplies from me.

What's wrong with me?

As we walk, I hold up the picture of Link for Jamie to see. He takes it from me gently and turns the print around. There on the back, in scrawled handwriting, is a list. *Names.*

'Links crew, I think,' he says passing it back to me. 'So much for her secret file.'

'Can I drop this back at my room before we go to see Michelle?' I ask Jamie. He nods. We detour past my room silently, and I slip the key into the lock and toss the folder onto my small cot-bed.

'Ready?' Jamie asks, leaning against the wall, a sly smile tugging at the corner of his lips. I step back into the corridor, locking the door behind me, and nod once.

'Let's go.'

twenty/eight

Jamie walks briskly beside me, leading the way. We don't speak. The torches we're carrying are the only lights in this long corridor, making it hard for me to read his expression. I'm getting better at finding my way around our clan hub, but it never ceases to amaze me how the people from down here remember their way around this rabbit warren.

We've been walking for about an hour and a half. My fitness has really improved since living down here, and I hardly feel any discomfort as we weave through the corridors. We're far from any clan activity here. It's eerie, like the catacombs we learnt about in school, where skeletons were kept after wars in ancient times.

'How long do you spend down here at a time?' I ask, trying to muster some sort of conversation.

'When Paula was in charge, I was doing about one month on, one month off.'

'Did the people down here trust you?'

'Mostly,' he says quickly. 'Who wouldn't?' He turns and his eyes crinkle, holding in a laugh. I feel the colour rise in my cheeks, and I'm glad of the cover of shadows. 'I *was* going to be living full time in the City once we were Partnered,' he says, answering the question I hadn't dared to ask.

After what feels like forever, Jamie stops and shines his torch a few feet ahead, illuminating a worn white line, a vague representation of a border. As I look out, I see nothing but darkness. My eyes focus on a pinprick of light, perhaps a distant torch.

'Please tell me you're coming with me,' I say, unease settling into my bones. *I'll be walking there with you.* That is what Jamie said . . . *isn't it?*

'No, I can't go with you. Michelle doesn't really like people from outside coming into her clan. It's *almost* surprising that she wants to meet with you.' He notices the panic on my face and puts a hand on my shoulder. 'But you're both Clan Leaders, so this is normal. Don't worry, I'm not *too* suspicious.' He looks around, eyes darting nervously. I feel lightheaded.

Then he starts laughing.

Some joke.

'You are going to stay here the entire time, though?' I try to keep the pleading out of my voice. He nods, and I can feel my palms getting sweaty as they hang limply by my sides.

'What do I talk about? What do I *not* talk about?' The questions tumble out, and I feel lost. 'What did Kit mean about pointy teeth?'

He chuckles softly and steps closer, putting his other hand on my left shoulder. 'You'll see. Just make sure you go in there with your eyes open. It's a chance for you to look around; see another side of the Underground. Take in Michelle, see how she does things. It's her opportunity to do the same.'

I take a deep breath, and I'm hit with every worst-case scenario my brain can conjure.

'You've been down here for weeks, Teddy. You have allies. You have Kit.' He pauses, pushing a loose strand of hair away from my face. 'You have me.'

'What if she's working with Link and it's all a plan to kill me?'

'You really think I'd send you to your death if I thought that was likely?' He lets go of my shoulders, and I immediately miss the weight of his hands. 'You're the toughest girl I've ever met. You've made your transition down here seem easy. Seriously, if they didn't know where you're from, they'd never guess.' I swallow.

Is he right? Do I fit in down here?

I try to slow my breathing, but I can't help the rush of panic that keeps bubbling to the surface. I feel his warm hands on my shoulders again.

'I think you need to believe in yourself,' Jamie says, smiling.

I bite out a laugh, but it doesn't sound like my laugh.

It sounds far away and manic.

'I know that sounds a bit woo woo, but I'm serious.'

I look away from him, into the darkness on the other side of the clan line, and squint to get a better look at the moving light. Jamie puts a hand on my cheek and turns my face gently back to his.

'Listen. Michelle isn't so difficult. All you need to do is *be yourself.* Everyone knows you're new down here, there are no crazy expectations. You're smart, you know how to talk to people. You just did it there with Rita. Michelle is young, and she was born down here, she likes fun and novelty. Lean into that.'

I feel like there's a lead weight in my stomach, and I'm worried that if I break his gaze, the weight will drag me down deeper into the molten core of the planet.

'You were born for this,' he says, and I close my eyes, feeling the warmth of his breath on my cheeks. I'm not sure if he means what he's saying or if he's just trying to distract me. Whatever his intention, *it's working.* 'I don't know where all this doubt is coming from. Everyone who takes the time to know you loves you. Zelda, for one, can't stop singing your praises. Don't let one small group affect how you feel.' I start to scoff, and he stops me. 'Hey – I'm serious. Link and his followers are just one small group in the grand scheme of the Underground. Win Michelle over, and you'll have more backing than Link could dream of.'

I open my eyes again. His face is earnest, light lines of worry carved across his forehead. 'We would all be dead right now if it weren't for you – Michelle included. *She owes you.* Everyone down here does.' He shrugs. 'It's just that some people don't realise the huge personal risk you've taken to save us.'

'Alright,' I say, putting my hand across his mouth. 'Enough with the pep talk or my head won't fit in this corridor anymore.'

He chuckles again, flicking off his torch, and I start to let myself relax. I look out into the darkness and see that the light is getting closer, casting a long shadow of a man, still quite some distance away. Jamie's words are rattling around in my brain. The idea that I saved the Underground has never occurred to me. *Maybe he's right.* It was *my* plan, after all.

Maybe I am the right person to lead?

I turn back to him and open my mouth. Before I have a chance to speak, I feel his warm lips pressing against mine. My eyes widen and then close as I lean into him. I let my hand slip into his hair, my fingers curling, pulling him closer. His arms snake tighter around my body, and his lips part, offering and tempting, leaving me hungry for more. His hand is on the back of my neck, drawing me even closer. I don't know what I had expected a kiss to feel like, but this . . . It's something else. I can't find any words to describe how it feels as my thoughts are clouded by the warmth of his lips, his arms.

I press closer again, and then – his touch is gone.

✕

I stagger back, gently touching my fingers to my swollen lips. Jamie pulls out his torch again, flicking it on. The figure with the lamp is fast approaching now. Jamie whispers something to me under his breath, but I miss it, busy trying to smooth my hair, hoping he can't hear my heart rattling around in my rib cage. He grabs my hand and presses it against his lips, stilling my nervous energy.

We step forward as our visitor comes into view, glowing in the yellow light. 'You are going to be brilliant,' says Jamie. 'You're going to make her fall in love with you, just like –'

Just like what? I want to ask, but I don't get the chance. Now that the lantern is closer, I can see two people are approaching. *Great.* I stand back as Jamie steps forward to talk to them. With all our lights here now it's much brighter, and I can see them better. They must be twins. They have midnight-black skin and hair. One of them has red ribbons braided into his hair, which is tied up in little buns across his head. The other brother has green braided into his hair, twisted flat against his scalp in the most beautiful and intricate patterns, the green woven through like little rivers. I feel awkward loitering behind Jamie as he laughs and jokes with them. *Everyone likes him.* An unexpected wave of pride rushes through me, and I'm quick to push it away. He's not mine to feel proud of.

'Hey, brother,' Red says as they clasp arms.

'Too long, Ricka, and you, Herma.' Jamie clasps Herma's arms now too. 'How's it been?'

'Keeping green, can't complain.'

'Seems like it's all moving well?'

'Nothing a little help can't handle.' The conversation is beyond me, but it seems like Ricka just made a joke.

As they start to laugh, I take a small step forward.

'This the girl?' Herma asks, looking at me with piercing eyes. There are scars on both his cheeks, healed into two sharp lines across the top of his already angular cheekbones. They make him look older and very intimidating.

'Yes,' Jamie says, putting his hand on my back to shepherd me closer. 'This is Teddy, Clan Head of Ember.' Jamie turns to me with a warm smile. 'You'll go with them now. They're good guys, you'll be safe. I'll be waiting here when you return.'

'*If* I return,' I mumble, and Jamie gently grabs my chin again.

'Stop. It. You'll be back here soon, with Michelle as your new best friend.' He tilts his head, as if something just occurred to him. 'Maybe that *is* what Kit was worried about after all. Maybe she was just jealous.' He winks.

With his hand still cupping my chin, I look into his eyes, willing him to kiss me again.

He won't, not in front of these people.

He bends forward, gently pressing his lips against my own. Heat washes over me and, at that moment, time stops. I stop.

'Bye,' I barely manage to whisper as he steps back, and I turn to follow my guides across the border. One of the twins looks around, a smile playing on his lips as he wiggles his eyebrows at Jamie suggestively.

I look back one last time, but all I see is darkness. Jamie must have turned his torch off to conserve the battery.

I wave into the darkness anyway.

twenty/nine

We walk for about twenty minutes, guided only by the lantern Herma holds. After we reach the first clan light, he switches the lantern off. Their lighting system seems *way* more advanced than ours. Looking around, I can see that most of the lights are LEDs set on poles that look like the streetlamps up in the Metropolis. I look at the lantern Herma is holding by his side. *It's fake*, I realise. It looks like an oil lantern, but it has a cluster of LEDs inside. I'm interested in why they don't just use a standard torch.

'How do your lanterns work?' I ask.

I get no response as the two brothers walk silently in front of me.

'What's it like living here in Gaia? Do you all share mealtimes?' *Nothing.*

I cross my arms. I don't know why they were being all jokey and friendly with Jamie but are ignoring me.

'I know you guys can talk.'

Herma turns around and looks at me, one eyebrow raised.

'You're a sassy one,' he says. I put my hands on my hips. He turns back, and I notice the patterns in his hair all finish with beaded tendrils dangling around his neck, clicking softly as we walk. We continue forward a few paces. I try again.

'How long does it take to get your hair done like that?' I ask.

Ricka turns this time, flashing me a stern look. When he turns back around, I notice that the ribbons braided into his hair are covered in rhinestones. I take a step closer to get a better look. In that instant, a shadow darts into my peripheral vision, and I'm sent sprawling backwards across the floor. I gasp, trying to get air back into my lungs, and try to move, but there's something on me.

Someone.

A huge man is crushing me, his dead weight impossible to shift.

I try shouting, but it comes out like a wheeze.

'Hey!' Ricka shouts, rushing back to where I'm pinned. He rips the man off me, and I notice that my assailant is covered in blood.

'What do you think you're doing?' Ricka says, pushing the man. He staggers, clutching his bloody stomach.

'Look, I'm sorry, I don't mean no trouble.' He stumbles at another approaching form, and I notice a massive gash across his shoulder. I turn to find the twins facing another man, both with blades drawn. *I didn't see their weapons while we were walking.* The sheaths, now so obvious, hang empty by their sides.

'Let me past,' the approaching man growls. 'Let me past, you fools!' he shouts, a bloody dagger in his hand.

I look at my hands and see they're covered in blood from where I pushed against the man. I feel a wave of nausea roll my stomach.

'We'll give you a three-count then you're out,' Ricka growls. I glance behind me and see that the bleeding man has already gone, darting down a narrow alley.

'Three!' Herma shouts. *That wasn't a count.* The brothers lunge forward, swords out, but the other man has also gone, darting down another alley. I look around, suddenly acutely aware of my surroundings. Lanes and alleys branch off the corridor as far as the light will let me see, narrow and inconspicuous.

No wonder I didn't seen the man coming.

'Outskirter scum,' Herma mutters under his breath.

Ricka offers me a hand. 'Hurt or healthy?' he asks as his eyes scan me, presumably for injury. I take his hand and he pulls me to my feet, ignoring the stickiness of the blood coating my fingers.

'Thanks,' I say, wiping my bloody hands on my jeans.

'Hurt or healthy?' they ask again in unison.

'Ah – healthy,' I say. 'Seriously, I'm fine,' I lie. *What the hell was that?* The brothers nod and continue walking. I stop for a second, looking back. 'Shouldn't we go and see if that guy's okay?' I ask, jogging to catch up, tucking my hands under my armpits to try to stop them trembling. No response. I nod curtly to their backs.

Got it. Mind my own business.

I knew something was going to happen. But what else is ahead of me?

✖

By the time we're in what looks like the clan's central hub, my hands have stopped trembling. I let them hang by my sides as I follow the twins' brisk pace. The corridors are wider here – they don't really feel like corridors at all, they're more like Underground streets, with ceilings that seem even taller than the ones in Clan Ember. I look up at the network of pipes. Michelle's clan run the water supply for the Underground, so somewhere here they have big tanks of water, with hydraulic systems slowly siphoning what we need out of Metropolis's water basin. It's then distributed via pipes and containers to the other clans.

I look around and am struck by the difference to the tunnels of Clan Ember. It is bright. *So* bright. There are tall lamps everywhere, with hundreds of LEDs beating down. I close my eyes for a second and feel the warmth – it's almost enough to trick me into thinking I'm standing out in the sun. We weave through a gathering of people, all smiling and laughing.

'Dance with us, girl!' a tall woman says, grabbing my hand. I jerk it back, more out of habit than reluctance, but she doesn't seem to mind. Her friends step forward, laughing, and swirl around me, holding onto their skirts like brightly coloured wings. I spin, caught in the middle of them. For a second I'm smiling too, then I feel a rough hand on my arm.

'Come on, Ember,' Herma says gruffly. I wave goodbye to the women, but they don't notice at all, they're lost in the music – music! I can hear it everywhere. The steady beat of drums fills me to my core, so different to the drums I've become familiar with in Clan Ember. I see a group of men sitting around with big white buckets turned upside down in front of them. Heads bobbing, they all hit their buckets at different times, creating interesting patterns with the sound. They look up when we walk past.

'Oi!' the closest man says, smoke coming out of his mouth as he talks. 'You coming to the round session tomorra?'

The boys nod and keep walking. I want to stop and listen, to feel the beat and move my body to the rhythm, but the twins are well ahead of me now. I run to keep up. Soon a flock of children run in front of me, weaving around my legs and pulling at my arms. They're wearing colourful clothing. One little girl yanks my arm so hard I drop onto one knee. Up close, I can see that her dress isn't new or clean. It might be brightly coloured, but it's nothing more than dirty rags, hanging off her body. I look around and see that all the children are dressed in the same rags. They start climbing on me.

'Hey –' I say, trying to pull a little boy off my back. His leg hits me in the temple. 'Stop that.' I feel a hand in my pocket. Then another. I try desperately to get the children off me, but it's like they're connected: each one knows what they need to do.

'Begone!' a voice calls from somewhere outside of the web of children. 'Drop it and go before we find your families.'

It's Ricka. He stands, one hand on his hilt. The children scatter, screaming and laughing as they disappear down the surrounding alleyways. 'Get up, keep up, you're a stranger here. A target. You need to be careful.' He doesn't offer me his hand this time. I stand, picking up my torch from the dirt floor.

'You could have warned me about them.'

'Your warning is us here escorting you. For most people, *that* is enough warning.' Then he's off again. I take pains to keep up this time.

Nothing and no one will distract me.

Our path here seems to be more straightforward than in Clan Ember. While Ember is a knot of twists and turns, Gaia feels like everything is laid out on a simple grid. I'm almost confident I could make my way back. The number of people around us has increased, and most people move silently out of the brothers' path.

Out of fear or respect?

All the walls we pass have been painted white – multiple times if the peeling flakes of paint are anything to go by – and the doors are all shades of yellow, blue and green. After a few more minutes the street opens into a plaza. Hundreds of people mill about. I can hear more music: strings, brass, and fast drumming. Couples dance around a fake fountain, made from sculpted plastic water bottles. Everywhere people are laughing and eating together under colourful bunting. The smell of food fills my nostrils, and I realise how hungry I am. I look around, trying to find the source, but one of the twins taps my shoulder.

'This way,' Herma says. I follow them as they slip down a nondescript alley. There are no light posts here, and they switch on their LED lanterns.

As we start winding through the narrow alleys, my confidence about finding my own way around is fast dissolving.

I'd never make it back on my own.

The laughter and music have melted away behind us, and now all I can hear is the sound of our footsteps. We move quickly, left-right-right, and left again. There are too many turns for me to keep up.

'Stand here,' Ricka says, stopping abruptly. He turns my shoulders to face the wall. I do as I'm told and hear tapping and the clinking of metal behind me. 'Turn,' he says. I obey. Where previously there was only a wall, there's now a blue door. I take a step forward and brush my fingers over its perfect wooden surface.

'But how?' I whisper.

'You wait here,' Herma says while his brother unlocks the door. They disappear through it, closing it behind them.

A second passes. Then another.

It's so quiet.

I wonder if all Clan Heads have quarters this far away from the clan's main hub of activity.

Perhaps it's because people are afraid of them . . . or maybe it's to protect themselves.

thirty

*I**t's been too long.* I clench and unclench my fists as all those worst cases flood my mind again. *What if this is a set-up?* I try to calm myself by thinking about Jamie waiting for me at the border, but that slips into remembering what happened at the border . . . which sends my pulse racing for a different reason. I press the backs of my hands to my flushed cheeks.

After what has felt like an eternity, one of the twins returns, but he looks different – *he* is *different*. This third boy has blue wound into his hair. They must be triplets. He opens the door for me without a word, gesturing for me to enter.

'Hello,' I say awkwardly, stepping into a large courtyard. I hear the door bolt slide into place as he closes me in.

'My name is Carn. Follow me,' he says. As we walk, I look at his tunic. It's the same as his brothers', tight on his muscular body, almost shiny, with a short sword on the hilt. We walk a few metres down a short corridor until we reach more big doors. I notice him straighten his shoulders as he pushes one of the heavy doors open. It swings wide, revealing a room about the same size as our dining hall, except the floor and walls are covered with blue and white tessellated tiles, and the room is sparsely furnished. I'm startled when Carn announces loudly, 'Teddy, Probationary Head of Clan

Ember, Your Majesty.' *Your Majesty?*

I copy my guide's actions and bow.

'Teddy, may I introduce you to my sister, Michelle, ruler of Clan Gaia – keeper of no prisoners.' *Sister?* I look up, slightly confused, and watch the brother with blue in his hair march off to stand beside his brothers, who are sandwiched between two women holding towels and some fresh fruit. At the back of the room, my eyes rest on the raised platform in the centre of the wall. It's covered in cushions made from exotic silks, and there's a young girl lounging there. She must only be fourteen or fifteen, at the most.

As I eye her perched there, eating some of the delicious-looking fresh fruit, Jamie's words ring in my head: *She's the youngest Clan Leader in the Underground*, and Kit's warning too . . . *youngest and most dangerous.*

Could this be her? The notorious Michelle?

I take a tentative step forward, and the girl finishes her grape, smiling broadly. I stop. Her canine teeth are filed sharp, and there's a little gem glistening on each one. She stands up, and I force myself to keep moving. She is tiny, wrapped in a golden sari. Her tight black curls are pulled back from her face with a silk ribbon, springing and popping like a black cloud around her head. I try to avoid looking at her teeth, but it's almost impossible.

Why?

'So, you must be the new lover of Jamie?' the girl exclaims, her voice soft but loud. I feel the heat of my blush as she stands and then begins to sashay her way down from the podium of cushions, closing the gap between us. She grabs both my forearms and kisses me elaborately four times from cheek to cheek, her nails digging into my shoulders as she pulls me in for an embrace.

'And the *contentious* new leader of Clan Ember.' She pulls back, holding me at arm's length. '*Fascinating*,' she murmurs.

I feel dizzy from her fruity perfume, and my shoulders sting where her nails dug in.

'You are *fabulous*,' the word rolls off her tongue like honey, 'absolutely darling. I had no idea what to expect, but *you are better. Better* than any of my imaginings.'

'I'm happy to meet you too, Michelle,' I say, forcing a tight smile. *I called her Michelle.* I start to panic. *Am I allowed to call her Michelle?* She doesn't say anything, just walks me to the door, her arm linked through mine and her hand clenched over the top firmly. We walk until we reach a fork in our path, where Michelle turns left and leads me into a small garden. Except it isn't a garden. I brush my fingers across the leaves. *Fake.* She throws her head back and breathes deeply, as if it were fresh air. Guiding me over to a small stone bench, we sit, and I wait. After a moment's awkward silence, I shift under the headlamp. I tug at my shirt, which is starting to stick to me.

'So, why did you want to meet me?' I ask, breaking the silence with my bold question.

She smiles again, her sharp teeth flashing at me.

'I wanted to meet the competition.' Her tongue plays with the pointed edge of one tooth, and I can't hide my surprise. She laughs and puts her hand on my arm, her nails lightly raking across my white skin. 'I kid,' she chuckles lightly. 'I just wanted to meet you.' She bops me on the nose. It's patronising and calculated, and I see immediately why Kit and Jamie told me to be careful. 'There have been a few rumours flying around about the new leader of Clan Ember, and I am not one to listen to idle gossip.' *I bet you are.* 'I knew your predecessor Paula, unfortunately.' She shakes her head. 'What she did to the Underground is . . . is unforgivable.' She spits the words out. 'It wasn't her Underground to sell out. *I'm* not hers to sell out.' She's standing now.

'There's a reason I got rid of her,' I say. I grab her arm and pull her back onto the bench.

'I know that,' she croons, placing her hand on top of mine. 'Thank you.' Her eyes brim with sympathy. *Or is it pity?* Maybe it's because she understands the burden of being a leader in the Underground.

'Regardless, Teddy, it's still hard to shake that kind of history. You will need to work hard to convince people of your trustworthiness.' She points her finger at my chest.

'Of your *value.*'

She's right. Maybe that's why people have been resistant to me. They're scarred by their experience with Paula. Michelle interrupts my thoughts.

'I think it's about time that we had some more clan collegiality, to show our respective peoples that we're all friends – working together!' She smiles, then breaks into raucous high-pitched laughter.

I narrow my eyes, trying to work out if I've missed something. *Surely she's having me on.* A woman walks over to us. Her short green hair is pulled back from her face with little clips, and she's wearing the same black uniform as the triplets, with one exception – no sword. She holds out a tray. Michelle picks up two long-stemmed glasses and offers one to me. 'Blue drink?' she asks, pushing the glass into my hands. 'Try it, it's really delicious.'

I take it, not wanting to be rude, but give Michelle a puzzled look.

'Yes, I *know* it doesn't look blue, but it tastes blue. So, I called it "blue drink".' She smiles, then tinks her glass against mine. 'Drink up.'

I lift the tall, fluted glass to my lips and take a sip. Sweet, floral flavours. Nothing blue.

'This is amazing –' I say. 'I – I can't describe it.' Not a lie.

Michelle smiles knowingly as she picks up a grape from the tray.

'I know,' she muses. 'They made it, just for me. I missed my old world so much.' *Old world?*

'You can't be older than fifteen?' I ask. She shoots me a look.

'I'm fourteen, but I'll be fifteen in March, thank you very much, and yes, I'm from a tropical island.' She looks away.

I let the unasked question hang between us.

'Yes, I'm a True, but my family were from a tropical island, and I've always felt a great affinity to that. When we moved here, they brought a tin filled with old photos and trinkets, memories of their life before they moved to the Metropolis, and before the great war.' Her eyes are misty, lost behind the veil of memory, and she suddenly looks much older. 'That's why I say "my home",' she explains wistfully. 'It *should* have been. Selfish adults stole it from us, just like the selfish people up there steal our right to live our lives the way we want to. I'm sure you understand what I mean. Coming from up there and all.'

She points a finger up, then stands abruptly and throws her glass at the ground. It smashes, and I can't help the small squeal that escapes my lips. I stand up. A second later the triplets run in, swords drawn. They relax when they see the shattered glass.

'Clean!' Ricka shouts behind him, into the arched doorway he came through. A few seconds later another man runs in wearing a black tunic. It's simple and loose-fitting, different from the others. The man silently picks up the shards of the glass. When she's satisfied the glass has been cleared, Michelle sits back down.

Something settles deep within me – a message.

This isn't a 'meet and greet' at all. This is a warning: *Mess with me or my people in any way, and I will end you.*

✗

'Now, I will show you the pride and joy of my clan,' Michelle says, finally breaking the silence we'd settled into. She laughs gently and takes my hand, pulling me after her. We exit through the large wooden doors, and she begins leading me back through the maze of her home. She turns and flashes another smile, her bejewelled canines glinting under the bright lights. 'This place can be a bit of a rabbit warren if you're unfamiliar.' She winks at me.

As we manoeuvre through the streets of her clan, Michelle is treated like royalty. Walking alongside her offers a new perspective on the general unease in her district. Everything looks like it did before, but now the sheen has worn off, allowing me to see the reality of tattered clothes and dirty white walls.

As she passes, the people don't look happy or celebratory. *They look frightened.*

I also notice some kind of caste system in the colours people are wearing. I wonder if this has anything to do with the colours her brothers wear.

Michelle seems oblivious to any of the apparent discontent as some people sit on corners with sallow faces. She merely smiles at the children chasing us with their palms outstretched. The people are showing respect, keeping their distance, but I can sense something is brewing.

I feel a tug at my arm, and I notice Michelle has stopped. 'And this is it,' she says, gazing up at three massive plastic tents looming over us.

I follow Michelle inside the milky green enclosure. The air is hot and damp. Giant globes hang from the ceiling, throwing off heat like portable suns. They're shining over rows and rows of crops. I recognise a few from pictures in books at school. Corn, tomatoes, potatoes. But there are many I don't know. Michelle is glowing as she looks at the foliage surrounding us, her fingers gently stroking the green leaves. For the first time, she looks childlike, actually happy, and I realise this is the real Michelle. My thoughts are interrupted by a man hobbling towards us, a huge grin taking up most of his face.

'Good morning, Your Loveliness.' Something about the way the man smiles makes my skin crawl, and I don't know how she manages to put her hand forward for him to kiss with his wet lips. He straightens up, leaning against his stick. His shirt is blue and white, striped, and clean, but I can see the yellow of sweat stains along the collar and beneath his armpits.

'Kenny, I would like you to meet my friend, Teddy. She's the leader of Clan Ember.'

The man turns his deep-set eyes to me and takes a deep bow. I feel myself shift uncomfortably under his gaze, the humid air making the back of my neck sticky. He smiles, and I see his yellow teeth. His tongue flicks over them so quickly I wonder if I've imagined it.

'The marvel you see here,' she says with a swoop of her arm, 'is the reason you got to enjoy my delightful blue drink.'

I still have no idea what she's talking about, but I get the feeling I'm about to find out as Michelle takes my hand and pulls me around with such gusto, I almost trip on the twisting tubes and pipes that layer the floor. We wind around rows of fruit and vegetables.

'This is where it all comes from, the food we eat in Clan Gaia.' She holds my hand, leading me through to the next tent. Kenny follows close behind, his heavy breathing the only sound.

'Each tent has a different climate,' he explains, licking his lips.

'This tent will feel more normal to you. The left is the

most humid tent, and the right is very, very dry.' *Where are they getting all this equipment?*

Kenny slips back out through the green plastic curtains, and I'm relieved.

'This is my favourite room,' says Michelle as we pass through the curtains into the humid tent. She spreads her arms out and tilts her face up towards the solar lamps. I can feel the beads of sweat instantly start rolling down my spine.

There is a reason only one clan does pick-ups. The more people who are exposed above, the harder it is for us to monitor.

'It's amazing!' I say, feigning enthusiasm.

Michelle turns, genuinely beaming.

As I walk down one of the aisles, I gather the courage to ask, 'How have you managed to get it all set up?'

She wanders off, ignoring my question. I take a deep breath in and exhale slowly.

I look at Michelle while she hovers over some brown leaves, plucking them off with her sharp nails and dropping the dead leaves on the rubber mat covering the floor. If she's sending her people up too, that means there are twice as many people on the surface until the produce tents are set up to serve the entire population of the Underground . . . But how long will that take?

She must have much bigger secrets if she's showing me this.

'I want to give you one of my little rubies,' she says, holding up a little cherry tomato. Her voice is as silky as her dress. The bright red glossy fruit shines against her dark skin as she rolls it around in her palm. 'Try it,' she insists, holding it up. It's red and plump, almost bursting between her talons. Before I can protest, I find the bright fruit rolling in the palm of my hand. I consider my options. I doubt it's poisoned, though the thought does cross my mind. It feels more like a bribe or a proposition. I pretend to examine the little red fruit, acutely aware of her scrutiny. I bring it up to my lips and pop the tiny tomato inside my mouth.

The flavour explodes in my mouth, the little seeds cool and

sweet on my tongue. Michelle holds up another cherry tomato and pops it into her mouth, balancing it between her sharp canines. She winks at me for a second, then it bursts, and she closes her eyes, relishing the flavour.

'How good was that?' She's practically shouting.

'So good,' I say through a forced smile. Then, without thinking, I say, 'You're running your own pick-ups, aren't you?' The question just pops out.

Her eyes flash, but before she can respond, Kenny bursts into the tent, sidling up to Michelle. He whispers something in Michelle's ear, sending the loose wisps of her hair quivering.

She looks at me. 'It would appear something has happened in that wasps' nest of a clan you have. You've been asked to return.'

I nod once, ignoring the insinuation in her tone.

'Nice to meet you, Michelle,' I say. She doesn't reply, just laughs that high-pitched giggle that's been grating on me all afternoon.

'I will see you again soon,' she croons as she follows me out.

'I'm sure of it.'

thirty/one

As I step outside the plastic tent, I'm met by Michelle's brother, Herma. He nods in my direction once, then starts moving. I quickly follow, casting a backwards glance to Michelle, who is flicking her tongue over one of her sharpened canines.

Is that sweat on her brow?

I have to run to keep up with Herma as we wind through the streets of Clan Gaia. My thoughts are spinning, and I hardly notice the chaos and colour surrounding us.

What kind of emergency could there be?

Michelle's smiling face is fresh in my mind. *If she thinks I'm weak, she'll try to poach my clan.*

I almost trip on a little boy standing in front of me.

'Something for me, miss?' he says, holding up empty hands.

'Shoo!' Herma shouts. The child scampers off, bare feet kicking up plumes of dirt. I had decided I would be up-front with Michelle, telling her about the 'attacks' against me. If she knew we suspected the dissent was being led by Link, and that we were onto it, it would prevent her from thinking I was weak. But I didn't get a chance.

I gulp down air. It's darker here.

'Ten metres that way,' Herma says, stopping and pointing into the darkness.

'You're not coming?' I pant. He shakes his head and turns, his long legs leading him back the way we came, taking the light with him. I start moving again, shoving my hand in my pocket to retrieve my torch.

'Shit,' I mutter in the darkness. *That little brat stole my torch.*

When I finally reach the clan line, I can only tell I'm there because of the texture change underfoot. The pressed dirt gives way to the familiar feeling of hard cement. I take a moment to slow my breathing. Then I look around.

'Jamie?' I call out.

Nothing.

'Jamie!' I spin around too many times. 'Look, this isn't funny. Someone stole my torch, would you just come out? Please?' Still nothing. I can feel the familiar knot of panic rise in my chest. *What the hell am I going to do? This is how I die.*

My morbid thoughts are interrupted by a light bobbing towards me.

I run towards it. 'Thank goodness you're here,' I say, allowing myself the luxury of a smile. I look past the light, but the face I see isn't Jamie's; it's that of a boy. A runner – the same boy who interrupted Paula that first night I was in the Underground.

What was his name?

'I'm Andy. Follow me,' he says.

'Where's Jamie?' I demand. 'He said he'd be here waiting. Is he okay?'

The boy gestures for me to follow and takes off jogging through the corridors, snaking his way around bends, always weaving a few steps ahead. I trip a couple of times, and call out for the boy to slow down and tell me what the hell is going on, but he won't answer. I speed up and grab his shoulder.

'They told me you'd be like this,' he says, not meeting my eyes.

'Who told you what?' I snarl.

'Kit . . . and Jamie. They said you'd be mad – asking questions.' He smiles sheepishly, and I let go of his shoulder with a frustrated growl. 'They told me to tell you they're both fine, and that you need to go to your room,' he adds, his eyes darting anywhere but my face.

Go to my room?

I push past the boy. The lights are becoming more frequent now, and I recognise where we are. But everything seems dirtier, just as Michelle's clan looked the second time I walked around. The green–black walls are slimy and slick with trapped moisture. Even the corridor feels too close compared to the bright wide-open streets

I was just in.

I spare a glance over my shoulder. Andy is catching up. He's about ten, his light blond hair almost white under the yellow glow. He puts his torch away and speeds up, his hair flapping around like the wings of a fledgling bird.

He's a runner. Of course he won't talk.

Kit told me about runners on my first day down here – *children who are fast and know how to keep secrets.* I try to focus on the sound of my boots hitting the cement. To focus on being faster than this kid. The sound of our footsteps thudding rhythmic ally on the dusty floor echoes around us.

We finally get to the corridor of my room – my old room.

'Hey,' I say, slowing my pace to a brisk walk, 'why is it so quiet?'

Andy gives me a sideways look then starts running again. 'Shit.' I reach out, grabbing his arm, and pull him to a stop. 'Tell me.' He struggles awkwardly. 'At least tell me *where* they are. You don't have to tell me what's happening – just tell me where they are, so I know they're safe.' I try my best to look concerned and not cross. I hold his gaze for a few moments.

Gotcha.

Andy sighs.

'Dining hall. That's where all the stuff's happening.' He puts his hands up defensively. 'Don't ask me what. That's all I'll say.' *I don't need to.*

Before he can stop me, I take off down the corridors; right – left – right – right.

'Wait!' I hear Andy shout somewhere behind me. I keep going. *Almost there.* I can feel my legs tiring. *I've covered a lot of ground today.* I draw in a deep breath and force my body to keep moving as I round the last corner and head down the main corridor that leads to the dining hall.

I don't know what I expected to see, but this is not it.

The tall metal doors are wide open, prevented from closing by the hundreds of bodies spilling out into the corridor beyond. It looks like every single person from Clan Ember is here. It *sounds* like it, too. People are gathered, snarls plastered to their faces as they push, call and jeer, stomping their studded boots. Those smaller or younger are sitting on people's shoulders to get a better look at whatever is happening inside.

I can hear Andy calling from behind me. 'Teddy, wait! Please!'

I know I should feel bad for him, but I feel worse about being kept in the dark. Kit and Jamie are trying to keep whatever is going on here from me.

Why?

A rush of anger shoots through me.

Isn't this supposed to be my *clan?*

I drop to my hands and knees and start crawling through legs, trying to avoid being trampled and kicked. Even if Andy does follow me, there's no way he'll be able to find me in this tangle of bodies. I can see that everyone is facing one area, towards the centre of the huge room. I try to stand up, to get my bearings, but people keep pulling me back.

'Stop pushing,' one man shouts in my ear, grabbing my neck and forcing me back onto my knees. I feel a sharp pain in my side.

'Get out of there, you creep,' a woman snarls. She gnashes her teeth and I scamper to get away, accidentally headbutting someone's shin. I dodge another kick and see a small opening. I stand up.

'Nice one,' someone growls behind me. The press of bodies is hot; the smell of old sweat, overpowering. I continue squeezing my way through the crowd. The room is filled beyond bursting point. I'm almost close enough to see the front.

Suddenly, I hear a high-pitched scream. *'Did you see that?'* someone beside me says. I press forward, trying to piece together fragments from different conversations.

'Nothing unexpected from that *type . . .'* I force my way past the

leather-clad arms of an exceptionally tall man, his orange beard tucked into his black leather belt.

'We should have tighter rules, make an example of them . . .' I try to avoid breathing through my nose as I keep moving through the mass of sticky flesh. *An example?*

Finally, I see what everyone is talking about.

Not what.

Who.

thirty/two

I feel blood rush to my face as rage courses through me. My breaths start coming fast and shallow.

Link.

And there, lying in a crumpled heap at his feet is a girl, about fifteen, in a dirty torn pink dress. He stands over her, his face brutal, crueller than I had thought possible. A piece of chain hangs from one fist, and he's flanked by two boys, one a child, no older than ten, the other at least seventeen. *My age.* I want to grab the girl and run, but I can't. My feet are glued to the floor. I don't want to make the situation worse.

I need to find Jamie and Kit.

I scan the crowd, but I can't see anyone clearly. There is so much to take in; everyone is jeering and shouting. I'm about to get down on my hands and knees again when I spot them, standing up the back, on the benches by our table. They haven't noticed me.

My heart sinks, and I feel a flush of shame that my friends could just be standing there, watching this.

I put my head down and start pushing my way across the packed room. The air is hot, and my neck is getting sticky with sweat. More and more people keep arriving, and I can feel my breathing become restricted as bodies press in from all sides. *People will start passing out soon.* I'm startled when a man beside me pulls a punch, and a small fight breaks out. As I duck to get past drawn elbows, the crowd begins to roar, and I look around, trying to see what's happened. Link is standing in the centre of the crowd, his arms raised like a gladiator, the chain links taut between his fists. His mouth hangs open as he roars with the crowd. I take advantage of the distraction and begin shoving my way through the crush of bodies. It's hot, and violence hangs in the air as tensions are pulled tight.

More small scuffles start breaking out. I can see Kit clearly now; her cheeks are flushed.

With panic or excitement?

Jamie's eyes are wild, looking around. Then it hits me.

They don't know what to do.

I'm mere metres away from the table when I feel someone grab my shirt and I jolt to a stop. I whip around and find I'm face to face with a girl, her dark eyes glowering beneath a cloud of bright red hair.

Petra.

'Where are you going, *Sunlight scum*?' She manages to grind the words out through clenched teeth, her right hand drawn into a fist. I try tearing out of her grip, but she's strong. Instead, I let my body go slack, dragging her down towards the ground, and then shoot back up, throwing my elbow into her nose. I hear a crack and grab her arm, shoving her spiked cuff into her cheek. She screams in pain and rage, and I take the opportunity to get lost in the crowd before she has a chance to retaliate. My thumping heartbeat fills my ears.

I can't believe I just did that.

I can hear obscenities being shouted behind me, but I don't waste time finding out who they're aimed at.

Kit is not going to be happy about this. Now I've given Petra a *real* reason to hate me.

I reach the bench and clamber up behind them, suddenly realising how tired I am. I elbow Kit.

'Oh fuck,' she says, grabbing Jamie's arm. His eyes widen as he realises I'm here.

I can see everything from the table. The youngest boy walks up to the girl and spits in her face, then Link kicks her in the stomach. She rolls back over, and the younger boy kicks her again.

'What the hell is going on?' I shout at Kit over the ruckus. 'What's wrong with you? Why are you just standing here?' I feel the pulse in my neck pumping so hard I'm sure it's about to burst.

'You don't understand,' Jamie shouts over the clamour, trying to grab my arm.

'*You* don't understand,' I respond, jerking away, my hands in tight balls by my sides.

I try to slow my breathing; dig my nails into my palms. 'Someone needs to stop this,' I shout.

'Teddy, this is clan business, go back to your room,' Kit demands.

Go back to my room?

Everything in the room slows. I see myself walking down the steps at my Job Placement, Jamie putting my gloves on at our Partnership. Kit's staring at me like I'm a spooked animal. Jamie reaches his hand out again, and I take a step away, out of reach.

'No,' I say, pushing through them to get to the front of the table. 'Like you say, this is clan business.'

thirty/three

I take in the chaos around me, drawing in a deep breath. *I must stop this.*

Cupping my hands to my mouth, I begin to shout.

'Enou –'

'Alright creeps. Get the hell out of my dining hall!'

An old man steps out from the kitchen doors with a huge metal pot and ladle in his hands. When no one stops, he raises the pot above his head and starts clanging, killing the deadly buzz in the room.

It is a horrible sound, and people cover their ears and start shoving each other, trying to get out of his way. The old man continues clanging and weaving his way through the web of bodies. Everyone's attention is on him now.

I catch sight of Link, who looks furious. He's lost his audience.

The clanging continues, and the crowd begins to disperse. Some people seem reluctant to leave, loitering by the walls, whispering behind their hands.

'I said GET OUT!' the old man booms again, his curly silver beard quivering. The build-up at the huge doors becomes a stream of bodies leaving, many cursing and swearing as they go. I try to spot Petra in the crowd, but I can't see her.

The little trio in the centre of the room are still poking and prodding their prey; the girl is curled up tightly, resembling a dirty pink ball. Link is crouched next to the girl as the old man approaches.

He puts a heavily spiked boot on Link's shoulder and pushes, and Link falls onto his hands. The older of the two boys spins around fast.

Deadly.

But the old man isn't scared. He pokes him in the chest with his ladle. 'I told ya to get out,' he growls, loud enough for everyone to hear. 'If you and yur circus don't get out of my dining hall now, you'll become part of the sausages I'm making for dinner!'

He leans down, grabbing Link by the scruff of his collar. 'Ya HEAR ME, BOY?'

A wave of emotion passes over Link's face. He looks around the room, and his eyes meet mine.

Don't look away.

I don't, despite the chill that freezes me from the inside.

Link shrugs himself out of the old man's grip and whistles to the two boys. They stalk away, leaving the girl behind on the floor, blood smeared around her.

The old man looks at us and I square my shoulders, waiting for his next move. I recognise him now; he's the chef, Lew. He occasionally stops to ring his pot and ladle in the ears of reluctant leavers as he approaches our table. Once he's within comfortable earshot, he calls out, 'Hello, you lot.' He sits down on the free bench beside us. 'I don't think you made the right decision, Kit.' His voice is laced with reproach.

I ignore the old man and run to the girl. I slip on some of the blood and come careening into her side. She groans.

'Sorry,' I mutter, carefully rolling her onto her back.

This is the second time today that my hands have been covered in someone else's blood.

'Kit! Get over here and help me!' I shout, pushing my anger down.

Not now.

Bruises are already blooming across the girl's exposed skin.

'KIT!' I scream.

'I did what I had to do –' I hear Kit saying somewhere behind me. Someone presses a cold cup of water into my hand.

'I'm Lew,' the old man says, putting a warm hand on my shoulder as I take the cup.

'Teddy,' I mumble, pressing the cold metal against the girl's flushed cheeks.

'I know who ye are, girl. Just surprised we haven't been introduced yet.' He levels another disapproving glance at Kit.

Tears prick my eyes. I hold the cup to the girl's lips. 'We need to get her out of here before Link comes back to finish whatever he started,' I say, looking around frantically.

'No one will touch her while we're here. Not even Link,' Lew says softly, kneeling beside me. He passes me the tea towel he had thrown over his shoulder and I start gingerly wiping some of the blood from the girl's face.

'KIT!'

'I was trying to do the right thing. To protect Teddy,' she says, kneeling down beside us, checking the girl's pulse. 'It's steady.' She sits back on her heels quietly for a moment, scanning the girl, calculating. She starts from her shoulders, gently moving and squeezing her limbs. 'I did this to protect you,' she says, throwing me a quick look. I can't see her expression.

Protect me?

'I knew you'd interfere.' Her shoulders slump. 'I thought if I could get the attention off you and onto an Outskirter, people might realise you're not the enemy.' She can't meet my eyes.

'You think an Outskirter dying is a fair price for my acceptance as leader?' I ask.

'The clan-less,' Lew explains, producing another tea towel and securing it around the girl's head, stemming the flow of blood from a nasty gash above her brow. 'They are people who 'ave done things that betray their clan. Not bad enough to die, but not forgivable. There's an element of truth to what Kit 'ere is sayin'. There are people who 'ate Outskirters more than they 'ate Link, so you'd lose 'em from your side.' Lew shakes his head, and a sour expression twists his lips.

Jamie walks over, carrying a bowl of steaming hot water. Careful to avoid his gaze, I dip my tea towel into it and start cleaning the blood and dirt away properly.

'I didn't mean for this girl to get hurt,' Kit cries out. 'Not like this. When I heard from Tony that she'd been caught stealing from a clan kid, I just let Link handle it. I thought having a public hearing might make things better – I assumed she was older, not a child.' I can feel Kit's pleading eyes boring into me, but I refuse to look at her. 'I'm a *healer*. I don't wanna hurt

people, I wanna fix them!'

I shake my head. I don't know where to start.

Lew stands up, his hulking form towering over us. 'I think the real issue is, it weren't your decision to be making.' Kit scowls.

'You're not Clan Head,' he tells her matter-of-factly, then looks at me. 'Kit thought she was doing you a favour. Ended up making things a whole lot worse.'

I follow his gaze across the room and notice Link creeping in, his arm around Petra. Even from here, I can see the blood oozing down her face. They move quickly over to the counter, and the kitchen hand passes them two glasses of water. Link shoots us a look as they hobble away.

'What on earth happened to her?' Jamie asks.

'I did,' I mumble. 'She attacked me while I was making my way through the crowd. I had to get her off me, so I elbowed her,' Jamie narrows his eyes, 'and shoved her spiked wrist cuff in her face.'

Kit gasps and Lew chuckles.

'I think you broke her nose,' Jamie replies. I nod.

I look at Link and Petra loitering near the doors, gossiping with Leelo and a few other people I don't recognise. Petra's hair matches the blood crusting around her nose. She sees us and starts screaming obscenities. Link shoots daggers my way and drags her back out into the corridor.

Lew clears his throat. '*Anyway*, like she said, Kit thought yur not bein' here would keep ya outta people's heads, but she *clearly* underestimated yur resolve and misjudged the 'ole situation.'

'I knew that leaving her with Michelle was going to be the best bet,' Kit mumbles.

'So I'd be safely locked in my room and not ruin your plan? Then why did someone come to get me?'

'I didn't know you'd been called,' Kit says, looking at Jamie.

'I didn't want to leave her there if I wasn't waiting,' he says, raising his hands defensively. I put the dirty tea towel down, pressing my hand to the girl's warm cheek.

'You *told* her to come back?' Kit says, standing up.

'I don't think she should be kept in the dark about things.'

Kit doesn't respond. I look between them, then spin back to Kit. 'What else are you keeping me in the dark about? No wonder no one likes me!'

Lew puts his hand on my shoulder again. The weight is surprisingly comforting.

'And whatever ya thought was gonna happen today went too far, lass,' he says to Kit, gesturing to the girl on the floor. 'Plus, ya stripped Teddy of 'er right to be present. Her right to *lead*.' 'I was trying help,' Kit says, her hands on her hips.

'So what else haven't you been telling me in your attempt to "help"?' I ask, staring at her. She looks away.

'There was a moment,' Jamie says, 'a fraction of a moment when we saw how young this girl was. It could have been stopped.'

'I thought it would distract them from you,' she whines. 'Make Link the bad guy. I didn't realise how much people would . . . love it.'

'I'm struggling to understand how anyone could justify this.' I gesture to the girl, her head resting in Jamie's arms, and Lew shakes his head slowly.

'Ya come from a different world to us. Down here, these 'skirters are outside the rules and boundaries of the clans. Makes 'em free to live how they please, which is a gift, but it's also a curse 'cause it leaves 'em unprotected. They can be used by clans-folk however they see fit. S'all part of tha' risk.'

'She's just a child. She might have been born clan-less –'

'So I'm the bad guy? I was *trying* to help you!' Kit steps forward, trying to grab my arm, but I snatch it away.

'Calm down, lass,' Lew says, and swats her with his tea towel.

Kit ignores him, tears pricking her eyes. Lew goes on.

'It seems like this Underground is being ruled by young folk now. Us oldies don't mind that, *but* I think you're all fools if you don't even wanna at least listen to the wisdom of yur elders, even if you refuse to be ruled by 'em.'

I stare at Kit. The girl on the floor coughs, her breathing laboured.

'She needs to get to the medical centre now,' I say. Kit nods. 'Jamie?' He bends over and scoops the girl up in her arms.

'What did she steal?' I ask as we follow Jamie out of the dining hall.

'Snuck in and tried to take some snacks and a container of drinking water,' Jamie says over his shoulder.

'Outskirters don't qualify for supplies,' Lew explains from behind us, where he's dragging yet another tea towel along the floor, mopping up the blood.

The girl groans and Kit rushes to her side, pulling her eyelids up to check her eyes. 'We need to hurry,' she says.

'Best they can do is beg or barter,' Lew says, stopping at the doorway.

'Or steal . . . this girl just happened to get caught.'

'It's hard to understand,' Lew says with a gruff-but-gentle tone. 'But to fit in down 'ere ya gonna need to learn to respect the difference in our cultures. This is just *our* clan. Everyone has their own traditions and ways ta handle 'skirters.' He raises an eyebrow. 'Why d'ya think yur new friend Michelle has such pointy teeth?' He smiles, his eyes getting lost behind his bushy eyebrows. The bloodied men flash in my memory, then the girl groans again. Jamie hastens to follow Kit as she speeds off towards the medical centre.

'How did you –'

'Not much I don't know 'bout down here, lass.' He winks, then puts his hands on his hips. 'Look, I'd hazard a touch'a understanding on both sides'll help mend this.' He turns my shoulders, directing me to where my friends are almost out of sight. 'Kit's a born healer – not a leader. She'll see that no lasting damage is done ta the girl. I'm just sorry ta say, she didn't realise how outta hand this'd get. *Despite* my warning her.' I spin around.

Warning her?

But the old man is gone.

✕

I walk into the medical centre and see Jamie standing in the far corner. Kit is crouching beside the young girl, and two people dressed in the donated, once-white medical jackets are helping her clean and bandage the girl's wounds. I notice that Kit is using a bandage and a splint – the girl's arm is broken.

She looks up at me but doesn't smile. I look away. I'm not here for her.

'She did think she was doing the right thing,' Jamie says softly, coming up beside me.

If she knew me, she wouldn't have done that.

'I can see she tried to do the right thing. But it backfired spectacularly,' I say.

He nods, a smile playing on his lips.

'What?' I ask.

'Good work with Petra,' he says. He looks at me, his eyes bright. I want to smile, to laugh about it with him, but I can't.

'You said you'd be there waiting for me.' Any hint of a smile leaves his face.

'Once this started unfolding, Kit sent a runner asking for me to come and help. I had to make a choice.'

'You did,' I reply, my voice cold.

'Not the choice you think. I sent that note to bring you back, saying there was an emergency.' Jamie reaches out his hand, but I step away. I know that he went against Kit, that he tried to help me, but he didn't do anything to help the girl.

'I knew you wouldn't go to your room.' *He wanted me to show up.*

'Well, now Michelle thinks we're compromised. I look weak to her, so well done.'

Kit walks over, her brow furrowed.

'Well done, both of you.' I turn and walk out through the milky-white plastic curtains, leaving the smell of bleach and blood behind me.

thirty/four

It feels weird, prepping to go above ground after what happened yesterday. I can feel my stomach churning with nervous anticipation. I was excited about our trip to the surface, but now, after yesterday's events, I just feel sick. The idea of spending time with Kit has my nerves on edge, but judging by her bright, bubbly energy, Kit has seemed to have slept everything off.

'I bet meeting Michelle wasn't as exciting as today will be!' She grabs my hand and pulls me up, spinning me around her. With all the chaos surrounding yesterday's incident, I still haven't had a chance to tell Kit or Jamie anything about my strange visit with Michelle. 'It will be your first time going up to the surface since you've been down here. I'm going to have to keep you on a leash so you don't try to run away.'

She hugs me tight and flashes a 'peace' sign to Jamie, who's standing outside the room, holding our torches, which he just loaded with fresh batteries.

'You're gonna be super careful, right?' he asks as we step out with our empty backpacks strapped to our backs. 'Remember what Zelda said. The Jubilee has the Council on lockdown. Double the guards, and new cameras everywhere.'

Kit rolls her eyes. 'We'll be fine, worry-wart! You should be more concerned that Teddy might remember how much more fun she has with me than with you.' She gives me a sly wink, and I smile at her tentatively.

'I doubt it,' he says, and my gaze slides to his. I feel my stomach flip again, and not out of worry this time. 'I doubt you'll have as much fun with Kit as you *could* be having with me,' he murmurs as we watch Kit run down the corridor to chat to her cousin Leelo and her boyfriend. Jamie puts his finger on my chin, turning my attention

235

back to him and his intense gaze. 'I know you said you had some reading to do last night. I'm not sure if you ended up getting a look at that Partnership booklet your Mum left for you . . .' he trails off as Kit walks back. I know I'm blushing.

'Are you okay?' Kit asks, looking at me. She turns to Jamie. 'Is she okay?'

'Just excited, I think,' he says, his eyes glinting with laughter. 'What did *Leelame* want?'

'She said she really wants to help us with pick-ups,' Kit says, swatting Jamie with her torch.

'And you told her no,' I say, trying not to be too smug as Jamie nods in agreement.

'Actually, I told her yes.'

'What?' Jamie and I say at the same time.

'Why would you do that? You told us yourself how useless she is.' I don't even care if I'm being harsh. The success of the pick-ups is my biggest drawcard. I can't have some kid jeopardising them. 'It's *my* neck on the line here. Plus, after yesterday . . .'

'I fucked up, okay? I get it. Yesterday was a huge mistake – *my* huge mistake. But I want to make it up to you guys. I've been explaining what we do to Leelo, quizzing her. She remembers stuff, and even has some good ideas.'

'You're kidding me.'

'What? Other people can have ideas, Teddy.'

'You've been telling her what we do? This is super private stuff, secret business. I can't believe I have to even say that to you!'

'What were you thinking?' Jamie asks. Kit's eyes start to fill with tears, and I fight to keep myself from saying more. Jamie doesn't hold back, however. 'She's friends with Link, Kit. Her boyfriend is hardcore in Link's crew, and I've hardly seen her around without him.'

'Her boyfriend isn't *her*. Sheesh, men are so obsessed with other men. She is *my cousin*. I trust her and I told her not to tell Link anything. Besides, I know yesterday was out of control, but I don't think Link has it in for Teddy as much as you two think he does.' I take a step back, unable to believe what she's saying. 'I think we just need to find a way to work *with* him, so he feels included and less threatened. Then he won't go all killy-killy.' She shrugs. 'I mentioned it to Leelo, and she seemed to think she could be a good bridge between our two mindsets.'

Kit plays with the straps of her pack. I run my hands through my hair and snatch my torch out of Jamie's grip. 'Let's go,' I say, already halfway down the corridor. *I just want to get this over with.* I can hear Jamie and Kit exchanging words, but I'm too far away now to hear what they're saying.

I don't slow when I hear Kit jogging to catch up.

'Remember who your friends are,' I say before she can open her mouth.

Even family cannot be trusted.

✗

We stop outside a nondescript metal door, and I wait for Kit to fish out a key and unlock it. She slides the key into the lock, then turns to face me.

'Despite your clear lack of confidence in my decision- making, you really don't need to worry, Teddy. It will all work out. I promise.'

I nod, but I wish she hadn't said it. I hate that word.

Promise.

No one ever keeps them.

Kit fusses with her pack. I tighten the straps on her pack, passing her another empty backpack.

'This is simple. Drop off the bags and grab two medical supply packs. Easy.'

I pull tighter than I need to.

'It's just – you've never done this,' she says slowly.

'I'm not an idiot,' I say, grabbing another pack to add to my front.

'Yeah,' Kit mumbles, grabbing a black beanie – my idea – to cover her bright hair.

I grab a beanie too, tucking my hair out of the way of the bag's straps. We look each other over.

'Ready?' I ask. *Kit is not the enemy*, I remind myself.

'Yeah, I guess. Are you?' she asks.

She wasn't convinced about me coming to the surface. *You're just not ready*, she'd said when we were making the schedules a week ago.

'Of course,' I say. 'Let's go.'

✕

We start weaving our path towards the exit. It's a weird route. We walk down a short corridor that ends in a locked door.

Once we're through the door and inside the small room, Kit locks the door behind us. In this glorified closet there is a single metal ladder dropping down from a gridded grate in the City. I can only remember being in a similar room once before, when I arrived here with Jamie and Kit after leaving my life in the Metropolis. Now Kit and I are going in the opposite direction. Up. Kit gestures for me to follow her, and we start our agonising two-hundred metre climb up the ladder.

The silence fast becomes awkward, so I decide to speak.

'Are we just going to do this in silence?' I ask.

She doesn't reply.

Focus on your climbing.

My arms start burning after forty rungs. The same slimy residue that coats the walls along our corridors coats the ladder too, and my hands are soon coated in flakes of rust and slime.

'Are you going to keep hating me for what happened?' she says finally, breaking the silence.

'I don't hate you,' I say. 'I'm just —' I sigh. 'Anyway, it wasn't just that. It's everything. You're trying to shield me from my job. You can't hide me away from everybody.' I didn't realise how much I'd needed to say that.

'You don't know what it's like down here,' she says as we ascend.

'I never will if you keep running interference.' I can feel my hands cramping and try loosening my grip.

'I'm trying to *protect* you,' she says again.

'You keep saying that, but it's not your job to protect me. I made a choice to do this. Now you have to let me.' I stop moving. 'It's *my* job. It's *my* risk. You didn't want to be Clan Head, you wanted me to do it, so now you have to let me.'

I hear her groan, low and resigned.

'I came Underground to help save everyone here. I don't think people even know that, or understand what that means.'

She stops, swinging out, holding on with one hand and looking down at me.

'Okay,' she says, 'you're right.'

I narrow my eyes in the dim torchlight.

'I've been trying to hide you away, to protect you, but I'll stop.' She swings back and continues to climb in silence.

That's it?

I consider asking her to explain the sudden change, but decide not to probe. When we finally reach the top, I feel a moment of relief, and let go with one hand. As I do, my other hand slips. For a second, I feel air rush past me. I reach up in vain, then Kit's hand grabs my wrist and I slam against the railing, clawing my way back onto the ladder.

'Thank you,' I gasp.

'Just trying to *protect* you,' Kit says wryly.

I let her help me out of the hole and onto the road. I'm immediately struck by the fresh air. I breathe in deeply.

'A little help?' she says from the grate. I help pull the metal pothole cover back across, then wipe the slimy rust flakes onto my pants. I look around, trying to get my bearings. All I can see is a recharging station for vehicles. Cool fresh air caresses my face.

I've missed this.

'Come on,' Kit says beside me. 'We don't have time to gawk.'

I let her set the pace, leading us through streets I don't recognise. The houses here are small and close together – different from anything else I've seen in the City. They're all connected by the same waist-high metal link fence; there's not a single white fence in sight. The grass, when there is any, is overgrown and unruly. *This makes no sense.*

'You didn't think all of the Metropolis looked like your privileged little pocket, did you?' says Kit.

'What are you talking about?' I ask, confused.

'This City isn't all fancy people like you. There are all sorts up here too – still boring, lifeless drones, but they're different from your . . . *type.*'

We weave through the streets, and I consider what she means. *There's so much I still don't know.*

That ball of anger simmers deep within me. *Still.*

'You know, I have no idea how you lot do it – life without music, or books. Eugh, so *boring!*'

'Shhh,' I hiss, grabbing her arm. She stops abruptly, and we listen. It sounds like the crackle of radios hissing – then silence. We wait for another beat. The wind picks up again, and the sound returns.

'It's just the wind,' Kit says, shrugging. 'Or some animals.' We keep walking. 'In the Underground, we let ourselves really *live*. We won't be defined by some moronic government. We will not be controlled!' she says, pumping her fist in the air.

I cut her off. 'Your city isn't all peace, love and butterflies either, you know.'

She doesn't respond.

thirty/five

We move in silence, and I look around, trying to absorb as much of our new surroundings as possible.

'In here,' Kit whispers, and we slink into a small public park. It's nothing like the parks I remember growing up. They were all vibrant garden beds and tall leafy trees. This park is just some weeds amongst yellowing grass and scraggy bushes. In the middle, there is a half-dead tree, and a decrepit bench underneath. This is not the Metropolis I know.

We take our empty packs off and drop them onto the bench. *No supplies yet.* There's a sound behind us. Kit grabs my shoulder and pulls me into the nearest bush, a rogue branch pulls off my beanie. I snatch it back and snag my skin on a thorn. I look at Kit, frowning, but she presses a finger to her lips and points out towards the bench.

I peer through the dense tangle of thorny branches, and moments later two people walk into the park, their own hats pulled low over their faces. All I can see are their eyes. They drop their large packs at the bench and turn quickly, springing off into the night, taking the empty packets with them.

'Efficient,' I mutter, getting ready to collect our delivery.

We need to get out of here.

Something about this place gives me a terrible feeling. But Kit grabs my arm, pulling me back into the shrubbery.

'Wait,' she whispers. 'Let's just sit for a bit. Make sure no guards are coming.'

I nod reluctantly and settle in.

For a while, we talk about anything: Tony, Rita, the new messengers – some of whom seem less reliable and might need a job swap. We discuss the access points. I want to have 'portal guards' when we go to do pick-ups, to make sure no one sees the team and tries slipping into the Underground. I shift on the scratchy grass. The more we talk, the more I'm assailed by that feeling of otherness. I'm part of the process, but still an outsider. Kit was right though; my knowledge of the City makes a huge difference. Understanding when and how things are done. It blows me away how quickly people forget things once they start a new life Underground.

And Trues – well – they live completely lost in their own version of reality.

'How was your meeting with Michelle?' Kit asks.

I explain everything I saw in Clan Gaia – from the moment the strange man covered in blood ran into me, to the creepy gardener who showed me the produce tents. 'She has big tents set up, growing vegetables hydroponically,' I explain. Kit looks surprised.

'Why did she show you?' she muses.

I don't answer and look out into the darkness.

What if Mum comes to surprise me?

I don't dwell on the thought; I know I'm just setting myself up for disappointment. We haven't heard anything from her since our last meeting.

'I didn't want that girl to get hurt,' Kit says breaking the silence. She looks at me with sad eyes. 'I spoke to Link, and he said they'd run a fair trial. Make her tell us where she was from, what she did and why she did it. Maybe get her to do some work or something as payment . . . cleaning or something. We've had clan-less do that before.' I shift uncomfortably. Nothing she's saying sounds particularly believable, based on the Underground I've witnessed.

'I don't know how you could have trusted Link.'

'It wasn't just him. The other two boys were there, and they'd agreed to keep it all clean.' I roll my eyes. 'I know you don't believe me.'

'I just find it hard to believe you thought Link would be fair in any sense of the word.' She slumps back.

'I know. It was stupid. I did what I could to fix up the girl. And I gave her a pack of food and some water, and got her some new clothes, too, before we let her go back.'

'Go back to what?' I turn around. 'What does she have to go back to? A life living between clans, begging for charity and stealing food, hoping she doesn't get caught? Actually, that sounds pretty familiar to me.' I gesture to the park we're waiting in.

'I know it seems like that to you, but these people aren't in a clan for a reason. Most of them are really violent or belligerent, and flagrantly flout any leadership or order.'

'So, they're all just like Link?'

She laughs softly at my comment, and I smile despite myself. It's nice to hear her laugh again. I hate this tension that keeps popping up between us.

'I know you didn't do it on purpose,' I say. 'I'm just disappointed that you didn't step in when you saw it get out of hand.' I take her hand and give it a squeeze.

'What's that?' Kit hisses, grabbing my arm. I hear it too, a rustling from across the street. I strain my eyes to see if I can make out the source, but it's too dark.

'If it's guards, then they've already heard us,' I say.

Kit scans the area, her eyes wide. 'I don't think guards would be loitering in the bushes.' She narrows her eyes, trying to see in the dark.

I make my decision. The meds are too important, and no legitimate Metropolis citizen would be hiding in the bushes. I slink up to the bench, hoist one of the full backpacks onto my shoulders and do up the straps, trying to take some of the weight off my back. Kit joins me and does the same. We don't take our eyes off the bushes.

As we approach the footpath, I get a better view of the shrubbery that lines it. I peer down the street and notice that the tall streetlamps illuminate the different garden fences all the way up and down the street. Kit draws a breath to speak, and I smack my hand against her mouth, harder than I intended.

There *is* someone – maybe two people – in the bushes. I step forward, but I'm too late to see their faces. They turn and jump a fence. I start after them, but they're moving too fast.

Wait, what was that?

Please be wrong. But I know I'm not. It was just a flash, but that's all I need. An unmistakable glimpse of red and blue woven across two scalps, glinting under the moonlight as the bodies melt away into the darkness.

Michelle's brothers.

'Move,' I say under my breath. Kit needs no prompting. I turn and find she's already halfway to the next streetlamp. I race to keep up as Kit expertly leads us back. We wind through more unfamiliar streets.

How many times has she been here before?

We arrive back at the entrance, both gasping for breath. The pack is heavy on my shoulders, and I can see the straps digging in on Kit's, too. Together we heave the metal grate open. I climb in first, then Kit swings down on the other side of the ladder, and we each use one free arm to pull the grate back, securing us in darkness. The dank smell hits me as I start climbing down. Above me, Kit pulls out the key and locks the portal shut.

'Do you have your torch?' she calls. I pat my pockets.

'No,' I say. Losing two in two days is decidedly not good.

I keep moving down, by feel only. I hear a click, then a little bead of light sways around the enclosed space. I look up, watching Kit clip a torch onto her belt, then we move quickly in silence.

'That was weird!' she says, jumping the last five rungs to the bottom.

'Did you see them?' I ask cautiously.

'Yeah,' she says, wiping her dirty hands onto the rust covered door. 'But who were they?' I'd assumed Kit would have recognised them too, but of course, she's never been to Michelle's clan.

'Let's get out of here,' I say, shifting the heavy pack. 'We'll get rid of these, and then I'll tell you.'

'I have to take these bags to the sorting station,' Kit says impatiently once we're back in the corridor. 'I don't need you running off to play the hero or trying to shank any enemies.' *As if I'm the loose cannon here . . .*

I narrow my eyes at her, but she's smiling.

For the first time in two days, I let myself really see my best friend. She's broken and damaged, and I need to remember that.

She doesn't even have the luxury of perspective that Jamie has.

'Come on – let's drop this stuff off.' *Still trying to boss me around, though.*

I feel my stomach gurgle as the scent of *something* wafts towards us. *I am never missing meals again.* 'Can we just have something to eat first?' I ask. Kit spins around, dwarfed by the huge packs.

'What did you say?' she says wryly, cupping her hand dramatically to her ear. 'Can we just see Jamie first?' I ignore her, shouldering past.

'Either I come with you and loiter around the sorting station while you flirt with Tony, or we eat now and then I leave you alone.'

She pulls a face and starts stomping towards the surprisingly delicious scent wafting up the corridor. Her silence isn't exactly a confession, but I know *something's* going on between Kit and lazy Tony from the sorting station.

'Fine,' she huffs, throwing her hands in the air. 'Let's go eat.'

thirty/six

The energy in the dining hall seems to have returned to normal –
whatever that is down here. I drop my bag down on the floor
beside my bench then take up a position in the growing line. There
is a small band of musicians setting up drums and guitars.

Walking back over to our table with my plate piled high, I slide
onto the bench, my tired legs grateful for the break. I spoon hot rice
into my mouth and feel some of the tension melt out of my muscles.
Looking around the room, something seems surreal. It's eerie
watching people eating their dinner and laughing as if nothing
happened in here yesterday.

Am I the only one who cares?

I tell Jamie and Kit about seeing Michelle's brothers at the
pick-up.

'So what, people are spying on us now?' Kit says.

'This doesn't make sense,' Jamie says, putting his fork down,
eyebrows furrowed.

'This was the first time we'd used that location.' He looks up
at Kit. 'Wasn't it?'

'Yes,' she says. 'Someone's ratted us out.' She shoots a look in
my direction. 'Someone's been telling Michelle about our new
delivery sites.'

A group of girls walk past our table, giggling and shooting shy
glances at Jamie.

What do they want?

'Maybe her brothers overheard something when I dropped
you off,' Jamie says. Kit slams her boot on the bench next to him.

'I don't think you said anything,' I say slowly as the memory
of what *did* happen floods back. I glance at Jamie. *I wonder if he
remembers.* I can feel my cheeks getting warm as I remember what his

246

lips had felt like, pressed against mine. His hands against my neck . . . I pick up my cup, taking a drink to cover my face.

Kit doesn't notice.

'I think it's someone in our little circle,' she says, pulling her knife out of her shoe and tossing it from hand to hand.

My mind flits through the limited list of suspects. I linger on the idea of it being Zelda.

I hope it's not her.

Zelda's always so kind, offering to show me new places, and she genuinely seems interested in how I'm settling in and talking about my experience growing up in the City. The more we talk, the more I realise that there *is* a lot that I don't know about the Metropolis.

Kit stands up, holding her empty plate. 'It wasn't me.' 'Obviously,' I say. 'But whoever it was, we need to find out. Michelle has only done this to protect herself, but someone from our side is working with her . . .' I let the thought trail off. I don't need to explain.

'Well, I'm done talking about it,' Kit says, shoving the blade back into her boot and grabbing our empty plates. 'After everything that's happened today, I can safely say I never want to meet Michelle, and I. Am. Done. Done with all of it and all of you.' She turns to leave.

'Hey, what did we do?' Jamie calls out in mock hurt, but Kit ignores him.

Jamie catches my eye. 'Other than that, did it go *smoothly*?' Something about the emphasis he puts on the word makes me realise he's not talking about the pick-up itself.

'Yeah, we spoke. I think things are – better now.' He nods, and I hear Kit's footsteps as she bounds back over.

'You know, whatever she was doing it for, it's not okay. She has that whole hydro-whatever set-up happening, which is some serious rule-breaking, as far as clan agreements go.

Unless she's planning on sharing the produce around.' 'What?' Jamie asks.

'I'll tell you later,' I say, waving my hand dismissively as Leelo approaches.

'Hey, Leelo,' Jamie says, picking up his glass and taking a long drink of water. I raise an eyebrow at the girl.

'So, did you speak to them? When can I start?' No hello, no eye contact.

'Well, we haven't figured out our plans exactly,' Kit says. I shake my head at Jamie and notice Kit rolling her eyes at us. 'But I'll probably be able to let you know tomorrow. Alright?'

'Sure. Just make sure you give me enough time to arrange my Stix games.' She turns, stomping off in her heavy boots.

'She will be the death of me,' Kit grumbles.

'What are you going to tell her?' I ask, once Leelo's out of earshot.

Kit doesn't answer, hoisting her pack onto her shoulders.

She then grabs mine.

'I know you two don't like her, but she can't work in the medical centre anymore.'

'Why?' I ask, not buying it.

'She has a bit of a problem with, you know –'

I shake my head. 'She's got a lot of problems, but I don't think any of them would impact her ability to work there.'

'She has an issue with *seeing* blood,' Kit explains. I raise an eyebrow.

'Well, let's give the useless girl a chance, huh?' Jamie says, raising his cup. 'Why don't you see if she'll help you with those bags?'

'I'm not a damsel, Jamie,' Kit says, smiling while giving him the finger. Then she turns and exits the dining hall, stumbling under the weight of the bags. I let out a long sigh.

thirty/seven

As always, I'm escorted back to my room.

'So . . .' Jamie says. 'This is awkward.'

I can tell by his tone that he's joking, but it still feels weird, especially with the gaping half a metre between us. I close the space and elbow him.

'Hey, watch what you're doing with those! I've seen the damage firsthand.' He holds his hands up in mock surrender.

I shrug. 'I do what I have to.'

He laughs, throwing his arm across my shoulders and pulling me into his side.

'You're definitely not one to hold back on poking the bear.'

I laugh, but underneath the joke he's right. I'm sure my encounter with Petra has only helped fuel the fires of Link and his gang.

I open my door and Jamie follows me inside, closing the door gently behind him. I hadn't explicitly invited him in, but there was something between us now, and I didn't know if I was supposed to say anything about it. I sit on my bed and start unlacing my boots, while he walks slowly around my room, touching my stuff. 'I totally forgot! I still haven't told you about how meeting Michelle went.' Trying to distract myself from the nerves racing through me.

He spins around with curious eyes. 'You had *stuff* going on. But I am curious.'

'Michelle was *interesting*. I actually think I might come to like her. But I need to see her again. We've got . . . unfinished business.'

He steps closer, lacing his fingers through mine and pulling me to my feet. 'Something to do with the hydro-whatever Kit was talking about?'

'Yes,' I say, not pulling out of his grip. I try to focus my thoughts, but my attention is caught on the space between us – or rather, the lack of it. I suddenly feel very hot, engulfed by the radiant heat rolling off his body.

'I knew you'd be brilliant,' he says, taking a step closer. I feel my breath hitch. I want to lean into him, to reach up and – I smile, then pull my hands free.

I don't know what any of this will mean for us, for our – my *new group of friends.*

'It was bizarre – she had fresh fruit.'

'That's not pos–'

'I know, but she did. I ate. Not just fruit, vegetables too. I didn't just taste it, she showed me where and how she was growing it. In these massive hydroponic tents, three of them – they would have only just fit inside the dining hall. It was –' I pause, realising I truly mean what I'm about to say. 'It was *inspiring*. Something that I think we could do to help benefit everyone down here.' I sit back down on the bed. 'That's why I need to see her again. She can't be sending people above ground. Her clan aren't familiar with the City – and now, with all those increased patrols and the cameras, they could jeopardise everything we're doing, risk the Sympathisers. That's why I need to go back.'

He nods, a peculiar look on his face.

Is he impressed?

'What?' I ask, narrowing my eyes.

'I think you're amazing,' he says matter-of-factly. 'I think you're doing better than anyone could have expected – even Kit!'

I hadn't expected a compliment like that. 'Better than even *you* expected?' I ask, unable to take the compliment without twisting it into a joke. He shrugs and offers me a sly smile, then starts walking around my room again. I try to ignore him, the way his attention zeroes in on my few belongings.

I pull my legs up and lean against the wall behind me.

Please don't go.

I close my eyes.

'You've been drawing?' he asks. I open my eyes again and see his hand poised over my sketchbook.

'Yeah, nothing good,' I say dismissively.

His fingertips linger on the leatherbound book for a second before he picks it up and starts flicking through the pages. Jamie stops on a page and turns it to face me. 'I like this one.'

I can feel the colour rise in my cheeks again. It's a self- portrait from the waist up, my reflection from the mirror on my wall, showing my body, its shapes and curves, capturing a moment of who I am now. My cheeks are burning as he looks between the picture and the real me. It feels like he can see through me, and his eyes are bright with mischief.

'Alright, enough being nosy.' I stand up to grab the book from his hands, but he holds it high above his head. I can feel his chest rising to meet mine as I reach up, pressed against him, and he lets me grab it from his hands. I can feel his breath hot on my neck as I lean past him, putting the book back on my desk.

'Are you going to say anything about what happened *before* I visited Michelle?' I ask softly, trying to keep my voice neutral.

'What happened?' he says, his lips grazing my ear.

I feel an electric current rush through me again, my brain going into overdrive.

'I don't know,' I murmur, leaning back to look into his eyes, desperate to slip my hands into the soft waves of his hair. 'Did something happen?'

'Can't remember,' he says softly, pushing past me and stepping across the narrow room.

I grab his hand before he has a chance to sit down on my bed and pull him back to me.

He has my back against the door in an instant, and I suck in a sharp breath as his lips press against the soft spot under my jaw. He kisses a hungry path down my neck, his hot tongue flicking across my collarbone, then his teeth gently grazing the delicate skin. I don't think – I try, but I can't – and then his lips are against my ear. I feel his warm breath before he speaks. 'Is something happening?' His words come out ragged. I arch my spine.

Nothing he does feels like enough.

I draw back, just an inch. 'I – I don't think we should do this.' My voice is barely a whisper. I feel him nod, his face still buried in my neck. 'Not just yet.' He pulls back, straightening his shirt, but before he can step back, I reach forward again, twisting the thin material in my hands as I pull him towards me. Then my lips are against his. An approving growl slips from his throat. I thread my hands into his hair and let everything slip from my mind, focusing only on the pressure of his body as he leans against me, pressing me against the door.

This is not enough.

I can feel tears pricking my eyes. I know we need to stop. I reach forward and press my lips against Jamie's neck, gently kissing along his jaw. I swear he shivers under my touch.

'We'll wait until this is over,' I say, trying not to let my voice break.

'*This?*' he asks, sitting down on the edge of the bed. I smile at his dishevelled hair and shirt. *I must look worse.*

'The probation, Link, whatever Michelle is doing. This whole time is . . . tense, and we don't need another thing for Kit to lose her shit over. I think she's only holding on by a thread as it is.' He nods in understanding. 'But I do want this,' I add, desperate to clarify.

'Don't worry, I got that,' Jamie says, straightening his shirt. It takes all my willpower to turn around and gently open my door.

'I think you should probably go.' *Don't go.*

He sighs heavily. 'Probably,' he says. 'I'll see you in your new room tomorrow morning. We'll need to tell Kit about you heading back into Michelle's clan. And come up with a plan to figure out who our traitor is.' His lips form a sly smile. I'm still blocking the door. He crosses the distance between us in a step and pulls me into a bone-crushing hug.

'Goodnight,' he whispers in my ear. Then the door shuts behind me, and he's gone.

I walk over and examine myself in the mirror. My hair is like a bird's nest, and my cheeks are flushed. I can still feel Jamie's hands lingering on my hips.

 I can't wait for this week to be over.

thirty/eight

In three days, we haven't gotten anywhere. We're no closer to knowing who our snitch is, and we haven't heard back from Michelle after I requested another meeting with her.

I stand up from the small card table that Kit and I have been hunched over for the last half hour, where we've been rearranging a paper version of the storage room. I stretch my back, doing lunges around the room to stretch out. The large space that was Paula's storage den has been cleared. The side room now functions as my bedroom, and this main room has become our private meeting room. We are all grateful to have a private space, now that we know there's a traitor in our midst. The three of us have become so paranoid, we haven't told anyone I'm staying here. I was comforted to discover that not many people even knew about this room to begin with.

Kit looks up, watching me stretch, then jumps up to join me. I have been practising the yoga moves she's been teaching me, although she's still way more flexible than I think I'll ever be.

The door groans as it's pushed open and Jamie walks in. 'Sorry I'm late,' he says, then cocks his head to one side as he takes in our downward dogs.

'Perve,' Kit says, springing back up and mock-punching him in the stomach. He doubles over, then barrels into her, picking her up and gently slam-dunking her into the lounge.

I look away.

They're like brother and sister, they've been friends for years.

I run my hands through my hair and pull my chair back, sitting down hard.

'Look at this,' Jamie says, spreading a large map of the City on the desk. Kit stalks over and we stare at the map he's just unfurled.

Different locations are circled in red, blue and green.

'So . . .' I ask, crossing my arms. 'You found a map.' I glance at Kit, and we share a smile.

'You have *no* idea what's going on?' Jamie asks, his eyes bright.

'No, I don't. You just got here.'

I don't bother keeping the annoyance out of my voice. He rolls his eyes, and I notice the two of them sneak a look at me, and then at each other. Jamie nods, and Kit starts to speak.

'See this?' She points to a red circle on the map. I nod. 'This, and this, and this?' She points to all the red circles on the page.

'They're all drop-off spots,' Kit says, pulling out a chair and sitting down. I look at the map.

She's right.

'And these are our new drop-off spots for *this* week.' Jamie points to the green circles.

'Those ones in blue, they're the spots for next week,' I say, understanding dawning. He's marked our fortnightly rosters, all the three-month cycles we planned to make everything less traceable to any Council officials who might be looking too closely.

'What are those purple ones?' I ask, pointing to a few I hadn't noticed earlier.

'That's where *someone else* has been doing pick-ups,' he says, leaning both hands on the table.

'Extra pick-ups, according to our Sympathiser intel,' Jamie adds.

'Michelle,' I whisper.

'So, Michelle has been double-dipping,' Kit says, her eyes narrow slits.

'Paula took advantage of the clans' trust, and now they don't trust us,' I say, slipping my hand into my pocket to feel the smooth surface of the dagger I always carry now.

'Those tents in Clan Gaia are *huge*, not to mention getting seeds and seedlings from food growers in the City would have been awfully expensive.'

'Maybe she has some generous friends up there,' Kit says, still scowling.

'These were established plants, heavy with produce – that's months of growing time. I went on a school trip to some "City farms" once. They use water, crushed rocks and fertilisers to grow the plants, instead of dirt like in the old days. But it still takes the same amount of time for the plants to grow and fruit.'

Jamie nods, but Kit shoves her chair back across the cement floor with a horrible scraping sound.

'I still don't understand why she showed you. Doesn't this mean she's exposing herself? She's obviously been doing this for months. Who knows what else they're stealing?'

She walks away from the table, leaning against the wall. 'Well, at least we know she's doing something dodgy, and we can smash her for growing the veggies. Maybe then she'll reveal who her mole is.'

'I don't want to rush into anything just yet,' I say.

I love Kit, but now's not the time to be impulsive. If I learnt one thing from the City, it was that being passive was the most important tool to have tucked away. I think of my mum, the poster woman of the Metropolis. *Make them think you don't feel anything, let them think they own you until the time is right.* I don't think Kit has that skill. She's always too eager to please or destroy. Despite her air of confidence, I'm starting to realise that's all it is – *hot air.*

'I think she wants me to join in,' I say. Kit's scowl deepens. 'No, I'm serious.' I stand up. 'She's testing the waters to see how I'll react, and since I'm new . . .' I trail off.

'Either that or it's some kind of weird reverse blackmail?' says Kit. 'She's showing you how clever and powerful she is, perhaps?'

I hadn't considered that.

'I don't think Michelle would do that,' I say, shaking my head.

Kit rolls her eyes, leaning against the back of the chair. 'She's already flexed her leadership muscles.'

'Did anything happen at the pick-up today?' I ask Jamie in an attempt to turn the conversation. He nods.

'Mark and I noticed two shadows watching us. Carn and

Herma.'

'What about the spy on our end?'

'We don't know yet. Although I would put all my money on it *not* being Zelda or Mark,' he says, leaning back and crossing his legs.

I agree with Jamie.

'Why don't we just say what we're all thinking,' Jamie goes on. Kit and I turn to look at him. 'It's obviously *Leelame*,' he says.

I nod slowly. Aside from the three of us, Leelo, Zelda and Mark are the only people who know the intimate details of our supply collection, and everything had been running smoothly until Kit started introducing Leelo to our systems. Then, as if on cue, we had company on every pick-up and Michelle suddenly wanted to meet me. Jamie interrupts my thoughts. 'I need to talk to a few people; we can't make any accusations without facts to back them up. It will only create *problems*.'

He gets up from the table, his muscles tensing beneath his thin black T-shirt. He catches me staring, and his eyes glint when they meet mine. 'I'm going to ask a few questions and suss out what I can.' Kit rolls her eyes. She hasn't said anything since Jamie threw Leelo's name in the ring.

What's she thinking?

I notice Jamie hesitating near the door. I look up and he smiles at me, sending my stomach into a twist of anticipation. When Kit turns to start pacing again, he shoots me a wink, then the door opens and he's gone just as quickly as he arrived.

✗

For the rest of the afternoon, Kit and I chart the locations of the next supply collections with an orange marker. When we tire of that, we start sifting through the last few piles of supplies Paula had hidden away: more boxes of tissues, baby onesies and an assortment of cold and flu meds.

'This would have been great for the flu season that just passed,' Kit mumbles, throwing the last blister packet on the pile. She leans back against the cracked paint on the walls fanning out behind her like wings. 'I guess we should go to your room and pick up your stuff?'

I nod in silent agreement.

'What do you think about the Leelo theory?' I ask tentatively. Kit shrugs.

'Wouldn't surprise me.' I wait for her to say more, but apparently, for the first time ever, she's done talking.

✂

Piling empty packs onto our bodies, we lock the door behind us and start weaving through darkened corridors back to my old room.

I'm happy to be living out here, far from the main hub of the clan. It feels safer. *Secret.*

'It's going to be good being out here,' I say.

Kit turns to me, surprised.

'Really?' she asks. She pauses like she's going to add something, but she doesn't, and we keep walking without talking.

She always underestimates me.

She gestures to one of the slurs that's scrawled on the wall: *solar eclipse the bitch.*

The number of Sunlight haters seems to be growing; more and more graffitied messages appear scrawled across our clan walls. Yet the targeted attacks haven't been an issue since those notes were screwed to my door. Most dissenters are more interested in ignoring me than goading me. *Maybe attacking Petra was the right move.*

Despite the challenges we might have, nothing is more important than my friendship with Kit. *Right?* I reach forward and grab her arm, squeezing gently. She doesn't stop, or turn, just keeps walking.

'It's like they've forgotten they came from the Metropolis too,' I say. 'Every single person down here came from there at some point, either through parents or their grandparents, if not directly!'

Kit doesn't respond, and I feel the familiar weight of my worry settle across my shoulders like a mantle.

It's all in your head.

But I can't seem to shut the voice up. I can't stop hearing its poisonous whisper.

She agrees with them.

We keep walking. More people are pushing past us now; some smile at us, others leer in my direction or look pointedly at the vandalism.

After everything they've been through, I thought the people would be craving some sort of order.

To protect themselves, if nothing else.

I honestly thought they'd appreciate the extra food and medical supplies, but it seems like the more these guerrilla vigilantes make me the enemy, the more people want to go back to the chaos of before. I consider the way Paula cultivated that disorder to her advantage.

Link isn't any different to her at all.

'So, you don't know?' Kit says, stopping short, hands on her hips.

'Sorry, what?' I hadn't been listening.

'I asked if you know how Jamie feels about you,' she repeats slowly, as if we're speaking different languages. I feel blood rush to my cheeks and am grateful for the dim lights in Clan Ember.

'I didn't hear,' I say. 'What do you mean?' *Does she know that something's happening?*

I don't even know what's happening.

'Don't answer a question with a question!' She pushes my shoulder, hard enough to show me she's not joking around.

'I think he's great,' I say. *Simple. Non-committal.*

'That's not what I asked,' she responds, her voice low and threatening.

I push past her and continue walking silently. *Just keep moving, she'll keep moving.* Kit's words keep ringing in my head. *Do you know how Jamie feels about you?* I think about his hands on my hips, the heat from his breath, and my arms prick with goosebumps.

'You're not a good friend,' she says. I spin around and face her.

'What?' I demand.

'You never trust me with your secrets.'

'I have no secrets that you don't know,' I say, hating myself for lying.

'Then tell me what's going on between you and Jamie.' I look at her, her eyes glassy, begging me to tell her what she already knows. *She loves him.* I think of all their flirting and fighting . . . *She told me they were like siblings.*

'Do you love him?' I ask, my voice no more than a whisper. I feel everything drop inside me. She rolls her eyes and walks away, shaking her head. 'Kit!' I call out, but she ignores me, huffing loudly. I go to grab her arm, but she stops, and I crash into her.

She pushes me behind her like she's trying to shield me. I look around her shoulder, my mouth falling open. My door is covered in red paint. It's fresh, still sticky, and the lock has been busted. Kit tries the handle, but the door won't open.

'It looks like it's been drilled out,' she says, kneeling in front of the mangled lock, the rage rippling out of her, tangible in the narrow corridor.

I thought these attacks had stopped. I squat down and examine the lock. It hasn't been drilled out; it's been filled up.

'What is that?' Kit says, trying to scrape some of the debris away with her fingernail.

'It looks like metal shavings,' I say. Kit pulls her knife out of her boot. We look at each other for a moment, silently agreeing to a truce. She flicks the blade open and pokes the tip into the clogged-up lock.

After several minutes she's cleared the lock enough for me to fit the key in. It's stiff, but after a bit of jiggling and some spit, courtesy of Kit, we manage to open the door. Everything inside is just as I had left it.

'At least they didn't touch anything,' she says, picking up my pencil and sharpening it with her knife. I consider asking her to stop.

I'm still shaken from the discussion we just had, the idea that she loves Jamie.

It doesn't change anything.

I poke my head back out into the corridor.

'We must have just missed them,' I say, slamming the metal door shut with a clang. 'Any one of those people we passed could have done this, or been part of it.' I try to remember who we passed, but I was trying so hard to ignore them. *Did that girl who passed us have red paint on her jeans?* Her head was down. All I remember is that she had blue hair. I look around my little bedroom-cell and sigh.

'You're sorry to leave this?' Kit asks, misunderstanding.

'Not at all,' I say, opening the sad excuse for a closet. 'I'm just thinking about the next fool who has to deal with the room. It comes with a terrible graffiti problem.' She barks a laugh, and we start packing without speaking.

'I do love him,' she says, breaking the silence as she rolls up my bedding. 'But not in the way you mean.' I meet her gaze and then turn back to folding my few clothes. We work silently, stuffing everything into my two backpacks.

'What are these?' I turn to face her then let out a low whistle. In everything else that had unfolded over the past few days I forgot to mention the notes to her. 'They're just notes from some Links creeps.' '*Why* didn't you tell me?' Her voice is cold.

'They were on the door one day when Jamie walked me to my room.'

'So Jamie knows about these?' she says, not a hint of play in her voice. '*Jamie* sure has been walking you to your room a lot.'

'*You* were working in the medical centre. Jamie walked me back at *your* insistence. When we got back here, there were some notes left on my door. I told him not to tell you. He was already freaking out; I didn't need both of you getting all parental and even more controlling.'

'I'm only trying to protect you,' she says, crossing her arms. 'How many times do I need to explain that pretty much *everything* I do is for you?'

'I didn't ask you to do any of this. I'm sick of being wrapped in cotton wool. I'm not worried about some notes from kids. There are bigger issues we need to address. How is freaking out over a couple of notes useful?'

'Then why keep them?' she asks.

I slam my bag down on the empty bed frame, sending the spring off in a violent ripple.

'So I have them – as proof – evidence – if I were to need it.' I snatch my notebook from the desk and the notes from her hand, shoving them both into the backpack. She walks in front of me, trying to block my way, but I shoulder her out of my path.

I'm sick of her treating me like I'm a child, or her puppet.

'You know what. Why don't you just sit down and shut up,' I snap. She opens her mouth to protest. 'You think you know me, know what's best for me, want the best for me, but you're forgetting a few things. I lived in the Metropolis, breaking their laws every day of my life for *seventeen years*. No one found me, no one called the MSC on me – and my father is one of the highest-ranking councilmen. He works for *the Mayor*. My mother, the darling of the City, is a *Sympathiser*, just as my grandfather was before her – in fact, he wasn't *just* a Sympathiser; if what Mrs Lowry says is true, he was one of the founders of all this.' I spread my arms wide, indicating the whole Underground. 'I have made more changes to *help* this hellhole in the few weeks I've been here than you've probably seen happen down here in all the time you were blindly following Paula. She tortured you, abused you and took advantage of *everybody* who risked their lives up there just so you would all survive – and for what? For her own personal gain.' I notice tears welling in Kit's eyes. 'And *I* stopped her. So next time you think I'm just some delicate, useless, Metropolis doll, think again. I am not a child. I am not your puppet, and I am not going to be lectured by you again. *Got it?*'

She doesn't say anything as tears spring to her eyes, slowly spilling over and rolling down her ashen cheeks. I fight the urge to rush over and hug her.

'I don't know what your agenda is, I don't know what your problem with Jamie and me is – whether you're jealous or you actually just don't like me. But either way, it doesn't matter, because

I'm here now and I'm in charge. If you want my job, that's fine. *Kill me.*'

She snaps her head up, locking her wet eyes with mine. I'm the first to turn, clenching my trembling hands into tight fists around the straps of my bags.

'You coming?' I ask gruffly, hefting the larger of the bags onto my back and stomping towards the door. 'Or are you going to stay here and sulk?' *I can't look at her.*

She shoulders past me to grab the other bag and bedroll. I hesitate, then drop my bag and put my hand on her shoulder, half expecting her to shove me away. She doesn't. Instead, she turns and faces me, her eyes still wet with tears.

'I need you to last as Clan Head because the Underground won't last without you,' she says, her voice a whisper. 'I need you to last because –' her voice breaks, 'because I won't last without you.' She turns away, gripping the door handle like it's giving her strength, and I watch another tear slip down her cheek. 'Just don't – don't fuck this up.' She shifts the pack on her shoulder and opens the door.

Andy is standing there, about to knock.

We all shout and jump back, tripping on each other. Andy looks as startled as we do.

'I – I have a note for – for Teddy.' He's polite, but he still won't look at me.

Has Link got to him now too?

I snatch the note from his hands.

Or he's still sore about the other day . . .

Kit walks quickly back into the room, wiping her face on the sleeve of her coat.

'Who's it from?' she asks, her eyes ringed red.

My dearest Teddy,

I'm sorry our catch-up got interrupted and was cut short! I do hope to see you soon. Maybe I could come and visit you in your new chambers. I would love to tell you more about the system we have set up here, I'm sure I can trust you have not revealed too much to anybody. Not yet at least . . . until you have heard the full story.

I pass the note to Kit. 'Wow!' she says after a moment. 'She is something else. There is no way that crazy lady is coming here.'

'How did she know about my new chambers?' I ask, feeling a chill run down my spine.

'Same way she found out about the pick-ups probably,' Kit says. 'Whoever our snitch is isn't just talking about the pick-ups. They're talking about everything we have going on.'

'But no one was supposed to know about that,' I say, unable to shake the ice-cold mantle of unease that's wrapped around my shoulders.

Kit shrugs. 'It looks like somebody found out.'

thirty/nine

We have been standing here for almost an hour, waiting for Michelle's party to arrive. Kit shifts anxiously beside me. I can tell by the way she keeps tucking and untucking her short hair behind her ears that she still doesn't like my plan.

Two days ago, after Andy gave me the note from Michelle, I sent a note right back:

We'd love to have you. Could you come in three days?

– Teddy

Kit lost her mind in response. *What are you thinking? We can't have her here – you can't possibly trust her.* I let her rant, then asked her to trust me. I know Michelle likes a show, and I plan to give her one.

We were an hour early because Kit insisted Michelle would come early, just to show us up. But there's still no sign of her.

Jamie is back in the dining hall finishing off the last details, making sure we've minimised any risks. We've organised an early fight-night to keep most people locked down. Both Jamie and Kit were sure it would offer an adequate distraction to any clan members who might otherwise get mixed up in some counterproductive *welcoming* tactics.

I try clenching and unclenching my icy fingers. Mark and Zelda wave, smiling in our direction. Leelo sulks behind them. Today she's wearing extra tall boots, and towers over all of us, despite being the youngest here.

I smile at Zelda as she squeezes in between Kit and myself. 'Good morning,' she says warmly, patting me on the back and giving Kit a hug. I notice Kit relax slightly. Mark comes up beside me, and Leelo hovers somewhere behind Kit.

Always excluding herself.

'Mark, Leelo,' I say, smiling at them both. 'Glad we're all here. Is Lew ready for lunch?'

'All ready to go,' Mark says with a smile. 'He told me to mention he's boiling the *good rice* today.' He wiggles his eyebrows, and I grimace as we all laugh. Except for Leelo. The only time I've seen her laugh is when she's hanging around Petra and her friends in the dining hall. I beckon for the girl to step closer. To my surprise, she does, but not towards me. She slinks over to stand on Kit's other side. Far away from me.

Typical.

The only reason we reluctantly decided to let her work with us was because Kit feels responsible for Leelo losing her job at the medical centre. She's not responsible, of course. If Leelo's uncomfortable around blood, that's her problem. But I have to admit, so far, when we've given her tasks, she's been quick and silent.

Still, something isn't right.

I glance at Kit as Leelo clears her throat unnecessarily loudly. Kit closes her eyes and clenches her jaw. We've discussed Jamie's suspicions a few more times, but every avenue of the investigation has come up dead. There were large periods over the last few days when no one knew where she was. Even though we can't prove anything, I trust my feeling about this.

'Did you hear about the anti-Sunlight group?' Mark says. Zelda reaches around me and shoves him in the side. 'What?' he asks, confused.

'Sorry about him. He only has a few brain cells in his head at best of times.'

'What did you hear, Mark?' I press, ignoring Zelda's comment.

'Just rumours that Link's been meeting with people who don't *love* you being down here.' They sound like the same people who have been doing their artwork on the walls around our clan. Part of our clean-up over the last three days has been scrubbing the different slurs off the walls, or getting others to cover the graffiti with their own art.

Everyone in the clan has had a job as part of our clean-up, preparing Clan Ember for Michelle's visit. I didn't realise that all our doors were copper until Andy rustled up all the runners and they got to work polishing the tarnished doors throughout the clan. The tiles have been wiped clean and all the globes either cleaned or replaced, so that the glimmering light casts a warm glow over our tiled walls and copper doors. I have to admit, our clan is quite beautiful in its own dark way.

As Mark speaks, I watch Leelo. Her eyes dart back and forth, hanging on his every sentence, narrowing when he voices his criticism. I notice Kit watching her too.

'What else have you heard?' Kit says, turning to face him. 'Did they mention any names, other than Link and Petra?'

But he doesn't have a chance to answer. I notice a little cluster of bobbing lights fast approaching from across the border, and shut the conversation down.

'Shhh – they're coming.' I straighten up.

Michelle arrives almost exactly as Kit had predicted, complete with an entourage. But something none of us foresaw are the gifts. Three of the guards in her party are holding boxes filled with fresh produce. I hear Zelda gasp when she sees the bright jewels of fruit and vegetables piled up in their arms.

'Teddy!' Michelle cries out, pulling me into a theatrical embrace as if she's meeting her dearest and oldest friend. She kisses me four times again, then pulls me back, holding my hands. 'It is *so* wonderful to see you again!' I can't tell if she's acting or genuinely excited to see me. 'Now,' she says, dropping my hands and stepping back, appraising our small group, 'who do we have here?'

I introduce Zelda and Mark. Leelo gives her a curt *hello*, then Michelle steps forward.

'Ahh, yes, nice to meet you all,' she waves to them absently.

'And you must be Kit?'

I see Kit clench her jaw.

Please behave, please behave, please.

'Yes, Michelle, and it's so great to be finally meeting you.' She thrusts her hand forward and takes Michelle's, clutching it tightly. Michelle's sharpened canines shine in the light.

'Let's get moving, shall we?' I say, leading Michelle into the clan and leaving our respective entourages to traipse behind us.

Lew is preparing a special lunch in honour of Michelle's visit, and some people have been invited to join us. Jamie came up with that idea. He said it will make me seem more human. I'm sceptical, but regardless, a fancy lunch could help raise morale, and it's the least I can do to repay everyone's hard work in getting the clan ready.

Surprisingly, I feel proud as I show Michelle around. I'm not sure if she's been here before, but after the last three days of cleaning, the corridors smell less of dead air, and the whole clan seems to have more life to it.

'I had no idea your clan was so eclectic,' she says as we pass bright rows of copper doors. 'Everything looks so – fresh!'

I smile and nod, throwing Kit an *I told you so* look over my shoulder. 'The mood lighting really works with the dark green tiles,' Michelle notes as we weave through the corridors. 'I'm glad I wore gold, I match perfectly.'

Mood lighting – as if the bunker lights were a choice.

Somewhere behind us, I can hear Kit choking on a scoff. I glance at Michelle. If she heard, she doesn't show it.

✄

Finally, we reach the sorting station. I had floated the idea that this would be a great place to show Michelle how much goes into our duties of managing the Underground supplies. Rita and her staff are busy bustling around the stacks. Adults sit at long tables restitching clothing into more practical and interesting garments while young children sit at their feet, collecting scraps. We move to the side as people carrying heavy boxes make their way into the sorting station, stacking them onto the metal shelves that run down the length of the room. I step in, Michelle close on my heels.

As we wander around the stacks and sorting bays, I watch her out of the corner of my eye, trying to gauge her reaction, looking for something to indicate suspicion, or even guilt. There's nothing.

Michelle smiles at the children who look up at her in awe.

Some of the older people say hello or hold up what they're working on for her to inspect. She smiles and nods, and something inside me can't let go of how sincere she seems. One little girl rushes over with some fabric that's been cut and resewn into a scarf.

'A gift?' says the little girl, who couldn't be older than four. Michelle picks the child up and invites her to put the scarf around her neck. I step closer, not wanting to interrupt this moment, but the vice around my stomach tightens. When she puts the girl down and turns to face me, smiling her dangerous smile, I respond with the broadest, most genuine smile I can muster.

Fight fire with fire.

I wave at Rita, and she comes over to join our group.

'Michelle, this is Rita, she manages everybody here – makes sure everyone in the entire Underground gets what they need.' Rita steps forward with a hand outstretched. Michelle smiles at her, then looks at her hand. After an awkward second, Rita folds her arms. I guess Michelle only touches *ranking* members of our clan.

'So, what do you do with the extra supplies?' Michelle asks tightly, her lips still poised in a predatory smile. 'Do you keep them?' Horror flashes in Rita's eyes.

'Oh no,' I say with my hand out, stepping forward. 'We don't have enough for extras.' I hold Michelle's gaze and then she breaks into a high-pitched laugh.

'Of course you don't! Now, are you going to show me your home?' she asks, taking my arm and leading me away from the confused Rita and out of the room, without a backwards glance.

I had never planned on taking her to my quarters; I'd been hoping she'd forget that little mention on her note.

'My home?' I say, feigning confusion as I lead our party towards the next stop on tour – the medical centre.

'This is it,' I say with a sweeping motion. I glance over at Kit, who's talking under her breath to Leelo. Leelo's smiling.

What are they talking about?

'Yes, yes, this is all lovely, but I mean your *new* quarters. You've been in *my* home; I'd like to see yours.' She pauses. 'Unless there's something you're hiding, Teddy?' I feel my pulse quicken, then every hair on my body jumps to attention when she suddenly bursts into the same high-pitched laugh.

There it is. The real reason Michelle wanted to come here.

The only reason?

I laugh along with her. 'Oh!' I exclaim. 'I didn't think you'd want to see in there. Honestly, I've only been in for a week, it's hardly worth looking at. I don't have any silk cushions or a fountain . . . Yet.'

She smiles, mollified by my reaction.

'I still want to see.' Her eyes turn hard.

'*Okay*, we'll go visit then.' I didn't love how openly she talked about the space, but *someone* here already knew, so I suppose it doesn't even matter anymore. I turn back to the rest of our party. 'Kit, could you take everyone back to the dining hall? Mark, maybe you could teach them that game, you know the one,' I say, waving vaguely.

'Stix?' he asks. Michelle's guards stare at her, waiting for their orders.

They don't want to leave her with me.

I notice her dismiss them with a subtle nod.

Kit narrows her eyes, then turns sharply and moves in the direction of the dining hall, her reluctance evident in her scowl.

'Oh, and Zelda,' I call out to the retreating group, 'please let Jamie know what's happening now and tell Lew we'd like lunch in about an hour. Ask him to include the beautiful gifts our guests have supplied.'

I watch everyone leave. Michelle turns, looking at our lights in more detail, muttering something about *vintage sconces*. Leelo hangs back, staring at me, her head tilted to the side. I smile as nicely as I can at her. 'See you later, Leelo,' I say, dismissing her.

'You didn't want me to keep my people with me?' Michelle asks once Leelo reluctantly follows the others. I turn my smile on

Michelle.

'Don't you trust me?' I start off towards my chambers, and soon hear Michelle's bangles clinking as she follows close behind.

✘

Michelle casts an eagle eye around the modest room.

Yes, it is larger than most clan rooms, but it is by no means opulent. Michelle walks around the space with curiosity. She picks up some of the foreign objects I've found over the past month, looking at them like they're artefacts in a museum. I sit at the desk while she turns an old CD case over in her hands.

'I haven't seen one of these before,' she mutters. She puts it down, then moves over to my bookcase, the one thing I do love in here. Jamie dragged it in, said it had been found during the clean-up. On it are five new-to-me books – all about different artists from the old world. One I had heard of from a school text: Van Gogh. He cut his own ear off. But his art was like nothing I could have ever imagined. I pored over the images every night.

'How did you know I had changed things down here, Michelle?'

Jamie and I had stayed up late putting away any documents, maps and other paraphernalia that we didn't want Michelle seeing – just in case she made it in here. Kit had also given me a new little knife. I'm acutely aware of its cold blade pressing against my ankle.

'You're smart,' she says, looking up. 'That's good.' She walks over to my table, fixing me with shrewd eyes. 'There are a few things that can help us in our position. Looks definitely help.' She waves graciously at herself and then in my direction, and she sits down. 'But smarts are key.'

We sit in silence while her eyes continue to explore the space. After a few minutes, she dips her hand into the little purse she has hanging from her wrist. I tense.

'Chocolate?' She holds up a small box of the finest looking chocolates I've ever seen.

'Wow,' I say. Kit would have her knife out to get at these.

Michelle picks one out of its little paper pan and holds it out to me.

'They're from my private collection.' I raise an eyebrow.

Her private collection. I wonder what else she has there. 'You know I can't stand that girl.'

'That girl?' I ask as Michelle drops the chocolate into my palm. She sighs and puts one in her mouth, then chews silently.

'You *know*, Leena, that drop-off girl of yours. I can't stand her.' She picks up another chocolate. *I knew it.* The informant.

Her informant. I can't help but laugh.

She doesn't even know her name.

'You mean Leelo?' I ask, reaching for another chocolate from the box she's still offering.

'I don't really care,' she replies vaguely. 'She snitches on you to me. I'm sure she snitches on me to someone else, and I wouldn't be surprised if she snitches on you to someone else too.' She puts the tiny box on my small table and dusts imaginary crumbs off her hands. 'Who *that* is, is a mystery to us both.'

'So, what do you know?' I ask, crossing my arms. Michelle smiles.

'New drop-off locations, rotating roster, limited pick-up group, the safety of Sympathisers, more frequent pick-ups but smaller collections.'

I nod. Basically, everything Kit has been telling her, to prep her for working with us . . . even before we approved it. I smile.

Don't let Michelle see behind your mask.

'And you knew about all of this when we met?' I ask, picking absently at my nails.

'Yes, I was just humouring you. But you're so sweet, it was easy.'

'Sweet.' *Great, she thinks I'm a sucker.*

She reaches out, dragging the small box back to her. 'Just one more,' she says with a sly grin. 'You see, Teddy, I have a few informants across the clans. They all come with a price. Some are higher than others; it depends on how *desperate* they are.' She puts the lid back on the chocolates and pushes them across to me. 'You can keep these.'

I smile and take the box. 'Thank you.'

She stands up and walks back over to my bookcase, pulling out the book on Van Gogh.

'So, what do you do about the Leelos in your clan?' I ask as she spins around, holding the page open on one of my favourites, the sunflowers.

'We kill them,' she says, snapping the book shut. 'Some habits are too hard to give up. Informants find that kind of life,' she hesitates, searching for the right word, '*exhilarating*. Besides, often the person they're telling has a hold over them – something they couldn't give up, even if they wanted to. A secret perhaps.'

I let her words roll around in my mind.

'I have nothing on Leela or whatever her name is, if you're wondering,' she says. 'She was just an easy target for me. Weak kid.'

'She's fifteen,' I say, standing up from the table.

'And you're seventeen, Teddy, yet you've got *nothing* on me.'

She's right. Kit's words ring in my head. *If you insist on having an ally, you might as well make sure it's one that will have some value to add.*

Michelle certainly meets that criteria.

She grabs my arm, nails digging into my skin. Her eyes burn into mine. 'You need to be *really* careful right now, Teddy.' Her words stun me. I twist my arm free, feeling like I've been stung. *What does she mean?* But before I can respond, she's smiling again and holding open a page of another book: *A Harem Beauty* by Francisco Masriera y Manovens.

'I think I want a painting like this done of me,' she laughs. I rub my arm where she gripped me, still shaken by her words.

Of course I need to be careful. I am careful. Aren't I?

'Should we go to lunch?' she asks, pulling me from my thoughts and turning my attention back to her.

'Yes,' I say, almost disappointed. Michelle puts the book away, and I notice a folded piece of glossy paper peeking out from the top of her small purse.

'You really liked that picture, huh?'

She spins around, her left hand flying to her purse as she tries to stuff the stolen page into the small bag.

'I'd like to give you the book.'

I lean past her and grab the book, holding it out. Her eyes linger on its crimson cover hungrily, but she shakes her head. I put the book back down with a shrug. 'Suit yourself.' We walk over to the door and I pull it open.

'Follow me,' I say, glancing out into the darkness. I needn't worry – hardly anyone knows I've moved down here, or that we're here now, but Michelle's warning has got my nerves on edge. I check, and the coast looks clear, so we step into the narrow walkway. 'Let's see what concoction Lew's put tog –' A hiss – smash!

Something explodes against the wall, sending orange sparks in every direction.

'Inside!' I shout, pointing back into the room. 'There's a fire blanket near the door.' Michelle runs inside to grab it.

I don't have time to worry about how dangerous it could be to have her in there alone.

She's openly spying on me, and she stole that page right in front of me.

I look around, shock paralysing me. A hedge of flames is now burning, creating a neat little fiery barrier that will soon block our exit. I take a deep breath and pull my shirt up to cover my mouth and nose, then jump over the flames, feeling heat bite at my shins. I run out into the corridor to see if I can catch anyone, but it's empty, and almost impossible to see with only the glow of the flames for light. I jump back over the growing inferno, smelling my pants singe in the flames.

I cleaned here. What the hell's feeding the fire?

I run back into my room, but it's hard to see with the billowing smoke. I fumble around, trying to find the extinguisher.

I know Kit brought one in. Where did she put it?

Behind me, I hear Michelle falling over the desk.

Bookshelf!

I cross the room in two steps and feel around until my hands meet the cold, smooth metal. I run back outside with the extinguisher and rip out the pin. It goes off with a foamy hiss, dousing the flames. Michelle runs out beside me, her mouth and nose covered by the scarf the little girl gave her. She's standing at the edge the remaining flames, fire blanket at her feet. I drop the metal canister with a loud clang and stomp out the last of the fiery embers. The smoke is still wafting up. I pull at the corner of the blanket, revealing the remains of a homemade fire bomb.

'That was too close,' I huff, wiping my ashy hands on my pants. 'Maybe we should skip lunch. I think you should go h–' But she's not listening to me.

I follow her gaze, which is trained on the wall, and feel a gasp catch in my throat.

Bright gold paint drips down the wall, glowing from the light seeping out of my chamber:

BRN

BRN

BRN

'Wow,' Michelle says, her voice hollow. 'You really need to get your people into line. Otherwise, someone's gonna wind up dead.'

She turns to face me, poking one long finger into my chest, and starts giggling.

'You.'

forty

Michelle and I decided not to talk about what happened. We went to lunch like normal, and then she left. She hadn't wanted the tour anyway; she had just wanted to speak with me. *To warn me.* Tension ripples through my body, and goosebumps break out across my flesh as I stare at the gold letters drawn on the wall.

We were in there. They could have trapped us. Smoked us out. I shake my head. I'm just about to start cleaning up the smelly ashy mess when I hear the heavy footfalls of someone running. I tense, pulling the small knife from where it's jammed in my boot. Whoever it is, I'll be ready for them.

I almost cry out when Jamie flies around the corner, sweat glistening on his brow. He wipes his forehead with the sleeve of his denim jacket and runs over to me, taking my face in his hands. His eyes scour me for any sign of damage.

'I just heard what happened. I was distracted guiding everyone out and helping Lew clear up, why didn't you tell me at lunch – are you okay?' he asks, his words spilling out a mile a minute. He's breathing heavily.

He ran here for me.

'She warned me. Michelle, just before the fire bomb. She warned me to be careful.'

He pulls me close, resting his head on top of mine. After the fire, Michelle said something I still don't fully understand. *Be wise with who you tell, I don't want your situation getting worse. Not if we're going to be working together.* What did that mean? *Working together?*

'Where's Kit?' I ask after a moment. Jamie shifts his arms and pulls back.

'She's with Link.'

'What?'

'They were in a deep conversation when I was leaving the kitchens, she waved me away so I don't know what it was about.'

Uncomfortable with that new piece of information I pull away, hugging my arms to my body.

What were they talking about?

'Do you know who it was?' he asks, draping his arm across my shoulder and standing back to look at the huge letters, still sticky on the tiled wall.

I shake my head. I can feel my muscles tensing at the memory – adrenaline starting to pump its way around my body again.

'Only you and Kit were meant to know I'm here, although Zelda, Mark and Leelo would have heard Michelle ask me to bring her here.'

'Leelo,' he snarls.

'Who we now know,' I turn to face him, 'is officially Michelle's informant.'

'What?' Jamie says, his eyes boring into mine. 'Michelle *told* you that?' I nod, and Jamie shakes his head, pacing in front of the wall. I reach out and take his hand, forcing him to stop.

'I think we need to come up with a plan,' I say. A sigh escapes before I have a chance to stop it. He gives me a sympathetic smile, then walks me inside.

I follow him over to the old couch beside the bookcase, ignoring the mess Michelle and I made fumbling around in the smoke. I flop down in the middle of the soft couch and Jamie perches on the arm, his knee still bouncing.

'We need proof,' I say. 'If we don't have proof, Link will help Leelo and twist it back on me.' Jamie nods. 'And we all know my word isn't proof enough. Michelle won't say anything, I'm sure.'

'That's not going to be easy.'

I sigh, leaning my head back against the wall.

'She's been weird lately.'

Do you know how Jamie feels about you?

Kit's words linger in my head.

'Who?' He asks.

'Kit.'

Jamie nods slowly. 'She's been dealing with a lot of big changes,' he says, tapping his knees.

'She's not the only one,' I mumble. Jamie leans over and takes my hand. 'There are less than two days left of my probation,' I say. 'What's going to happen after that?'

'Let's just get through this hurdle,' he says, too quickly.

'What are you not telling me?' I lean forward, putting my hand on his knee, stilling him. He gets up and walks over to the desk, raking a hand through his hair, then turns around, his eyes filled with concern.

'It doesn't end, Teddy.' He straightens up and walks back over to me. 'Well, it might, but it probably won't. Link will keep fighting to take your position. We might have mis calculated things . . .'

I feel that familiar anger bubbling up from deep within my chest. *More things I haven't been told.*

'And so what, that's just life?' I stand up to face him. He takes a step forward, and I try to step back, but the edge of the couch presses into the back of my legs.

I'm stuck — in every sense.

'You'll be fine,' he says.

'You don't know that,' I say. It comes out as a whisper. I reach up and take his face between my hands. The fresh stubble is rough beneath my fingers. I draw my thumb across his lips, then pull him to me, pressing my lips against his mouth. His lips part gently, inviting more, and I feel his urgent hands across my back.

In a second, he has me in his arms, gently lies me down on the couch, his hands moving warm and sure across my waist. I feel his fingertips scrape across my bare skin where my shirt has bunched up. I take a breath while his lips press a line down my jaw, across my throat. His teeth gently graze my ear, then he starts kissing across my collarbone . . . then lower. A breath catches in my throat.

'I'm not going to let anything happen to you,' he says, his breath tickling my skin. He reaches a warm hand up and cups my cheek. 'I prom—'

I lean forward, stealing the word from his lips before he can say it.

He meets my enthusiasm in every way, pulling me closer to him, both of us hungry and desperate for more. My mind glosses over the idea of waiting for the *right time*, a better time. I let that thought slip away as the realisation sinks into my bones.

I can't keep waiting for things to sort themselves out, because there will never be a right time. I feel his knuckles graze my sides as Jamie gently tugs at the edge of my shirt. His eyes lock with mine, waiting. I nod.

This is my life now, and I want to live every moment of it.

forty/one

'Can you just tell me what *might* happen?' I ask, adjusting my position so I can see Jamie's face from where I'm lying, with my head on his lap. I ignore the scratch of denim against my cheek.

He pulls a loose strand of hair away from my face. 'Link can't eliminate you and automatically become the leader while you're on probation.' I nod impatiently. 'As of next week we have the vote, and then you'll officially be Clan Head.' I throw my hands in the air in a sarcastic *hooray*. 'Alright, sassy,' he says, playfully shoving me. 'Once you're officially the Clan Head, there is no protection, the rules reset – eliminate and take over.' *Bingo*.

Of course, I've known it from the start, but now it's not some abstract concept. It is here. And despite the discovery of Paula's stolen supplies and my improved systems, it seems I haven't made any progress building support in the clan.

'I've always wondered if they're just trying to scare me, so I won't make it, or hoping I'll become so frightened I'll just beg them to take over,' I say.

I can sense Jamie looking at me, and I glance up to meet his gaze. The warm light from my lamp casts a shadow on his face.

I smile. *I don't want to talk about this anymore.* For the last half an hour we've been debating the possible outcomes of – well, everything. But without a crystal ball, we have no way of knowing what might happen. I stand up and walk over to the desk, grabbing my sketchbook and a pencil, then I spin around to face him.

'I want to draw you,' I say, stalking back over to where he's sitting. He scoots closer, his leg pressed close against my own. I can feel his arm around my back, fingers brush against my side, toying with the hem of my T-shirt.

'Alright,' I say, pulling my legs up and turning my body to face him. He moves back, and I notice a flicker of disappointment cross his face. He angles his chin.

'Okay, Picasso,' he says. 'I'm ready.' *Picasso*. Another artist I would never have known about except for the books Jamie has collected for me. Every day I learn something new, something else that has been missing from my life.

The lengths the City Council has gone to quash all these things.

✗

Jamie sits, silent and patient, watching me while I sketch his face. We don't talk. Based on where his eyes keep darting, it's not hard for me to figure out what he's thinking about while my pencil marks the page with tiny strokes and lines.

'Tell me about your family,' I ask.

'What about them?'

'When did they move to the Underground? All I know is that you're not a True, but you've been down here since Kit was a child.'

'I moved here when I was seven.' He looks away, examining the wall intently. 'But I didn't come down here with my family.' I stop, my pencil hovering just above the paper. His eyes cloud over like he's lost in an old memory. 'My parents died, and there's no place for orphans in the Metropolis.' I swallow.

Is that true?

'Some neighbours came and took me away. They were Sympathisers. They sent me down here so I wouldn't be Sanitised like my parents were.' His voice breaks. 'I hid when they were collected. My mum shoved me under their bed. She knew they were coming. I still don't know why they were Sanitised, though.'

The pencil slides out of my fingers and makes an ugly line across the page.

'I –' I look up, and he reaches out to take my hand.

'You don't need to say you're sorry.'

'But I am.'

After a moment, I turn my notebook around, and he smiles.

A real smile.

'Can I have it?' he asks.

'No,' I say, taking the book back and standing up. Jamie's shoulder slumps a little. 'You can take another one though – any other one. I want this picture.' I give him the notebook and he takes it from me gently, as if it might fall apart in his hands. He gingerly flips through the pages.

'This one,' he says, holding up my self-portrait, the one he saw the other day. I think about everything that's happened since then. I want to stay angry and feel sorry for myself about the fire, but with Jamie around, my heart won't let me.

Gently he tears the picture out of the book, folding it and slipping it into his pocket. He stands up and walks over to where I'm leaning against the desk and opens his arms, waiting for me to accept his invitation. I lean forward and he envelops me in a hug, his cheek resting on the top of my head. I expect to feel that usual wave of comfort that comes from being close to him, especially now, but for a cold sliver of a second, I don't.

'Don't worry about the looks people are giving you,' he murmurs. I shift to look up at him, questioning. 'I know you've been avoiding the dining hall during peak times. But the more you isolate yourself, the harder it will be. You don't need to be frightened.'

I step back from him, putting my hands on my hips. I was *shocked* today when I saw that fire.

Not frightened.

Shocked and angry.

I'm not going to let them win.

Maybe that's what Jamie is saying I should tap into.

'It's easy for you to say,' I reply. 'Everyone loves you! I can't go there without one-third of the people openly hating me, one-third hassling me with problems they think I can just magically solve and the other third ignoring me altogether. Which, to be honest, is my preference at this point –'

'I get it,' he says, holding his hands out. 'You're not a people person right now. I just think, for the next couple of days, you should consider making yourself more present. You need to hold your head up and show them you're not afraid.'

'I'm not afraid,' I say. 'Let them tie me to a stake and burn me to the ground. I'll look them in the eyes while they do it,'

I scoff. 'Dirty liars.'

'Kit and I know you're not staying away out of fear, but nobody else does. Link could be using your low profile to his advantage.' He steps forward again, and I press my brow against his firm chest. 'I know there are a lot of angry eyes cast in your direction. I just think you need to show these people what a great leader you are.'

I look into his eyes and I know he's speaking his truth. He believes I'm meant to be here, that I *am* the best choice to lead this clan.

I was infected before I'd even snuck out, I realise. Long before ever meeting Kit or Jamie or Paula. I have been drawing since I could hold a pencil, and my grandfather, one of the original Sympathisers, encouraged me, and he was murdered for his work trying to save and protect people. People like me.

These people.

That is why I am here.

That's why Mum let me go.

It's been a week since we last heard anything from her. We leave a note in the packs asking for some info. So far, there have been no notes in return, and the increase in patrols means Jamie hasn't been able to pay her a visit. Maybe one of the neighbours found out she was a Sympathiser, maybe my father thought she was infected by me. A knot forms in my stomach.

Infection is a lie. There is no infection. It's just human nature.

'Okay,' I say. 'I'll come to breakfast tomorrow. At a normal time.' He takes a step back and presses his hands into my shoulders, squeezing gently. I swallow as his eyes take me in, as he looks over me slowly. Something has shifted between us and I know he can feel it too. He smiles, stepping forward. I snake my arms around his neck and feel his body stiffen in my arms. I gently press my lips against the soft part between his collarbone and neck and then kiss a trail up to his ear. 'Goodnight,' I whisper.

Jamie reaches down to kiss me. I reach up onto my toes, then I break the kiss, pulling away. His eyebrows pucker softly, and I notice the flash of something in his eye.

Hurt?

I cup his cheeks in my hands. 'I'll see you at breakfast.' Then I grab his shirt and pull him close, and press my lips hard against his. For a second I can't think about anything else except him. Then we break apart, breathless

He smiles, and I find myself wishing he didn't have to leave, that things could just be normal, but I need to be alone. I need to think.

I let Jamie go, and he stalks over to the door and slips out into the darkness. I watch until his shadow is gone, then I look at the letters sprayed on the wall. I don't stand there for long before I step inside and close the heavy door, making sure I've locked myself in.

What is normal?

Climbing into bed I stretch my arm across to the vacant space beside me on the bed.

Maybe I should have asked him to stay?

I roll over and close my eyes.

Jamie and I were going to be Partners. That would have been normal.

I think.

But that sort of normal meant suppressing human nature, human expression.

There's nothing normal about that.

forty/two

'Ready?' Kit asks as we pull on our hoods. Her pink hair protrudes from her hood in sharp spikes, perfectly matching the spikes on her mask.

Kit had bought in to the idea of wearing masks to hide our identities straight away, but Jamie was harder to convince.

Won't it look a bit much? he'd said at breakfast. *We aren't the bad guys . . .*

Kit had promptly reminded him that we, our team, are mostly girls and we are, in fact, doing lots of 'wrong' things by City Council standards, so theoretically we *are* the bad guys . . . well, bad girls.

'Let's do this,' I say with forced enthusiasm as we begin our ascent up the ladder. I can't shake a feeling niggling at me from the pit of my stomach.

Mark was supposed to be with us, but last night, while Jamie and I were . . . occupied, Mark tripped over some metal beams that were supporting a section of sagging roof in the main corridor. Somehow, he managed to completely tear a muscle in his leg. Zelda was also supposed to come today, but she insisted on staying with Mark. Two people down, we were forced to recalibrate: bringing Jamie *and* Leelo along.

It also meant we would have to forgo having a portal minder – something I really wanted on a big pick-up like this.

A risky pick-up.

I climb the ladder, one rung at a time, feeling the cold, flaky metal bite into my bare hands. I glance down and Jamie shines his torch up into my face, hanging on with one hand.

He grins at me.

Show off.

I keep climbing, trying not to think about how far we still have to go. I almost drop my torch from between my teeth when I feel a warm hand push against my butt. I twist around, shining my torch down so I can see Jamie's face. He smiles up at me, wiggling his eyebrows suggestively. I quickly turn my attention back to climbing, before one of the others notice.

This is the first time we're collecting supplies from the new vacant apartment procured through Mrs Lowry. It means there's a place where all the big deliveries can be deposited, since there won't be any space or time restrictions. If all goes well, this location will become one of our regular monthly rotations.

✕

After ten more minutes of gruelling climbing, I wait while Leelo and Kit open the grate above us. They heave it open, and we slip out into the night. The fresh air hits my face, warmer than it has been lately. The air smells sweet, like fresh-cut grass after rain.

Jamie climbs out easily, and Leelo pulls the grill closed after him. I objected to Leelo coming with us, especially since this would be her first collection, but Kit wants to keep her close. Plus, with Zelda and Mark out, we didn't have many options. I haven't revealed much information about the collection today – even Kit hasn't mentioned anything *that I know of* – so bringing Leelo is also going to be an experiment to see if any of Michelle's people spy on us here next time. I watch Leelo while she adjusts her empty pack. Her kohllined eyes dart around above her mask, taking everything in. *Or is she nervous?*

We pad across the City in our soft-soled shoes. It's been raining, and everywhere is glistening. I look around an unfamiliar street. The tall apartments looming over us look expensive but foreign. It is quiet and still, and the silence is making my hairs stand on end.

Just another corner of this city, I didn't know existed.

Who lives here?

Each building is covered with Metropolis propaganda: *We watch because We care! Sharing information saves lives! Your family aren't your friends.*

Kit stops abruptly, fist raised, the signal to hold.

In the cool streetlights, she looks fierce. I glance back over my shoulder nervously.

We haven't seen or heard any guards, which somehow feels worse. I feel Jamie's eyes on me, and my body heats as the memory of last night floods my brain. *Now is not the time.*

'Okay,' Kit says softly, and we continue padding through the streets. I watch Leelo like a hawk, analysing her every movement. She keeps low but her head darts around, like she's looking for something . . . or someone.

The lights of the buildings are reflected in watery puddles, distorted by every footstep we make. Kit is taking us on a deliberately winding route, and I'm happy to be following her. I want to slip my hand into Jamie's, but I'm acutely aware of Leelo's darting eyes. I shiver, and I can feel the rain seeping through my hoodie.

Kit stops again.

I crouch, listening for any sounds I might have missed.

Where are the guards?

She gestures for us to move quickly.

This isn't right.

We follow in single file until we're gathered in front of the tall glass doors at one of the towering apartment buildings. I fish in my pocket for the slip of paper containing the entry code. It was in the pack Mrs Lowry left after our last Sympathiser meeting. I step forward, keeping my head down.

Ignore the cameras. We'll be gone before anyone notices.

I reach out, my hand shaking and damp from sweat, and enter the seven-digit code, holding my breath.

We all sigh when the pad blips green and the glass doors slide open. We step into a large white foyer. Inside, the air is dry and warm. There are large pots with orange and yellow plants lining the walls. We all spin around, taking in the size of the space. It's huge, almost the size of my entire house when I lived in the Metropolis. There are two lifts at the back of the huge foyer, more pot plants on either side. We walk towards them, making sure to keep our heads down. Kit presses a button with an arrow pointing up, and the doors to the right slide open with a soft *ding!*

We step inside, but the doors don't shut. I look out into the blackened street beyond the glass doors.

'Welcome to Belmont Towers, your home. Select your level.' I look at the others anxiously. This wasn't in the instructions. None of us wants to speak. *There's always someone watching or listening. Or both.* We stand shoulder to shoulder in the small metal box, and I feel Jamie lace his fingers between mine. He squeezes my hand gently. 'Select your level,' the automated voice purrs again, not quite human. The doors remain open. Any guard walking past could look in from the street and see us, huddled in here together. My heart is beating so hard I'm sure everyone can hear it.

I notice that the keypad inside the lift is the same as the one outside the main doors. I let go of Jamie's hand and pull the crumpled piece of paper out of my pocket again. I push forward, then enter the seven-digit code on the number pad.

Errrrrrrrrp. The door buzzes and slides shut, the movement agonisingly slow.

'Welcome home, Mrs Jennifer Angela Lowry,' the voice croons, then we launch up. The movement is so sudden we all grab onto the sides to steady ourselves. Kit lets out a squeak of surprise when the lift comes to a sudden stop. I can feel my ears popping.

'Level seventeen. Remember: We watch because We care.' Kit sticks her head out and looks up and down the hallway.

Clear.

We move in single file, jogging softly down the corridor, our feet leaving impressions in the perfect white carpet. The white walls gleam, broken occasionally by shiny black doors with silver numbers on them. When we reach door ten- seventeen Kit puts her fist up again. I pull out the piece of paper and pass it to Jamie. He steps forward, smoothing it on his leg, then types the code into the keypad. There's no blip or flash of green before this door slides open.

forty/three

The lights flicker on when we step inside the apartment. The air inside warm, like a sunny afternoon.

I look around. I don't know what I was expecting, but this isn't it. I guess part of me expected Mrs Lowry's flair for old-school colour and, well, oldness, but this apartment is new – *brand new* – never been used, and *completely* empty.

There is no obvious sign of any supplies. Kit and I start looking in all the cupboards.

Maybe the Sympathisers wanted to hide the goods in case we were discovered.

Jamie opens the cupboards and drawers in the kitchen, which are also empty.

'It's amazing,' Kit says, genuinely in awe. There are pale red lines across her cheeks where the straps of her mask have been pressing down.

'I know. I think I prefer this to my room down there.' I point down, then it hits me. We're up so many floors. 'Kit, there are *so* many people beneath us.'

'Yeah, I know,' she says, continuing her search through the cupboard near the front door.

'No, I mean literally beneath us, in the apartments below.' Her eyes widen in understanding, and she slaps her hand across her mouth. I nod, and we make our way back into the lounge room, gently lifting our feet on the plush carpet.

'We need to be *really* quiet,' I say in a whisper. 'People are living all around us. If they know this place is empty and then start hearing voices . . .'

Jamie nods in understanding. I glance over at Leelo. She's leaning against the wall, not looking for supplies at all. I look back at

Jamie, standing at the entrance to the kitchen.

'She's feeling a bit off I think,' he says, jutting his thumb in Leelo's direction. 'Nervous.' *We all are.*

This is the most exposed location we've ever collected from, and I can't work out why there's nothing here for us to collect. *Where are the supplies?*

'I don't like this. We should go,' Kit says, pulling her mask back on. Her eyes are bright. Jamie and I copy, pulling our masks up over our faces.

'Leelo, are you ready?' I ask, my voice muffled. 'We've got to go now – there's nothing here, something's wrong.' I draw in a deep breath, trying not to lose my patience. 'Come on.' I offer my hand to help her up. She ignores me, putting her mask on, not taking her eyes off the door. 'What are you loo–' Before I can finish my sentence, there's a bang on the door.

'CITY PATROL! OPEN UP!'

Kit's already tugging at one of the windows and Leelo springs into action, helping her open the stiff window.

'MRS JENNY LOWRY, THIS IS CITY COUNCIL. OPEN THE DOOR.'

Jamie starts moving towards the door.

'What are you doing?' I ask, grabbing him by the arm. 'We need to leave now.'

'Hurry!' I can hear Kit calling from the window.

I glance behind, not releasing my grip on Jamie's arm. Leelo is already out of sight and Kit is hunched in the window frame, using her shoulder to keep the window from closing.

'Jamie, we need to go. Now!' I say, pulling my mask off so he can hear me through the hammering on the door.

'You go,' he says, pushing me away. 'You need to go; I'll buy you some time.'

I look at him in disbelief. 'They'll kill you.'

'Or they'll kill you,' he whispers, his fingers pass gently across my cheek. 'I've made my choice.'

He pulls down his mask and brushes his lips softly against

mine. It's over in a second, and then his lips are gone, and all I can taste are my salty tears. He turns me away and pushes me back towards the window, and I half run, half stumble when the guards shout again.

'WE'RE GOING TO BREAK DOWN THE DOOR NOW. YOU HAVE PUT YOURSELF AND YOUR ENTIRE FAMILY AT RISK.'

I think of Mrs Lowry's little granddaughter and her son. *Have we put them at risk? In being here? In existing?* I reach the window and call out Jamie's name as Kit pulls me onto the fire escape. The door bursts open just as the window slams shut and Kit pushes me down beside her. I don't have a chance to break my fall, and I taste the sharp tang of blood. I glance at Kit and see her eyes fill with tears. I pull myself up and peer back into the room, instantly wishing I could look away, but I can't.

The room floods with the City Guard, their grey forms looming like storm clouds. They gather around a black figure slumped on the floor.

Jamie.

One of them kicks him in the stomach, then another joins in. I can hear jeering, and I bite the inside of my already bloody cheek to stop from crying out. Kit is grabbing my arm, tugging at me — she's telling me we need to go, we need to take the head start Jamie's buying us.

The shadow of someone walking over to the window spurs us into action. Somehow, I manage to find the strength to start moving, then I stop and turn back, keeping low. The guard near the window has turned, walking away.

I call out to Kit in my loudest whisper, desperately waving my arm to try and catch her attention. She comes back to the window, and I can feel her nails digging into my arm as we watch. Jamie is being dragged to his knees, his hood and mask ripped off. His hair is messy and blood trails down his neck. Kit looks at me and her eyes flash in despair. All the guards are watching the spectacle; they're not looking at the window. Kit stares at Jamie hunched on the floor, then she springs to life, pulling at my arm, begging me to come with her.

I don't move.

I can't move.

I watch one of the guards. An old man, his grey beard clipped and neat.

What's in his hand? He holds up a black gun in his un wavering hands and presses its barrel to Jamie's forehead.

I reach forward, a scream bursting from me. Kit freezes then pushes us both down   petrified that guards will hear and rush to the window, to us, but my voice is lost in the explosion of the gunshot.

✗

I don't know how I reached ground level. I can't remember climbing down the fire escape.

Jamie is dead.

Leelo grabs my shoulders, shaking me. 'What happened?'

I hear the sharp barking of orders above us and feel someone pulling me.

'Run!' Kit screams, and we take off into the night.

'The guards got Jamie,' I hear Kit say with ragged breath.

'They got him.'

Leelo leads us through the darkness.

'I don't know how they knew,' Kit says over and over again.

My pants are sticking to my legs, wet from splashing through puddles.

Someone set us up.

I look up, but neither girl is speaking.

Someone set us up.

It's in my head.

Jamie is dead. Someone set us up. Jamie is dead.

Somehow, we reach the ladder. I feel the sting of rust on my grazed hands as I climb down. My arms are numb. My legs are numb. I listen to the sound of Kit and Leelo talking anxiously above me. Their voices blend into the vibration of the ladder as our hands and feet clamber rhythmically down it.

Down, down, down, into the Underground.

I feel a giggle bubble up from inside as I sing it to myself. It catches in my throat as the gunshot still rings in my ears and my tears blur my vision again. Kit moves behind me, her breathing ragged with sobs. *Jamie's dead.*

forty/four

I can't move.

Every part of my body feels locked.

'Teddy, I can't get down,' Kit croaks from above me, her voice raw, and I realise I'm still clinging to the bottom rung of the ladder.

How long have I been here?

'Where's Leelo?' I ask, looking around the small space.

'She's run to get help.'

I unfurl my fingers and fall back against the wall. We're in a portal room. It isn't as dark as I remember, or maybe Leelo has left her torch. I can't see where the light is coming from.

'We need to go,' Kit says, clearing her throat. I reach for her, but she steps away. I can see the shock in her eyes. 'We need to tell everyone what's happened.' She says it with no emotion.

We shouldn't.

I open my mouth to explain, to tell her why that's a bad idea. We need to get Zelda and Mark, we need a plan, but Kit's already walking me down the corridor back to the main walkway.

We were set up.

'We need to get to the dining hall. That is where Lew will be. He'll know what to do,' I say, but Kit ignores me, marching forward. 'Where's Leelo gone?' I ask her again.

I can't remember.

Kit turns, rolling her eyes, then fixes me with a cold stare.

'I told you, she's gone ahead. To tell everyone what's happened. Don't play dumb.' 'Dumb?' I say, stopping.

'Someone set us up!' she snaps, and walks ahead.

'Kit,' I call out, reaching out for her arm, but she swats me away.

She couldn't think it was me? The face of the older guard flashes in my head. *I recognise him.* He was there, that night with Jamie, when we were watching at Maree's cafe. He was one of the men who was laughing with Link and talking to Paula, the night I left the City. This guard is a part of that same tentacle.

They already know we're down here. They know Link.

'I need to go to my chambers,' I say to Kit, but she ignores me.

'Kit,' I call after her. She turns around.

'Look, I'm upset too, Teddy, but there are things that need to happen.' I recoil at the implication in her tone. The icy way she looks at me.

She blames me.

'We need to go and talk to the clan. As our *supposed* leader, I thought you'd understand that.'

But this is bigger than me. It's bigger than this petty clan war. I try catching up, but I can't get my legs to match my racing thoughts.

'Please, you've got to trust me,' I say to her back, but she starts away faster than I can keep up. I pull the hood off and throw my empty pack against the wall then bend forward, drawing in a full breath.

I need to calm down.

I lean against the cold tiled wall and slide to the ground, pulling my fingers through my damp hair. Then I just sit. Watching Kit walk away.

I try to focus on my breathing as tears sting my eyes, demanding to be set free.

✕

I'm roused from my brooding by the sound of nearby shouting. I slowly stand up, leaving the empty pack on the floor. I begin moving through the deserted corridor towards the noise.

When I reach the tall copper doors of the dining hall, the shouting is almost deafening. I try to find a familiar face in the crowd. I feel my eyes sting with tears.

I'm looking for Jamie, but he's not here. Jamie is dead, and someone set us up.

I look out into the sea of people again, searching for Lew, or Zelda, someone, *anyone.*

Finally, I spot Kit. She's standing on top of a table, in between Leelo and Petra, with Petra's arm around her. I look around at the crowd again, and it finally clicks.

It's me.

They're shouting about me.

Everyone is pushing and shunting to either get away from or get closer to me.

I notice Link climbing up onto the bench beside Leelo. She starts whispering frantically in his ear. I catch the smirk on his face as he nods, then turns to the crowd, pointing one finger in my direction.

'TRAITOR!' he screams, the veins on his neck bulging with the effort, his hands spanning out around him, spurring them on as they shout it back. I feel the bodies around push me closer to him.

'Traitor, liar, Sunlight scum!' he chants, and the crowd chant it back, driving me closer and closer.

'Traitor, liar, Sunlight scum!'

I feel a hand on the back of my leg and an elbow in my back.

Traitor, liar, Sunlight scum! Someone reaches forward, snatching at my chest, pulling at my shirt. *Traitor, liar, Sunlight scum!* I feel nails clawing at my neck.

I look up to the table where Leelo, Kit and Petra are standing, with Link in front.

'Kit!' I call out.

She hasn't heard me.

'KIT!' I scream again, but she refuses to look at me.

'Traitor.'

The crowd seems to be growing, undulating around me, preventing me from getting away.

'Liar.'

I feel the warm spray of spit as a bearded man steps forward to shout in my face.

'Sunlight SCUM!'

The words hit me like stones, throwing me back and forth as the crowd circles around me. I spin around, looking in vain for Lew. I imagine him running out of the kitchen, pot and ladle in hand. Stopping this. Stopping them.

I cover my ears again. I feel something press sharp into my chest and open my eyes. Petra is in front of me, smiling, her yellow teeth golden under the light.

'Now everyone will see you for who you really are.' With each word, she stabs me in the chest with her sharp red talons.

'Murderer!' she shouts, looking around, and the crowd screams and jeers.

She's enjoying this.

She pulls back, and her closed fist meets my cheek before I have a chance to react. The hot tang of blood fills my mouth. I run my tongue across my teeth and spit. It lands on her shoe. Petra's eyes flash, and then her hand is around my neck, squeezing. I gasp for air, my eyes searching desperately for Kit.

Look at me. Please, look at me.

'Enough!' Link's voice booms. Petra lets go, and I collapse to the floor. She shoves me again, wiping her shoes against me, the studs on her boots tearing my pants. I get up as fast as I can, squaring my shoulders, ignoring the ache in my jaw. I narrow my eyes at Petra. She runs back over to the bench, climbing up and wrapping her arm across Kit's shoulder again. I can't help the tears that squeeze out from my eyes, but I refuse to back down.

I take a step forward, and for a second, I notice Petra tense.

But before I have a chance to do anything, Link steps in front of me, his chest inches from my own.

'Interesting how the tables can turn,' he drones, his sour breath filling my nostrils.

'You need to stop this,' I snarl. I can feel the warm blood dripping out the corner of my mouth.

'Why?' he asks with a sleazy smile. 'Even your friend agrees, *you're* the reason we lost our dear, sweet Jamie.'

I glance up at Kit, who finally meets my eyes.

'Even she agrees, it really does look like you. Set. Him. Up.'

With each word, Link waves the long, sharp dagger he'd used during the swearing-in ceremony, *weeks ago*. I can feel heat flush my neck, the tipping point on the rage I've been trying to control.

'You don't seriously believe that?' I say, shouting over his shoulder, locking eyes with Kit again. 'Why would I do that?'

Link pushes me back with one hand. I grab his wrist and notice the rings on his fingers are caked with dried blood. I let go. I stare at Kit, and she meets my gaze for a second.

What are you doing? I implore silently.

She shrugs as the crowd starts shouting and jeering again. It's a movement so subtle I think, maybe I *didn't* see it. Then she puts her arm across Petra's shoulder, and I feel a sob catch in my throat. Link seizes his moment.

'She saw you leave him to be taken. Kit and Leelo were opening the door to help you all escape, but you kissed him and walked away. You didn't seem too concerned about the guards knocking on the door. Leelo said she didn't even see you *try* to get him to come.'

Leelo had already left us. 'Sweetie, you left him there.' I spit in his face.

He wipes it off with the back of his torn sleeve, leaving a thin line of my bloodied saliva. He walks over to the table and sits on the bench, clicking his fingers twice. 'Take her.'

Two stocky men I don't recognise grab my forearms, dragging me back.

'Let me go,' I shout, struggling in their grip. 'I said get off me,' I snarl, kicking my leg, but their grip is too strong, and I'm half dragged, half carried away. I bend my neck around desperately, craning to see Kit. 'Kit!' I call out. I see her, just for a second. Petra puts up a hand, sarcastically waving goodbye. Beside her, Kit stands with her arms crossed over her chest.

The moment our eyes meet, she bows her head and turns away.

Away from me.

I don't bother fighting the tears now. The men drag me through the mass of bodies as I scream. People's arms and legs are flying everywhere, some trying to get at me, others in retaliation as fights break out in other parts of the room.

I keep screaming and kicking as they drag me down the corridor, away from the dining hall, until I feel a thump on the back of my head.

forty/five

'How could you let them do this?' I ask.

It's taken her two days to visit me.

Two days since Jamie —

I know there's no point in asking. I can see it in her vacant eyes.

She believes their lies.

'How could you think I would be guilty of any of this?' I say regardless. Kit turns her back on me.

'The Teddy I thought I knew would never have sold her friend out to secure her own position.'

'What?' I spit. 'What are you talking about?' She has a manic look on her face now.

'I know what you did.' Her eyes are wild, and her hands fly around as she speaks. 'I even know why! What I don't understand is how you thought you'd get away with it.'

She leans against the wall furthest away from me in the dingy room that is my prison. It's as close to a cell as I can imagine. The ceiling is only just taller than me at the highest point. I want to ask Kit why she never told me about this room . . . *rooms?* There's a door that I presume leads to a corridor and more cells. My room has a small 'open' area, where Kit is now standing before the bars that cage me in. Not meeting my eyes, she starts to speak.

'I know it was part of your plan.' *My plan?*

'What plan?' I fight the urge to scream. I *must* stay calm.

'To eliminate Jamie.' She looks up, meeting my shocked gaze. 'You were clever,' she begins, twisting her fingers together.

'Becoming friends with us. *Special* friends with him.' I open my mouth.

'There's no point denying it. I know something was going on

between you two. You've never cared about anyone else but yourself. I saw you kiss him before we walked away.' *He kissed* me.

It doesn't matter.

I shake my head. 'You told me he was like your brother,' I say.

'Yes, he was. He was *my* family. Why would I want *you* to steal him from me?'

I have no answer. Kit takes my silence as an admission. 'It was very clever to use Paula as ammunition against me.' She clasps her hands together in front of her stomach.

I stand up and grip the bars between us.

'Ammunition?' I manage to choke out. 'These are lies, Kit – you know me better than this.'

How long have they been drip-feeding her their story?

'I just examined the facts,' she snaps defensively. She breaks my gaze and starts running her perfectly manicured fingers up and down her arms.

How long has this been part of Link's plan?

'You were obviously going to make it look like you had tried to save him, but in the end, that was clearly all too hard. You're just like Paula. You used us to try and buy your way back into the City.' She hesitates, as if she wants to get close, but doesn't move. 'You did it. *You* alerted the guards.' Her eyes are cold. 'I bet Mrs Lowry herself was in on it.'

I take a step back. I know I'm still a stranger to her, compared to Jamie, who she'd known practically her whole life.

Show them what a great leader you are. That's what Jamie told me. *What would he say to me now?*

Link knew Kit was broken and took advantage of her. Jamie had said it: *she doesn't want to be alone, she's afraid of being persecuted because she's different, but aren't we all?*

'Don't look so upset,' she says. I look up, hopeful, but she stands before me like a stranger. 'Even the brightest star goes dark, eventually.'

How could she fall into their hands? Even I had to admit it was clever. *Take away the people closest to me.*

'Isn't it obvious?' I say. 'This *plan* is all Link. Make it about *me* trying to manipulate the clan. Blame *me* for what *they're* doing.' I roll my neck. 'And what about Leelo? You know for a fact she was a traitor, leaking intel to Michelle. She was working for Link too, the whole time – it's so obvious!' *I just need to get her to remember.*

'No, *you* told us Leelo was the traitor.' She laughs, and it sends a shiver down my spine. 'I trust my cousin over a stranger. It was you all along.'

I shake my head. The black walls surrounding me seem closer than they did moments earlier, and I can feel my breath rising in my chest as panic sets in . . . again.

'Listen to me,' I say slowly. 'I know terrible things happened to you. You trusted Paula, and she hurt you.'

Her hands go instinctively to her arms, then she jumps forward, grabbing the bars in front of my face.

'You don't know anything!' she snarls. 'You need to stay here. You're dangerous. Perhaps you were even working with Paula, and you betrayed her! It all seems too neat, too convenient that you – you Sunlight *scum!* – just swanned into leadership down here.' She shakes her head. 'All with the help of your mother and your grand plans . . . I'm just sorry I was ever stupid enough to trust you.' She grits her teeth as if fighting back tears. 'Now, because of *you*, Jamie is gone. Jamie, who was family.' She bangs the heel of her hand against the bars, then steps away. I fall against the wall, using it as a crutch before my legs betray me.

'He was my . . .' I don't finish my sentence.

What was he to me?

I feel a swell of anger rise within. He had been stolen away before I even had a chance to find out.

'Exactly,' she drawls, stepping away from the bars as I step closer, continuing our dance. 'Jamie was nothing to you. That's why he was so easy for you to kill.' She stumbles, as if the recoil of her words is too powerful for even her to handle. I try to swallow, but my mouth is dry.

'Get out,' I say. I can see Kit gathering her words, but I've had enough. I know what story Link and Petra are trying to spin. I know the lies and stories they're weaving, and Kit has let herself be swallowed up by them.

Looking for that family she's never had.

I can feel my knees starting to tremble, but I won't let her see me fall. I step forward and grab the bars right where her hands were moments earlier.

'Get. Out.' The words hardly make it past my clenched teeth. I know she's heard me. She turns without a second look and the door slams shut behind her. I hear locks clicking into place.

My friend is gone, and with her, my last hope.

forty/six

I can feel the dirt in my throat, my tongue dry and cracked. It hasn't taken long for me to become dehydrated. I can't remember the last time I drank, and with no clean water and no edible food . . . The door swings open and a young guard steps inside, but is quickly shoved away. I see a familiar bearded face.

'Teddy, are ya okay?' Lew asks, stooping down to peer through the bars. The guard steps forward, but I can see his hesitation. He doesn't want to take on Lew.

'Get OUT!' Lew bellows, and the guard hastily scampers away. 'Teddy, what canny help ya with, how can we fix this situation?'

I look into Lew's honest eyes, and I feel the pressure of the last few days start to rock me, my solid resolve about to crumble. I realise how pathetic I must look: a dirty-faced girl, hungry and broken, rejected by my best friend, and fed food an animal couldn't eat.

'And to think there were some people who thought I was going to be the one to lead the Underground,' I manage to whisper. Jamie's words linger: *show them what a great leader you are*. In my mind, I see him kneeling, the guard pointing a gun at his head.

Lew looks at me, dragging me back into the present with his steady gaze. 'I wanted to go back to get him. I didn't want to leave him there. Leelo had already left and, and we had to, to leave him there. With those monsters. He pushed me to the window, to buy us time – *me or all of us*, he said.' I feel my voice catch in my throat. 'I didn't want it to be him. I wanted it to be me. I didn't –' Lew reaches out through the bars.

'I know, I know,' he says, trying to soothe me, speaking in a tone you might use on a small child who's scraped their knee.

I'm not a child.

'You don't know. You don't understand. No one does.'

I feel like telling him about Jamie and me, about what we shared.

'I would never betray anyone – least of all Jamie!' I say after some time.

'You and Jamie?' he asks, gently probing. I try to answer, but my words get caught in my throat.

'I kept pushing him back. I wanted to wait for all this to be over, for everything to settle down.'

I don't know what else to say. I pull my arms back through the metal bars and crumple into a heap on the dirt floor, and finally the tears I've been bottling up begin to cascade down my face.

Tears for losing Jamie, tears for Kit . . . tears for myself.

I gasp for breath and see Lew produce a little cheesecloth bundle.

'Here,' he says, pushing the pile between the bars. 'Have some food. It doesn't look like they've been feeding you anything you could eat.' I look up at him and jerk my head in the direction of the bowl, filled with rotten – something. He gives a low growl.

'Thanks,' I manage to croak before biting at a tiny piece of bread. I've never been hungry like this before, but if I gorge myself on this food, I'll make myself sick. I also need to make it last.

While I nibble at some bread, Lew sits cross-legged, waiting patiently on the other side of the bars. 'I don't know how long I've been in here. The lights don't change,' I explain, jutting my chin at the single bulb illuminating my dirty cage. 'Kit came down once. To tell me that she wanted nothing more to do with me.' Lew's eyebrows shoot up. I guess it's news to him. 'She says I'm the reason Jamie's dead and that she made a huge mistake in ever trusting me.' My voice cracks. 'That she should have let Paula kill me when she wanted to.'

I slowly draw in a breath. 'Why did you come down here?'

'I want you out of here so you can take your place as the rightful head of Clan Ember,' he says.

I hadn't expected that.

'I'm gonna see Kit m'self. I can't honestly believe she thinks any of those things. Surely, she woulda known 'bout you and Jamie, if *I* could tell. The girl's thick, but she's not *that* thick.'

'How come they haven't gotten in your head?' I ask, brushing his comment away. 'I can't understand all the lies they're spreading.'

'I've been around a little bit longer than you and yur friends. You'll find that many older people here actually disagree with what Link and Petra are doing with the clan-less Outskirters. The way they're trying to round 'em up.' He sighs, rubbing his temples. 'If I'm frank with ya, we don't know what we can do about it. I've spoken to some of the other elders, and they like ya, but they don't know ya, and they're scared.' He pushes himself up from the ground, gripping his knees. 'No one is infallible, Teddy. But there are certain things you can only learn through experience.'

'I know that,' I say softly.

Jamie would have known that, too.

I want to tell Lew I loved Jamie.

I did love him – didn't I?

I remember his hands, the way they set my skin on fire. His confidence in my decisions. The way he looked at me. *I did . . .* I close my eyes . . . *And I think he loved me – but I didn't even get a chance to really know him.*

Another thing Link and the City have stolen from me.

I remember Lew is still here. Our eyes meet, and for the second time, I get the feeling he knows what I've just been thinking. Lew smiles kindly, the same warm smile he gave me when we defended the Outskirter in the dining hall, when I realised the true extent of Link's cruelty. He doesn't care about people, not even the people of his clan. *He's worse than Paula.* Or he will be. *I must stop him.* 'So, do you have a plan?' I say, surprising myself with the resolve in my voice.

'Thought you'd never ask,' Lew replies, smiling conspiratorially.

forty/seven

Two days later Lew returns, just as he said he would, bringing another small bundle. Once the guard leaves us, he opens the package and pulls out a metal file.

'How did you get it?' I say. He chuckles and puts the tip to his lips.

'Now, you never heard stories as a child?' he asks.

I shake my head, not following.

'Well, we do down here. We read. And I'm an old man. So, before the war and all these dark times, I had stories. When I was growing up, my favourite books were about daring thieves, and one book involved a great escape from jail. In the story, the robber gets a metal file brought to him in a cake. He manages, over months, to wear away at the grout around his window. Then he pushes out the metal bars and disappears into the night.' His eyes glow with the memory.

'So, you're expecting me to file my way out of here?' I ask, unimpressed. 'Over *months*?' Maybe I was wrong to put my hopes of escape in the hands of an old man. He pops one eyebrow, his eyes sparkling.

'You don't get it?' he says, eyes peeking out from under his bushy eyebrows. 'See those bricks?' He points to the crumbling wall behind me. 'You need to use this file to get the old mortar out. Get yourself a brick and when your dimwit guard comes in –'

'You've got to be kidding me,' I say, not bothering to hide my disappointment.

This was his big plan?

'Do you have a better idea, lass?' he asks, sitting down and crossing his arms.

'They don't actually come in – the food just gets slid under the

"

bars.'

He furrows his brow, thinking, then his eyes light up.

'Okay, you have a brick underneath you and pretend you're sleeping. Leave this,' Lew holds up the file, 'somewhere obvious, but out of reach so they must come in to get it, then boom!' I shut my eyes, trying to visualise how this will all unfold. It's actually . . . not the worst idea. It could work.

'Fuck, Lew! You're a genius!'

The old man's eyes widen in surprise at my language.

'You didn't think girls could swear?' I say indignantly.

He laughs. 'That's not swearing, lassie. I just didn't think *you* swore.'

He hands the file over, and I move quickly to stash it under my bedding. 'Link has announced himself as the official Clan Head,' he says as I settle back down. My mind rushes to the girl in the pink dress.

Link is no leader.

He fills me in on Link's recent escapades, rounding up any Outskirters who've been living in the outer corridors of Clan Ember and locking them in the empty supply closets. 'He's thinking of using them as unpaid workers.' 'Slaves,' I say matter-of-factly.

Lew nods. 'Basically.'

'No one should be punished for being clan-less,' I say. 'What does anyone expect them to do? If they're not given supplies, of course they're going to have to steal.'

He nods his agreement. 'But yur damned if ya do and yur damned if ya don't.'

I shake my head.

'It seems like yur in a bit of the same boat too.'

Before we have a chance to discuss anything more, there's a heavy thud on the door. I hurry to shove the food under the back of my shirt, tucking it in so it doesn't slip onto the floor. Seconds later, the door behind Lew opens and light streams in.

'Time's up, Lew.' An older clan member steps in, different from my usual minders. 'Our precious leader needs her beauty sleep.

She's going to be meeting the big boss soon.' Lew and I exchange a look.

He didn't know that.

We don't even have a chance to say goodbye before the man hustles Lew out into the hall, and with a jingle of keys, I'm locked up again.

✕

I nibble some more at the food Lew has brought, even indulging in some of the raisins he managed to add. I relish their sweetness as I shut my eyes and imagine I'm sitting in the park under the sun, feeling the warm rays sink into my skin. I open my eyes and glance up at the lone globe illuminating my own personal hell. I don't even care about the real sun at this point.

I think I'd pay to sit in Michelle's fake garden and feel the heat from her lamps sink into my cold, damp skin. Michelle, my *only* friend now. If you could even call it friendship. Kit's cold eyes flash across my mind again.

After my snack, I set to work filing away at the mortar around one of the bricks, which already looks precarious. If the guard is right and Link is planning to meet with me, tonight might be my only chance to get out. That skinny young guard will be back soon with my next meal.

Little bits of dried sand fly off the wall, and my knuckles become red-raw as I work. I'm glad for the distraction from my thoughts. I stop and reward my good progress with three more raisins, some bread and a little cheese. It's salty and delicious. Ordinarily, I would be wary of eating anything salty since the water isn't drinkable. But I'm feeling optimistic I'll have ample clean water soon, if this all goes to plan.

Wait.

I sit down for a second. What will I do when I get out? I groan as I realise what a half-baked plan we've come up with. I roll my shoulders. I'll go to the kitchens and find Lew. He'll know how to get me out of the clan temporarily. Maybe to Michelle.

I start working at the mortar again. My torn skin, dry from the sandy mortar, causes my fingers to slip, but I keep going. It feels good to work. I have been so numb, so *still* for so long. I hear a sound behind the wall and I stop, sliding the file into my waistband. The sound stops. Perhaps I imagined it. I look to the door, scanning for shadows beneath it, but there's nothing. I turn back to the brick again and resume scratching and scraping away.

✕

I stop for another break. The guard will be here soon. I slip the file into my waistband, hide the dust under my bedding, and wait.

✕

'Mealtime, your *highness*.' The younger of the two guards reaches out as if to hand me the metal cup he's holding. It slips from his hand before I can take it, and what looks like clear, fresh water splashes across the floor. I lick my dry lips.

'Oops,' is all he says before he throws the empty cup at me. It bounces off my shoulder.

'Here's something to eat.' The older guard frisbees the flat bowl of grey porridge under the bars, so fast it catches on a loose stone and upturns. 'Oh, dear,' he drones. 'You should know it's bad manners not to eat the food your hosts have offered you.'

'Fuck off,' I say, picking up the bowl and frisbeeing it back.

I freeze. The file has slipped out of the band of my pants.

He thinks I'm scared of him.

The two guards stand leering at me.

'You're a rude – little – Sunlight – bitch.' He punctuates each word, like throwing little rocks at me.

Don't move, don't move.

'Pussy.'

The two men laugh as they finally leave, locking the door behind them.

I grab the file from the leg of my pants, gripping the warm metal in my hands. I start filing again.

310

I really need to get out of here.

✖

I stand up straight and stretch my back. The brick's loose now. I just want to pull it out, but it's not like a baby tooth, it won't budge unless it's completely free. I get back to my scraping, finishing off the mortar, then I try pulling again. Finally, the brick releases itself from the wall, sending me falling back into the dirt and dust.

I don't waste time celebrating. I move quickly, putting the brick under my blanket.

What next?

I toss the file between my hands.

I need to distract them from the bricks.

I look around the small space, then it hits me. I step forward and start filing at the bars.

Make them think I'm trying to file my way out.

I run the file over one of the lower metal bars. It makes very little progress, but a huge mess. Shards of metal spray everywhere, twinkling even in the dim light.

Perfect.

I file at a few bars and then spread the filings around, in a little path towards the metal tool. I position it in the half-light beneath the hanging bulb, a poor attempt at hiding it. Once I'm happy with the scene, I finish off the rest of the food and stuff the cheesecloth in my pocket.

Jamie would be impressed. My heart aches at the thoughts I have been so desperately trying to suppress.

I can't think about him now.

Not yet.

I go back to my makeshift bed and arrange the blanket so it won't tangle my legs.

I need to be free to jump up quickly while the guard is bending down under the light.

I hug the brick, then practise jumping up a few times.

I'm tired, but I can't let myself fall asleep. Despite my best efforts, once I'm lying down, my eyes start to close. I can feel myself drifting off. I try to stay awake. *I must . . .*

forty/eight

I kick my legs out, and the sudden movement wakes me. The nightmare I'd been having is already slipping from my memory as my eyes adjust in the dim light.

Panic hits me. *Have I missed my opportunity?*

I stand up quickly and see that the file is still lying in the half-light where I left it. I look over at the food and water bowls to check, but nothing has changed. I push down my blanket and rub my eyes.

I feel better physically, having slept deeply for the first time.

I lie down again, no longer tired. I feel the buzz of anticipation set my body on edge.

I practise jumping up with the brick twice for good measure, then wait for the sound of the keys. I wonder who they will send today. I hope it's the boy. Not much older than fifteen, he will be a much easier target than the other guard, Owen, a huge burly man with arms the size of tree trunks. *I doubt he'd even notice if I clocked him on the back of the head.*

I find myself dozing off again, even though I'm not tired.
Maybe they're not coming back until Link wants to see me.
That will be a problem.

I stare at the door, highlighted by a thin line of light around its border.

✄

After what feels like an eternity, I hear clinking, and a flash of light trails over me. Maybe I'm dreaming again. I stretch out my legs, and my hands clench around something rough.

The brick.

I freeze, popping one eye open, then the other. The boy is

"

standing over me, each red mark of his pimply face like stars in a complicated constellation. He freezes when he sees that my eyes are open, and I see his leg poised, ready to kick me in the stomach.

This place really does have five-star service.

I throw off the blanket, shouldering him out of the way, and slam the brick square in his temple. He stumbles back, stunned. Before he can recover, I run behind him and kick him in the back of the knee, then lift the brick up with both hands and slam it down on the back of his head. I grimace as I hear his skull crack when he hits the ground. I check his pulse to make sure I haven't killed him.

He's still breathing.

Two huge angry bruises are already forming ugly purple lumps on his head.

Dragging him onto his back, I scrounge through his pockets to find the keys, a small notebook and a pencil. I shove these things into my pocket and also grab the small torch he dropped. As I walk over to the bars, I remember the brick.

Putting it back in the wall would be better.

I replace the brick, then tuck the file into the back of my waistband. I don't want to get Lew in trouble. Once I'm on the other side of the bars, I can't hold back the smile when I lock the gate, securing the boy inside the tiny cage.

I walk over to the main door and press my ear up against the cool metal.

Fear bubbles to life. I put my hand on the doorknob and turn it. It's unlocked. I press my ear against it again and decide to make my way to the kitchen to find Lew.

He'll know what to do.

I take a deep breath and step out into the corridor, fighting through the fatigue I feel as my limbs move more than they have in days. I had half expected to be in an antechamber, but instead I find myself standing in one of the main thoroughfares. If I go left, I'll walk directly to the medical centre. If I turn right, I'll end up in the main corridor, heading towards the dining hall.

I look at the door I stepped through and consider how close I am to everyone. Do the people even know what they're walking past every day? I had always assumed that door led to a supply closet — it's just a random little door, not a heavy copper one like most of Clan Ember's doors. Did Kit realise those cells were there before she visited me?

Why did she never tell me?

I look around. It must be late in the evening, because there's no one about and the lights have been dimmed to a gentle glow. I look left once more and think about Kit.

Once, finding Kit would have been the obvious choice.

Not anymore.

Ignoring the ache in my chest, I turn right and begin slinking through the corridors. The kitchen has a back entrance, for deliveries and staff. I try to remember how to get to it.

I start walking faster. I can't afford to waste time. I don't want to be seen, and I don't know how late or early it really is. It sounds like each step I take is the heavy clomping boot of a Metropolis guard, but I know it's just in my head.

I get to a crossroads and stop again, trying to decide which way to go. I think if I keep going straight, that will take me to the back of the kitchen. I tread softly, running across wide walkways and then sticking to the walls.

My eyes water as the lights get brighter.

Morning.

My heartbeat pounds louder in my ears with the passing of each bright light. I push myself onwards, moving faster and faster — every walkway and corridor is a potential threat.

I see the back door to the kitchen and fight the urge to whoop. I reach into my pocket, fishing for the stolen keys. I try the first three, but none of them work. I finger through the remaining eight and almost drop them when I hear a door open and slam shut.

Footsteps echo down the corridor, paired with occasional shouting. It seems like I'm not the only one who has trouble getting up in the mornings.

I have tried four more keys when I hear footsteps getting

closer. Voices start to fill the corridor. *Familiar voices.*

'I'm still not surprised.'

I recognise Leelo's whining voice immediately. The keys slip out of my shaking fingers and jingle as they land on the concrete floor.

'But his ideas, about the Outskirters, they're so –' I freeze. *Mark.* I take a deep breath and try the last key. 'They didn't choose to be clan-less.' The voices are louder now, and I'm confident I know who they belong to.

'They're barbaric, that's what they are.' *Zelda.*

Click. The door opens and I slip inside just in time to see through the crack: Leelo, Zelda and Mark, who's still hopping on crutches. A heartbeat later and they would have seen me. I click the door shut and turn the lock from the inside, closing my eyes as my blood roars in my ears.

What are Zelda and Mark doing with Leelo?

A shiver of doubt runs down my spine.

Anyone can betray anyone.

I shake the thought from my mind and start moving around boxes and tubs into the back room behind the kitchen. Skirting my way around a freezer, I notice a pantry the size of a small room. Suddenly I hear footsteps approaching from the other side of the freezer and look around frantically.

I must find Lew.

forty/nine

I've hardly taken two steps into the pantry before I feel someone's hand covering my mouth. An arm crosses over my chest, and I'm being pulled away from the glowing warmth of the pantry and shoved into a dark room. I struggle to break free, trying to bite the hand that's still gripping my face. Then it's gone. I whip around, grabbing the file from my waistband, and find myself face to face with Lew. Even in the low light, I can see his left eye is swollen, with pink and purple bruising around the lid, and his nose has been set with tape.

'What happened to you?' I ask, my voice a whisper.

'Don't worry about me. Yur not safe here.' Lew's eyes dart around the storage room frantically, as if he's expecting someone to pop out of one of the boxes. I open my mouth to ask questions, but he cuts me off. 'They know yur out.' I can see a sparkle in his busted eye.

'Apparently, they found that young guy passed out, black and blue, locked in your cell.' He gives me a fleeting conspirator's grin, then his eyes go dark at the sound of running outside.

'I've only been out for what, fifteen minutes?' I ask, trying to keep the panic out of my voice.

'A lot of things can happen in fifteen minutes. They think someone helped ya.'

It's not hard to guess who they think helped me, but Lew's injuries don't look fresh. *When did this happen?* Again, as if reading my thoughts, he waves his hand dismissively. 'I'm an old man.' He moves into the depths of the dark storage room that doubles as his office and sits down on the old wooden chair behind the tiny desk. 'I'm seventy-five this year, an' I've seen too much to sit 'round with me mouth shut any longer.' He prods his eye gingerly. 'I spoke up 'bout somethin' last night.'

I can hear more people stomping outside. The frosted glass walls don't provide much protection. It's only a matter of time before they check this room, even with the lights off.

'I think ya need to take shelter with that young one, Michelle. I know yur friends with 'er. Once yur there, you can figure out what to do next, about Kit.'

'Did you talk to her?'

He hangs his head, nodding slowly. 'They have brainwashed 'er something good. I'm sure you will be able to talk some sense into 'er. I tried to get it out of 'er, to figure out what she is thinking, but she doesn't seem to be thinking clearly at all right now. Regardless,' he waves his hand dismissively, 'I've known that girl longer than she's known 'erself and she can't honestly believe in the way Link runs things. She's a healer, for Pete's sake!' His fingers absentmindedly go to his nose. Kit must have set the break for him.

'This descent into violence is exactly what I kept telling Kit and Jamie would end the Underground. Us oldies have always known it would destroy this clan and the whole Underground.'

'I tried to explain that to them too. I don't think Kit ever understood. She's never known anything different. Those are hard beliefs to break.'

'Difficult and impossible are two very different things,' he says.

The voices outside are getting louder.

'I think she's in here!' I hear a gruff voice shout. More feet stomp in.

'We've got her now.'

I recognise the voice immediately. *Link.*

Lew turns to me urgently. 'You need to go, but first, take this,' he says, pressing a necklace into my hand. 'Fix it,' he says as I hold up the chain, studying it. There's a small silver moth with a broken wing hanging from the chain. It feels familiar. 'Fix the moth, Teddy,' he says. 'Your grandfather left it with me to fix many years ago. He had intended to give it to you as a birthday gift but –' His voice breaks off. 'I'm sorry I haven't fixed it yet. He'd want you to have it now, I'm sure.'

Emotion rises in my throat. 'You – you knew my grandfather?' I ask, pocketing the broken necklace.

He nods but before he has a chance to explain, I can hear raised voices. I turn to the door, pressing my ear against it. I will them to walk back into the dining room so I can slip into the corridor, but they're not leaving. It sounds like more boots are approaching. I look at Lew, and see my panic reflected in his expression. I need to hide.

I move quickly, opening one of the boxes on the floor, trying to be as silent as possible. I put one foot in the box and am rewarded with a loud pop as I stand on some bubble wrap. I freeze. Lew has his eyes closed, and one finger pressed to his lips. I lift my foot out of the box and almost fall over as the walls around us shudder. The knocking comes again, faster, vibrating the entire room. I jump away from the box, not bothering to be silent now. I look at Lew, panicking about what this will mean for him. He looks different now. No longer the cunning man who snuck me a file and helped plan my escape. He's frozen in terror.

There's more shouting outside. I can't tell if they're shouting at each other or trying to yell at me through the door. The walls shudder again. This time, though, they're clearly calling for us to 'open the hell up!'

I shrug at Lew. I can't out-manoeuvre these guys, there's no back door to slip through, and boxes aren't going to hide me.

I consider using the file as a weapon, but my combat skills – *What combat skills?*

The shouting has stopped. I can hear the soft clinking of a chain.

'Open up, old man. We want to have a chat with your girlfriend.'

I don't need to see through the door to know it's Link. I look at Lew again, knowing it might be the last time I see him, or anyone who actually cares whether I live or die. I'm struck by the thought of my mother. She has no idea what's happening down here.

I have no idea what's happening to her up there.

Link has started counting down from five, but I won't play his game. If I'm going down, I'll do it on my terms.

I take a deep breath and grip the doorknob.

fifty

'Hello, Princess. Going somewhere?'

One of the guys standing behind Link throws a left hook at me. I duck, and he hits his friend's shoulder instead. It must have hurt because he cries out, and there's just enough confusion for me to weave through the bodies of their gang. I take off, sprinting towards the back door of the kitchen, hoping it's unlocked. It opens without protest, but I don't have time to celebrate. Without bothering to check if anyone is around, I turn left and keep running.

I make it back to the main corridor and turn, heading away from the dining hall. I think I'm heading in the direction of my old room, and I'm fairly sure I'll be able to make my way to the border from there. Once the lights start to thin out, I feel better. I know the central clan hub is behind me, but I haven't seen anyone since I escaped from the kitchen.

I slow to a brisk walk and fish the little torch I stole from my guard out of my pocket. It doesn't offer much light, but it's enough to stop me from tripping over. The walls are starting to get that slimy look they have this far out from the clan hub.

I stop for a second and listen; I think I've out-run them.

I start running again.

The surrounding silence is broken by the echo of footsteps and shouting.

I pick up my pace.

I know if they catch me this time, they'll kill me. I keep running, the cold air burning the back of my throat, until suddenly, the wind is knocked out of me altogether. I cough, getting back up and wiping dirt off my hands onto my jeans.

'Hey, Teddy,' Petra singsongs as she approaches with a small group. They've all got knives out. 'Kit says to say hi.'

I ignore her, turning back to run the other way, but the glow of multiple torches is fast approaching as Link and his group arrive.

I'm outnumbered and surrounded. Turning back to Petra, I ask, 'How's your cheek?'

She scowls, touching her hand to the cluster of little scabs on her face. Before I can move, multiple sets of hands are on me, making any chance of escape impossible.

I won't give myself up that easily.

I fight back with animal ferocity, kicking and screaming.

'Get off me!' I spit at the man closest to me. He slaps me across the cheek. I recoil, but only for a moment, launching for his neck.

'Tie the bitch up!' a woman shouts.

'Get her down,' a man says. Moments pass, then I'm on the floor, a boot pressing hard between my shoulder blades.

'What are you doing?' I hear Link say. My cheek is pressed into the cold hard floor so I can't look up, but I can see his studded boot inches from my head.

I feel a sharp pain in my left temple.

✕

I open my eyes; my head is foggy. I try to move, but I can't. I twist my wrists against the cable ties binding me to the metal chair. Bright lights blare at me from all angles. My left eye won't open. I try rolling my neck, but the pain that shoots down my shoulders makes my stomach roil. A hiss escapes my lips.

I move my good – better – eye to take in the room as best I can.

This can't be happening.

I'm hit with a flash of *déjà vu.*

Everything is the same.

This is just like the first time I was in the Underground with Paula. I can hear someone talking, but the voice sounds miles away. I can feel hands slapping my head.

'Wakey, wakey!'

I blink rapidly, trying to focus.

Link.

He smiles, the skin on his face stretched taut around three long piercings. They look like sharp twigs. One between his eyes, one through his nose, and the last above his chin, and it scares the hell out of me.

'So, what is your plan?' he asks. I try to talk but realise there's black tape across my mouth. 'What's that?' he croons condescendingly, his dark eyes made more menacing by the black kohl lining them. 'I know you think you're the Underground's *saviour.*' He spits the word.

I shake my head, screaming into the tape.

'I also know you didn't set Jamie up. After I arranged for Mark's little . . . accident, Leelo assured me Jamie would be the replacement. It was easy at that point. Paula thought she was the only one with guard connections.' He lets that new information hang in the air, and my mind rushes back to the night at Maree's cafe, when Link was laughing and talking to all the guards. 'That poor guy would've ended up in the Council's hands eventually, regardless of if you had gone out *that* night or not. It was all part of my plan. You being there to watch it was just a tasty treat.' He rubs his hands together, the rings cracking against each other with the movement. 'I think the Sympathisers are a liability, a useless waste of time. We get the dregs of the City. Where is the good stuff? Well, that is all available for us at any time from their storage warehouses, and the factories. I always wondered why Paula didn't go straight to the source, but I guess she had another plan in mind. So, I'll ask you again, Teddy, what is your plan?'

I quit struggling and focus on calming my ragged breathing. Petra steps forward, into the ring of light, and I can see the dirty blade of a knife as she dances it in her fingers expertly.

I hold her gaze.

He's only telling me this because they are going to kill me.

'He asked you a question, Teddy. It's rude to ignore someone when they're talking to you.'

I jut my chin, indicating my current situation.

'Oh, yes, I can see you're in . . . a bit of a bind!' She cackles. 'But maybe if you just help us out.' She leans forward, drawing the tip of the blade across my cheek. I try to keep breathing slowly . . . *In and out* . . . I feel the blade draw down my other cheek . . . *In and out* . . . Her breath is hot against my neck . . . *In and out* . . . She reaches forward and rips the tape off my face. 'Don't be a bad girl now.'

I can't help coughing when my mouth is free again. I feel a hot trickle of blood down my cheeks where Petra drew the knife across my skin.

'So,' Link says, standing behind Petra now, his hands on her shoulders, massaging them. 'What is your plan?' Petra looks up at him, and I consider their likeness.

Jamie was right. Maybe they are *brother and sister?*

'I don't know what you're talking about,' I say, disappointed my voice sounds so thin and raspy.

'I don't believe you,' Petra replies in a sing-song voice through clenched teeth. Link strokes her head, his long nails pulling through her wild hair.

'Nor do I, pet,' he says, without breaking eye contact with me. It makes my stomach flip, and feel like I might throw up. 'Maybe she needs some convincing?' With that, he's behind me in a flash. I feel his nails drawing over my skull as he grips my hair in his hands and pulls. The strain on my neck is excruciating. He keeps pulling, stretching my neck further back than it should go. I feel Petra sit down on my lap, pressing her blade against my exposed neck, flat and cold.

'I'll ask you again,' she says. 'What is your plan?'

'I don't know what you're talking about,' I force out through the pain.

Link shoves my head up, and the blade is gone from my throat, but a scream rips from my lungs as Petra plunges the long blade into my thigh. Pain licks through me so fast I can *see* it, flashing white, blinding me. I twitch and buck, fighting back the rising bile.

Petra jumps off me, and then the burning pain in my leg really starts as blood bubbles hot and sticky around the knife, which is still in my leg. Link's voice is loud my ear.

'I didn't want it to get to this so soon. But if you're going to be difficult . . .' Link steps away, and I hear heavy footsteps as someone else approaches. I try blinking hard, washing the pain from my mind, but the room is still swimming in white.

Someone highkicks the knife and it tears out of my leg, taking a chunk of my flesh with it. I hear a dull thud against the far wall and bite my teeth down. My thoughts blur, and I gag. The acrid smell of my own vomit is filling my nostrils, and I feel a hard knuckle meet my right shoulder. No, not just a knuckle, something sharper and more rigid. An image of Link's blood-caked rings flashes in my mind. 'This could have been avoided,' he says, sounding disappointed. 'I think there was even a chance we could have worked together.'

'I would never work with you,' I manage to croak. 'Never.'

'Pity,' he says. And then they're gone, and the door slams shut.

✗

The blood pumping out of my thigh slows to a weeping ooze. My eyes are still squeezed shut. I'm not squeamish around blood, but I really don't want to see Petra's handiwork. My throat still stings from the vomit. I hear the door open again.

I'll defy them.

'Ready to talk yet?' Petra asks. I open my eyes a sliver and four Petras swim in and out of my vision as I struggle to keep them open. I've lost too much blood.

'Poor Teddy. You're not looking your best. But you're in luck – we're done for today. We'll be back tomorrow,' she whispers in my hear.

She laughs, a grating sound, then I hear footsteps as she moves away. I catch a blurry glimpse as she walks back, and see the knife in her hand again. I flinch as she raises the knife towards me, but she just cuts the cable ties that bind me to the chair. Like a puppet with no strings, I collapse to the floor.

Where's Link? I'm obviously not worth his time.

'Let's go, boys,' Petra croons to her men, who hover over me. 'She won't be any fun now anyway.'

I close my eyes again, listening to three pairs of footsteps moving towards the door. *One stops.*

'Oh, and by the way,' she says, 'we're it for visitors. There won't be any food or water tonight. We don't want you attempting any more getaways.'

I hear her shrill laugh as the door slams shut, its copper ring humming in the air around me.

I try using the chair to help me sit up.

Come on. I feel every muscle screaming at me. *Come on!*

But the pain is too much.

fifty/one

I weave in and out of consciousness for a while. I feel white-hot and wet, as sweat breaks over my body. It's getting harder to stay awake. My eyes are . . . so heavy.

After a while, I start hearing things. I imagine someone's saying my name. *Mum.* I see her face in front of me, her eyes filled with concern.

What is she doing down here? I try to tell her to go away. *It isn't safe down here.* What would she think, seeing me here like this? Broken. Dying. Accused of destroying the very thing I gave up my life for. I ignore the searing pain as a sob racks my body. I will die, and they will celebrate it. Perhaps Mum won't even know. No one will try to find her. The Underground will collapse, I know it. I tried. *Maybe I didn't try hard enough.*

No one's coming to help me.

'Teddy. Teddy!' A hot hand presses my cheeks, sending pain shooting up to my temples.

I try opening my right eye and manage to crack it just wide enough to see Kit crouched by my side. Her face is centimetres from mine, tear-stained and wide-eyed.

I take her in. Her usually bouncy pink hair is flat, and her favourite jacket is covered in blood. *My blood.*

I look down at my body and see I'm covered in blood and vomit. Something close to nausea stirs within me again.

'Please sit still,' she mumbles, trying to get a bandage out of its packaging. 'I'm going to fix you up.'

She drops it and picks it up twice before it's open, her nails getting in the way as her hands shake.

I sit, unable to move anyway, while she cleans and patches me up. I feel like a bear that's been attacked by a dog. All torn, my stuffing spilling out.

I'm only partly listening to the things she's saying . . . *After what they did to Lew* . . . I suck in sharply as alcohol stings on my cheek . . . *Link wants to kill the clan-less children* . . . I try to swat the alcohol swab away, snatching at her wrist, but my hand and my brain aren't communicating . . . *punishing the Outskirter parents* . . . more pain, this time in my shoulder as she rotates my arm. *Pop!* Back into its socket . . . *I knew they were twisted, but not sick* . . . My ears ring.

'I was so hung up on Jamie's death. I needed it to be someone's fault.' She's gripping my face in her hands, gently dabbing at my left eye. 'I wanted there to be a reason, so I took the easiest story to believe.'

That's *what was easiest? To betray me?*

She stops working and looks into my eyes, her hands still gripping my head. I want to push her away, to scream at her to get off me, but I can't make my body move.

'I need you to know how sorry I am. I made a huge mistake, I know that now.'

Even at a whisper, I can hear her voice break.

My heart breaks too.

'You did,' I say, putting all my energy into my arms. I shove Kit away and she falls back, hurt flashing across her face, but at least she has the decency not to look surprised. I need to leave, and I don't want to tell Kit where I'm going.

'Bye,' I say prematurely. But my legs are a pulpy mess; they refuse to cooperate.

'You're not going anywhere,' she replies, reaching out.

She just won't take a hint.

'At least not on your own.' She moves towards me again, and I don't have the energy to shift back. I see she has her satchel with her, the same one I've seen her wear before. She pulls out a little glass bottle filled with some orange liquid. 'This will make you feel better,' she says as she holds it to my lips. I take a sip of the sweet drink. She's right – almost immediately it takes some of the heat out of my face. 'You're dehydrated,' she says.

I hear a soft tapping on the door and freeze. Kit puts her hand up. 'Relax, it's just Zelda.'

'How?' I ask, but she's already at the door. Moments later she returns with Zelda in tow. Zelda tries to conceal her horror, but I must look bad.

'Do you have the bag?' Kit asks.

Zelda nods, holding a stuffed black backpack. *My* black backpack.

'I put the main stuff in it.' They exchange a look, then turn back to me.

'So, you were planning to get to Clan Gaia, to seek refuge with Michelle, I guess.'

Kit isn't asking, so I shrug, not bothering to hide my halfbaked plan.

I'm obviously not going to make it there alone.

'Lew said it was my best shot.' I don't recognise my voice, and it hurts to speak. Kit holds up the little glass bottle and instructs me to keep sipping it as she cuts away at my pants.

'Why are you here?' I ask. It's less painful to talk now. Kit interrupts before Zelda can reply.

'She told me about what happened in the kitchen. She was in the dining hall with Mark and Leelo when Link went on his rampage.' I watch Zelda quietly nod. '*She* never doubted you,' Kit says, avoiding my eyes.

Zelda smiles. 'My grandma taught me a few tricks before she died. A few ways to tell someone's true spirit.'

'Yeah. Unfortunately, I didn't have a grandma to instil such faith in me.' Kit looks down. 'I got swept away in my pain.' She grabs my hand. '*Our* pain.'

I try to pull my hand away, but Kit's grip is too tight. She looks genuinely distraught.

'I don't know how I could have sided with Link. Against you! It's insane. I just walked away when you were locked in that cell. Just left you there.'

Zelda puts a hand on Kit's shoulder as Kit breaks down.

'She took some convincing, but after Lew first came back to the medical centre . . .' Zelda explains.

'What did Link do to him?' I ask. I need to know. Just the thought of Link sends my neck into a spasm.

'They –' Kit's voice breaks. 'He's not dead.' I feel my heart constrict. 'He's in the medical centre but he will be okay,' she says firmly, more to herself than to me. Her watery eyes meet mine.

'We need to get out,' I say, clawing at the chair, trying to pull myself up. 'Before Petra comes back. They can't know you two helping me.'

I'm almost standing when a wave of nausea hits me – *my leg*. I spew up the orange liquid I'd just been sipping. I grimace at the burning feeling in my throat.

Less soothing on the way up.

'You need to stay sitting down,' Zelda says soothingly, easing me back onto the metal chair.

'They're not coming back, not tonight at least,' Kit says. 'They're having a big party. To celebrate –' She pauses. 'They've had parties almost every night. Lots of drinking and fighting. I usually stay away.'

They help me out of my disgusting clothes. Zelda tries to distract me with stories about Link's debauchery and his drunk army, Kit washes me down with damp cloths. I feel bloated and tender all over. I hiss at the pain radiating from my thigh. At one point, I look down at the wound. It's a mistake.

Zelda quickly responds with a hand on my chin, making sure I don't look away from her bright face. I tune out her chatter – it's too hard to focus through the pain.

'This is all we could find,' Zelda says, holding something up, breaking my reverie. I look at the black long-sleeved jacket. It was one she had given me when I first moved down here. It has a long plastic zipper and leather buckles at the neck to close the collar over your face.

The girls begin carefully threading my arms through the sleeves like I'm made from tissue paper. I look at the pieces of my old pants on the floor. There was no other way to have removed them, not without disturbing the cut that's now covered by a cooling salve and bandages.

I really liked those pants. They were the last pair of plain black jeans I had from above, the last remnant of my old life.

Kit scoops up the pants before I have a chance to mention them.

'I made these for you. A little while ago,' Zelda says, stepping in front of me. 'I was waiting for your official swearing-in as Clan Head to give them to you.'

I don't know what Zelda is talking about. All I can see is a brown paper package in her hands. I shake my head, sending another shooting pain down my spine.

She opens the package and holds up a pair of pants made from a sort of plaid material. Red and black patches of the same fabric cover sections where the cloth looks thinner, and zippers have been used to help bridge some of the gaps. 'This fabric has been in my family for generations. It's the fabric of my clan,' Zelda says. Seeing my confusion, she explains, 'In Scotland, in the old world. Clan Wallace.

'My family come from a great line of warriors.' She stands straight, filled with pride. 'It became a tradition that when they fled their country, every bride would have some of their clan's tartan sewn into their wedding dress.'

I look at the pants, as bright as fresh blood, confused.

Why would she do this for me?

'My grandma told me three things before she died. One: that I should never stand down for a man. Two: that I was destined to continue our family's line of witches; and three, that I would be led back into the light by a great leader, and I needed to do whatever my heart told me to in order to support *her*.' Zelda puts the pants into my hands. 'You're that great leader, Teddy. You're our saviour. We won't get out of here without you. I just know it.' I rub the smooth fabric between my fingers. 'You are born for the Sunlight. I know you're going to take us all back there.' I can't speak.

Tears fill my eyes as I let my friends help me pull the pants on. Only this time, the tears are not from pain.

The pants fit perfectly. I look at Zelda, completely in awe of her talent and strength.

'Thank you,' I say. It feels inadequate, but I can't think of anything else. Together, they walk me back over to the chair, which Kit had wiped down. I sit down, and they kneel in front of me.

'So, what's next, boss?' Kit asks, a smile playing on her lips.

I want to relax, but I can't forget what she's doing. I sit up straight, despite the pain. *Not yet.*

'I need to get to Michelle, to buy some time while I get a plan together.' They nod. 'It seems like Link hasn't managed to brainwash everyone, so you two need to stay here and find out how many people are still on my side. Or not on his side, at least.'

I pull together all my strength, standing up. I turn to face the door.

'They wanted blood; I gave them blood. If they want fire, *I'll give them the sun.*'

acknowledgements

Firstly, I'd like to thank you Mat, Matthew, Matty, Matais. You have never doubted me or told me that my ideas are too big or unrealistic or too grand. Thank you for pushing me every day to do more and achieve my dreams and goals. I am so grateful to have you in my life.

I'd also like to thank my parents, who despite the challenges that I have posed, being the eccentric human that I am, have both always supported my dreams and provided me with the resources and encouragement or necessary space, to learn and grow and be me.

I owe a great debt to my grandparents, who have never stopped supporting, loving, and encouraging me to be a better person. Providing me with music lessons, taking me to them and forcing me to practise, even making me look up words in the dictionary to find the spelling . . . well maybe that one didn't work. But the unlimited fount of love you've all provided me is a gift I will always cherish.

To Kimbles, who read this manuscript MULTIPLE times. You always provided insight and encouragement. Thank you. I love that you're in my life.

To Callum and Roxy, who both read the first version of this book that no one should have had to read. I'm sorry and thank you.

To Katy, my kindred spirit and sister.

To Lewis, I thank you wholeheartedly for everything you do to help make this imaginative world a reality. You're a fantastic human being.

To all the different women of writing wisdom who imparted their guidance to help me become a better writer and learn my craft and make this book the best it can be; Glenda, Maya, Kate and Vanessa. Thank you.

To Eric, you are a champion and you're my champion! Thank you for always having my back and providing the truth bombs I don't always want, but usually need.

To Marlene, you *get it* and I love you for that.

To my agent Suzie, thank you for hearing me when I said I want to be an author AND a musician, not just a musician who wrote a book.

To my New Leaf Agency family, including but not limited to Dani, *and* to Zoe at the Bent Agency, thank you all for being on my team.

To my publisher herself, Claire. You have made this process so easy and enjoyable for me. Thank you for your support, enthusiasm, joyful disposition, and wisdom. I hope to always love words as much as you do. To the next one!

To my editor Danielle, despite my frequent, desperate emails you still talk to me! You always have the answers and never seemed to be bothered; I am so grateful for that.

To Charlotte, you're the champion I didn't know I needed. I'm still waiting for the embosser to arrive.

To Adrik, thank you so much for your patience with my fluid planning and your acceptance of all my hair-brained ideas.

And to the entire publishing team – you love this book as much as I do, THANK YOU. I am so happy knowing my characters are working amongst friends.

Finally, maybe you thought I forgot about you? To all my OUTSiDERS. I hope you know how much I love you all.

So, here's to everyone who feels like Teddy, like a circle inside a square. Trust me, I've never fit in and, quite frankly, now I would never want to.

Keep being you because the world is better because of it.

Keep Watching. Keep Listening. Keep Breathing.

the story continues in . . .

Scan this QR code to find out more and listen to the sounds of the Metropolis.